T0301102

CAN'T RUN, CAN'T HIDE

Also by Yrsa Sigurdardóttir

The Thóra Gudmundsdóttir novels

Last Rituals

My Soul to Take

Ashes to Dust

The Day is Dark

Someone to Watch Over Me

The Silence of the Sea

Standalones

I Remember You

The Undesired

Why Did You Lie?

The Prey

The Freyja and Huldar Series

The Legacy

The Reckoning

The Absolution

Gallows Rock

The Doll

The Fallout

About the Author

Yrsa Sigurdardóttir works as a civil engineer in Reykjavík. She made her crime fiction debut in 2005 with Last Rituals, the first instalment in the Thóra Gudmundsdóttir series, and has been translated into more than thirty languages. The Silence of the Sea won the Petrona Award in 2015. Can't Run, Can't Hide is her seventeenth adult novel and the first in the Black Ice Series.

About the Translator

Victoria Cribb studied and worked in Iceland for many years. She has translated some forty-five books by Icelandic authors including Arnaldur Indridason, Ragnar Jónasson and Sjón. In 2017 she received the Ordstír honorary translation award for her services to Icelandic literature.

CAN'T RUN, CAN'T HIDE

Yrsa Sigurdardóttir

Translated from the Icelandic by Victoria Cribb

HODDER &
STOUGHTON

First published in Great Britain in 2024 by Hodder & Stoughton Limited
An Hachette UK company

First published with the title *Lok lok og læs* in 2021 by Veröld Publishing, Reykjavík

1

Copyright © Yrsa Sigurdardóttir 2020
English translation copyright © Victoria Cribb, 2024

The right of Yrsa Sigurdardóttir to be identified as the Author of the Work has been asserted by her in accordance with the Copyright, Designs and Patents Act 1988.

All rights reserved. No part of this publication may be reproduced, stored in a retrieval system, or transmitted, in any form or by any means without the prior written permission of the publisher, nor be otherwise circulated in any form of binding or cover other than that in which it is published and without a similar condition being imposed on the subsequent purchaser.

All characters in this publication are fictitious and any resemblance to real persons, living or dead, is purely coincidental.

A CIP catalogue record for this title is available from the British Library

Hardback ISBN 9781399722834
Trade Paperback ISBN 9781399722841
ebook ISBN 9781399722858

Typeset in Sabon MT Std by Manipal Technologies Limited

Printed and bound in Great Britain by Clays Ltd, Elcograf S.p.A.

Hodder & Stoughton policy is to use papers that are natural, renewable and recyclable products and made from wood grown in sustainable forests. The logging and manufacturing processes are expected to conform to the environmental regulations of the country of origin.

Hodder & Stoughton Limited
Carmelite House
50 Victoria Embankment
London EC4Y 0DZ

The authorised representative in the EEA is Hachette Ireland, 8 Castlecourt Centre, Castleknock Road, Castleknock, Dublin 15, D15 YF6A, Ireland

www.hodder.co.uk

This book is dedicated to my mother,

Kristín Halla Jónsdóttir

Many thanks to Eva Björg Ægisdóttir for the loan of her characters from West Iceland CID in Akranes, who appear here in a supporting role. One could call this an attempt to create a sort of Marvel Cinematic Universe for the world of Icelandic crime fiction. By the way, I heartily recommend Eva Björg's books: they're great.

Pronunciation guide for Icelandic names and words

Akranes – AA-kra-nes
Alvar Grétarsson – Al-var GRYET-ar-sson
Angantýr Gunnarsson – OWNG-gan-teer GOON-nar-sson
Ása Bjartmarsdóttir – OW-ssa BYART-mars-DOE-teer
Berglind (Begga) Mímisdóttir – BAIRG-lind (BEG-ga) MEE-mis-DOE-teer
Bogi Lúthersson – BOY-yee LOOT-er-sson
Bói – BOH-wee
Borgarnes – BORG-ar-nes
búálfur – BOO-owl-vur
Dísa – DEE-ssa
Einar Ari Arason – AY-nar AA-ree AA-ra-sson
Ella – ELL-la
Gerdur – GHYAIR-thur
Gígja – GHYEE-ya
Glymur – GLEE-mur
Gunnar Sigurdsson – GOON-nar SIG-oorth-sson
hangikjöt – HOWNG-kee-KYURT
Hördur – HUR-thoor
Huldar – HOOL-dar

Hvalfjördur – KVAAL-fyur-thur
Hvarf – KVARV
Idunn – ITH-un
Ingigerdur (Inga) Jónsdóttir – ING-kee-GHYAIR-thur (ING-ga) YOHNS-DOE-teer
Íris – EER-is
Jónsi – YOHN-ssee
Karl – KAADL
Karólína (Karó) – KAA-roh-LEE-na
Kjalarnes – KYAAL-ar-nes
laufabraud – LOHV-a-BROHTH
Lína – LEE-na
Lubbi – LOOBB-bee
Midsandsbryggja – MITH-sands-BRIG-kya
Midsandur – MITH-san-door
Minna-Hvarf – MIN-na KVARV
Mosfellsbær – MOSS-fells-byre
Reykjavík – RAY-kya-veek
Reynir Logason – RAY-neer LORG-a-sson
Robbi (Róbert) – ROBB-bee (ROH-bairt)
Sævar – SYE-var
skafrenningur – SKAAV-renn-ing-goor
Sóldís Sigursveinsdóttir – SOHL-dees SIG-oor-svayns-DOE-teer
Týr Gautason – TEER GOHT-a-sson

Chapter 1
Wednesday

An unusual stillness reigned over the farm at Hvarf. There was no sign of life. Not even the faintest breath of wind stirred the hairs on his head. Leaden clouds hung unmoving in the sky or changed shape with such infinite slowness that the shifts were barely perceptible. Karl was struck by a sudden odd fancy that time itself had slowed down. He switched off the weather report on the car radio. The announcer had moved on to the shipping forecast, listing the names of the various sea areas, which held no interest for Karl. His single stint on a trawler as a young man had convinced him to spend the rest of his life on land.

He took his hat from the passenger seat and got out of the car, but didn't immediately put it on, as he wanted to listen with his ears uncovered. The silence was absolute: most of the birds had left long ago, either migrating south to the sun or moving closer to the shore, to the easy pickings in the towns and villages. The voices of the rivers and streams were choked by icy fetters, the tourists were snug at home, and the livestock was shut up in byres for the winter. Even the waves in the nearby fjord were muted.

But the family who lived at the farm ought to be home, and he would have expected to hear some indication of their presence by now. All four of them couldn't still be asleep in the middle of the day. When Karl last spoke to Ása and Reynir, just under a week ago, they hadn't said anything about going away. And since trips weren't that common when you had a farm, as he knew from experience, the subject would definitely have come up. On the rare occasions when he himself had a holiday planned, he couldn't talk about anything else for weeks beforehand, whether his audience wanted to hear about it or not.

The family's cars were both parked in the yard, buried under thick quilts of snow – an SUV with jacked-up suspension and a sporty little number purely for summer use. At least, Karl hadn't seen them touch it during winter in the year and a bit that the family had been living here. Which made sense. Personally, he wouldn't take it out in snowy or icy conditions for fear of ending up in a ditch. The SUV was another matter – a luxury vehicle that had apparently cost the equivalent of a decent tractor. Karl wouldn't mind putting that through its paces in deep snow or on black ice, if only to see what you got for your money. Eye-wateringly expensive cars like that were a rare sight among the farming community. But then this was no ordinary farm. And the people who lived here were anything but ordinary farmers.

One look at the buildings was enough to tell you that. Unlike most Icelandic farms, it boasted outsize, ultra-modern living quarters that the couple had built for their family, connected by a glassed-in corridor to the more conventional, two-storey farmhouse that the previous occupants had found sufficient for their needs. But the new owners had different requirements. The family lived in the modern building and reserved the old house for guests or members of staff, though up to now there had been few visitors, and the only employees had been assistants, who hadn't lasted long. Karl hadn't liked to ask why they had quit, but he guessed the isolation must have got to them.

Karl was no architect, and the design of the buildings was none of his business; but he had strong views, all the same, on the corridor connecting the two houses. The buildings were in such stark contrast, one belonging to a past rooted in careful thrift, the other the offspring of modern excess. To join them together seemed to Karl as incongruous as harnessing the farm's two horses to the sports car.

A whole army of tradesmen had been marshalled for the job of renovating the old farmhouse, the byre and the other outhouses, though there was no doubt in Karl's mind that it would have been cheaper to knock down the old buildings and start again from scratch. But the property's energetic new owners had wanted to preserve as much of the original appearance as possible.

The new house was a different story. Its design paid no homage to Icelandic farming culture or the history of the area. On the contrary, it was huge, with soaring ceilings inside. There was nothing remotely low-key or economical about its design or construction. Although the bulk of the structure was made of concrete, at the rear, invisible from the yard, was a large glass room, housing the industrial-sized kitchen and an open-plan dining and seating area with a fireplace. The new owners had told Karl that it was envisaged as a space where they could cook, eat and relax in close communion with nature. He had merely nodded, while thinking to himself that these were the kind of people who would pay good money to stay in a glass bubble in the middle of a bog for the same purpose. He couldn't understand it himself, preferring to experience nature without any barriers – even transparent ones.

The couple had been living here with their two daughters for just over a year now, and during that time his opinion of them had undergone a transformation. He no longer dismissed them as the type with more money than sense. He still couldn't get his head round half of what he regarded as their hare-brained schemes, but he liked them. It was hard not to. The wife, Ása, was lovely; quick to laugh at herself and her attempts to adapt to her new circumstances. Her husband, Reynir, wasn't as outgoing and often seemed a bit distracted, yet he came across as sincere.

From the pristine surface of the snow, Karl thought that no one had crossed the yard since yesterday's heavy fall. But as he approached the front door, he saw that this wasn't quite correct. There were tracks leading from the modern house to the small byre that housed the farm's few animals, apart from the chickens that lived in the henhouse behind the new building.

The fact that the animals had been fed was a clear sign that the family were at home. If they'd gone away, they would have asked one of their neighbours to take care of the farm, and in that case the tracks would lead from the car park in the yard to the byre, rather than from the house. Besides, Karl assumed that he and Ella would have been chosen for the task, as it wouldn't be the first time they had done Ása and Reynir that favour.

But no one had heard from the family for nearly a week. That was why he was here now, and why he had called by the day before yesterday too. A loud barking erupted from the byre as Karl approached the front door of the house, followed by a high-pitched yapping from the same source: the two family dogs, one a border collie, the other a tiny scrap that reminded Karl of nothing so much as one of those hanks of sheep's wool you sometimes see caught on barbed-wire fences. When he had dropped round the day before yesterday, hoping to find the family at home, they had made the same racket, but from inside the house that time. They were friendly dogs, with no obvious purpose in life except as pets, and were sometimes loose in the yard to welcome him when he arrived. But because they were shut in now, they reacted to the visitor as any dog would – by barking. It didn't mean anything. Still, it was odd that the dogs weren't either running around outside or in the house. He couldn't ever remember them being shut in the byre before.

A gut instinct told him something was wrong and he had learnt not to ignore the feeling. It had never let him down, as far as he could remember.

Karl contemplated the unusually large front door for a moment or two before knocking. This set the dogs off in a second volley of barking, in unison this time. The two cows joined in with a loud mooing, but fell silent when he knocked again. Karl couldn't shake off the idea that the animals in the byre were listening, waiting as expectantly as he was for the door to open. Nothing happened. He pressed his ear to the wood but couldn't hear any sound of movement inside. He straightened up. There was no telling how loud a noise would have to be to pierce this solid block of oak.

Abandoning the door, Karl peered through the nearest window. A light was on inside the house but there was no sign of life. His feeling of unease intensified, driving him to do something that, until today, he would never have dreamt of.

He bent down to the letter box and pushed it open. Its very existence was an error, as the architect who designed the new farmhouse had clearly never lived in the countryside. Since the couple were equally ignorant, they hadn't corrected the plans. No one in the neighbourhood had letters delivered through their door; instead, the post was left in the mailbox on the main road by the turn-off to the farm.

Karl was just opening his mouth to call through the narrow opening, when he recoiled. A familiar smell had reached him on a waft of hot air. A faint whiff of death, and it didn't come from dried-out pot plants. He'd smelt it more often than he cared for: the sweetish odour of putrefaction given off by all dead animals that lay unburied for any length of time. It wasn't that strong, however, and if he hadn't been a farmer he might not have twigged straight away. But he was in no doubt: something inside the house was dead.

Karl withdrew his hand and the flap snapped shut with a loud click. This time there was no barking or mooing from the animals in the byre, just an eerie silence mirroring the one inside the house. Karl had an unsettling sense of being totally alone.

He licked his dry lips, ran his hands through his hair, rubbed his unshaven cheeks and tried to work out what to do. That smell didn't necessarily mean anything, he told himself. There could be some meat rotting on the kitchen table. Perhaps the family had been planning to have a barbecue, then fallen ill, and the meat had been sitting there too long at room temperature. An absurd idea – but better than various other scenarios Karl was trying not to think about. He reminded himself that it didn't pay to dismiss absurd ideas. Life was rarely straightforward.

He decided to walk round behind the house and see if he could spot anything through the glass walls. The blinds were never drawn. In fact, he had only just stopped himself from pointing out to the couple that they could reduce their heating costs if they closed them, belatedly remembering that money was no object to them. They had drilled down to the natural hot water supply and installed their own geothermal heating system, so they could simply turn up the thermostat if necessary.

The snow was untouched behind the house too. No one had emerged through the French windows on to the deck outside the glass room since the last snowfall. The hayfield in the distance and the mountains to the east were white as far as the eye could see; the panoramic view the couple set so much store by was as pure as spotless linen.

But Karl hadn't come here to admire the scenery. He turned to peer through the glass wall, his gaze travelling over the minimalist kitchen: no upper cupboards, no handles on the doors or drawers of the units; if it hadn't been for the incredibly complicated chrome coffee maker and the tap over the sink, the furnishings could have been mistaken for a continuation of the seating area around the fireplace.

There was food on the kitchen table that hadn't been cleared away. Karl felt a rush of relief. The family must be at home and alive. They'd eaten a meal, then gone to bed. Ill, presumably, because he had never before seen anything left on the table after mealtimes. Now, though, he could make out an open carton of milk, a glass, a plate, a loaf of bread and a block of cheese, still in its packaging. No sign of any putrid steaks, though. Perhaps the family had been struck down by gastric flu and he'd misinterpreted the unpleasant whiff he'd smelt through the letter box. But although he hoped this was the explanation, deep down he knew he'd never confuse the two: nasty though the smell of vomit and diarrhoea could be, the odour of decomposing flesh was infinitely worse. The faintly floral note that accompanied the rotten stench almost suggested someone had tried to mask it with perfume.

Karl stood there irresolute, wondering what to do. The most sensible course of action would be to get the hell out of here. He didn't want a member of the family to walk into the kitchen and catch him peering through the windows. But as he was backing away from the house, he had second thoughts. Ása and Reynir were the most fastidious people he'd ever met: they'd once sought his advice on tackling the stink of manure from the byre, asking if there was a spray or air-freshener that could disguise the pong. He had broken the bad news to them that nothing of the kind existed; they would just have to get used to it. People who asked questions like that would never let their home reek like a charnel house in a heatwave. Without a shadow of doubt, there was something very wrong here.

Karl walked briskly over to the French windows and tried the handle. If he barged in on the family while they were sleeping, that was too bad. It would be even worse having to admit to Ella that he'd had another wasted journey. He would never get away with telling her less than the whole truth: everything had seemed fine, apart, that is, from a slight odour of rotting flesh.

The glass doors turned out to be unlocked. Karl shouted Ása and Reynir's names through the gap. The faint – but horrible – smell poured out with the humid heat, condensing into mist in the freezing air, and he grimaced as he waited for an answer. But there was no response.

Karl stepped inside before he could lose heart and called again. Still no response. His eye was caught by some dark marks resembling footprints on the parquet by the door. This was as out of place as the taint in the air, since the floor was normally sparkling clean. He followed the trail of footprints with his gaze. Noting that they led through the kitchen and further inside the house, he decided to follow them.

Although Karl had been invited inside before, it had only been in the communal areas – the living room and the sleek, stylish kitchen. He wasn't familiar with the layout of the rest of the house, except that there was a separate bedroom wing, which was where the footprints led. The connecting door was closed, but he noticed a number of scratches on it. They were vertical and ran down the wood in two separate clusters, a patch of smaller ones lower down and some longer, deeper scratches beside the door handle. He was in no doubt that they had been made by the dogs, the result of countless vain attempts to get through the closed door. He was also convinced that the scratches were new, as the couple always had any damage repaired instantly.

Karl put the crook of his elbow over his nose, then opened the door to the bedroom hallway. It was as he'd feared: the stench was sickening here and he felt his heart begin to pound.

There were several doors, all of them closed. He followed the footprints to one and opened it, still holding his arm over his face. It turned out to be the master bedroom. Karl froze on the threshold. A woman, who appeared to be Ása, was lying on the unusually large bed. The sheets were rumpled and the double duvet had been pushed to the foot of the bed, where it drooped to the floor. The pillows had been scattered; two were on the floor, one was standing up on end by the headboard. Ása herself was lying on her back, in nothing but a vest and knickers. One of her legs hung down to the floor like the duvet, the other was bent at the knee. Her arms were in a strange position, one thrust straight out from her body, as if reaching across the empty place beside her; the other bent at the elbow, the fingers touching her chin. Her once-white vest was dark with dried blood, like the bedclothes, and rucked up to reveal her abdomen, which was a ghastly shade of luminous green. In contrast, her legs and any other areas of exposed flesh were grey, bloated and streaked with dark veins. As a farmer, Karl was accustomed to the sight of death, but the animals he dealt with were covered in fur, with little naked skin to be seen. He knew enough to stay away from the woman, though.

Karl couldn't be a hundred per cent sure that it was Ása, as her face was as deformed as her limbs. In fact, it was worse. There was a deep gash extending from the crown of her head down to the middle of her forehead. Her tongue protruded a little between her colourless lips, and her dull, bulging eyes had rolled back into her head as if she had been trying to get a glimpse of her head wound in her last moments. But one thing was clear: she hadn't died a natural death. Further testimony to this, had it been needed, was provided by the blood splashed all over the walls and floor. Even the ceiling hadn't been spared.

Karl clamped a hand over his mouth and reversed sharply out of the room. Fighting back his nausea, he forced himself to look in the other rooms in search of the girls and Reynir. The first door he tried turned out to belong to the older daughter, and when he saw her, he lost control. The jet of vomit that exploded from his mouth spread over the congealed blood on the floor. He threw up again as he half fell out of the front door into the yard. He had seen more than enough.

He wiped his mouth on the sleeve of his coat, then got in his car and took out his phone with trembling hands. Discovering that there was no signal, he threw the phone on the passenger seat and started the engine, afraid he was going to be sick again. As he reversed frantically to turn round, his gaze fell on the buildings. The curtains were drawn in one of the upstairs windows in the old farmhouse, yet he could have sworn that they had all been open when he had first driven into the yard.

Karl turned the wheel and roared away as fast as he dared in the wintry conditions. As he pulled out of the drive on to the main road, it began to snow.

Chapter 2
Before

Sóldís wasn't used to travelling long distances by taxi. On the few occasions when she splashed out on a cab, it was to get home from clubbing in town at weekends, knackered, her thoughts hazy. This was different. For one thing, it was no ordinary taxi. The car was unmarked and much smarter than the ones Sóldís was used to taking. A chilled bottle of water had been waiting for her in the back, and there were magazines in the seat pockets. Not that she'd touched them, as there was an inexhaustible store of material on her phone if she'd been in the mood to read.

For another thing, although you'd hardly have guessed it from the semi-darkness outside, it was morning, and she was neither tired nor the worse for wear. But there was something reminiscent of those drunken cab rides home: her thoughts were a little incoherent, all at sea. A random thought would bob to the surface, call attention to itself, then vanish back into the depths, to be followed by another. Sóldís found it impossible to pin any of them down.

Was she making a colossal mistake? Perhaps she should have swallowed her pride and stayed in town. Suppose there was no internet connection on the farm? She might remain stuck on her Master's thesis. She wondered how she would get to the shops when she ran out of something, or to Reykjavík if she needed to. And whether the couple's daughters would like her. Or Jónsi would track her down. Should she use her faint reflection in the car window to put on some make-up? Or not?

So many questions but no answers as yet.

Sóldís dropped her gaze to her trousers. She had decided to dress down, in a hoodie, worn jeans and trainers, to convey the impression that she was ready to pitch in and turn her hand to anything. She was going to the countryside, after all. But now she was having second thoughts. Would it have been better to wear a smart outfit? Would her new employers think she was being disrespectful by not making more of an effort on her first day?

Sóldís pushed the thought away with a sigh. It was too late to do anything about it now. She twisted round and snatched a glance out of the rear windscreen. There was nothing to see but the road unwinding behind them, same as the last time she'd looked. They'd passed very few cars; in fact they seemed to be the only people heading out of town this early on a Sunday morning. She caught the driver's eye in the rear-view mirror.

'Are you expecting to be followed?' He sounded amused but his gaze was serious.

'No. No, of course not,' Sóldís lied. But she kept worrying that Jónsi had found out about her little act of revenge. She was afraid that the moment the taxi pulled up in front of her new employers' house, her ex-boyfriend's car would screech into the yard behind them. Her stomach tightened. Her first meeting with the family mustn't be marred by a screaming match on the doorstep. The idea was absurd, but since when had common sense been a match for one's fears? There was no getting away from the fact that Jónsi had totally lost it when he discovered that she had deleted all the saves in his favourite computer games. The message he'd sent had been crystal clear: *I'll kill you*.

Although she didn't actually believe he'd follow up on his threat, he might well be furious enough to hunt her down and scream abuse at her in front of witnesses. The prospect held no more appeal for her right now than being killed.

Seeing that the driver still had one eye on the mirror, Sóldís tried to appear relaxed. But since this state was foreign to her, even at the best of times, she wasn't sure how to fake it. She decided to strike up a conversation in the hope of distracting herself.

Her opening was about as feeble as you could get: 'Is it much further?'

'No. Quarter of an hour. Or thereabouts.' When the man said no more, Sóldís prepared to be left in silence again with her thoughts. But suddenly he spoke up again: 'You haven't been there before?'

'No. This is my first time.' Sóldís looked out of the window at the flank of the mountain they were passing. It was so steep that the snow that cloaked the rest of the landscape hadn't managed to get a purchase there. Apart from the odd patch of white, the mountainside was a desolate grey. There was just enough light now for her to pick out the largest boulders in the band of scree that was making its infinitesimally slow descent to the valley floor. 'I've only talked to them on the phone,' she added. 'It all happened very fast.'

'So you're going to work for them?'

'Yes, for a two-month trial period to start with.'

'Do you mind my asking what the job is?'

Sóldís recalled the complicated non-disclosure clause in her contract. She'd had to read the lengthy paragraph several times to work out what it meant, but she still wasn't a hundred per cent sure what she was expected to do. Or rather, not do. Surely it wouldn't prevent her from telling someone what her job involved? As far as she could work out, the restrictions had mainly related to the family. She was not permitted to talk about them to other people, to post photos of them on social media or to discuss them in any way, in public or in private. 'I'm just supposed to help out,' she said after a pause. 'With this and that, you know. Take care of the animals. Help the girls with their Icelandic. Cook some meals, clean and so on. The job title is "general assistant".'

'I see.' The man shot her another glance in the mirror but this time his eyes had crinkled in a smile. 'They're nice people, and they've done the place up in style. It's a bit remote, but if you like that sort of thing, you should be fine.'

Sóldís was almost certain there was nothing in her contract to prevent her from asking questions about the family before she met them. She'd tried googling them, but with little success. Almost all she'd found was news on the business pages about the sale of their company abroad. The sums mentioned reminded Sóldís of the kind of numbers that used to be bandied about in her sixth-form astronomy course – too mind-bogglingly large to grasp. She had also tracked down the woman, Ása, on social media, where she seemed to be quite active, posting rather impersonal, highly stylised photos. Sóldís would have absolutely no problem identifying the family dogs, but wouldn't be able to recognise a single member of the family themselves. She could walk past them in the street without having a clue who they were. 'Do you know them, then?' she asked the driver.

'I work for them too. But not like you. Just from time to time. Picking up packages from Reykjavík, or the occasional employee or visitor. I run a car service, you see, and they have an account with me. They call and I jump to it.'

'Are there any other people working for them, apart from me?' The couple hadn't mentioned anyone except the four family members.

'No. Not as far as I know. I expect it'll just be you.'

An awkward silence ensued, and Sóldís got the impression that something was not being said. 'Do they find it hard to hang on to staff, then?'

There was a moment's delay before the driver answered: 'No, I wouldn't say that. But it is rather a lonely spot. Not everyone can cope with living somewhere that remote. It's no coincidence that the locals are flocking to the city. Humans tend to be social animals, after all. The countryside's days are numbered, I reckon. The internet is only prolonging its death throes.'

'Am I the first person they've hired for the assistant job?' This was the conclusion Sóldís had drawn from talking to the couple on the phone. Come to think of it, though, they hadn't actually said that. She'd just leapt to the conclusion. She had a tendency to fill in the blanks like this, to assume the best – as her relationship with Jónsi showed. 'Or have there been others before me who've given up and left?'

The driver hesitated. 'You're the third person I've driven up there for the job. First, there was a young woman like you, then a young man, who's just left. Neither of them lasted long. Keep that to yourself, though. If the couple want to tell you, they will, but please pretend you didn't already know.'

No doubt the driver had been made to sign the same kind of non-disclosure agreement as she had. 'I promise,' she said. 'Do you have any idea why they left? Just out of curiosity.'

'Not a clue. The young man must have organised his own transport. He left recently – about a week ago – and without any warning, from what they told me. But don't ask me why. On the other hand, I gave the young woman who was here before him a lift home to Borgarnes. She was silent the whole way. Didn't say a single word. Between you and me, I think they were both a bit odd. People get the idea that moving to the countryside is the answer to all their problems – it's quite common, you know. They'll have been running away from something, I expect, looking for a new start. But wherever you go, you can never get away from yourself. I expect they realised that in the end and that's why they decided to leave.'

The man broke off abruptly, as if it had belatedly dawned on him that Sóldís might think this was aimed at her. 'I'm not suggesting you're like that,' he added hastily. 'Don't take it the wrong way.'

'Oh no. No problem.' She wasn't in the least offended. On the contrary, she was thinking about the family she was going to live with and wondering what could have prompted them to move to the middle of nowhere. Could they be running away from something too?

They completed the rest of the journey in silence. The driver was probably kicking himself for having said too much. She, meanwhile, was preoccupied with wondering what her new life would be like. It would be the first time she'd ever had a whole house to herself: a restored farmhouse, apparently, that was normally used for guests. She'd been told she might have to share it with visitors from time to time but not often, and probably not at all over the winter. According to the couple, few people bothered to visit them outside the summer months, so the house would be hers until spring at least. And spring was still a long way off.

Which was why, when the car finally pulled up in the yard, Sóldís initially took more of an interest in the old two-storey house than in the imposing new-build. It was more to her taste, after all: a typical wooden farmhouse with white walls, a red corrugated-iron roof and a concrete basement level. She'd always preferred old things. Her clothes were evidence of that. She'd never been particularly stylish, a fact that came home to her when the front door of the modern house opened and she saw a woman, presumably Ása, emerging to greet her.

She was the type who's glamorous without even having to try – slender and graceful, with a pretty face and the kind of long, blonde, wavy hair that Sóldís could only dream about. She herself had thin, mousy locks that were flatter than Denmark, though they were also prone to getting static electricity in an attention-seeking kind of way. One of Sóldís's hands rose instinctively to her head. It was a pointless gesture since once her hair was standing on end no amount of stroking would smooth it down. Anyway, it wasn't as if this was a modelling job. And they'd already seen her during the one online meeting they'd had as part of the rather rushed interview process, although they themselves had kept their webcam switched off. Even when she got the job, she'd been informed over the phone; she hadn't actually seen them at any point. Still, at least they were aware of how ordinary she was – something Jónsi had flung at her in parting. She was about as exciting as tomato ketchup, he'd said. He wanted more: he wanted Béarnaise sauce. As stupid as it sounded, his words had cut her to the quick. And they still stung.

'Hello!' The woman came over, holding out a hand to Sóldís and wearing a wide smile. She had the kind of perfectly straight, dazzlingly white teeth that belonged in a toothpaste commercial. Though her hand felt silky-smooth, her grip was firm. 'Ása. Welcome. Did you have a good journey?'

Sóldís nodded. 'Oh yes, very.'

'Great. The girls are so excited about meeting you. They're in the byre. I told them not to charge out at you in case they put you off and you decided to turn tail and head straight back to town. Not that Íris is likely to fawn all over you – she's a teenager and doesn't like to show any enthusiasm. But I guarantee you Gígja will.'

Sóldís, mindful of what the driver had said about the last two assistants, managed in spite of herself to smile and act normally. 'I can't wait to meet them too.'

The driver lifted out Sóldís's case and closed the boot.

'Is that everything?' Ása asked, surprised.

'A different story from that lad.' The driver chuckled. 'You'd have thought he was moving in with you for the duration. I've never seen so much luggage.'

Sóldís felt her cheeks growing hot. 'I don't need much. I don't own much.' She didn't want to have to explain that she'd left most of her belongings behind when she walked out of the flat she'd shared with Jónsi. Too shattered to think clearly at the time, she'd taken only what she could stuff into one suitcase – though the driver had lifted it with such ease that the case might as well have been half empty. Of course, she could have gone back later to fetch the rest of her belongings, as she still had a key to their flat, but fear of coming face-to-face with Jónsi had prevented her. It wasn't only that she'd been unable to resist that little act of vandalism on his games console on her way out of the flat. It was also that an encounter at this stage could mean nothing other than total humiliation for her, now that it was no longer any secret what Jónsi thought of her. She'd rather say goodbye to her few meagre belongings than risk bumping into him again.

The awkward moment was brought to an end by Ása clapping her hands, smiling and asking if Sóldís would like to start off by getting settled in. There was no rush, and it would be perfect if she came over to the main house for lunch at twelve. Then she could meet the other three members of the family and have something to eat, before being given a tour of the property.

Sóldís accepted this suggestion gratefully. It would give her time to catch her breath and explore the old house that was to be her home for at least the next two months. The driver accompanied them to the door, where he handed Sóldís her case and said goodbye. Then, while Ása's back was momentarily turned, he slipped Sóldís his card: 'Just in case.' He gave her a slightly awkward smile, at the implication that she too might want to quit her job early, and walked back to his car.

She slipped the card into her coat pocket and followed Ása inside. Her living quarters turned out to be far more luxurious than she had been expecting. The couple had given the impression that the old house was a bit primitive, but it had clearly been given a thorough revamping, including a fresh coat of paint and new parquet floors. The furniture, which consisted mainly of old, restored pieces, was in good condition, and the windows were brand-new, as were the two bathrooms and all the kitchen appliances. The house even had a special TV room, and Ása explained that Sóldís would have access to all the main streaming services, both Icelandic and international. There was a good internet connection too, because, as she informed Sóldís, they'd had cable installed. And they'd had their own phone mast built as there hadn't been any signal here when they first moved in. Ása mentioned this casually in passing, as if nothing could be more natural, just as an ordinary person might mention that their phone contract came with unlimited data. People with her wealth obviously inhabited a totally different world.

The amenities were so superior that Sóldís didn't know what to say. But her silence didn't seem to matter because Ása talked non-stop while they were doing a tour of the house. She gave Sóldís her choice of the three bedrooms, recommending that she take the largest, which had the most wardrobe space.

Then, apparently remembering how little luggage Sóldís had brought with her, she tactfully changed the subject.

When they had seen everything except the cellar, Ása clapped her hands again, opened her blue eyes wide and smiled. 'So, that's the house. Not exactly state-of-the-art, but I hope it'll do.'

Sóldís nodded eagerly. 'It's fantastic. Absolutely fantastic. I'm sure I'll be happy here. How could I not be?'

Although Sóldís's enthusiasm was genuine, Ása looked a little surprised. Once she had gone, Sóldís did another circuit of the house, paying special attention to the bedrooms. Two were on the ground floor, while the largest was upstairs and had a bathroom next door. Sóldís felt inclined to follow Ása's advice, but before she made up her mind, she tried lying on the made-up beds in the two downstairs rooms. Perhaps she would feel more comfortable in a smaller space. She would be sleeping alone and there was no chance of that situation changing any time soon. That had been clearly stipulated in her contract: no visits from boyfriends. Which was easy enough when there weren't any.

She didn't take to either of the smaller rooms. She lay and stared up at the ceiling, then got to her feet and peered into the drawers in the bedside table and chest, then into the wardrobe. All were empty apart from the wardrobe in the second room, which turned out to be full of clothes on hangers. Inspecting them, she saw that they belonged to a man – a young man, she guessed. They couldn't have been more different from her own cheap, boring apparel that served no purpose beyond covering her nakedness and keeping her warm. Most of these garments had prominent designer labels and were smarter than anything she had ever owned.

Sóldís frowned and closed the wardrobe. The clothes presumably belonged to some male relative or friend of the couple, who must be as rich as them if he could afford to leave all this designer gear behind. There was something depressing about not taking your clothes with you. It occurred to her that this might have had nothing to do with the owner's extravagance or lack of respect for his clothes; he might simply have been in a hurry to leave. They could, for example, have belonged to her predecessor, who had apparently left without saying goodbye. On second thoughts, that was unlikely. A man who dressed in designer gear was unlikely to accept a job as a dogsbody in the depths of the countryside. Then again, she recalled the taxi driver saying that the young man had brought a massive amount of luggage with him. Perhaps he'd been well off but had got into financial difficulties. It happened. In that case, the clothes might be his. Maybe he'd taken the most essential and would be back to collect the rest later.

Sóldís resolved that, as soon as she got a chance, she'd suggest the clothes be returned to their rightful owner. Presumably he'd want them back while they were still in fashion. If, on the other hand, they belonged to some rich relative who had deliberately left them behind and subsequently bought himself a whole new wardrobe, they could be donated to charity.

She carried her suitcase upstairs. It only took her a couple of minutes to unpack. The wardrobe up here was empty and she wondered why the owner of the clothes hadn't opted to stay in the largest room. Perhaps he had, but the wardrobe in here hadn't been big enough and he'd had to spill over into one of the downstairs ones. At any rate, she'd have thought that the type of guy who wore designer gear would have gone for the biggest room. Unless, of course, the clothes had belonged to a visitor and one of her predecessors had already been occupying the upstairs room when he came to stay.

Sóldís flopped on to the big double bed in her new room. As she lay, quietly luxuriating in the superior mattress, she couldn't help wondering about her two predecessors. She'd give anything to know their reasons for leaving. She just hoped the driver had been right and that the problem had lain with them rather than with her employers, their daughters, the house or the area.

Sóldís felt a rush of apprehension. She focused on breathing: in, out, in, out. Staring at the ceiling panels, she distracted herself by counting the knots in the wood, her ears tuning in to the creaks and groans of the old house. Her great-grandfather always used to say that a loud creaking in the house timbers was an omen that the owner was going to die. Oddly enough, this memory helped to calm her nerves. It was such a ridiculous superstition. Everyone was going to die sooner or later, so a prediction like that would always come true in the end, whether or not your house had creaky timbers.

Of course it would be OK. More than OK. It would be fun, and that was exactly what she needed right now. She continued her deep breathing, in through her mouth, out through her nose.

Gradually, it began to work. Her anxiety receded and she reminded herself that the feeling wasn't a foreboding of anything. It was simply the realisation that she would be alone in a strange house, far from the city and everyone she knew. Another disorientating factor was bound to be the speed at which her circumstances had changed. She'd phoned the employment agency immediately after leaving the flat she'd shared with Jónsi and explained that she was looking for work in the countryside. It had been the only way she could think of to put as much distance between herself and her former life as possible. Then she had sent in her rather sketchy CV, thinking that the most she could expect was an offer of work at a hotel in a week or so. But no more than a few hours had passed before the agency had rung back to tell her about this position. The phone interview had taken place the next day, followed by another in the evening, then the online meeting the day after. Three hours later she was employed and arrangements had been made for her to start in the morning. All done and dusted.

Sóldís had no regrets about not requesting a longer time to consider the offer. It had been no secret that the couple were looking for someone to start straight away, and any delay or foot-dragging could have resulted in them hiring someone else. Besides, it was quite clear to her that a chance like this was heaven-sent. The decision had been a no-brainer. Having a live-in job meant she wouldn't be forced to crash with friends or relatives while she was finding herself a new flat and a new life. That was all the incentive she needed.

But because it had all happened so fast, the change in her circumstances hadn't sunk in yet. Hence her anxiety.

It would take a little time to adjust to the situation. But Sóldís would manage.

Of course she would.

Chapter 3
Wednesday

The windscreen wipers were fighting a losing battle with the sheer volume of snow. Týr had already had to stop twice to clear them and would probably have to do so again soon. The clumps of ice building up on the glass left streaks that grew wider with every stroke. But that was nothing compared to the first leg of the journey, when it had been all he could do to hold the car on the icy road as it was battered by violent gusts of wind on the Kjalarnes peninsula. His knuckles had whitened on the wheel, and the intermittent yelps from the passenger seat had done nothing to help matters. Apart from that, Idunn had barely opened her mouth during the drive.

At first, he'd attributed her silence to nerves brought on by the hazardous conditions, but he was beginning to think that the woman was always like this. She came across as a classic introvert; all his attempts to draw her out had been met by monosyllabic replies. She stared, tight-lipped, into the dark, snowy void ahead, ensuring that their eyes never met, because eye contact was a sure invitation to conversation. He guessed that her unsociability was the reason why the other officers answering the call-out had seemed relieved when he offered her a lift. You couldn't exactly accuse her of being a bundle of laughs.

Týr slowed down as the GPS announced that they were due to turn right soon. He had checked the route on the map before setting out and knew that the turn-off was shortly before the head of the fjord. He had never driven round Hvalfjördur before, always taking the tunnel when he travelled north or west from Reykjavík, and the visibility was so poor that it would be easy to overshoot if he wasn't careful. Since there was only a single lane in either direction and no hard shoulder to speak of, he'd rather avoid having to turn round. If he did, he reckoned they'd have a fifty-fifty chance of ending up in a ditch. He should have kept up with the convoy of police vehicles but, out of consideration for his passenger, he had slowed down and got left behind. It was quite a while since he had last seen the red glow of rear lights, so there was no chance of tailing the car in front, like a duckling following its mother.

As Týr took the right turn, Idunn finally broke the silence. 'Is it much further?' He was so startled that he took his eyes off the road for a moment to glance at her. She was still staring fixedly through the windscreen, though if she'd lowered her eyes to the satnav on the dashboard, she could have seen the answer for herself.

'No. About fifteen minutes.' Týr tightened his grip on the steering wheel as the car skidded slightly on the bend.

Idunn went on: 'I'm getting worried about the return journey. I can't stand snow and ice, and I've had it up to here with blocked roads.'

It occurred to Týr that he might have got his companion wrong. Perhaps Idunn was the chatty type after all and had just been suffering from nerves. He'd have liked to pass the time by talking but feared that he was now in for the kind of conversation he found hardest to sustain: a conversation about himself and his background. *Oh, really? You grew up in Sweden? How come? And what made you move back home?*

As far as he was concerned, moving to Iceland had meant *leaving* home. But he'd discovered that for most Icelanders 'home' meant Iceland. It couldn't be anywhere else. Even spending more than half your life abroad, like he had, made no difference. If you were Icelandic, you were supposed to regard Iceland as home. Perhaps he would one day. But for that he would have to stay on in the country, and, as matters stood, there was no guarantee he would. He had acted impulsively after a messy break-up, without pausing to consider the decision about his future that it would inevitably leave him facing. The move had at least made one thing clear, though; it had provided him with the necessary distance to recognise that his relationship had reached the end of the road. He'd faced up to the fact that neither of them had been happy and that splitting up had been the only sensible solution.

The downside of the move was that he was now wretchedly lonely and still hadn't managed to build up any kind of social network in Reykjavík. His few remaining relatives had dutifully stepped up to begin with, before gradually withdrawing into their own lives once the novelty of his presence had worn off. He couldn't blame them. Although he'd met them during his summer holidays in Iceland, he wasn't a fixture in their lives. And as much as he longed for companionship, he didn't like the idea of being regarded as a charity case, so he tried to avoid imposing on them.

He'd made up his mind to stick it out in Iceland for a year, and meant to stand by this decision. But if things went on like this, he'd be forced to admit that his attempt to reconnect with his roots had been a mistake and to return to Sweden with his tail between his legs. Still, even that would be better than struggling on in his lonely state. Maybe it was also time to face the fact that his roots might not actually be here. Maybe he didn't have roots anywhere. Raised by Icelandic parents in Sweden, he was neither wholly Swedish nor wholly Icelandic.

To complicate matters still further, he was adopted and had no memory of his birth parents, who had disappeared prematurely from his life. His mother had died of breast cancer when he was four, and his father had been killed in an accident not long afterwards, though Týr suspected this might not have been the real cause of death. His adoptive parents always became evasive when he tried to elicit the details of the accident that had cut his father's life short. Týr was convinced he'd either killed himself or been a junkie and died of an overdose, and that they were trying to shield him out of a misguided desire to be kind. Matters were complicated further by the fact that his birth father hadn't been cohabiting with his mother, and had been reluctant to acknowledge his son, so Týr's adoptive parents knew next to nothing about the man.

Týr knew far more about his birth mother. Her memory had been kept alive by her sister and brother-in-law – his adoptive parents. On the mantelpiece in their home there had been a handsome urn containing her ashes, and next to it a photo of her smiling broadly, oblivious to the tragic fate that awaited her. Her sister and brother-in-law, who had no children of their own, had taken him in when he was left motherless. And his father, having no apparent interest in him, had been quick to sign the adoption papers. Foolish as it was, Týr found it hard to accept this rejection. But it didn't matter – in fact, it had probably been a stroke of luck for him because it would be hard to imagine better parents than his adoptive ones. Growing up, he had been perfectly aware of this, and nowadays he had no interest in discovering anything about his birth father. Reaching this stage had felt good. Since the man hadn't given a shit about him, it was only fair that the feeling was mutual.

But that still left him with the problem that he had never put down roots anywhere.

To forestall any questions from Idunn about his unusual background, Týr decided to take charge of the conversation himself. The easiest option was to talk about work, as this was the only thing they had in common and it would lessen the chances of them straying on to personal matters. 'What information did they give you?' he asked. 'Is it possible we could be looking at an accident?'

'I assume I was told the same as you: several members of the household have been found dead inside the farmhouse, and the man who made the discovery is claiming they were murdered. I haven't a clue if he's right. Perhaps it's a case of carbon monoxide poisoning and the injuries the man thought he saw were simply the result of decomposition.'

Týr nodded. Since Idunn was a pathologist, she presumably knew what she was talking about. His criminology studies had only touched on the examination of bodies, and he had no regrets about not having learnt more. As far as he was concerned, other people could take care of that side of the job. Yet, even so, he doubted the witness would have failed to discern the signs of decomposition, especially since he was a farmer. He must be used to seeing the carcases of animals, at least.

'Pretty grim, however it happened.' Idunn exhaled heavily, and the sound reminded Týr of the countless times he'd done the same. It was unavoidable in his chosen profession. An involuntary reaction, as if his body was trying to expel the bad impressions of its own accord. It never worked.

Out of the corner of his eye, Týr saw that Idunn had turned her head and was studying his profile. He threw her a quick smile to take the edge off the discomfort it was causing him. He wanted her to know that he knew she was staring.

'I have to ask you something,' she said. 'I hope you won't find it rude.'

Týr told her to fire away. He guessed what her question was going to be: it was the one he got asked more than any other. And he was right.

'How did you get that scar on your forehead?'

'Not by doing anything exciting, I'm afraid. I just fell off my tricycle when I was a kid. I was peddling along full tilt without looking where I was going. The front wheel hit a hole in the pavement and I was thrown over the handlebars. I split my forehead open. Bad luck – but it could have been much worse.'

'You could wear a fringe, then no one could see it.'

Týr had tried that. All the photos of him as a boy showed him with a long, thick fringe down to his eyebrows, but at the age of twelve he'd realised how naff it made him look, and ever since then he'd worn his hair short. 'I just put up with people seeing it. It doesn't matter. Sometimes it can even be a useful icebreaker.'

'I wasn't asking as an icebreaker. I just have a special interest in wounds. That's why I wondered. Wounds are a big part of my job, though not usually healed ones like yours.'

Týr only just stopped himself from raising his eyebrows at this.

Idunn seemed to realise how odd her comment must have sounded. She added: 'Do you get asked about it a lot?'

That was easy to answer. 'Yes. So I'm used to it. It's not a touchy subject.'

'Ugh, tell me about it! When I meet people for the first time, they always ask me the same question too, so I can save you the bother and tell you the answer now: I specialised in forensic pathology because I find it a fascinating field. More interesting than conventional medicine. I'm not that keen on people – living ones, I mean.'

'I see. I wasn't actually going to ask, but that's good to know.' This wasn't entirely honest. Týr had in fact been wondering and would no doubt have raised the subject at some point. On the drive home, probably.

He couldn't think of anything else to say and they lapsed into silence again.

The snowfall appeared to be easing off at last. Týr found he could make out more in the beam of the headlights than just the short stretch of road immediately in front of the car and the nearest marker post.

'What a criminal way to treat animals,' Idunn muttered suddenly, and Týr peered through the side window, following her gaze. He glimpsed what looked like a herd of horses huddled together for the scant warmth afforded by each other's bodies. There was no sign of any shelter in the field, but perhaps it was obscured by the falling snow.

Týr returned his attention to the road. 'I expect the horses can cope or they wouldn't be out here. Their owner must care about them. And they're tough beasts.'

'You reckon?' Idunn sounded sceptical. 'Know a lot about horses, do you?'

'Me? No.' Týr laughed for the first time since he'd answered this call-out. The thought of him choosing riding as a hobby struck him as so absurd that he couldn't help himself. 'What about you? Are you into horses?'

'No.' The answer was curt and didn't seem to invite any follow-up. Though perhaps Týr was missing his chance to throw the conversational ball into the air again. Well, if so, that was tough.

The further they got from the main road, the worse the driving conditions became. Týr passed a sign saying Minna-Hvarf and knew that this meant they were getting close. He'd been warned not to turn in there but to keep going. Shortly afterwards, they reached the correct turn-off. A signpost bearing the name Hvarf showed that they were unmistakably on the right track. The farm was well named – *hvarf* meaning 'out of sight' – as it was situated in a small valley, hidden from the road.

The access road hadn't been ploughed and Týr was grateful that he'd been allocated one of the big police four-by-fours with elevated suspension. He did his best to follow in the wheel ruts made by the cars that had gone ahead but didn't always succeed. He and Idunn were flung from side to side as the vehicle yawed as if they were navigating a rough sea. Idunn clung to the handle on the roof, using her other hand to prevent her big camera from being thrown off her lap. Týr merely tightened his grip on the wheel.

The farmyard turned out to be large, so there was no shortage of parking spaces, despite the crowd of vehicles already assembled there. Týr recognised two of them from the convoy, both four-by-fours like the one he was driving. In addition, there were a couple more police SUVs, presumably belonging to the local force. Then there were two other vehicles, one a small family car, the other an SUV, both buried in snow. At a scene like this, he'd usually expect to see the big van belonging to forensics as well, but a decision had been made to delay sending it until the snow let up and the access road to the farm could be ploughed. Whether that would be later this evening, during the night or tomorrow morning, only time would tell. Until then, they would have to examine the scene as best they could with the instruments they had been able to bring along.

The view was dominated by a brightly lit, modern house that completely dwarfed the other four buildings, which consisted of an older, renovated farmhouse connected to the new house by a corridor, a byre, a sheep shed and an outhouse.

A frantic barking broke out in the byre as Idunn and Týr stepped out of the car. But it quickly died away as they walked over to the modern house, where a group of people had gathered under the porch. Týr wasn't surprised to see so many there. The farm was on the patch of the West Iceland Police, so, in addition to his colleagues from Reykjavík, there were representatives from the local CID based in the small town of Akranes on the coast some forty-five kilometres away. The locals had taken the decision to request back-up from the capital as soon as they were alerted to the number of bodies and the gravity of the case.

There was an unpleasant smell hanging in the air around the porch, and one of the women in the group, noticing Týr's involuntary grimace, gestured to a large patch of vomit on the heated pavement. It had been cordoned off with police tape to prevent anyone treading in it. 'The bloke who discovered the scene threw up on his way out,' she explained. 'Inside the house as well.'

And that extinguished any faint hope Týr had been cherishing that the scene wouldn't be too hideous.

The group standing by the door were all kitted out in white protective suits with their hoods up, masks over their faces and goggles over their eyes. One of them handed Idunn and Týr clear, sealed bags containing the same kind of gear, which they proceeded to put on.

Idunn cut a strange-looking figure once dressed. She had stuffed her mane of extremely long, thick, curly hair inside her hood, which made her head appear several sizes too large for her body. The strap of her camera scarcely fitted over it as she attempted to hang it round her neck, but no one commented and most of them tactfully looked away.

It was hard to recognise any member of the group since all that could be glimpsed of their faces were the eyes behind their goggles, but Týr managed to identify several people nonetheless. He knew his boss, Huldar, by his height, as he towered over everyone else, and similarly he was able to pick out his tiny colleague, Lína. Another female officer could be recognised by the colour of her skin. She was black, which made her stand out. Her name was Karólína and she had joined the force at the same time as Týr. The two of them, along with a man of Polish origin, had been hired as part of a campaign to increase diversity in the force. The initiative had been launched by Huldar, and although Týr didn't think much of his talents as a manager, he had at least done a good job in this respect. Týr was lucky to have been taken on, but then he'd been helped by the lack of applications. His Swedish connection had been enough to mark him out as different from most of the people currently working with the Icelandic police. And the changing character of Iceland's criminal underworld, which was increasingly beginning to resemble that of their neighbouring countries, meant that he was valued for his experience abroad.

'Everybody ready?' asked one of the masked personnel. Týr didn't recognise his voice, but the man introduced himself immediately afterwards as Hördur, head of West Iceland CID in Akranes. After that, he introduced two other members of the group, Elma and Sævar, who worked with him. Sævar had unusually dark eyebrows; Elma was fairer. She was the woman who had pointed out the vomit. Once Idunn and Týr had shaken hands with the Akranes detectives, Hördur added, with marked emphasis, that he was in charge of the investigation. In spite of the request for back-up from Reykjavík, the Akranes team evidently had no intention of surrendering their control of the inquiry. This was a matter of indifference to Týr and, as far as he could tell, to Idunn as well. They snapped on their masks while Hördur was addressing the group: 'Right, those of you who have just arrived from Reykjavík, be warned that what you're about to face in there is pretty unpleasant.' His voice was grave and tinged with sadness. 'Please don't touch anything. Just follow me and stay with the group. We've already taken a lot of pictures, which will be shared with you later. If you want to take your own, could you please nominate one member of your group to take responsibility for that or we'll all be blinded by the flashes.'

'I take my own photos. Regardless of what you decide to do.' Idunn was gripping her camera as if afraid it was about to be confiscated. To prevent an argument breaking out about whether priority should be given to the Reykjavík police or the pathologist, Hördur backed down and allowed two cameras.

There was a wreath on the front door made of bare twigs decorated with dried berries. From it hung a small plaque bearing the inscription: *Home is Best*. The wreath and its message couldn't have been more ironic in light of what awaited them inside.

It took a little while for everyone to enter. Most baulked at the faint but unmistakable odour of death. Then, quickly pulling themselves together, they began, one after the other, to don plastic shoe-covers prior to stepping over the threshold. There was a bit of jostling before they were all inside and following Hördur through a large entrance hall, past the family's shoes and a row of coats hanging from pegs. Týr found himself staring at a brightly coloured child's anorak and a hat with a large pompom. It was a relief to get past and into the house proper.

But things didn't improve there. Everywhere Týr looked, there were signs that this had been the home of children. Although the place was unusually clean and tidy, there were clues all over the place, from the wax crayons on the gleaming wall-mounted dresser to the small, colourful sock lying in the middle of the floor, and the framed child's drawing on the wall facing the entrance. There was a stuffed toy rabbit on the floor by the shelves, its head and long ears drooping, its face invisible. It had a dejected air, as if it knew its time was up. No one would want a cuddly toy that had belonged to a dead child.

There was complete silence among the police officers as they took in the cavernous room beyond the entrance hall. The ceiling was so high that it could easily have accommodated two normal storeys, but judging by the size of the place from the outside, the owners could afford to be extravagant with the space.

Nothing they could see prepared them for what was coming. The only indication that they were in the right house was the nauseating smell. There were no bloodstains on the smooth, shiny-white walls, no sign of broken ornaments or furniture overturned in a struggle. Apart from the children's toys, you'd have thought the owners had been expecting an estate agent's photographer, not a killer. Perhaps Idunn was right when she had spoken of carbon monoxide poisoning.

From the lofty open space, they passed through the connecting corridor into the old farmhouse. Here the proportions and design were more conventional, with normal ceiling heights and modest-sized rooms. Hördur led them straight to the door of a ground-floor bedroom, from where they could see the body of a young woman sprawled on a neatly made bed. She was dressed in a T-shirt and pyjama trousers, and lying face up, with her feet on the floor as if she'd fallen over backwards. Her mouth was open, her lower jaw sagging as if she had seen something that made no sense to her.

Judging by the smooth duvet cover and pillows, the young woman hadn't been in bed when she was attacked. Týr thought she had either been getting ready for bed or else fled into the room, pursued by her assailant. But one thing was crystal clear: her demise owed nothing to carbon monoxide. Her terrible wounds left them in no doubt that she had died at the hands of another human being.

'We can't be sure who she is,' Hördur told them, 'but it seems likely that she worked for the couple – as an au pair or something. Upstairs, there's a room we think was hers. The bed there has been slept in, and there's a phone on the bedside table that must have belonged to her. Admittedly, there's nothing in the wardrobe, but there's a suitcase in the room that appears to have been recently packed. Otherwise, the room is empty, apart from a page torn from a book that's lying on the floor. The logical conclusion is that she was intending to go away. Possibly just for her weekend off, but obviously that didn't happen.' Hördur was silent as he let this sink in. The young woman had so nearly escaped the horror. 'It looks as if she woke up and came downstairs to find out what was going on, only to come face-to-face with her killer. But of course that's just a guess at this stage.'

They lingered long enough for Idunn and the detective who was taking pictures for Reykjavík CID to capture the body and its surroundings in exhaustive detail. Idunn took considerably longer to complete this process than the police officer. In contrast to her silence in the car, she kept up a continuous commentary as she worked, directing her words not to the group standing watching from the doorway but to herself, describing everything she saw. Happening to glance at the others and noticing their puzzlement, she rolled her eyes behind her goggles and explained that she was recording her observations on her camera.

Having received permission from Hördur to touch the body, Idunn tentatively took hold of the young woman's arms and legs and bent them. She measured the temperature of the room and the body of the deceased. Since she was reporting all this aloud, they learnt that the body was more or less at room temperature, and since it would have taken less than twenty-four hours for the body to cool, Týr knew that Idunn was recording this detail purely from a desire to be methodical. To tick all the boxes. Because there could be no doubt that the dead woman had been lying there for much longer than a night and a day. The sickening stench and the signs of putrefaction could not have belonged to the recently deceased. Idunn didn't appear to have had any difficulty moving the limbs either, which indicated that rigor mortis had eased off. So the young woman must have died no less than forty-eight hours ago. If Týr had to guess, he'd say longer.

When Idunn had finished, Hördur ushered them back into the modern house and from there into the bedroom wing. There was police tape cordoning off a trail of bloody footprints, but luckily the corridor was wide enough for them to pass. The sights that met them in the rooms leading off the hall in this wing were no less gruesome than the first crime scene, and Týr began to fear that the nightmare was never going to end. It was as if they were in some kind of hell in which every door concealed a scene of horror worse than the one before. His eyes couldn't get used to the sights confronting them or his nose the cloying, suffocating stench of death.

The mask provided almost no protection. There was a smell of vomit too from a puddle by one of the doors, which Elma, the female officer from Akranes, pointed out, explaining that it had also been made by the man who discovered the bodies. After seeing what was inside the room, no one was surprised by his reaction.

The scenes in the rooms of the teenage daughter and her younger sister were distressing enough, but even these didn't prepare them for the savagery with which the woman in the marital bedroom had been attacked. There was no way of guessing the motive, but the injuries suggested a frenzied assailant. Týr found it hard to imagine the hatred that must have motivated the assault. The longer he studied the woman's body, the more terrible he found the spectacle. And the flashes regularly illuminating the luridly mottled, bare-veined, bloated flesh did nothing to improve matters. Týr felt so dizzy he was afraid he was going to lose his balance, but clutching at the doorframe or leaning against the wall for support was out of the question. He didn't want to make himself unpopular with forensics, who would have to go over everything in here in microscopic detail and would not take it kindly if the crime scene was contaminated.

He concentrated on breathing in through his mouth and out through his nose, which helped a little. Then Idunn's voice broke into his consciousness and he was forced to listen to her describing the large gash which extended from the dead woman's crown to her forehead, almost splitting her skull in two. As she pondered aloud what kind of weapon could have been used, he blurted out: 'An axe. It was made by an axe.'

Idunn broke off and turned to look at him. Although Týr could see nothing but her eyes, he thought she was surprised by his interjection. As surprised as he was, perhaps. He hadn't intended to say anything; the words had burst from him involuntarily. He was well aware that it wasn't his place to tell Idunn what to think. Feeling his cheeks grow hot, he was grateful for the mask that concealed most of his face.

Idunn didn't comment on his interruption but merely returned her attention to the corpse with an almost imperceptible nod. But his words seemed to have caused her to abandon her speculation about the murder weapon for now. Instead, she commented that, based on the evidence she had seen in the marital bedroom and the girls' rooms, the attack must have been made at night. The victims had been in bed, very probably asleep.

Týr carefully suppressed a sigh of relief when Hördur announced that they had finished with the bedrooms and that there were no more bodies in the house. It was the first time in his career that Týr had been so badly affected by a crime scene, although he had witnessed plenty of distressing sights in Stockholm before being transferred to economic crimes. He felt a violent longing to be outside in the open air, and assumed that this was the result of claustrophobia, another first for him. The explanation wasn't hard to find; every aspect of these murders was so excessive, whether it was the number of victims or the sheer brutality of the attacks. And there were children among the dead, which violated every instinct.

Hördur showed the group into the kitchen next, following the trail of bloody footprints. The room turned out to be as over the top as the rest of the house. Everything was immaculate and free from clutter here as well, the only sign of life being the food packaging and leftovers on the table. It didn't appear to have been the family's supper, since the leftovers consisted of a carton of milk, a block of cheese and a paper bag containing a sliced sourdough loaf. To Týr, this looked more like a midnight snack.

'I don't suppose it will have escaped any of you that the husband is not among the deceased,' Hördur said. 'Before you arrived, we conducted a thorough search of the premises. Indoors, anyway. And we believe there are two possibilities. One is that he made a break for it and the killer caught up with him somewhere outside the house. If so, his body will turn up by daylight.' Hördur gestured to the trail of footprints that led to the French windows in the glass wall. 'In other words, we believe the footprints belong to the husband. He either left this way after doing the deed or – if he wasn't the killer – while it was still going on.' Hördur didn't say anything for a moment, and the eyes of the others followed the dried-up marks across the floor to the glass doors. 'If he was the killer, he must have made his escape this way. Left the country, presumably.'

'That's fairly likely, isn't it?' asked a voice behind Týr that he recognised as belonging to his boss, Huldar. 'The guy's rolling in money. For all we know, he could be holed up somewhere in the tropics by now. Planning to get himself a new face and a nice new life.'

Týr frowned inadvertently, making his goggles twitch. Hördur, catching the movement, asked what was on his mind. Týr replied, reluctantly at first, uncomfortable about contradicting Huldar in front of strangers: 'Although I don't have any evidence, I think it's more likely that the man's dead. This incident has all the hallmarks of a familicide – the kind of murder where the father decides it's best his family should die, and wipes out the lot, before topping himself.'

It was Hördur who answered: 'It could have been an aggravated burglary,' he said, sounding sceptical. 'Or a revenge killing. I think we'd do better to avoid generalisations at this stage.'

'I'm not generalising. I'm just pointing out what seems plausible to me.' Týr had never worked on a familicide, either during his short spell of duty in Iceland or, previously, in the Swedish police. But he had learnt about such cases during his studies and found them interesting, though it would never have occurred to him that he would one day take part in investigating one. He decided he might as well plough on, now that he had started. The stifling feeling of claustrophobia had receded slightly the moment he opened his mouth. 'In familicides, the victims are typically attacked in their sleep, as seems to have been the case here. Another feature that appears to fit is that the family members are usually murdered in one continuous attack, lasting a relatively short time. Not one today and another tomorrow. I think it's pretty clear that these murders were all committed the same night. And, more often than not, the perpetrator – or family annihilator – is the father, who also seems to be a likely suspect in this case.'

'And?' Hördur prompted. All eyes were on Týr now.

'Well, if that is the scenario here, the man will almost certainly have taken his own life. Maybe by walking off into the wilds in the hope of dying of exposure or finding some other means of killing himself.' Týr turned slightly to stare into the impenetrable darkness beyond the glass wall. 'I doubt he'll have shot himself, because if he'd had access to a firearm, I assume he'd have used that to kill his family.'

Idunn nodded, drawing the others' attention back to her ridiculously large head. 'I agree. Do we know anything about their finances? Could they have been facing bankruptcy, in spite of all the conspicuous signs of wealth?'

Again, it was Hördur who replied. 'We haven't got that far yet. It's my understanding that they were fantastically wealthy. But of course that's no guarantee that their financial situation hadn't taken a turn for the worse.'

'I'd be interested to know what emerges.' Idunn fiddled with the camera and Týr guessed she was switching on the voice recorder again. Then she continued: 'Money worries are a very common motive for family murders. The killer has a warped belief that their family needs to be spared the fallout from bankruptcy. It's more common among the wealthy than the poor. Particularly among people who've been extremely well-off. Having to take a drop in their standard of living to be on a par with the rest of us seems like a terrible prospect to them. Unendurable, even.'

'We're getting a bit ahead of ourselves here.' There was a note of irritation in Hördur's voice now. 'This is Iceland, remember.'

The petite Lína chipped in at this point: 'There has been one case of familicide in Iceland.' All heads turned to her and it was apparent, even through her mask and goggles, that she was gratified by the attention. She elaborated: 'In the middle of the last century. A chemist poisoned his wife, his children and himself. He had three children, if I remember right.'

None of the Reykjavík team was in any doubt that Lína was right: she could always be trusted to be accurate about this kind of detail.

'Who's the most likely suspect in these sorts of cases?' Hördur asked, apparently coming round to Týr's suggestion.

'The father, as Týr said,' Lína replied. 'With very few exceptions.'

Since no one else seemed to have anything to contribute, Týr spoke up again: 'There's another thing. Money troubles aren't always at the root of it. There's also the possibility that room is being made for a new partner, that one of the couple has had enough and wants to make a fresh start, for example. Or sometimes parents oppose their teenage child's choice of a boyfriend or girlfriend, so the teenager decides to get rid of them. But in that case the kid usually tries to pass it off as the work of an intruder, in which they themselves were also injured but survived. That's extremely unlikely here, though, as the teenage daughter is dead and there doesn't seem to have been any attempt to make it look like a break-in.'

Idunn turned to Hördur. 'Was their marriage solid? Did the teenage girl have an undesirable boyfriend?'

'No issues as far as we know. But, as I said, it's early days.' Hördur took out his phone and asked for Idunn's number, which he entered into his contacts. 'I'll get in touch when we know more.' Holding up his phone, he peered at the screen. 'The connection's still down. I wonder if the mast's out of order.'

Týr couldn't care less about the phone signal. All he could think about was the appalling butchery that had taken place in this house and his increasing desperation to get out. He couldn't shake off the sensation that the walls and ceiling were closing in on him, even though he knew it was an illusion.

Huldar now intervened, bringing them back to the question of the missing man: 'So the father could be somewhere in the vicinity? Wounded, possibly, and pretending to have been hurt in the attack? Waiting for us to find him? If so, he must have seriously misjudged how long it would take for his crime to be discovered.'

Before anyone could answer, a loud click rang out in the big, glass room, making them all jump. It was followed by the unmistakable sound of a cuckoo clock. They had passed one in the hall leading to the kitchen. The cuckoo rang out nine times, then broke off; then there was another loud click, presumably as its little door closed again, hiding the cuckoo from view.

Once it had fallen silent, Idunn walked briskly over to the kitchen table and the remains of the meal. She bent down to the open milk carton and Hördur yelped: 'Don't touch anything!'

Without so much as glancing his way, Idunn pulled down her mask and sniffed at the spout. Then she replaced her mask and surveyed the group: 'My grandmother has the same kind of clock.'

Týr was so wrong-footed by her words that the walls abruptly stopped looming closer. He noticed the others cocking their heads quizzically too. It appeared he wasn't the only one who suspected the pathologist had lost the plot, an impression only heightened by her comically large head. But when Idunn resumed, it turned out that she was perfectly sane.

'Off the top of my head, I'd say the victims have been dead for four, maybe five days. Or thereabouts. But a cuckoo clock like that needs to be wound once a day. So how come it's still going?' Idunn pointed to the milk carton. 'And the milk's still OK. Now, I'm no expert in the preservation of foodstuffs, but if it had been standing on the table at room temperature for several days, it should have turned sour.'

'Couldn't it have been left there by the man who reported the bodies?' Lína piped up.

'Does that seem likely to you?' Idunn retorted. 'Would any of you have stopped for a snack after seeing what we've seen here? Or taken the time to wind up the cuckoo clock?' When no one replied, she continued: 'I thought not. But do ring the farmer and check. Who knows? Perhaps he was starving, and likes to keep track of the time.'

There was a pause, broken by Hördur, who said in tones of revulsion: 'If it wasn't the farmer, it has to have been the killer, doesn't it? Does that mean he's been here the whole time?' No one replied, but Týr guessed they were all thinking the same thing: what kind of person would be capable of butchering four people, then living among their bodies for days afterwards?

Chapter 4
Before

'Ninety-nine, a hundred. Coming!' Sóldís removed her hands from her eyes and turned away from the wall. She hadn't actually needed to stand there with her hands covering her face but she had done it to oblige Gígja, who took their games of hide-and-seek very seriously. Sóldís was keen not to jeopardise their three-day-old relationship. Gígja was beginning to trust her. For example, she was no longer worried that Sóldís would cheat. At first, the little girl had wasted part of her precious hiding time by checking up on Sóldís to make sure she was obeying the rules of the game. Sóldís knew this because she could hear the thudding of the little girl's feet as she spied on her. Gígja would never make it as a ninja.

This was their third game of hide-and-seek in a row today; yesterday they had played it four times. Gígja got rather more out of the game than she did; Sóldís's biggest challenge was to conceal her boredom.

Despite an initial slight wariness, the little girl had taken to Sóldís quickly. And now, after only three days, it seemed that her trial period was over. Mind you, quite a lot could be achieved in that time. Sóldís had once managed to fall head over heels in love over the August bank holiday weekend. It had taken her the next three years to understand that her feelings weren't reciprocated.

Íris was a tougher nut to crack, which was no surprise as she was a teenager. Sóldís was young enough herself to remember what it was like to be too young for some of the things you wanted to do and too old for others. And to regard anyone who wasn't the same age as you as a loser. So Sóldís didn't take it personally when Íris rolled her eyes at her suggestions or sighed over their Icelandic lessons. There was no point getting annoyed about it.

Sóldís looked down at Bói and Lubbi, the two family dogs, who stared back at her, eyes bright with anticipation. They'd obeyed her order to sit beside her while she was counting. She couldn't imagine what they thought she was doing, but then they had limited insight into most of the things humans got up to.

'Gígja and I are playing hide-and-seek,' she explained to them, and the dogs both tilted their heads enquiringly. 'Let's find Gígja.' Recognising the name, the dogs eagerly swept the floor with their tails. Sóldís clapped her hands and they jumped up, wild with excitement about what was going to happen next. The game always seemed to take them just as much by surprise as if they hadn't taken part in all the previous ones.

They followed Sóldís out of the bedroom on the ground floor where she had been counting while Gígja hid. The girl had decided yesterday that today they should play in the old farmhouse, and Sóldís hadn't objected. Well, actually it had given her a moment's hesitation. The old house was supposed to be her quarters, and, although it was far too big for her, she felt the others shouldn't take it for granted that they could just waltz in without knocking. Well, not all the others. Up to now, only Gígja and her mother had had any reason to come over. Ása had brought a large pack of loo paper and put some rolls in the bathrooms. She'd also brought a bag containing various things to eat that she had put in Sóldís's fridge. On neither occasion had she bothered to knock. Clearly, she felt that, as the owner, she was well within her rights to enter.

On the second occasion, Sóldís had remembered that she wanted to show Ása the clothes that had been left behind in one of the downstairs bedrooms. Ása had followed her in there, opened the wardrobe and regarded them for a moment or two. Then she had run her hands through the garments as if searching the pockets. She hadn't found anything, or at least there was nothing in her hands when she closed the wardrobe and said she'd see that the clothes were returned to their rightful owner. Sóldís merely smiled at her, trying not to show how odd she found this behaviour. Ása didn't mention who the clothes belonged to, nor did she give Sóldís a chance to ask. The following day, Sóldís had taken a peep inside the wardrobe out of curiosity and discovered that it was empty. The hangers were still there but every single garment had vanished. Ása must have removed them while Sóldís was occupied in the byre or the henhouse, or on a walk with Gígja. She hadn't been aware of the intrusion, which would have been the third in as many days.

In spite of this, Sóldís felt it wouldn't be appropriate to lock the doors. Ása had told her there was no need to in the countryside; the farm was so remote that no one would find their way there by accident. Anyone who did come round had a reason to be there. Sóldís had refrained from pointing out that not every visitor had respectable motives. What about debt collectors, for instance? She had been afraid that if she said this, Ása would burst out laughing. People like her only owed money to the types who would hire lawyers in suits to call in their debts, not broken-nosed thugs with tattoos on their necks, knives in their ring-bedecked hands and the next dose of steroids in their jacket pocket. Still, Ása's airy dismissal of her concerns meant that Sóldís didn't feel she could lock the front door. And definitely not the connecting door between the two houses. Not even at night. Silly though it was, she was afraid Ása might wake up before her and find the door locked. Sóldís didn't want her employer to get the idea that she hadn't listened to her, or that she suspected the couple of anything underhand.

Nevertheless, she knew she would be driven to locking herself in sooner or later. The front door, at least. It was hard to sleep, knowing that there was only an unlocked door between her and the overwhelming darkness outside.

Sóldís had never experienced true darkness before. In the city, the outriders of daylight – street lights, the glowing windows of night-owls, illuminated advertising hoardings and the headlamps of cars – all stood guard against the encroaching menace of the night. But there was nothing like that out here. The blackness wrapped them in its smothering folds like a seamless shadow. When she looked out of the window after dusk, she might as well have had her eyes shut for all she could see. Anything could be happening out there.

No doubt it would have been different if the moon hadn't been thickly veiled in cloud. She could at least have discerned the pale contours of the snowy landscape. But would that necessarily have been an improvement? Which was preferable, seeing a movement out there in the gloom or imagining that something was on the prowl unseen? Sóldís was inclined to think the former, after experimenting with shutting the curtains the night before. It had turned out to be a mistake because then she'd been assailed by the irrational fear that a figure was standing just outside the window, waiting for her to open the curtains. It made no difference that she was sleeping upstairs, which meant that logically there was no way anyone could peep in her window without the aid of a ladder. No, she found she actually preferred staring out into the black void.

'Coming! I'm coming to get you,' Sóldís called in a loud, clear voice as she set off with Bói and Lubbi on her heels. She paused in the hall and listened for any sound of Gígja, but all she could hear was the dogs panting. So she began the hunt, noisily opening the hall cupboard and announcing that now she was going to find Gígja. It was important to stoke up the tension and enhance Gígja's pleasure in not being where the seeker apparently expected to find her. It was also essential, when Sóldís identified the correct hiding place, to emit a groan of frustration and declare that she was ready to give up.

Sóldís paused again to listen but couldn't hear a sound. Even the dogs seemed to be holding their breath. For once there was complete silence in the house, yet when she was alone in bed, she couldn't sleep for all the creaking and shifting of the timbers. That first night she'd thought she'd never drop off, and kept expecting a figure to materialise in the doorway. In the darkness, she'd had the odd illusion that the knots in the wood were eyes, and in the end she'd had to turn over on to her side to avoid looking at them. Her great-grandfather's words about creaking timbers no longer seemed fanciful. Eventually, though, tiredness had conquered her fear and she had drifted off, not stirring until her alarm clock raucously announced the new day.

The next morning, in a calmer state, she had been able to come up with various rational explanations for the uncanny noises in the night. They must have been caused by the difference in temperature between day and night, which caused the timbers in the house to expand and contract audibly. The following night she had got to sleep earlier, comforted by this explanation into assuming that she wouldn't have any difficulty – even if the bed started creaking of its own accord when she was lying perfectly still. After two nights of fitful sleep and a long day's work, she was so shattered that there was no danger of her lying awake.

It looked as if this job wasn't going to be quite the cushy number Sóldís had envisaged, which didn't bode well for her thesis. It wasn't that her employers had deliberately misled her; she'd simply failed to grasp the extent of her daily duties. There was no way that tending the animals, keeping the outsize house clean, cooking, child-minding, looking after the dogs and teaching the girls could all be achieved within normal working hours. Not to mention winding up the cuckoo clock every morning. At least the teaching was a shared burden, as Ása took care of most of it. Sóldís was only responsible for Icelandic, where both sisters showed considerable room for improvement. Although they spoke the language fluently, without a foreign accent, they were a long way behind their age group in reading and writing. Íris was at a much greater disadvantage than Gígja, as she was older and had missed out on more.

According to Ása, Íris was an outstanding pupil who got top marks in most subjects, particularly excelling in the sciences, so Sóldís shouldn't have too much trouble tutoring her in her mother tongue. But after sitting with Íris over her schoolbooks, Sóldís had to disagree. No doubt it was a new and unwelcome experience for a bright kid like Íris to find herself struggling, so it wasn't really surprising if she quickly grew demoralised and complained that Icelandic was stupid and pointless. Sóldís's main task was to convince her of the opposite. It would take time, but hopefully, if she persevered, she would make progress in the end.

Sóldís was less concerned about Gígja, though she showed signs of having mild ADHD, which made it hard for her to concentrate. Her parents had omitted to mention this. To be fair, Sóldís wasn't sure they even realised. If they did, they were in denial. At some point she would have to raise the subject with them, though she wasn't looking forward to it. She was in no doubt that Ása and Reynir, being super-intelligent, focused and ambitious themselves, took it for granted that the same would be true of their daughters.

She reminded herself that most of her duties were easier to achieve. The byre, the hens, the kitchen and the housework required nothing more than elbow grease. Quite a lot of elbow grease, but the chores weren't complicated. Still, when you added it all up, the pay suddenly didn't seem quite as generous as she'd first thought. All things considered, her hourly wages were barely more than she'd make as a cashier in a supermarket. On the other hand, at least she got free meals and accommodation, and was spared having to deal with rude customers.

The best thing about this whole adventure was not having to meet anyone from her previous life. There was no danger of bumping into an old friend who might start asking questions about her break-up or innocently enquire how things were going. Sóldís wasn't ready for that conversation yet. Not without turning red and maybe even shedding a tear. The last thing she needed right now was to make a fool of herself in front of her friends. Perhaps they'd laughed at her when Jónsi had described their break-up. She suspected she was being a bit hard on him and their mutual friends – but still. Having this time out would give her a chance to pull herself together and then she'd be able to put a cheerful face on things the next time she encountered any of them. Even Jónsi. She hadn't heard from him since he sent her that furious message, and this suited her just fine.

In the circumstances, having a chance to retreat from the world in safe company weighed more heavily than any desire for shorter working days.

Sóldís went into the sitting room, which didn't offer many good hiding places. She checked behind the sofa and the two armchairs. The dogs followed her like shadows, still utterly mystified about what she was up to.

She ruled out the kitchen with equal speed, as all the cupboards were full and there was no room in them for even a small child to hide.

Next, Sóldís went into the other downstairs bedroom. There was nobody there either, or in the guest loo. That ruled out the ground floor. The only door she hadn't opened led down to the cellar. Up to now, Gígja had hid either on this floor or upstairs, and it was unlikely that she had deviated from habit. In their previous games, she had twice hidden in the same place, so she didn't appear to be particularly inventive.

This was to be the last game of the day since Sóldís needed to head over to the new house to help with supper. Deciding to liven up the proceedings, she went over to the cellar door, took hold of the handle, opened it and shouted: 'I know you're in the cellar! I'm coming down there.'

For once the dogs weren't glued to her heels. They hung back, peering doubtfully into the darkness beyond the door. From upstairs there came a faint cry: 'No one's allowed in the cellar! And, anyway, I'm not down there.' Gígja could have left out the last part as there was no doubt about where her voice was coming from.

'Yes, you are! I know you are. You're just trying to trick me!' Sóldís called in reply. Then, becoming aware of an unpleasant odour rising from below, she raised her arm to her face and buried her nose in the crook of her elbow. So that was why the dogs were hanging back; they must have noticed the smell as soon as she opened the door.

It grew stronger. Sóldís hastily shut the door. This had ceased to be funny.

'No one's allowed in the cellar. Daddy says so. Anyway, I'm up here,' Gígja yelled, apparently misinterpreting the slamming of the door.

It seemed to dawn on the dogs that Gígja might be calling them, and they raced off up the stairs, Bói bounding ahead of little Lubbi, who could only manage one step at a time. Sóldís lowered her arm from her face, glanced back at the cellar door with a grimace, then went off in pursuit of the dogs. 'Aha!' she shouted. 'Now I'm definitely going to find you!'

Although the dogs had given away Gígja's hiding place by whining and barking in the bathroom, Sóldís humoured the little girl by pretending to search all the other upstairs rooms first: her own bedroom, the TV room, the room with all the bookshelves and the two armchairs, and a store cupboard full of sheets, towels and cleaning fluids.

Only after that did Sóldís enter the bathroom. The dogs were standing, tense with excitement, by the bathtub that also served as a shower. The shower curtain had been pulled across, and it didn't require a sixth sense to work out where Gígja was hiding, but Sóldís pretended not to find her straight away.

In the end, though, it was time to take hold of the shower curtain, encouraged by the barking of the two dogs, who must have thought she was braindead by now.

Before jerking it aside, Sóldís observed the final rule of the game: 'Bother it, I've looked absolutely everywhere,' she said with an exaggerated sigh. 'I'm just going to have to give up.'

Sóldís's arm was almost pulled out of its socket as the shower curtain was whipped aside. 'Ta-da! I'm here, silly!'

The dogs went mad with joy at having been proved right. Gígja clambered out of the bathtub, beaming to reveal the big front teeth that she had yet to grow into. Her fine, shoulder-length hair floated around her head, crackling with static electricity from the plastic curtain. She certainly hadn't inherited her mother's luxuriant mane; it had more in common with Sóldís's limp locks. Gígja gazed at her eagerly. 'Again! This time I'll be "it".'

Sóldís shook her head. 'Sorry, no can do. I need to go over to the main house and start getting supper ready. You can help me if you like.'

Gígja's expression showed what she thought of this. She started whining and pestering Sóldís, as kids will, but in the end, recognising it as a lost cause, she latched on to the idea of cooking instead. 'Let's bake something! Let's bake a cake for supper.'

Sóldís smiled at her, and was about to say that she wasn't sure how this suggestion would go down with her mother, when she was distracted by the sight of a smartwatch on the child's wrist. It was far too big for her and she hadn't been wearing it at the beginning of the game. 'Where did you get that watch, Gígja?'

'I found it.'

'Where?'

'Here. On the side of the bath.' Gígja held out her thin wrist to show Sóldís. 'It's Alvar's watch.'

'Who's Alvar?' Sóldís examined the watch. She guessed Gígja must have tried to squeeze into the cupboard under the sink and found it there. This was the bathroom Sóldís used herself and there definitely hadn't been any watch there that morning.

'Alvar used to work here. Like you. Mummy thought he was better than Berglind, who used to work here before him. But Daddy thought Berglind was much better. I like you the best. The others couldn't be bothered to play with me.' Gígja withdrew her arm, smiling at Sóldís. 'You're much more fun.'

Sóldís smiled back, unsure how long she would manage to stay at the top of Gígja's popularity list. For now, she had the advantage of novelty but that wouldn't last for ever. 'I expect Alvar wants his watch back. Let's ask your mummy or daddy to give it to him. He must be very sad about losing it.'

Gígja's expression showed what she thought of the claims of prior ownership. 'Maybe he left it behind on purpose. Maybe he didn't want it any more. Maybe he wants me to have it. I'm never allowed to buy anything or have anything new. Mummy won't let me.'

Ása had told Sóldís that she was trying to cure the girls of their materialism. Back in the States, she and Reynir had been far too indulgent, and Amazon packages had appeared daily. But now that the parents no longer needed to feel guilty about being away from home so much, it was time to get the girls' shopping mania under control. 'I think Alvar will want his watch back, Gígja,' Sóldís repeated. 'He must be very sad about losing it.'

This time it worked. Gígja nodded, though she looked disappointed. 'Yes. Maybe. He was in a big hurry. He didn't even say goodbye. He just went away.'

* * *

Reynir's reaction continued to niggle at Sóldís as she chopped the vegetables for salad. He had been sitting in an armchair by the fire in the big glass room, book in hand, classical music blasting out of the sound system, when Sóldís had handed him the watch and told him where they had found it and who they thought it belonged to. He'd stuffed it in his pocket, muttering that he'd see it was returned. When Ása appeared, turned down the music and asked what they were talking about, he'd said, 'Nothing,' and lowered his eyes to his book.

The armchair by the fire seemed to be Reynir's base. When he wasn't in bed or closeted in his study, he was sitting there, listening to funereal music. Either reading a book or staring absently out of the window. There had been a vague reference to his illness before Sóldís took the job, but no further explanations had been forthcoming. In the three days she'd been working here, no one had referred to the big scar that disfigured his scalp, so she wasn't sure if it was linked to his illness or some terrible accident. Not that it made any difference to her, since nursing was about the only duty that wasn't in her contract.

Following the smartwatch incident, Sóldís concluded that all the designer clothes in the wardrobe must be Alvar's. It would be too great a coincidence if he had left the watch behind and someone else had left the clothes – unless more than one person had departed in a hurry. The thought made her so uneasy that she deliberately pushed it to the back of her mind.

The cucumber on the chopping board had been reduced to tiny chunks. Sóldís put down the sharp knife. Dusk was falling and the open-plan room was reflected in the big glass wall that divided it from the wintry world outside. Sóldís noticed in the reflection that Reynir had stopped reading and returned to his favourite habit of staring out of the window. When their eyes met, she hastily lowered hers, but not before she had caught the mirthless grin he sent her.

Acting as if she hadn't noticed it, Sóldís tipped the chunks of cucumber into the salad bowl, hoping her embarrassment didn't show. She had found his smile deeply unsettling, even creepy, like the look a spiteful child might wear before treading on a spider. But perhaps it had just been distorted by the glass – after all, windows weren't manufactured to be faithful mirrors.

Before Sóldís set to work chopping a fiery red pepper, she shot another glance at the window. Reynir's grin had vanished and she thought he was now lost in contemplation of his own reflection. He was no longer a disturbing sight; from his expression he appeared to be preoccupied with a worrying thought. He had slipped his hand into the pocket containing the watch, and she couldn't help wondering if his worry was connected somehow to that.

Later, as she was tidying up after supper, she saw something that convinced her she had been right. In the bin she caught a glimpse of white plastic that looked like the watch strap. After a quick glance around to check that nobody was looking, she pushed the rubbish aside and saw that it was indeed the watch. It couldn't have fallen in there by accident when Reynir scraped the leftovers off his plate because it had been carefully concealed under the things that were already in the bin.

Sóldís fished the watch out of the rubbish, being careful to keep it below the kitchen counter. She snatched another look around in case anyone was watching her and wondering why she was rummaging in the bin. But Reynir was still staring abstractedly into the darkness, so Sóldís ran her finger around the side of the watch, found a tiny button and tried turning it on. She'd never owned a smartwatch herself, so she didn't know what sort of information she could learn from it or even why she was doing this. In no universe would a smartwatch contain the answers to her questions. Certainly not in the universe she currently occupied. The screen remained black and a second attempt gave the same result. The battery had run out of juice.

Sóldís licked her dry lips, returned the watch to the bin, then spread the rubbish back over it, not knowing what else to do. Quietly, she closed the cupboard.

Chapter 5
Thursday

The slide on the screen showed pictures of the victims when they were alive. One was of the family celebrating Christmas in an unidentified living room, the other was of the young woman who had worked for them. That photo had been in the police system, dating from when she had last renewed her passport. As in most photos of the kind, she looked as if someone had pointed a gun at her head.

'The victims.' Týr's boss, Huldar, was running the team briefing. 'Ása Bjartmarsdóttir, thirty-seven years old. Her daughters by Reynir Logason: Íris, fifteen, and Gígja, eight. And this is Sóldís Sigursveinsdóttir, twenty-five, who worked for them, helping out around the house. The fate of Ása's husband, Reynir, also thirty-seven, is not yet known.'

All those present stared at the screen. Týr studied the faces of the two women and girls, trying in vain to glimpse any resemblance between them and the bodies he had witnessed at the scene.

'So far, we don't have an exact time of death, but they probably all died the same night, which the pathologist thinks was several days ago – at most a week. The post-mortems will shed more light on this, but as a considerable amount of time had passed before the bodies were discovered, we can't expect much precision. A day either way. Maybe more than one.'

Huldar paused to clear his throat before continuing: 'From their clothes, it appears they were asleep or about to go to bed at the time, and their bodies were all found in bedrooms. The blood splashed up the walls provides us with incontrovertible evidence that this was where the killings took place. No blood was found in any of the other rooms, apart from the footprints leading from the couple's bedroom through the big glass room to the French windows opening on to the deck behind the house. If we subsequently detect traces of blood elsewhere on the property, we can assume that it was cleaned up with the intention of misleading the police. Forensics are on to it. Personally, I can't see what purpose that would have served, since no attempt appears to have been made to conceal the murders. Though, having said that, there was a strong smell of decomposition in the cellar of the old farmhouse, which suggests that one of the bodies might have been lying in there for a while, though it's left no visible traces. But there could be a different explanation. Like I said, forensics are on to it.'

Huldar turned from the screen to face the group. He looked bug-eyed from exhaustion, like Týr and the other officers who had been at the scene. None of them had got home until late the previous night. 'The murder weapon was a sharp instrument. A heavy one. An axe was one suggestion, but we'll have to wait for the results of the post-mortem.' Huldar briefly met Týr's eye as he said this. 'All we know at this stage about the people involved is that the couple were both software engineers. They went to the US for their postgraduate studies and ended up staying on. They set up a successful company and would probably have remained there if the husband hadn't developed a brain tumour. But as a result of his illness, they sold up and moved back to Iceland. The sum their company changed hands for hasn't been made public, but it's clear that we're talking billions of krónur. And since the sale was reported in the media, it's possible that news of their wealth led to a break-in. Nevertheless, the most likely scenario is that the husband was responsible, so we're going to pull out all the stops to find him – alive or dead. But I don't need to tell you that until his guilt has been confirmed, we need to keep an open mind.'

Týr knew this would be tricky. When you already had a strong suspect, it was hard to muster the enthusiasm to pursue other lines of inquiry. Everyone wanted to be involved in investigating the most likely lead; no one wanted to be on the losing team.

The flow of information continued: 'The family's assistant, on the other hand, was a penniless student, training to be a teacher. She'd finished a B.Ed. and started a Master's degree. She'd only been working for the family for a short time and was single following a recent break-up. At this stage we don't know if it was amicable. Nor do we know if Ása and Reynir had fallen out with anyone. Or why anyone would have wished such a grim fate on the family.'

Since there was nothing more to be said on this subject, Huldar proceeded to show them photos from the scene. Only a few of those present had been at the farm the evening before, but the unforgiving slides conveyed much of the horror.

Týr looked away. He'd had enough trouble trying to put these images out of his head last night as he lay in bed, unable to sleep. When he did finally drop off, the scenes from the house had merged into his dreams and given him nightmares, though he couldn't remember them when he woke up early this morning, weary and unrefreshed. Instead of turning over and trying to get back to sleep, he had stuck to his resolution of going to the gym before work. A hard workout often helped revive him after a bad night. The healing power of aching muscles lay in the fact that the pain distracted him from his tiredness.

The briefing was winding up. Huldar had recapped the little that was known so far about the murders and the victims. He'd followed the slideshow of gory atrocities with a verbal repetition of the same information, in almost the same words, presumably so that the meeting wouldn't seem embarrassingly short. And now he'd been reduced to waffling.

Tomorrow's meeting was bound to be more informative, since by then they would be in possession of more facts. A search had been launched for the missing husband over a wide area around the farm, and checks were simultaneously being made to see if he could have left the country. Meanwhile, forensics were on their way to the scene to collect samples. Although there would be a delay before the full results of their investigation were available, some findings might be of immediate interest. The police were also hoping that a concrete lead would come to light when the circumstances of the family and their assistant were put under the microscope. If nothing else, their digital trail and the interviews with their next of kin should help to clarify things and narrow the investigators' focus. So far, they only knew the basic background facts about the people involved, not what they had been doing during the crucial days leading up to the murders. Nor did they have any idea what motive the husband could have had – if, indeed, he was the killer.

Huldar brought up a final slide listing Reykjavík CID's responsibilities in the investigation, and reminded those present how important it was to maintain a good relationship with the local force in Akranes. No one should forget that

Reykjavík were there only to assist, not to run the inquiry. Lastly, he said a few words intended to rally the team, which fell hopelessly flat. Nothing could lift the mood of despondency in the room. Murder inquiries involving children were always especially hard.

Týr leant forward to get a better view of the screen. The list of assignments was quite long – so long that the font had been reduced to cram them all on to the slide. But by straining his eyes he could see that there were a couple of jobs that might suit him, and only two that he definitely didn't want to do: he had no desire to be sent back to the countryside to assist the local team, and he didn't want to investigate the family's finances. He'd done a stint in the economic crimes unit in Stockholm, and a more tedious job was hard to imagine. He'd almost gone out of his mind with boredom and had quickly requested a transfer.

To ensure that he wouldn't get drafted into economic crimes in his new job in Iceland, he had deliberately omitted his brief experience in this field from his CV. It had helped that during the interview process no one had asked him to list all the departments he'd worked for in the Swedish police. His basic training was in order. He'd worked for the Stockholm police. And, according to his referees, he was even-tempered, polite and easy to get along with. Last but not least, he was physically fit. In other words, he fulfilled all the criteria.

The allocation of tasks began. To Týr's relief, he dodged the family finances. But here his luck ran out, because he and Karólína were given orders to go back out west to assist the local CID. He suspected that this was because he hadn't yet managed to gel with the team here in Reykjavík. It wasn't that he didn't rub along OK with his new colleagues or that there was any bad blood between them, and he certainly wasn't being bullied or ostracised in any way, but during the six months he'd been working there, he simply hadn't managed to develop the kind of rapport with the rest of the team that they had with each other. But then most of them had known each other for years, and in a tight-knit unit like that there's rarely a gap left for an outsider to fill. He would fit in eventually, but it would take time.

The same was true of Karólína, whereas the Polish man, who had been hired at the same time as them, had clicked with the others more or less from day one. By partnering Týr and Karólína on a job, Huldar was no doubt trying to bring them together, on the basis that if they became mates, no member of the team would be left out in the cold. To be fair, Týr could think of many worse people to be partnered with. Karólína was conscientious, hard-working and good at her job. She was sporty, like most of the younger officers, and came across as serious, though Týr didn't know if this was by nature or a result of the sobering sights she was regularly forced to witness in the line of duty. Her only fault was that she was a bit quiet – like him. If they were partners, there would be more silences than was usual between two police officers, but he didn't mind that. He hoped she wouldn't either. Although he found it hard to tell her age, he guessed they were near contemporaries.

* * *

Their assignment turned out to be even worse than he'd feared. As if having to liaise with a police team they didn't know wasn't bad enough, they would also have to stay in the Hvalfjördur area. Rooms had been booked for them at the hotel closest to the crime scene, to spare them the drive back and forth to Reykjavík in dodgy winter weather during the three days Huldar reckoned they would need to spend out there.

Týr was no great fan of hotel rooms and would have preferred to sleep in his own bed at night. Then again, he thought, seeing as he wasn't particularly happy with the flat he was living in, perhaps the hotel would make a nice change. The flat belonged to his parents and used to stand empty most of the year since they lived in Sweden. They'd decided to hang on to it when the family originally moved abroad. He'd been twelve at the time and remembered little apart from the emotional upheaval associated with moving – the excitement about going to live in a new country, coupled with the wrench of being parted from his friends and classmates.

He knew every centimetre of that flat, every crack in the walls, scratch on the parquet, pattern on the towels and piece of furniture, far more intimately than he cared to. He had intended to make some changes when he moved back to Iceland, rather than remain stuck in the past. And the flat represented the past. Since moving to Sweden, his parents had always made a big deal about going back to Iceland on visits and spending as large a chunk of the summer there every year as their jobs would allow. Partly this was because there was nowhere else they themselves would rather be, partly because they wanted Týr to cultivate his ties with the country and keep up his Icelandic. Yet, to his surprise, they had been less than thrilled when he told them of his decision to try living in Iceland. From their expressions, you'd have thought he'd said he wanted to relocate to a rock in the middle of a crocodile-infested river and devote himself to swimming practice. It was the same look they'd worn when he first told them he wanted to study criminology. They had been hoping he would follow in their footsteps and become a doctor, but nothing could have been further from his mind.

He would have to find a tactful way of breaking it to them that he was planning to look for another flat – if he decided to settle here. There was no point telling them the truth, that he was searching for himself and didn't feel he'd find himself in their old home. Still, eager though he was to get the move over with, he'd probably put it off until late spring, when his parents were due to arrive for their annual summer holiday. By then, with any luck, he'd have made a decision about his future, and he'd also be able to fall back on the excuse that he didn't want to be in their way; they should have the place to themselves. That wouldn't seem strange to them as it was years since he'd last lived at home.

Huldar supplied Týr and Karólína with the address of their hotel and the keys to the four-by-four Týr had been driving the previous evening. He also gave them the telephone number of Hördur at West Iceland CID in Akranes and told them to put themselves in touch with him. Their orders were to go home and pack for three nights away.

* * *

Karólína used the drive to Hvalfjördur to examine the social media accounts of the wife, Ása, and the assistant, Sóldís. She couldn't find the youngest child or the husband on any of the usual platforms, and the older daughter had kept her accounts locked. According to Karólína, there was little to be gleaned from their public profiles. Sóldís hadn't posted anything about the farm, and her older posts had all consisted of harmless photos and captions that wouldn't provoke anyone. What Karólína could see of Ása's posts was also unremarkable: stylised photos of country life, with sentimental captions, several of which Karólína read aloud for Týr's benefit. He couldn't see the point of them, but then he'd never been a fan of the kind of pocket philosophy that was supposed to encapsulate some essential truth but always seemed wide of the mark to him. Perhaps he was put off by all the emojis scattered throughout the text. His ex-girlfriend used to love that kind of thing.

'The last photo Ása posted is a bit odd.'

'Oh?' Týr shot a quick glance at Karólína, who was holding the phone screen towards him, but he was forced to turn back to the road before he could get a proper look. From what he'd seen, it had appeared pretty conventional. A wood fire and two steaming mugs, arranged on a table next to some other stuff. In the background, a glimpse of a snowy scene through large windows.

'This must have been taken in their glass room. Nothing odd about that. But there's a red blur outside, like a movement, and beyond that you can just make out the shape of a dark figure that looks as if it's staring in the window.'

Týr snatched another sideways glance but Karólína was now busy zooming in on the photo. 'Is there anything odd about that?' he asked. 'Isn't it just part of the set-up?'

Karólína didn't answer for a moment. Then she said: 'Maybe. Except there's a snowstorm outside, which makes it hard to work out what you're seeing. The background's out of focus. Her photos aren't normally mysterious like this. They're usually very obvious: you see exactly what you're intended to see. And the caption seems a bit out of character. It just says: *It's good to be safe indoors when danger lurks outside.*'

Out of the corner of his eye, Týr saw that Karólína was peering at the photo again. 'It's a man, I think. Or, I don't know, it could be anything really. The background's too out of focus.'

'Perhaps she was talking about the weather. That can be dangerous.'

His remark effectively shut down the conversation. In the ensuing silence, Týr concentrated on driving and Karólína put her phone back in her pocket and stared out of the window for the remainder of the journey. They turned off before the Hvalfjördur Tunnel and took the old road around the fjord, the steep white slopes to their right banded with black rock strata, the sea to their left mirror-smooth today. On the opposite shores of the fjord they could see the long, blue-green potrooms of the aluminium smelter at Grundartangi, followed by the occasional house, a single church and a cluster of Second World War barracks. Nearer at hand, the little island of Geirshólmi came into view. It was said to have been the lair of a band of robbers a hundred-strong during the Viking Age, which Týr found hard to believe given its tiny size. Scarcely any more credible was the tale of the ringleader's wife, who was said to have swum ashore from the island with her two small children, fleeing from an attacking force. Then again, it wouldn't have been the first or last time someone performed an extraordinary feat to save their children. In comparison, Týr thought, the atrocities at Hvarf seemed even more far-fetched than these old stories, especially if the father, Reynir, was the killer, as all the evidence suggested.

The hotel turned out to be no more than a handful of tiny summer cabins, three in total, plonked in the middle of a field. The shapes of concrete foundations could be glimpsed under the snow on either side of the huts, testimony to earlier, more ambitious plans for a long row of similar cabins. Týr wasn't sure if this could really be classed as a hotel, but one thing was certain: if the planned expansion ever took place, the reception would need a bit of a makeover. At present it appeared to be housed in the cowshed.

After knocking on the door of the farmhouse without success, Týr and Karólína went in search of signs of life. Finally, they tracked down a middle-aged woman in the cowshed. She was dressed in wellingtons and a threadbare jumper, and had a mop of rather wild, curly hair. She looked like someone who didn't suffer fools gladly.

The woman glanced up from her task. Eyes widening at the sight of Karólína, she announced in English: '*We have only one room available.*'

It wasn't the first time Týr had heard Karólína being addressed in English. Since she spoke perfect Icelandic – she was, after all, an Icelander – it must be galling to be constantly taken for a tourist in her own country. Karólína smiled thinly, visibly suppressing her irritation, and replied in Icelandic: 'We're from the police. We understand rooms have been booked for us. Our names are Karólína and Týr.'

Unlike other people Týr had seen in this situation, the woman didn't appear remotely embarrassed by her faux pas. 'That's right. I got a phone call.' She wiped her right hand on her trouser leg and greeted them. As she took Karólína's hand, she added: 'You don't look much like a police officer.' Judging from her expression, the woman thought there was a good chance Karólína might be a fraud. What possible reason she'd have for impersonating a police officer, Týr couldn't guess. Perhaps the little cabins were in such hot demand that there was a risk someone might try to trick their way on to another person's booking.

'Well, I assure you I *am* from the police. I just don't happen to be in uniform. Our car is outside and it's marked, if that helps at all.'

Týr bit back the urge to ask the woman if she was referring to the colour of Karólína's skin. He wasn't sure his colleague would appreciate his interference. It would only make the situation more awkward, and, in any case, she was more than capable of speaking up for herself. But Karólína didn't challenge the woman. She just seemed keen to end the conversation. No doubt she had learnt long ago that some battles weren't worth fighting.

The woman waved a hand dismissively, as if prepared to take the car on trust. 'I was just saying. Anyway, I'm Gerdur.' She eyed Karólína, as if still a little doubtful. 'You speak very good Icelandic. You've hardly got any accent at all.'

Karólína smiled thinly again. 'That's because I *am* Icelandic. The two tend to go together.'

Gerdur nodded, still unpersuaded. Then she turned to Týr, her gaze focusing on the scar that ran from his hairline across his forehead to end up between his eyebrows, as if pointing to his nose. 'Talking of accents, I reckon I can hear a bit of a lilt when you talk. Are you not from these parts either?'

'Yes and no. I've lived abroad. That's all.'

'Hmm.' Again, Gerdur seemed dubious but didn't ask any further questions. 'Right. Come with me.'

They left the shed and the friendly lowing of the cows, and crossed the yard to the farmhouse. On the way, Gerdur turned to look at their car with its police markings. They'd obviously passed the test.

Týr and Karólína waited in a tidy hall while Gerdur was fetching the keys to two of the cabins. As she handed them over, she explained that there was a duvet and pillow on each bed along with a towel. However, it seemed someone had failed to pass on the message about bringing their own sheets.

When Týr reached out to take the keys, the woman abruptly withdrew her hand. 'Are you here about the murders?'

Týr saw no reason to conceal the fact, so he answered that yes, they were. But instead of being rewarded with the keys, he got another question: 'Do you know who killed them?'

'I'm afraid we can't discuss that.'

The hotel owner was still withholding the keys. She seemed determined to use them as a bargaining chip. 'When did it happen? That can't be a secret. And how? Were they shot? That's what I heard.'

'Same answer, I'm afraid. We're not at liberty to discuss any aspect of the case.' Týr held out a hand for the keys. 'Did you know them at all?'

'Well, yes and no. I knew who they were. No one in the neighbourhood could fail to notice when they bought the land, let alone when they built that socking great house of theirs. There was an endless procession of vehicles and machinery coming and going along the valley, which is pretty unusual in this neck of the woods.'

'Were they unpopular?' Týr was still standing with his hand outstretched, but the woman showed no sign of surrendering the keys.

'No, not really. We're getting used to that kind of thing – all the local property being hoovered up by types with more money than they know what to do with. At least this lot were Icelanders. Which is better than foreign billionaires treating the country like a Monopoly board.' She stared hard at Karólína, as if this was aimed at her.

Karólína seemed to take it that way. 'I'm Icelandic, remember? And no billionaire. I'm certainly not about to hoover anything up.' This time, she didn't smile, but Gerdur seemed to relax a little.

After a moment, Gerdur continued: 'At least they didn't fence the whole place off like the bloody foreigners do. And they built a house on the land. They didn't give any cause for complaint, really. Though personally I'd rather have seen the place taken over by someone who meant to run it as a proper business, not play at farming like they did. Two cows, two horses and a handful of hens, so I've heard. And a couple of goats too, which apparently lived in cushier accommodation than many people. No, there's no point in that kind of hobby farming.'

'So they got on well with all their neighbours?' Týr prompted. 'There was no tension between them and any of the local farmers or owners of the summer cottages in the area?'

Gerdur tightened her lips and, after a moment's silence, handed him the keys. 'No. None.'

Týr was good at spotting when he was being lied to. And he was being lied to now. But he just took the keys, and he and Karólína said goodbye without further comment.

Chapter 6
Before

Sóldís could feel the luxurious warmth of the underfloor heating through her thin socks. She paused in the connecting corridor, closing her eyes in appreciation. If she ever acquired a flat or house of her own, she wanted to have heating like this. A vivid memory came back to her of the icy bedroom floor in the flat she had shared with Jónsi. She used to get out of bed and tiptoe barefoot into the other room to beg him to come to bed and warm her up. He almost never obliged, though, preferring to play his computer games in the living room. In hindsight, it was incredible that it had never dawned on her that all the affection in their relationship had come from her.

There was no sound from the new house. Nothing but the ticking of the big cuckoo clock in the hall. Sóldís wondered if she should turn round and go back to her own quarters. She really didn't want to go into the kitchen and discover that Ása and the girls had gone out for a walk and that Reynir was sitting there alone with a book.

Still, there was no music playing, which made it unlikely that he was there, so she decided to go ahead and check. If she didn't, she knew she'd only end up browsing social media and risk giving in to the temptation to spy on Jónsi. It was this that had driven her off the sofa in her quarters to come and see what the family were up to. Watching Jónsi going about his life as if nothing had happened was doing her head in. She'd hoped at least to see some signs of regret in the photos he posted. A hint of sadness in his eyes, something fake about his smile. But far from it. She felt more dispirited every time she scrolled. It was hard to face the fact that she'd been no more important to him than a bit of fluff he'd brushed off his shoulder and instantly forgotten. He hadn't even been able to sustain his fury at the way she'd sabotaged his games console, to scream at her down the phone or send her further abusive messages. Evidently she was too insignificant in his eyes even to be angry with for long. No, she thought, it was better to risk an encounter with Reynir than to waste any more emotional energy on that bastard Jónsi.

Sóldís went into the kitchen, thinking that if she saw Reynir alone in his chair, she would go smartly into reverse. But if Ása or the girls were there, she would invite Gígja to go for a walk with her in the snow. A blast of cold fresh air would do her good. Of course, Sóldís could have gone out on her own, but she wanted company, someone to distract her so she wouldn't have time to think or wallow in her misery. She'd presumably gain some brownie points from her employers too, as it was Sunday and therefore supposedly her day off. She wasn't required to perform any duties between Saturday lunchtime and Monday morning.

Sóldís smiled to herself when she found Ása alone in the kitchen, busy with something at the kitchen table. She had her back turned and didn't notice Sóldís until she cleared her throat. Then Ása spun round, as if startled. She tried to smile but betrayed herself by hastily wiping a tear from her cheek. In her other hand, she was holding a large camera. Her face was bare of make-up, her hair scraped back in a bun, but even without making an effort, and a bit puffy around the eyes, she still looked good. Sóldís became aware of her own scruffiness. There was an indelible stain on the front of her worn sweatshirt and she hadn't felt like taking a shower that morning. To make matters worse, she had black circles under her eyes from all the sleepless nights.

'Hi. Phew! You made me jump. I was so absorbed in what I was doing.' Ása sniffed a little as she beckoned Sóldís to join her. 'Come in. Please. I could do with a bit of company.' She gave a wan smile.

Arranged on the table in front of her was a tableau consisting of two mugs of coffee, an apple pie, a bowl of pistachios in their shells, an open book, a scarf and a few bare twigs in a silver vase. The mugs had been placed side by side, so they were touching. Viewed from the right angle, they appeared to be leaning against each other like a loving couple. On the other side of the table was a wide-bowled wine glass with red dregs in the bottom. It couldn't have been part of the still life or there would have been more wine in it.

'What do you think?' Ása took two steps backwards, made a frame with her fingers and squinted through the distorted rectangle at the collection of objects on the table. 'I thought I'd take yet another winter picture to post online but I'm not sure. It's a bit lifeless. It mustn't look too obviously staged.' Ása turned to Sóldís. 'Does it?'

There was no denying that it did. But since it was a well-known fact that most photos on social media were staged, what did that matter? Provided that the photo could maybe, possibly, conceivably be the result of a serendipitous moment, it would pass. So Sóldís assured her that it didn't. She knew Ása had been crying, and she didn't want to upset her. Sometimes a white lie was justifiable. But the next moment, regretting her lack of honesty and aware of how uncharitable people could be in their comments, she added that maybe the picture would look better with the fire in the background.

'Good idea.' Ása's smile looked genuine this time. She snapped a few more pictures, making sure she got the glowing hearth in the frame. 'Hey! Would you like a glass of wine?'

Sóldís was about to say no, then changed her mind. She was no wine drinker, more of a beer or breezer kind of girl, but it occurred to her that she would benefit right now from the care-free feeling of being a little tipsy. She had such a weak head for alcohol that it wouldn't take much. 'Yes, please. If that's OK.'

'Of course. You'd be doing me a favour. I won't have to feel guilty about drinking alone.' Ása fetched another glass and an open bottle from the kitchen island. The bottle had a very posh-looking label, which led Sóldís to expect some kind of heavenly nectar, but the wine proved far too powerful for her taste. It was so heavily oaked that she might as well be sucking on a piece of wood, but she was careful not to make a face. 'Where is everyone?'

'Reynir's gone for a rest. He's been a bit under the weather. His health is . . . He's . . .' For a moment, Ása looked as if her tears were about to spill over again, but she pulled herself together. 'Íris is moping in her room and Gígja went outside to build a snowman. But she got bored by the time it reached the size of a football and started running around instead. Much to the dogs' delight.'

Ása took a slug of wine, wiped her mouth with the back of her hand, and continued: 'You know, life is so strange. At your age I thought everything would turn out well as long as I was conscientious, careful, honest and kind. As long as I avoided cigarettes and drugs, drank in moderation, went to the gym and worked hard at my studies. But no. It's not enough. Things will go wrong, whatever you do.'

Sóldís couldn't think of any suitable response to this, guessing that Ása was referring to her husband's illness. She didn't know what had happened and didn't want to risk putting her foot in it. Given how miserable Ása looked, his health must be deteriorating, which would make it a sensitive subject. Instead, she asked if Ása would like her to try to get Íris to snap out of her bad mood.

Ása gave a short bark of laughter. 'Thanks for the offer but I wouldn't want you to waste your time. When Íris is in one of her moods, it's best to leave her alone to get over it.' She took another sip and Sóldís followed her example. The wine tasted better now that she knew what to expect.

Outside the glass wall, Sóldís caught glimpses of Gígja through the curtains of falling snow. Only when her game brought her close to the big windows could the little girl be seen properly, but even then the air was so hazy with snowflakes that she appeared out of focus. The same was true of the two dogs who were racing back and forth with her in a confusing game of tag. The order of who was chasing who kept changing, with no apparent logic. They would vanish behind a thick curtain of flakes, only to reappear shortly afterwards with their roles reversed.

Ása was also gazing out of the window, watching her daughter. She broke the silence when the blizzard swallowed Gígja up again. 'Funny. Íris would never have played like that at her age.' She swallowed another mouthful of wine, then went on: 'The girls couldn't be more different. As you've probably noticed.'

Sóldís nodded and sipped her wine. She didn't say anything, but then she wasn't expected to. Ása elaborated: 'Gígja never worries. As far as she's concerned, everything will turn out OK. I don't know if she even realises that anything could go wrong. As a result, she's always happy. I wish I could learn to be like that. I don't want to dwell on the negatives; I want to focus on the positives, on the good in this life.' Ása swivelled her glass, watching the red liquid obeying the centrifugal force. 'Fat chance of that ever happening, though. Not with things as bad as they've been recently.'

Sóldís was careful not to show her surprise. She'd got the impression Ása had a dream existence. She and Reynir seemed happy together, they had two healthy daughters and they weren't exactly lacking in worldly goods. Although Reynir had been ill, Sóldís had assumed he was on the mend. Come to think of it, though, she had no actual evidence of this; she'd just taken it for granted. She cast around for something positive to say. 'You've got an amazing house.'

Ása looked at her for a moment, then smiled and gave a brief laugh. 'Thanks. You know, you're all right.' She clinked glasses with Sóldís. 'Cheers!'

Sóldís returned her smile and took another sip. Gígja and the dogs drew near to the glass wall again; the little girl's red anorak and the black patches on Bói, the bigger dog, were the first things Sóldís could make out. 'The shot might work even better with Gígja in the background,' she remarked. 'Playing with the dogs in the snow. That would add a bit of life.'

Ása's smile was more genuine this time. Raising the camera to her eye, she snapped a picture. The next moment, there was a bang as something hit the glass, and Ása dropped the camera back to her chest.

Gígja was leaning against the window, hands over her head, mittens pressed flat against it, her face squashed and distorted. Not exactly what Sóldís had had in mind as the background to the photo.

The little girl was moving her lips but no sound could be heard through the thick glass. A patch of mist formed and her lips left a smear. Bói's nose left a similar mark as he appeared at her feet and peered inside as well. Little Lubbi, keen as ever not to be left out, stood up on his hind legs with his forepaws on the window and stared inside too. Neither dog seemed particularly bothered by the snowflakes blowing into their eyes. They both shook them off simultaneously, Bói more violently than Lubbi, who lost his balance and dropped down on to all fours.

Sóldís automatically fell into the role of servant and hurried over to open the door. 'What were you saying, Gígja?'

'Can we have some cocoa?'

The dogs seemed to understand the question because they gazed at Sóldís with imploring eyes. 'Not right now,' she said. 'Later. But only you. Dogs can't have chocolate.'

Gígja gestured behind her. 'I wasn't talking about them. The man wants cocoa too.'

'Which man?' Sóldís hugged herself as the icy air forced its way inside. 'There's no one out in this weather. Not here, anyway.'

'Yes, there is. He's over there. I saw him. He'd like some cocoa. He's going to help me build a snowman. It's too difficult for me on my own.'

Ása came to stand beside Sóldís. 'Don't be silly, Gígja. Who do you think would be out in our fields in weather like this? Either come in or stay outside. We can't keep the door open any longer. The cold's getting in.'

Bói turned and barked into the snowstorm. Sóldís and Ása both looked up from Gígja's red cheeks to peer through the thick mist of swirling flakes. It was hard to work out distances in these conditions but there was no question that there was a figure standing there. Not close enough for them to see his face – they could only make out his vague silhouette.

Sóldís felt the hairs prickling on her arms. The shiver that ran through her body had nothing to do with the open door.

'Come inside, Gígja,' Ása screeched. 'Now!'

'But—'

'No buts.' Ása's voice was loud and shrill with fear as she pushed Sóldís out of the way, grabbed her daughter by the shoulder and yanked her inside. The dogs followed, showering the parquet with snow, but for once Ása ignored it. She closed and locked the French windows, then she reached for the switch that controlled the blinds. They began to roll down over the glass walls for the first time since Sóldís had arrived at the house. Up to now, there had been no reason to block the view out.

Or the view in.

Sóldís realised that, whatever her employers might say, the time had come for her to start locking the doors to the old house.

Chapter 7
Thursday

Karólína had invited Týr to call her Karó, adding that no one called her by her full name except her grandmother and their boss, Huldar. Týr had nodded and made a mental note to take her up on her invitation, as he didn't want to be the third person on that list. He hoped this was a first step towards reducing the awkwardness that had so far characterised their relationship. Apart from their exchange about Ása's photo, they'd failed to find much to talk about on the drive up from Reykjavík. Their paths had barely crossed during the six months they'd worked in the same office. He had mainly been involved in investigating cases linked to organised crime, she'd been working on sexual offences. The only thing that linked them, apart from working for the Reykjavík police, was having Huldar as their boss. But neither subject provided much material for a conversation, as they didn't know each other well enough to be frank. And the subject of the current investigation was soon exhausted, because they knew so little as yet. But now, at last, they had a practical problem to discuss: where to find a shop that sold bedlinen.

Týr had rung Hördur at Akranes CID and received orders to go and see the man who had discovered the bodies. His name was Karl and he had asked to be excused from coming into the station for a formal interview on the grounds that he was still in shock. Since it was vital to talk to him as soon as possible, Hördur had decided that someone would have to go to see him. The formal statement could wait. Týr had been given the address of the farm where the man lived, along with rough directions that he had memorised without too much trouble. Out here in the middle of the countryside, there were fewer roads to get lost among than in town.

Karó had got in first with a request to drive, so Týr had to make do with being the passenger, a role he disliked, though he couldn't fault her driving. He preferred to be behind the wheel himself, especially when negotiating challenging roads like this one, which hadn't been ploughed. Clinging to the ceiling handle felt a lot more precarious than being in the driver's seat, and it was a relief when they reached their destination and the juddering and yawing finally stopped.

The farm dog greeted them with a marked lack of enthusiasm as they got out of the car. Despite the layer of snow covering the yard, he had managed to find some mud or dung to roll in. It was lucky he kept his distance, as Týr hadn't packed a change of clothes and couldn't afford to get his trouser legs dirty. Their 'hotel' didn't run to a laundry service – or indeed any other kind of service, as far as he could see. Karó, misinterpreting the looks he kept shooting the dog on the short walk to the house, told him there was no need to be scared; she was sure the dog wasn't fierce. Týr retorted that he wasn't scared of the dog but of the dirt. This didn't come out the way he'd meant it to sound, but there was no chance to explain. Karó was knocking on the door. She still had her knuckles raised when it opened.

A woman came out, looking noticeably sad and drawn. She greeted them and introduced herself as Ella. She seemed a little taken aback to see a black policewoman but didn't comment, just shook their hands as they told her their names. Then she showed them inside, pressing a hand to her chest as they took off their shoes. 'It's so awful I just don't know what to say. Who would do a thing like that?'

Týr left it to Karó to reply, thinking that it would be as well to establish from the outset that she spoke fluent Icelandic. 'We'll soon find out. The investigation is still in its early stages, but I assure you the killer won't escape.'

'It can't be anyone local, you know. That's out of the question.' The woman sounded as if she was trying to convince herself. 'Quite out of the question.'

'At this point, we need to keep an open mind.' Karó laid her shoes neatly by the wall and straightened up. 'Nothing can be ruled out as yet.'

Týr, seeing a look of alarm crossing the woman's face, chipped in: 'We're here to talk to your husband as a witness. That's all.'

This seemed to have the desired effect. The woman turned to him, looking a little less worried. 'He's absolutely distraught. I've never seen him in such a bad state before. He's waiting for you in the living room. I'm hoping it'll do him good to talk to you. If he goes over it with you, hopefully he can forget about it afterwards. No one wants to remember something like that. Why would they?'

Týr nodded. He couldn't agree more.

They entered the room where Karl was sitting. He stood up when Týr and Karó appeared at the door and introduced themselves. Seeing that the man was surprised not to recognise them, Týr explained that they were from Reykjavík, not Akranes. Karl was unshaven, his face puffy, and his hands were visibly shaking.

Karó began by asking how he was doing and reminding him that he would have to go to the police station in Akranes at some point to give a formal statement. Then she got down to business. She enquired why he had gone round to the farm yesterday and asked him to describe what he had found there. Karl repeated the story Týr had read that morning in a brief report outlining what he'd told the police last night. Almost word for word.

He and Ella hadn't heard from the family for several days, so he'd wanted to check if everything was all right. He'd gone round two days earlier, on the Monday, for the same reason, but hadn't seen any signs of life then either. He'd also tried to ring them several times. When the phones were still dead yesterday afternoon, he'd been concerned enough to call round again. He'd arrived at the farm just after five in the afternoon as he'd wanted to be home again in time for supper. But of course that wasn't to be.

His account of how he'd come to be inside the house, and what he'd seen there, was also consistent with the report, but it packed far more of a punch to hear the man describe the horror in person than to read his words in Times New Roman on a computer screen. Naturally, having witnessed the aftermath of the bloodbath with their own eyes helped them to appreciate the shock the man must have felt.

Karó said nothing while Karl was talking. When he lapsed into silence, her question was to the point: 'I understand from what you said yesterday that you didn't know the couple very well. But that doesn't seem to square with your account. It's clear that you were concerned for their welfare. Not many people would bother to make two visits and repeated phone calls and spend so much time worrying about a family they barely knew. What kind of relationship did you have with them?'

Karl didn't seem to resent her question. 'I'd say they were acquaintances of ours. Not close friends or anything like that.'

Karó nodded, then went on: 'How and when did you get to know them?'

'Oh, it was shortly after they moved to the district. I don't remember exactly when, but I came across Reynir one day after he'd skidded off the road on the black ice we had last winter. I towed him back on to the road and we got talking. He invited me to drop by for coffee and I took him up on it not long afterwards. They mentioned they were planning to run a hobby farm and I gave them advice from time to time. That was all. I didn't know them that well, like I said, but well enough to know that they were very decent people. And they had two young daughters – so of course I was worried.'

'It didn't occur to you that they might have gone away on a short trip?' Týr asked. 'To Reykjavík or abroad?' He was butting in, but Karó didn't appear to mind. They hadn't had a conversation beforehand about how to organise this interview or decided which of them would be in charge, though Karó had led the questioning up to now.

'No. I assumed I'd have heard about it if they had. They usually got in touch and asked us to feed the animals when they were going away. You can't just go gadding off without making arrangements when you have livestock. Besides, Ása had booked a haircut with my wife for herself and her younger girl on Monday, and they didn't show up. That had never happened before. The only time previously that she'd been unable to attend, she'd let Ella know. So that added to our concern.'

'So your wife is a hairdresser?' Karó made a note in the small pad she was holding.

'Yes. She did her training back in the day. Now she does it as a sideline for people in the district – the ones who don't feel like trekking all the way to Reykjavík or Akranes. She's got a small set-up in the basement – just the one chair. She doesn't have many clients.'

Karó looked up from her notepad. 'Then maybe we should have a chat with her as well. Ása might have told your wife something of interest while she was having her hair cut. Is there anything you talked about with the couple that could shed any light on what happened? Were they involved in any disputes? Were you aware of any tensions in their marriage?'

Karl was silent for a few moments before responding to this flood of questions: 'I'm sure Ella will agree to talk to you. But as far as I know there was nothing wrong. They never mentioned anything like that – not to me. And their marriage seemed like a happy one. Though . . .' He trailed off, looking pensive.

Týr and Karó watched him intently. Týr guessed that, like him, Karó was hoping Karl had witnessed the couple quarrelling, or worse. But when the man spoke again, it was about something else.

'Without wanting to suggest that it has anything to do with this business, the fact is that not everyone in the district was a fan of theirs. Some people felt they interfered in things that were none of their business – things they knew nothing about. Mind you, that was mostly Ása. Reynir kept a low profile, but then he's ill. But, you must understand, it was nothing serious. Just a difference of opinion about the treatment of livestock.'

'Could you explain more clearly?' Týr couldn't follow what the man was trying to say.

'The quarrel – well, disagreement – was about a piece of grazing land. Hvarf, the farm the family bought, used to be part of a larger property that two brothers had inherited and divided up between them. I tried to avoid getting dragged in myself, but I do know that before the family bought it, one of the brothers had permission to graze his horses on the other brother's land. The pasture changed hands in the sale, though. Ása and Reynir weren't satisfied with the arrangement and claimed that there had been no mention of any grazing rights when they bought the place. But I'm not the right person to describe the disagreement. You should have a word with the man involved. Obviously, he knows all the ins and outs of his dispute with the couple.' Karl's gaze swung from Karó to Týr as he added: 'But, for God's sake, don't mention that it was me who told you.'

'Who is this man?' Karó's hand hovered over her notepad, ready to take down the details.

'Einar Ari, he's called. Einar Ari Arason. He lives at Minna-Hvarf.' Karl looked from Týr back to Karó again. 'He should be familiar to the police.'

'Ah.' Karó stopped writing and met Karl's eye. 'As far as I'm aware, he hasn't crossed our radar in the Reykjavík police, so you'll have to be a bit more specific. Are you suggesting that he's violent?'

Karl shifted in his chair and pulled at his collar as if it was too tight. His unease about having to discuss his neighbour like this was understandable and very common. People were naturally afraid that their words would find their way back to the person in question, and that there would be repercussions. 'He's got a temper on him,' Karl conceded. 'He's a nasty piece of work. I'll say no more.'

'Did he use threatening behaviour towards the couple?' Týr asked, ignoring Karl's reluctance to talk about him. 'In relation to the disputed grazing land?'

'Not that I witnessed myself. I only have Ása's word for it. Apparently he made various threats, but as far as I know he didn't carry any of them out.'

'Like what?'

Karl blew out a breath. 'He didn't threaten to kill them. It was just the usual rubbish. Like how he'd make their life so difficult they wouldn't want to stay in the district. That he'd sue them, that kind of thing.'

'All over a piece of grazing land?' Karó didn't try to hide her surprise.

'No. There was more to it than that. It was mainly to do with his treatment of the horses. Ása wasn't happy. She said it almost amounted to animal cruelty. But believe me, their quarrel had nothing to do with that terrible business at the farm. It's not possible. Einar Ari's a bully, not a monster.'

Although Týr felt he should keep an open mind at this stage, he was inclined to agree with Karl. It was hard to see how an appalling atrocity like the murders could have arisen from a dispute over some grazing land or a difference of opinion about animal husbandry. On the other hand, he reminded himself that people had been known to commit murder with far more trivial motives. Still, it was much more likely that the husband was the killer. This angle about the bully from the neighbouring farm would in all probability turn out to be a waste of time.

Karó resumed her questions, focusing on the timeline now – on when Karl had last seen or heard from the family. Since it was doubtful that the post-mortems would provide the police with a precise time of death, they would have to rely on other kinds of evidence. Týr reckoned that the family's internet usage would give the best indication of when it had happened. Dead people don't go on the internet, whereas the living have frequent recourse to it – if they're not permanently online.

According to Karl, he had last seen the family on the Thursday of the previous week, exactly seven days ago, or six days before he found the bodies. He had met them on the Hvalfjördur road as he was on his way to Reykjavík and they were coming back from somewhere. They had stopped and had a brief chat, but then a car had appeared behind him and he'd been forced to move on. Now that he came to think about it, the couple had seemed to be in a hurry, though they hadn't said why. He added that although he hadn't seen them since then, that didn't mean they hadn't been alive and well afterwards. He hadn't gone over to the farm until Monday, three days ago, when Ása didn't turn up for her hair appointment. He hadn't seen anyone on that occasion, but he was fairly sure they'd been alive then – possibly just gone for a walk – because he'd heard the dogs barking inside the house. But when he came back two days later, they'd been shut in the byre. This would suggest that the victims had died after he dropped by on Monday, but that didn't fit with what Týr knew about the state of the bodies. Decomposition had been too advanced for them to have been lying there for less than forty-eight hours. The pathologist's provisional findings, reported at this morning's briefing, had supported the idea that the victims had been dead for several days.

'About Reynir.' Karó looked up from her notepad. 'Was there any sign of him during either of your visits?'

'No. Like I said, I didn't see anyone. Obviously I'd have told you if I'd met him.'

'I meant, did you hear anything to suggest that he was in the house, or see footprints in the snow or anything like that? Or anything to indicate that he'd recently left? Wheel marks left by a car that could have picked him up, for instance?'

Karl shook his head. 'No. Nothing like that. Though I do remember thinking, as I drove away, that someone had pulled the curtains in the old house. But I wasn't myself, as I'm sure you'll understand, so I can't be sure I didn't imagine it.' Belatedly, he twigged. 'Hang on. Are you saying Reynir hasn't been found? They said on the radio that you were investigating four deaths. I just assumed Reynir was one of them.' When Týr and Karó didn't answer, he asked: 'You don't think *he* did it?'

'We don't know anything for sure yet. The investigation is only just getting off the ground.' Karó abandoned the subject of Reynir and started asking questions about the young woman who had been working for the family. Karl said he'd never talked to her, only seen her from a distance. Then he asked in tones of disbelief whether she was a suspect. Karó explained that she wasn't, but carefully avoided mentioning that she had been among the victims. According to his account, Karl hadn't entered the old house, so he wouldn't be aware of what had happened to her. But he seemed to have put two and two together now.

'One question, Karl. Is it possible that you had something to eat while you were in the house? Bread and milk, maybe?' Karó licked her lips, searching for a tactful way of broaching the subject. 'People can do some strange things when they're in shock.'

It took Karl a moment or two to grasp what she was asking. 'Did I have something to eat? Is that what you're asking me?'

'Yes. Did you? It wouldn't be a crime if you did.'

'No. I did not have anything to eat. Of course not. I'm not crazy. There was food on the table when I arrived, bread and some other stuff, if I remember right. A plate and a glass. A glass of milk. But that had nothing to do with me. How could you even think that?'

After this the conversation became increasingly sticky, because Karl kept harping back to the food, asking how it could even enter their heads that he would have raided the fridge after finding the bodies. He reminded them that he'd been sick twice.

Clearly, there was nothing to be gained by continuing, so they said goodbye to Karl, agreeing that it would be better not to interview his wife, Ella, straight away. They were worried that if they did, it might be interpreted as muscling in on the Akranes police's jurisdiction, as they hadn't received any orders from Hördur to talk to her.

As Karó turned the car round and drove away from the farm, it seemed the shyness between them was history. At last, they had something concrete to talk about. 'I bet the food was left there by Reynir,' she said. 'Imagine. That he was actually capable of sitting down and eating a snack after butchering his family.'

'He did more than that, I reckon. He went on living with the bodies for several days. If what Idunn said yesterday was right, the food was too fresh to have been sitting there since they died.' Týr turned to Karó, studying her attractive profile. 'It sounds like we're looking for a seriously disturbed individual.'

Karó concentrated on the snowy track leading from the farm to the road. 'There's another thing. There was no glass on the table yesterday. Or plate. Which suggests that Reynir must still have been in the house when Karl arrived – if Karl remembered the detail about the glass and plate correctly. But why remove them? I can't think.'

Týr shrugged. 'If he's as crazy as everything suggests, maybe he put them in the dishwasher before leaving the house and making his getaway.'

'Damn.' Karó speeded up a little to shake off the farm dog which was running after the car, barking wildly.

Týr turned and looked through the rear windscreen as the dog halted in the middle of the road and watched them drive away. He barked once, then turned and trotted off home.

Chapter 8
Before

The blinds were still drawn in the large open-plan room. Sóldís averted her eyes, keeping her back to the blanked-out windows. She didn't want to think about that shadowy figure outside. In spite of that, she was more than ever convinced that it was better to be able to see out than not, as her imagination was conjuring up far worse images than the vague form she had glimpsed the previous afternoon. In fact, she found it hard to recall the incident in any detail. It had all happened so fast, and the ensuing commotion had left her confused, especially after Ása had run to fetch Reynir. She had reappeared with him on her heels, newly woken and bemused – bemused enough to insist that they'd been imagining things, despite the combined testimony of his wife, his daughter and Sóldís.

Ása had stubbornly insisted in the face of his scepticism, and they had argued about it in a constrained way, as couples do when other people are listening. Finally, Reynir had let himself be persuaded, and crouched down beside Gígja to get her to describe the man. This had proved tricky, but in the end Gígja had said that it might have been the 'horse man'. Reynir had stood up without replying. Ása had followed suit, and an awkward silence had fallen. Sóldís hadn't liked to ask who the 'horse man' was, as this was obviously a touchy subject. When the couple finally broke their silence, it was to ask her to go to her quarters as they needed to have a private chat.

She had obeyed without a word, locking the doors firmly behind her, both the one to the connecting corridor and the front door of the old farmhouse. But the brief feeling of security this gave her hadn't lasted long. Locks were no barrier against fear. The knowledge that she was alone in the old house, thrown back on her own devices if anything went wrong, preyed on her mind. Doors weren't the only way of entering a building; it would be easy enough for someone to break a window if they wanted to get in. And she only made things worse by reminding herself that the world was full of bad people, the kind who wouldn't hesitate to hurt others and got a twisted kick out of threatening and intimidating their victims.

The more she tried to be sensible, the more panicked she became. Rationally, there was nothing threatening about a man being outside. Although the weather wasn't exactly suitable for a ramble, that didn't automatically mean that he couldn't have been out on a walk. But Ása and Reynir's reaction had suggested he hadn't been an innocent hiker: he was someone who meant them harm – the 'horse man'. Gígja had said it as if it was two words, rather than 'horseman', meaning a rider – unless that was just her slightly uncertain Icelandic. Sóldís couldn't begin to guess who he was or why the couple had been so rattled to hear him mentioned. Ása and Reynir were among the most down-to-earth people she'd met, the scientifically minded type who relied on evidence and facts rather than being led astray by their emotions. If they were rattled, there must be a genuine reason for it.

She hadn't felt any better once she was tucked up in bed. The wind had picked up and the noise sounded at times as though someone was whistling outside her window. The old house responded with creaks and groans that sounded for all the world like footsteps on the floorboards. Once, she heard an odd squeaking that sounded as if it came from the landing. This alarmed her so much that she had got out of bed and tiptoed over to the door, opening it a crack to peer out. But of course there was nobody there and no sign of anything wrong. She felt a bit foolish as she got back under her duvet, but almost immediately she experienced another wave of apprehension as bad as the one that had driven her out of bed. Her attempt to calm herself down by listening to a podcast didn't work either, as all it meant was that she couldn't hear what was happening around her. She'd rather have a bit of warning if someone was about to force their way into her room – which wouldn't be difficult as her door was unlocked. It had an old-fashioned keyhole but there was no key in it, or in any of the other internal doors in the old house, as far as she could ascertain. She'd have slept better if she could have locked herself in, and preferably bolted the door too.

Eventually, against all the odds, she had succumbed to sleep, released at last from her fears. The last thought she could remember having was that she should get out of here, resign and leave. That there was something wrong about the whole situation. She now put that down to her insomnia. Problems always seemed a thousand times worse when you were struggling to get to sleep.

When she turned up to work the next morning, no one had said a word about the previous evening's incident. It might never have happened. Yet the blinds were still pulled down over the glass walls.

Íris flopped forward on to the table and lay face down on a half-completed grammar exercise with a theatrical groan. The blonde hair she'd inherited from her mother swept over the desk, brushing aside the flakes of rubber from her eraser. She had been defeated by the twin delights of the subjunctive and the indicative mood.

'Let's take a break.' Sóldís could tell that there was little point ploughing on. A short break wouldn't kill anyone. 'Come on. Let's do some stretching.'

Íris looked up, her expression as scornful as when she'd collapsed in defeat. 'Stretching?'

'Or something. Let's stand up, anyway.' Sóldís got to her feet and Íris copied her – with another martyred groan, so Sóldís wouldn't make the mistake of thinking she was pleased with the suggestion. Though secretly she must be. 'How about we go into the sitting room? Chill out a bit.'

Íris shrugged her thin shoulders. Sóldís couldn't help feeling sorry for her and gave her a friendly smile. It must be tough being a teenager in such an isolated spot. Teenagers needed the company of their own age group. It was an essential part of their social development. In Sóldís's opinion, home-schooling the girls like this was madness. But it was none of her business. 'You can look at your phone if you like.'

Íris's eyes shone with sudden pleasure and she straightened her hunched shoulders. But the gleam soon vanished and the long-suffering look returned. 'What about Mum? I'm not allowed to touch my phone during the day when I'm supposed to be studying.'

Ása and Reynir had gone for a walk with Gígja. 'She's not here and I promise not to snitch. If she finds out, I'll take the blame – as long as you promise only to look at Icelandic content. Language learning can involve surfing the net sometimes.'

'But I don't want to surf, I want to check out social media.'

'Well, there's Icelandic stuff on social media. Don't you have any Icelandic friends? Or cousins, or people you follow?'

Íris shook her head. 'I've only got one Icelandic friend. Mum hates him.'

Sóldís doubted this was true. Hate was a strong word and few people felt genuine hatred, even if they had something against a person. Aware that she might be heading on to thin ice, she ventured: 'Is his name Robbi, by any chance?'

Íris's jaw dropped and she gaped at Sóldís. 'How did you know? Was Mum talking about him?'

Sóldís shook her head. She'd seen the name scribbled in the margins of Íris's exercise books and told her so. This was met by a look of outrage, as if Sóldís had been spying, which was unfair. The fact was you couldn't help seeing the repetitions of his name. But Íris cheered up again when they entered the sitting room. She flung herself down on one of the big sofas and lay on her back, holding her phone over her face.

Sóldís didn't have hers with her as she'd got into the habit of leaving it in her quarters during the day. She was on duty, after all, and knew that most employers regarded time spent on one's phone as skiving. From what Íris had said, Ása belonged firmly in this camp. Still, the advantage of the arrangement was that Sóldís couldn't give in to the temptation to look at social media all day, even if it meant she had nothing to distract her now. 'Tell me something, Íris.'

'Hmm?' Íris was engrossed, barely aware of Sóldís's existence.

'There were loads of clothes in one of the bedrooms in the old house. In the wardrobe. Do you know who they belonged to?'

'Clothes?' It was the only word Íris seemed to have taken in.

'Yes. Clothes. A wardrobe full of them. Expensive gear.'

'I haven't a clue.' Íris glanced up briefly from her phone. 'Maybe they're Alvar's. I think he left all his stuff behind when he went.' She made a face. 'And they're not expensive. They're cheap knock-offs. Just give them to charity if they're in your way.'

Sóldís bit back her irritation. 'Not everyone can afford expensive brands, Íris. The clothes may have been precious to him.'

'If he wanted to keep them, he wouldn't have left them there. He just couldn't be arsed to throw them away himself. I wouldn't leave my stuff behind if I still wanted it.'

'Sometimes people are in too much of a hurry to pack their things. Maybe he didn't have time.' Sóldís decided to seize this chance to ask Íris about her predecessor. It wasn't often that both Ása and Reynir were out at the same time. When they were home, Sóldís always had the feeling that they were eavesdropping on her conversations with the girls, so she avoided discussing anything that she wouldn't talk about to their face. 'He left in a real hurry, didn't he?'

Íris shrugged and the cushion she was resting her head on slipped out from under her. 'Yes, I think so. He left late in the evening or in the night. After I'd gone to sleep, anyway.' She added wearily: 'It's not like there's anything to do here in the evenings.'

Sóldís ignored this complaint: 'Did something happen? To make him leave without warning like that?'

'I don't know. I'm glad he's gone. He was such a loser.'

'In what way?' Sóldís knew that in Íris's teenage world, almost everyone was a loser, apart from her and her mates – the few she had left after moving back to Iceland.

Íris rolled her eyes as if Sóldís didn't understand anything. 'Just, you know. He wasn't *lit*.' She said the last word in English, with a pronounced American twang. 'He thought he was. But he was more, like, creepy. Then he had a fight with

Dad, even though he knew Dad was ill. A total loser, like I said.'

'He had a fight with your dad? What about?' Sóldís could think of several reasons. Reynir was a deeply uncomfortable presence about the house and sometimes said things that bordered on inappropriate. He asked Sóldís personal questions, like what her grade average had been on her B.Ed. course, what her parents did for a living and why she didn't have any brothers or sisters. Not to mention the occasion at lunch when he had asked whether she'd ever been in a relationship and which sex she was attracted to. Ása had hastily intervened at that point to change the subject. Then she'd murmured to Sóldís that Reynir wasn't quite the same since his operation but that she mustn't let it bother her. It was fine to ignore him. There'd been some damage to his prefrontal cortex when his brain tumour was removed.

'I don't know. I was in my room and just heard raised voices. They were yelling at each other. But Alvar started it, not Dad.'

It didn't actually matter what they had argued about or who had started it. The pertinent point in all this was that Sóldís's predecessor had quit after falling out with Reynir. 'What about the girl who was here before him?' she asked. 'Did she leave the job early as well?'

Íris's eyes narrowed. 'You mean Berglind? She was fired.'

'Do you know why?' Sóldís was prepared for Íris to snap at her or ask why she was being so bloody nosy, but she didn't.

'Mum couldn't stand her.'

If Íris was to be believed, Ása and Reynir had each in turn been the cause of an assistant's departure. Sóldís could understand it in Reynir's case, but up to now Ása had given the impression of being pretty easy to get along with and slow to anger. Sóldís's first thought was that Berglind must have broken the rules about social media. Perhaps she'd posted a photo or a video of the family that had angered Ása. 'Did she do something wrong?'

'I have no idea but she must have. You have to do something bad to get fired. Or at least I assume so.'

Sóldís nodded. She didn't imagine Íris had ever had a job. She wouldn't have had to spend her summers pulling up weeds as part of the youth employment programme that teenagers in Iceland were expected to take part in, or work on a till in the Bónus discount supermarket at weekends in order to save up for anything she wanted. Sóldís was pretty sure Íris wouldn't have to slave away in a restaurant alongside her university studies either and that her marks would be higher as a result. Her father wouldn't adopt a pitying look when he grilled her about *her* grade average. But since sharing these thoughts with the girl would not be appropriate, Sóldís merely said: 'Yes, that's how it usually works.'

Íris's phone bleeped and Sóldís was instantly forgotten. The girl read something on the screen that seemed to please her, as a rare smile touched her lips. Sóldís was fairly sure it was a message from Robbi. She slipped in another question in the hope that Íris would answer, despite being distracted: 'Who's the "horse man", Íris?'

Íris looked up from her phone at once. 'What?'

'The "horse man". Gígja was talking about a horse man when we saw someone outside yesterday. I forgot to ask her who she meant.' This wasn't exactly true but it didn't matter: Íris hadn't been there.

'Gígja's talking rubbish. She's just repeating Mum's bullshit. Mum's obsessed with that guy. She keeps imagining he's stalking her. Who do you think would bother? He's got better things to do. Anyway, he's not like that.'

'Who is he?'

Íris exhaled irritably through her nose. 'My friend's dad – Robbi's dad. Mum's just got the wrong idea. She doesn't get it.'

'Doesn't get what?'

Íris had no chance to answer. From the hall came the sound of the front door opening. That's all it took to make them both leap up and dash back into the kitchen. Quickly resuming their seats at the table, they started poring over the subjunctive and indicative again, as if they'd never been doing anything else. Sóldís, aware of her racing heart, realised how unexciting her existence had become. If life was a journey, she was the senior citizen with impaired vision who hogged the middle of the road, driving at half the speed of everybody else. She'd always been risk averse and opted for the safest course, but as a result she'd missed out on a lot – like feeling her heart beat faster from time to time. The biggest thrill in her life before she came to Hvarf had been the adrenaline kick at the supermarket till, when she couldn't pack her purchases fast enough and the next customer's shopping was piling up.

Perhaps Jónsi had been right after all: she was tomato ketchup, not Béarnaise sauce.

Trying to recover her concentration, Sóldís stared at the open textbook lying between them on the kitchen table, searching for inspiration, but the verbs didn't exactly come to life before her eyes. They were no more than letters on a page. It turned out not to matter, though. No one came into the kitchen to witness her lacklustre teaching. And she heard no further sounds from the hall or anywhere else in the house.

Sóldís looked at Íris. 'You heard the front door too, didn't you?'

Íris nodded. She looked round at the empty doorway. Then she made to get up, but Sóldís put a hand on her shoulder and said she'd go and check herself. She was just walking towards the hall when the bloody cuckoo clock sprang into action, almost giving her a heart attack. If it hadn't been for the incident yesterday, she wouldn't have been so jittery. Of course there was nothing strange going on: Ása, Reynir and Gígja must have come home and maybe opened the front door to chuck in a wet glove or unwanted scarf, before going over to the byre to check on the animals. The front door was locked; she'd heard the latch click behind the others when they went out for their walk.

But there was no wet mitten lying on the floor of the entrance hall. No scarf either. On the tiles just inside the closed door, however, there were two wet footprints. They were too large to have been made by Gígja. It must have been Reynir. But his outdoor shoes were nowhere to be seen and the only possible conclusion was that he had stepped inside, then changed his mind and reversed out of the house.

Sóldís decided to open the door and see if there was any sign of the family. She had opened it a crack before she suddenly remembered the man. What if he was standing outside? There was a peephole in the door that she could have looked through first but it was too late now.

But there was no stranger in the yard. There wasn't a soul. The only sign of a human presence was the line of footprints leading to the door. But there were no tracks leading away again.

Sóldís followed the trail with her eyes as far as the drive but could see no further because of the snow that had started softly falling while she and Íris were sitting at the kitchen table. As she watched, the heavy flakes started to fill in the footprints.

By the time the others eventually got home, the tracks leading to the door had vanished. And the wet footprints had evaporated from the heated hallway floor.

Chapter 9
Thursday

The sheets were more expensive than Týr would have liked, and designed with tourists in mind, judging by the print of the Northern Lights that adorned them. They were so garish they were bound to keep him awake at night. As if that wasn't bad enough, the lurid green reminded him sickeningly of the colour of Ása's abdomen, the very last image he wanted in his head before he went to sleep. He'd never feel the same about the Northern Lights again. Nevertheless, he inserted his card into the reader, thanked the sales assistant and returned to the car. As he got into the passenger seat, he chucked the paper bag on to the back seat.

'All sorted, I see.' Karó started the engine. She had made a quick exit after buying herself a set of sheets that were no less garish, featuring an orange picture of a volcanic eruption. Unsurprisingly, she'd felt uncomfortable in the shop, as the assistant had insisted on speaking to her in English, despite the fact that Karó had answered in Icelandic. Týr knew he wouldn't be able to stop himself intervening if things went on like this. He felt like an idiot standing there, pretending not to notice. Sooner or later he would have to raise the subject with Karó and ask how he ought to react. He didn't want to make the situation any more awkward.

'I rang Hördur while you were in the shop,' Karó said, 'and brought him up to speed with what we learnt from the interview. He's given us another job.'

Týr tried to hide his displeasure. The news was almost as frustrating to him as the meagre choice of bedlinen in the petrol station shop. He'd been hoping that he and Karó could have some say in what they did next. But, mindful of what his boss had said about the Reykjavík police playing second fiddle to Akranes on this case, he felt it was better to keep his mouth shut than to start whinging about it. If it had been up to him, though, he'd have gone straight round for a word with Einar Ari Arason from the neighbouring farm about his quarrel with the couple. Swallowing his frustration, Týr asked what Hördur had had to say about the farmer and Karó told him not much. The man was notorious locally as a bully with a bad temper. The police had frequently been called in to keep the peace, on one occasion because he'd threatened Ása in connection with their disagreement over the use of the land belonging to Hvarf. But Hördur had hastened to add that there was a major difference between that kind of unpleasantness and a series of horrific murders. Which was fair enough. Nevertheless, Einar Ari's dealings with the couple had cast a shadow on their otherwise peaceful existence in the area.

'We've been asked to go and meet a couple of engineers from the telecom company that installed the phone mast for Hvarf. They were sent out to restore the phone coverage for the area, but they think they've found evidence of sabotage. They're going to wait for us to take pictures and record the damage – in case it's linked somehow to the murders.'

Týr couldn't hold back. 'But what about Einar Ari? Doesn't someone need to talk to him?'

'Not at this stage. Hördur told me they're going to hold off until they know more about his disagreement with the couple. Apparently, Ása and Reynir didn't make any further complaints after the police had spoken to the guy and warned him to toe the line. So it seems likely that things calmed down after that. Still, who knows? It probably makes sense to be well prepared before approaching a character like him. And it may not be necessary to interview him at all if Reynir's found and turns out to be our killer.'

They started driving towards Hvarf and soon spotted a van with the telecom company logo. Karó parked on the side of the road behind it and they continued on foot, following the tracks of the engineers up a small hill to the phone mast. The men waved to them from where they were resting on a large rock that was bare of snow, then rose to their feet as Týr and Karó approached, folding their arms and watching as the two police officers clambered, panting, up the last stretch. The engineers, who were crimson in the face from the cold and clearly fed up with waiting, didn't seem overly impressed with their stamina.

The GSM antenna lay in the snow beside them, a white aluminium cylinder attached to a steel pole. Wires protruded in a wild tangle from one end, like a plant that had been torn up by the roots. There was a low, concrete base with a steel attachment, where the antenna had evidently been mounted. The spot was so windswept that Týr guessed the fastenings must have given way during a particularly ferocious gale. After introducing himself, he tried out this theory: 'Wasn't it just blown over?'

The younger engineer answered: 'Possibly. If the wind knows how to use an adjustable spanner. The nuts on the fastening were unscrewed before the antenna was pulled down. All the wires have been disconnected. That's why we called.'

Karó either didn't notice the barb directed at Týr or didn't care. 'Is that a common problem? Vandals tearing down equipment like this?'

'Never seen it before,' the older man replied, and his younger colleague nodded. 'Even the idiots who steal bikes or set fire to clothes-recycling containers want to keep their internet and phone connection. Besides, they're not exactly likely to be passing by out here. The person who sabotaged this mast did it to cut the connection.'

Týr gazed out over the surrounding countryside. He hadn't noticed on the way here but the fjord had curved gradually towards the east, so they could no longer see out towards its mouth and the open sea. The desolate, snow-covered landscape brought home to him what a backwater this district was nowadays. Its lifeblood had been abruptly cut off more than twenty years ago when the Hvalfjördur Tunnel opened, diverting the traffic that had once been forced to take the long, winding road round the fjord. All he could see now were a scattering of farms and an abandoned cafe that had once been a popular rest stop. The emptiness of the road told its own story. 'How big an area did the mast cover?' he asked, returning to the present.

'Just the one farm. It's called Hvarf and not without reason. Before the antenna was installed, the farm was located in a pretty big dead zone – by the standards of the network in general. All the other farms in the area can connect to different masts. So, if the intention was to cut the signal, it was targeted at Hvarf and nowhere else.' The older engineer pointed to the farm where the bodies had been found.

From up here, the buildings looked less imposing than they had down on the level. Týr could see a number of cars parked in the yard, and, further off, lines of colourfully dressed search-and-rescue volunteers combing the landscape for Reynir's body.

'Do they know when the signal dropped out?' Týr turned back to the engineers.

The men exchanged glances. 'Yes. That's clear.'

As neither seemed likely to elaborate, Karó prompted them: 'So, when was it?'

'On Friday last week, if I remember right.' The older man looked sheepish.

'Six days ago, in other words. Do you usually wait this long before repairing faulty antennas? Am I right that you're only here now because we asked you to come out?' Karó smiled to take the sting out of her question.

'Yes, you could say it's unusual. But then this is no ordinary phone mast. It was installed last year, specially for this farm. It wasn't top of our list, but the owners offered to cover all the costs, so they went to the front of the queue. We'd never had any complaints from the previous owner about the lack of coverage. But because the antenna is partly privately owned, we waited for the owners to get in touch about the repairs. It would have been difficult to charge them for the job if we'd just jumped to it, sorted it out, then sent a bill. But they didn't ring. Didn't send an email or anything. Nobody heard from them.'

'No. Nobody heard from them.' Karó met Týr's gaze for a second. No doubt she was thinking the same as him: dead people don't tend to get in touch with service centres.

* * *

The farmyard was a hive of activity. There were two vehicles belonging to forensics parked there, in addition to the cars of the deceased, a couple of police SUVs and a large lorry. The byre doors were open, and a pair of cows was being led over to the ramp at the back of the lorry. The people leading them were wearing protective overalls, gloves and masks, like those driving the beasts from behind. Týr assumed this was to do with the byre rather than the livestock. For all they knew, the killer might have gone in there and maybe even found the murder weapon there, if it had indeed been an axe. But of course all these precautions would be a waste of time if Reynir turned out to be guilty. Since he'd lived on the farm, his biological traces would be all over the place and their presence wouldn't tell the investigators anything on their own. In cases where the perpetrator knew the victim or belonged to the same family, this type of evidence had to be directly linked to the murders and impossible to explain by any other means before it would be admissible in court.

No barking met Týr and Karó when they got out of the car this time, so Týr assumed the dogs must have been removed from the premises. What happened to people's pets in cases like this, he had no idea. Maybe they would be taken in by relatives of the family, though apparently there weren't many relatives in this instance, as the couple had both been only children. And next of kin could hardly be expected to take in the larger livestock like the two cows.

A man Týr recognised from forensics in Reykjavík waved to them from the doorstep of the new house, then came over. 'Is there any news about the bloody phone reception?' he asked in irate tones. 'We've only got the one TETRA radio between us; the situation's totally unacceptable.'

Karó repeated what the telecom engineers had told them: they were working on restoring the signal but they wouldn't be finished for at least another hour or two, assuming the equipment hadn't been irreparably damaged. If it had, they would have to order replacement parts, which meant the antenna wouldn't be working again until tomorrow.

The man threw up his hands and gave an exasperated groan. Týr wondered how he'd cope in a real crisis. Karó seemed unmoved by the drama he was making out of it and merely asked if he had any news.

At this the man began to calm down. 'Not really. Of course, the buildings are teeming with biological traces. It'll be no joke trying to process them all. Possibly pointless too. We haven't come across any evidence to suggest that anyone other than the husband was responsible, and his traces will be all over the house, as you'd expect. So his DNA won't tell us anything, even if we find it in the bedrooms. But if the theory that he's our man turns out to be wrong, we won't have been wasting our time after all. Especially if the traces come from the bedrooms. Not many visitors are invited to get into bed with their hosts.'

'Is there anything else that might implicate Reynir in the murders?' Týr assumed not, but you never knew. He couldn't think of anything that would remove all doubt, short of a suicide note in which Reynir confessed to the crimes. But that was wishful thinking. Cases were rarely that open-and-shut.

'No, nothing conclusive. We found a pile of drugs that had been prescribed for him. They've been sent to Reykjavík for analysis, but we do know that one packet contained the sort of powerful painkillers that are often misused. There were sleeping pills there too. The rest were presumably connected to his illness.'

'What about his passport? Has that turned up?' Karó zipped her down jacket up to her chin when the wind abruptly veered round and started blowing into their faces.

'Yes, it has. It was in a drawer in the couple's walk-in closet, together with his wife's and his daughters'. That's good news, at least, since it means he's probably still in the country. Though we can't be a hundred per cent sure.'

The man was right. It was possible to travel within the Schengen area without a passport if the ticket was bought through an airline that didn't require that type of documentation. Yet the fact that Reynir hadn't taken his with him increased the likelihood that he was still in Iceland. Fugitives had to travel further than Europe if they were to have a realistic chance of getting away with their crimes.

The forensic technician turned and looked at the two cars that had belonged to the family. 'We've discovered something else. The car keys are missing. They're literally nowhere to be found. The spares too. And the keys to the snowmobile in the shed.'

Karó and Týr both turned their heads simultaneously to the cars. She got in first: 'Have you looked everywhere?'

'Yes. More or less. Though there's still the byre.' Before she could respond, the man added in a sarcastic tone: 'Maybe the keys are in the stalls just vacated by the cows, or in the dung store. We haven't sifted through the manure yet. But then, hello, who would keep their keys there?'

'No one, of course.' Karó shrugged. 'But the person who took them could have thrown them in there.'

'And another thing: the cable junction box has been destroyed.' The man shook his head. 'Weird.'

'Don't forget the phone mast. That was sabotaged too.' Týr contemplated the handsome modern house. In any other circumstances he would find it striking, but now the sight of it gave him the shivers. 'It's pretty clear, isn't it, that all this was done to isolate the family? So they couldn't phone for help or escape by car or snowmobile?'

'Or on horseback.' The man gestured to the byre. 'They owned two horses but those have gone missing like the keys. All I can think of is that they must have been let out for the same reason – so that no one could get away on horseback. Unless the husband took them.'

'Are we absolutely sure that they only had two cars at their disposal?' Týr asked. It was a long way to the nearest settlement of any size, and hard going, especially in the present conditions. If Reynir had wanted to escape, Týr couldn't picture him riding or walking. Not with two cars in the yard.

'According to the vehicle register, they only had these two. But he could have rented one. They're checking with all the main car rental companies now. But that's unlikely to produce any results.'

'Why?' Týr couldn't understand why the man seemed so sure.

'Because one of the snowmobiles is missing. There were two registered in their names but we've only found one. So the most likely scenario is that Reynir used it for his getaway. Which is going to make the search area a whole lot bigger than we'd bargained for. Unless the snowmobile was being repaired at a garage or they'd lent it out. We have to allow for that possibility.'

After a bit of a struggle the cows had finally been loaded on to the lorry. There was a loud outbreak of mooing before the animals quietened down and the men re-emerged. They put up the ramp, then slammed the doors of the cab. 'Were the horses valuable at all?' Karó asked. 'Might someone have stolen them?'

The man shrugged. 'Search me. All I know is that there are two stalls which recently had horses in them. There's a load of tack too. Saddles, bridles and so on. Of course, it's possible the horses were let out to graze by the owners before the murders happened, but that's unlikely. Stabled horses aren't usually let out during winter. And the weather's been so bad recently that it would make even less sense. No, we reckon it was all part of the plan to isolate the farm. To cut the family off – in case any of them survived the attack.'

The house seemed even more forbidding now and Týr averted his gaze. 'Is it clear when the family last went online?'

The man shook his head. 'No. Not as far as I'm aware. Their phones were sent to Reykjavík with the first samples, along with all the computers in the house. We can't expect any results until this evening. Or tomorrow. But seeing as all contact with the farm had been cut, the technology may only be able to tell us when the phone blackout began.'

'Possibly the internet went at around the same time,' Týr said. Then he elaborated: 'If they were like most people, they wouldn't have taken it calmly when the internet stopped working. If that happened after the phone signal dropped out, you'd assume they would have got in the car and driven until they could find a signal and report the fault. Then asked the company to send out an engineer. But, who knows, maybe the car keys had been hidden? Or the murders were committed almost immediately after the junction box was sabotaged.'

'It'll be interesting to see what emerges from the post-mortems.' The man's optimism that this might help with the time frame was misplaced. Idunn had already explained that they'd only get a very vague idea of the time of death from her. But Týr agreed that something of interest was bound to emerge.

He'd always been bad at waiting, especially in situations like this. He often wished life could be fast-forwarded like a film. Rarely did he wish it could be rewound. There was little in his past that he would want to repeat or try tackling in a different way. It almost certainly wouldn't change anything. His role in life was pretty insignificant, after all, more like an extra than a main character. Nothing he said or did, or failed to say or do, would have much impact on the world.

'Bloody snow.' Karó kicked the drift at her feet. 'I don't suppose they found any tracks or footprints by the house?'

'Nope. Anything like that has been obliterated.' Then, remembering something, the man added: 'Having said that, it seems two hens have been decapitated.'

'*Decapitated?*' Týr queried. His parents had made sure he spoke good Icelandic but every now and then he came across a word or compound that conveyed nothing to him or that he misheard. This must be one of those occasions.

'Yes. We found two hens' heads buried in the snow behind the house. On the deck. They must have come from the hen-house behind the building. There were several hens in there and a load of feathers in the chicken run.'

'Did they keep them for the pot?' It was clear from Karó's expression that she wouldn't have accepted a dinner invitation if they had.

'No. I very much doubt it. We found the headless chickens. Someone had tried to bury them behind the house. There was a spade by the wall and we used it to dig around until we found them. The ground must have been frozen hard, because they were only just under the surface.'

'Could you tell how long they'd been lying there?' Karó asked.

'No. But they've been sent to town for analysis. What for, I don't really know, as it's hard to see how they could be linked to the murders.'

'Perhaps they were foreplay. The first stage of madness. Or a trial run.' Týr reckoned there was every reason to examine the remains of the poultry. It couldn't be considered normal to chop the heads off your pets only to bury them afterwards.

Their conversation came to an abrupt end, as if the volume had been muted. They stood there, contemplating the house for a while, until eventually the man broke the silence to ask if they wanted to have a look around inside. It was the last thing Týr felt like doing, but before he could decline, Karó accepted the invitation for both of them.

They donned protective suits, although samples had already been collected from most areas in the two houses. On their way in, they encountered several members of forensics coming out, all clad in the same kind of overalls. A female officer told them to be careful and not to touch anything or enter rooms unnecessarily. They mustn't use the basins or turn on the taps anywhere as the traps hadn't yet been emptied or the sewage examined. It seemed probable that the killer had showered or washed after the bloodbath. She went on to say that the team was now going out to the byre to do a thorough examination there. Once they had gone, Týr and Karó's guide told them there was every indication that the animals had been fed and watered over the last few days, right up until the bodies were discovered. A vet had examined the cows and dogs and found them in good condition.

It all pointed to the same thing: Reynir had to be the killer. Who else would have fed the animals or continued living in the house, eaten a meal and wound up the cuckoo clock after murdering two women and two girls in there?

Just before entering, Týr pointed up at a small wall bracket and mount over the front door, with a hood that he was fairly sure must once have covered a security camera. The wires sticking out of the wall beside it suggested as much. 'Is there a security system in the house? Or CCTV?' Yesterday evening he'd been too preoccupied with the harrowing sights to pay as much attention to his surroundings as he usually would at a crime scene. There could have been cameras in every corner for all he knew.

The forensic technician followed his gaze and replied: 'Yes. It appears so. But they've all been taken down. We haven't found a single security camera in the whole building. It's impossible to say when it was done, though of course you have to suspect that it was connected to the murders.'

'There would be little point tearing them down afterwards.' Karó was staring upward as well. 'The recordings must have been saved, though. Unless the computer is damaged or missing too?'

'No. As far as we can tell, none of the computers are missing. The system was still linked up to one of the PCs that was taken to Reykjavík for examination, so it seems it was only the cameras that were taken down.' The man lowered his gaze again. 'Presumably before the killings took place, though, so I don't suppose the recordings will tell us anything. Like you say, what would be the point of taking them down afterwards?'

As they entered the hall, Týr found to his relief that the house didn't feel as sinister now. The forensics markers all over the place diminished the horror evoked by the evidence of the massacre. And portable floodlights had been erected here and there to banish the shadows. The smell had dissipated a bit as well, but the biggest difference was that the bodies had gone. Looking into the bedrooms, it was almost as if nothing untoward had happened – if you overlooked the blood splashed up the walls. The stained bedding had been sent off for analysis, along with all the mattresses. According to the man who guided them around the house, the mattresses had been as blood-soaked as the sheets.

The girls' rooms looked almost normal, and Týr allowed his gaze to linger on the furnishings: the decorations on the walls, the objects the girls had used as ornaments and the clothes hanging in the open wardrobes. He was immediately struck by the conspicuous age gap between the sisters: the younger girl's room was decorated in childishly bright colours, matched by the rainbow hues of the clothes in the cupboard and some of the pictures on the walls, which had clearly been drawn by her. They all seemed to depict happy scenes. In every single one, a big yellow sun shone from the sky, surrounded by rays. The subject matter was either cheerful people or smiling animals, or a combination of the two. The only downer was the brown spots of dried blood spattered across the drawings on the wall above her bed.

The walls were also adorned with *Star Wars* posters and it was clear that the little girl had been a big fan of the franchise. Most of the toys sticking out of the box on the floor were models of spaceships or characters from the films. The box and its contents hadn't been spared the shower of blood either.

Evidently Týr had been staring at the gruesome toy box too long, because the technician took it as implied criticism, as if he thought they'd overlooked the blood. 'It'll all be taken to Reykjavík on the next trip,' the man said defensively. 'There wasn't room for everything in the first batch because of the mattresses.'

Týr merely nodded and didn't bother to explain that he hadn't been doubting their expertise. He continued to scrutinise his surroundings.

One of the things that gave Týr pause was an exercise book on the girl's desk. 'Word List' had been written on the front in felt pen, each letter in a different colour. Opening the book,

Týr read several entries written in a childish hand. They didn't always follow the ruled lines and in some places a wrongly spelt word had been crossed out and rewritten: 'sadle' had been corrected to 'saddle', and 'gote' to 'goat'. Only a few pages had been filled and the rest of the book would remain forever empty. Most of the words related to animals or nature, and the most ambitious item he spotted was 'avalanche'. The girl had managed to write it correctly at the first attempt and Týr guessed that an adult must have spelt it out for her, judging by the mistakes in much shorter, simpler words elsewhere in the book.

Týr leafed through the blank pages until he got to the back, where he found a page on which was written, in much larger letters than at the front: 'Don't Look!' Ignoring this injunction, he turned over the page and skimmed the few words written there: *Kunt*, *Bich*, *Looser*, *Hore*, *Basterd*, *Shit*, *Theef*, *Arshole*, *Fuking* and *Bludy*. Clearly, no adult had helped her write these words. Where could she have come across this collection of swear words and insults? Judging from the phonetic spelling, she must have heard them rather than read them on the internet, say. Had they entered her consciousness via TV, rap music or her immediate environment? If she'd encountered them at home, it must have been through overhearing loud quarrels, but it was too late now to identify the source, since there was no one left to ask.

Týr drew the technician's attention to the exercise book. 'You should take this too.'

The teenage daughter's room couldn't have been more different – all dark colours and nothing on show that could be described as remotely cute. The clothes in the wardrobe were all in muted earth tones or black, and selected garments were displayed on hangers on the walls. Handbags too. Designer brands, which it was apparently no longer considered uncool to flaunt before the world. Like the little sister's drawings, these items had been splattered with blood.

If it hadn't been for the bedframe with the missing mattress and the dark stains on the walls, the room could have been the office of an agent in the fashion world. But, as is common with teenagers, in trying a bit too hard to come across as cool, the girl had overshot the mark. The effect was clichéd and self-conscious. No doubt in time she would have discovered the delicate balance that is required to achieve coolness, but now that would never happen. Somehow this made her room seem almost sadder than her little sister's.

They also looked into rooms Týr hadn't seen the previous evening. Each bedroom had a large en-suite bathroom, and the marital bedroom also boasted a walk-in closet. There was even a gym containing most of the standard equipment. One room turned out to be a wine cellar, another a spacious office. The computers had been removed but three large monitors remained, lined up side by side across two desks. On the floor in one corner was a gadget that looked to Týr like a small robot. It sported two big round lenses resembling eyes, two arms with grippers, caterpillar tracks for legs and a drawer at the front, its purpose obscure. 'What is that?' he asked.

The man shrugged. 'A domestic robot, we think. A bit more advanced than a robot vacuum cleaner. Or maybe just a toy.' He went over to a cupboard by one wall and opened it. At the bottom was a safe that he opened as well. 'This was closed but not locked. It contained some foreign-denomination banknotes – euros, dollars and pounds.'

'A lot of money?' Karó knelt down to peer inside. As there didn't appear to be much to see, she got back to her feet.

'Not that much. About two hundred thousand krónur – or fourteen hundred dollars – at a rough estimate. There were some papers too: their marriage certificate, the girls' birth certificates, that sort of thing.' The man shut the safe and gestured at the two desks. 'In addition to the currency, the house was stuffed with expensive gear that hadn't been touched. The computers in here were worth a fortune. Then there's enough silver tableware for dozens of diners in one of the kitchen cupboards, as well as jewellery in the bedroom drawers, pricey art on the walls, all kinds of collectibles and banknotes left lying around the place. We've pretty much ruled out a robbery as none of this stuff was taken.'

Týr looked around thoughtfully. 'Unless something else is missing that was worth more than the rest put together. So much more that it wasn't worth the thief's while to bother with any other portable goods.' He fell silent, waiting for the inevitable question. It came, after a brief pause.

'Like what?'

Týr shrugged. 'Haven't a clue. Diamonds, maybe.'

Chapter 10
Before

'Perhaps the tracks were made by a whore.' Gígja stared at Sóldís eagerly, waiting for her reaction.

Sóldís didn't disappoint her. She frowned. 'What did you say?' She guessed it must have been a slip of the tongue. Gígja's Icelandic was still a bit shaky at times. Sóldís racked her brains for something that sounded similar, which the little girl might have meant to say. 'Did you ask if the tracks were made by Thóra? Who's Thóra?' The family had never mentioned the name in her hearing.

'I don't know.' Gígja's face split in a grin. 'But I do know who Thor is. He's the one with the hammer.'

Sóldís brought the conversation back to what the child had said. 'What did you mean, Gígja?'

'Nothing.' Gígja smiled again, clearly pleased by the reaction the word had provoked. 'I was just being silly. I don't know what "whore" means. I just wanted to try it out.'

'There are some words it's better not to say,' Sóldís told her seriously. 'They can hurt people's feelings and make them angry or sad. We have to be careful with words. So try not to use ones you don't understand in future.'

'But I'm collecting words. Begga taught me to. She said I should write down all the new words I hear. Then I'll be the best at talking Icelandic. Better than Íris.' Gígja smirked at the thought. 'She won't understand and she'll have to ask me what the words mean.' The prospect clearly delighted her and her face split in an even wider grin. 'But I'm not going to tell her.'

Sóldís couldn't fault Berglind's idea for improving Gígja's vocabulary, even if an ugly word had accidentally found its way into the collection. But this wasn't the right time to encourage the little girl to continue the practice. It would be better to raise the subject again tomorrow, when Gígja had forgotten about the incident. Sóldís would rather not have to explain what 'whore' meant. Besides, she was too preoccupied by the mystery of the footprints that had appeared earlier. Her attempts to find Berglind and Alvar on social media had been futile. She had hoped their accounts would shed some light on their abrupt departures but there were too many people with the same names, and she had to admit that she was no good at internet sleuthing. The footprints she had at least witnessed with her own eyes. Somehow that made the question of their origin far more urgent than her curiosity about Berglind and Alvar.

It was getting on for evening now and Sóldís was still feeling jumpy. It didn't help that none of the others shared her conviction that an intruder had entered the house only to vanish into thin air. Admittedly, this detail of her story didn't exactly inspire confidence in the rest; she would have done better to embroider the truth and claim that she had seen footprints leading back away from the front door. When Ása and Reynir got home they hadn't believed her. According to them, they'd locked the door when they left, and no one could have got in without a key.

By then, the tracks had disappeared, both from outside the door and from the floor inside. There was nothing Sóldís could point to apart from their own footprints in the newly fallen snow. She'd insisted that the tracks had been around about there. The couple had surveyed the yard before returning their gaze to her, shaking their heads and looking awkward.

It wasn't until Sóldís had asked if it could have been the man they'd seen round the back of the house the day before that a look of fear had flashed across Ása's face. But she'd quickly controlled her features when Reynir sighed loudly and muttered that they weren't going to start on that bloody nonsense again, were they? After which he had stormed into the house and Ása had suggested, in a falsely cheerful tone, that they get on with making supper. No more had been said about the mysterious visitor.

But Sóldís had observed that Ása's hands were trembling slightly as she started getting the food out of the fridge. And she had shouted 'No!', when Íris wanted to pull up the blinds. So there was little point in her pretending not to be bothered. Sóldís knew better. It only stoked her own fears to know that Ása shared them. Discussing them would have been the best way to put them to rest but it seemed the subject was a no-go area. When Sóldís had tried to raise it while they were cooking, Ása had interrupted and started talking about something else.

So it was that Sóldís had seized the opportunity, once she and Gígja were alone together, to ask the little girl if she'd seen anyone during their walk. Reynir had got up from the table before he'd finished his meal, and Ása had pursued him into the other room. Íris, meanwhile, realising there was a risk she might be drafted in to wash up, had made herself scarce. Gígja, in complete contrast, had smiled widely and asked if she could help. She had even added '*please*' in English, as if Sóldís needed any persuading to accept her offer.

Gígja hadn't seen anyone. But she guessed that Sóldís's questions related to the footprints. This was hardly surprising, as the little girl had been with her parents when they got back from their walk and she couldn't have failed to notice the state Sóldís was in. She had peered at the snow and even, in her childish desire to help, claimed that she could see footprints. But of course there had been nothing there: the fresh snow had eradicated all trace.

Gígja's suggestion that the tracks might have been made by a whore arose from the same impulse. In her desire to find an explanation, she had brought out a word that she knew meant something bad, presumably because she'd heard it used in a negative context.

Sóldís let Gígja put the detergent in the dishwasher and switch it on. 'Thanks, Gígja. You're great.'

'I know.' Although this praise didn't come as any news to the little girl, she beamed anyway, pleased with herself. 'What shall we do now? Do you want to play *Star Wars*?'

Normally, Sóldís would have told Gígja politely that she was going to her own quarters to read a book. But the truth was that she couldn't face being on her own right now, especially not in the old farmhouse. At least being in the company of the chatty little girl would stop her ears from tuning into every creak or other unexplained noise and interpreting it in the worst way. She drew the line at *Star Wars*, though.

'Ask your Mum if you can come over to my side and watch a film. If she says yes, then we'll do that. But only if she says yes, mind.'

Gígja didn't wait to be told twice but scampered away and reappeared shortly afterwards, almost skidding across the shiny parquet in her eagerness to bring Sóldís the good news. She was allowed to watch a film. But only one for children. She added, sotto voce, that she wouldn't tell her mother if they watched a horror film. With monsters. Or mummies.

Nothing could be further from Sóldís's wishes. Shaking her head firmly, she said a children's film or nothing. Before leaving the kitchen, she gave the place one last check to make sure she hadn't overlooked anything. The couple were unbelievably picky about tidiness – well, Ása mostly. But the kitchen looked immaculate, just as they liked it – bare of clutter, the surfaces so sterilised they could have been used for an emergency operation. Even the air smelt of glass cleaner.

There was none of this sterility in Sóldís's quarters. On her side, the house and its furnishings were more cosily old-fashioned, less shiny and sharp-edged. The illumination was softer too, as there were no spotlights, though the yellowish light cast more shadows, which, combined with the creaking timbers, made Sóldís a lot more uneasy than in the ultra-modern surroundings on the other side.

Still, every cloud had a silver lining. Since seeing the footprints, she hadn't given a moment's thought to Jónsi. She was far too jittery to brood on her rejection. Or on the fact that her friends were ignoring her calls, probably worried that she wanted to crash on their sofas. When all she had wanted was to hear a friendly voice, discuss her situation and ask their advice. Should she stay or leave? Leave or stay? With any luck, Gígja's constant flow of chatter would distract her from obsessing over her dilemma, the footprints or the shadowy figure of the man in the snow. Sóldís could do with a break from the continual sense of disquiet and apprehension.

Gígja took a flying leap on to the sofa in front of the TV and drew her legs up underneath her. She was only wearing one sock. This didn't bother her, though it had annoyed her mother when they sat down to supper. Ása hadn't been able to concentrate on eating and kept darting glances under the table as if to top up her irritation. This had then been noticed by Reynir, who, unable to bear his wife's mania for order, had sprung up and stalked out of the kitchen without finishing the food on his plate. Usually, he put away his meals without paying any attention to the others, so clearly there was tension between the couple. Ása's expression as she followed him out of the kitchen had supported that theory.

Before joining Gígja on the sofa, Sóldís went over to the TV to fetch the remote control. She usually kept it on top of the television cabinet but, to her surprise, it wasn't there. She could have sworn she'd replaced it there yesterday evening when she'd given up trying to find anything worth watching. When she cast her mind back, she could picture herself putting the remote on top of the cabinet. But she must have remembered wrong; it's almost impossible to remember a specific instance of a habitual action. Like when she took the pill every morning. Five minutes later she couldn't remember if she'd taken it – not that that mattered any more.

Unable to see the remote anywhere, Sóldís began to feel increasingly disconcerted. She and Gígja pulled the cushions off the sofa and chair in case it had slipped down behind them. Sóldís kept trying to recall the details of the previous evening. On leaving the TV room, she thought she'd gone straight into the bathroom where she'd washed her face and brushed her teeth before going to bed. But the remote wasn't in the bathroom or on her bedside table or under the bed.

She and Gígja searched the rest of the old house, going through the kitchen, the book room, the bedrooms, the laundry, the storeroom and the downstairs bathroom, but the remote control was nowhere to be found.

'Íris must have taken it.' Gígja seized on the most obvious explanation she could think of. But then she always blamed Íris for everything. 'She hid my crayons once.'

At any other time, Sóldís would have told Gígja not to be so negative about her sister, but the little girl did have a point. Since the remote control was nowhere to be found in the old house, and it could hardly have vanished into thin air, it stood to reason that another person must have taken it, and there weren't many suspects to choose from. 'Have you been in here today, Gígja?' Sóldís asked.

'No. Not until now.' Gígja spread out her hands, palms upward. 'I haven't got it.'

'Of course not. You're helping me search, aren't you?' Sóldís tried to make light of the situation, but she couldn't help mentally reviewing the day and coming to the conclusion that Reynir was the only person who could have entered her quarters. He'd spent most of the day in his office or bedroom while she and Ása were teaching the girls or taking care of the household chores.

He could easily have nipped over to the old house without her noticing. She didn't lock the door to the connecting corridor during the day, as it hadn't even crossed her mind to do so. Up to now, she had thought any possible threat would come from outside the building, not inside. Why the hell should Reynir have taken her remote control? She clapped her hands and forced herself to smile. 'Never mind. Why don't we play cards instead?'

So that's what they did. The deck of cards turned out to be in its usual place in a drawer in the TV cabinet. They played several games of Happy Families, followed by Ólsen-ólsen, a version of Crazy Eights. Neither game was much fun with only two players but Gígja enjoyed herself, especially as she won more often than she lost, helped by the fact that Sóldís couldn't keep her mind on the cards and, in any case, had no wish to beat the little girl.

'Can I ask you something, Gígja?'

'What?' Gígja looked up from her cards.

'Who's the "horse man"?' Sóldís put the question as matter-of-factly as she could. She didn't want the child to realise that it was inappropriate of her to ask. That she shouldn't be trying to extract information that Gígja's parents seemed to want to keep under wraps. Sóldís felt she had no choice but to resort to this method since she had every right to know who the family thought might be prowling around their house. Though she wasn't a member of the family, she did live here. The information she'd managed to prise out of Íris hadn't been enough. The fact that the man was the father of Robbi, the boy Íris fancied, didn't explain anything.

'The horse man? You mean the bad man?'

'Yes, him.' Sóldís guessed that in the eyes of everyone in the family except Íris, he would probably be considered bad.

'I know who he is. But I don't know him.'

'Does he live near by?' Sóldís sent up a private prayer that the answer would be no. She didn't like the idea of him being one of their neighbours. She'd rather hear that he lived in Reykjavík.

'Yes. He lives on the farm next door. But that's quite far away.'

Sóldís sighed under her breath. 'In what way is he bad? Wasn't he going to help you with your snowman?' It was a mistake to ask a child two questions at once but it was too late now.

'I don't know if it was him. The man in the snowstorm had his hat pulled down over his face, like a bank robber, with a hole for his eyes.' Gígja slapped down her last card and smiled. 'Ólsen!'

Sóldís faked disappointment. Her heart had begun to pound and she regretted ever having raised the subject with Gígja.

She could have done without the knowledge that the man had been wearing a balaclava. What kind of person would walk around like that? Nobody, surely? At least, nobody harmless. She could forget about her hopes that it had just been some passing hiker. 'Why do you call him the "horse man", Gígja? Did he sell you the horses? Or did he maybe break them in for you?'

'Oh, no. Mummy would never let him do that. He'd kill them. He'd suck out all their blood until they were dead.' Gígja met Sóldís's eye. 'Your turn.'

Reminded of the game in hand, Sóldís hastily drew three cards without paying any attention to the one Gígja had put down. 'Pass.'

Gígja frowned. 'Are you trying to lose?'

'No, of course not.'

'Ólsen-ólsen!'

Sóldís allowed Gígja to gloat for a while, then, after a decent interval, she returned to that nonsensical comment about sucking blood. 'Are you sure you didn't misunderstand something your mother said, Gígja? Vampires aren't real, you know, and even in stories they don't go after horses. No one's going to drink your horses' blood.'

'He would. Mummy said so. I know what she said.' Gígja collected the cards from the coffee table and attempted to shuffle them. 'That's why Íris isn't allowed to meet the boy she likes. Because the horse man is his daddy. Maybe Mummy's scared he'll suck Íris's blood too.' A sly smile touched her lips. 'It would serve her right. Then her face would turn white. Like a ghost.'

This conversation was getting nowhere; they were talking at complete cross-purposes. Worried now that Gígja might mention it to Ása, Sóldís started chatting about something else in the hope that she would forget all about it. They played a few more games until eventually Sóldís called a halt and said it was bedtime. She had absolutely no wish to be left alone as she knew she'd only start thinking about the wicked horse man skulking around outside. Or about Reynir creeping into her house to steal her remote control. And then her imagination would go into overdrive, picturing all the weird things he might get up to.

It would be almost impossible to get any sleep tonight. But one thing she wasn't going to waste any time worrying about was that the horse man would suck all the blood out of her. That was a bit over the top, even for an inveterate worrier like her.

After delivering Gígja to her side of the house, Sóldís scuttled back through the glassed-in connecting corridor, keeping her head down for fear of seeing a shadowy figure outside. She closed and locked the door behind her, then double-checked that the front door was securely locked. That done, she was able to relax a little. She was safe, confident that no one could get in.

Until, that is, she remembered that it was Reynir's house. Which meant that he and Ása must have spare keys. She might as well not have bothered to lock the door. Her heart started pounding again and it took an effort to steady her breathing. There had to be a solution. Recalling that both doors opened inwards, she fetched two kitchen chairs and wedged one under each door handle. Now, even if someone tried to get in using a key, they would have to throw their weight against the door several times and smash the chair before they could open it. She couldn't fail to hear that. She felt slightly reassured, if not entirely at ease.

Next, she made the mistake of checking her phone, opening her inbox and clicking on an email from her supervisor. The woman asked how her Master's thesis was coming along and requested a brief status update. Sóldís didn't reply, as she hadn't given a moment's thought to her Master's since moving to the countryside. Any report would have to be on the brief side, consisting of two words: *No news*. She resolved to get to grips with her work and make up for lost time. Perhaps part of the reason she was so on edge was a bad conscience about being behind with her dissertation. Well, that was easily remedied, though it would mean knuckling down and no more playing cards or watching TV in the evenings. Perhaps it was a blessing in disguise that the remote control had disappeared. She put her phone back in her pocket to avoid the lure of social media and resolved to find something to read instead.

Going into the book room, Sóldís selected a title that looked unlikely to contain anything disturbing. She'd never come across the author before but it looked like one of those literary novels that dispenses with plot, so there was a good chance she'd fall asleep out of sheer boredom.

Her prediction proved accurate.

But it seemed she wasn't going to be granted eight hours' uninterrupted slumber. In the middle of the night, she surfaced to find the book open on her chest and the bedside lamp still on. She often nodded off like this, stirring for just long enough to put her book down and switch off the light, before turning over and going back to sleep. But now she gradually became aware of some hard object in her left hand. At first, her mind still fogged with sleep, she thought it was her phone. But it wasn't the right shape.

Sóldís opened her eyes wide and saw that she was holding the missing remote control. The creaking outside her room sounded disturbingly like feet descending the stairs. Yet again all her instincts were screaming that she needed to get out of here.

Chapter 11
Thursday

The poky cabin was entirely lined with pine – floor, walls and ceiling. The furniture had been chosen to match: a tiny kitchen table with three chairs, an uncomfortable two-seater sofa, a coffee table, bunk beds and a double bed so narrow that it barely qualified for the name, while at the same time managing to be just too big for the single Northern Lights fitted sheet. Even the twee furnishings in the kitchen corner and bathroom were made of pine. No doubt many would find it cosy, but Týr wasn't one of them. The overpowering smell mingled with a chemical odour, emanating, no doubt, from the varnish on the all-encompassing woodwork. Týr already had a headache and it was getting worse. He would have liked to open the door to let in some fresh air, but it was too damned cold and the wind was gusting, scooping up the loose snow and flinging it around to create the typically Icelandic phenomenon known as *skafrenningur* – like a blizzard from the ground up. Given half a chance, it would soon fill the cabin. A fine white powder was already collecting on the sills where Týr had cracked open the windows.

To make matters worse, the Wi-Fi connection was sluggish. The screen of Týr's laptop showed the frozen image of his boss, Huldar, his mouth open in mid-sentence. The sound was working fine, though, apart from the occasional tinny echo after he'd spoken.

As a rule, Týr didn't have any problems speaking Icelandic. He liked to kid himself that he had barely any trace of a foreign accent; he knew that wasn't actually true, but he reckoned people would have to listen hard to detect it. And it wasn't that common for people to hang on his every word or wait in suspense for him to express an opinion. He owed his good grasp of the language to his parents, who had never let him get away with speaking Swedish at home. Nevertheless, as soon as he got flustered, he had a tendency to stammer.

The connection re-established itself, and the sound and picture came back into sync. 'The tracker dogs started out well enough,' Huldar was saying, 'and seemed to be following Reynir's trail for a few metres from the house, but then they lost it and were useless after that. Of course, snow and freezing temperatures don't exactly work in their favour, especially when the trail is old. We haven't managed to track down the missing snowmobile either, at a garage or anywhere else, so we're guessing Reynir used it for his getaway. That would also explain why the dogs were only able to follow the trail for a short distance beyond the edge of the deck.'

'So it was Reynir who left via the French windows in the glass room?'

'Yes, judging by the reaction of the dogs. They were given one of his shirts from the laundry basket and apparently they immediately started sniffing along the trail of footprints. But the blood analysis should settle that question – assuming it is his. It could be the blood of his victims that he stepped in before making his getaway. I take it you agree that Reynir's our man?'

It was hard to read people's reactions in an online call but Týr thought his question about Reynir had hit a nerve. No doubt Huldar was tired after a long day and eager to wrap things up. Any input from Týr, however minor, would only delay matters. Still, he was grateful that his boss had taken the time to give him a status update. At least it showed that he hadn't forgotten about Týr the instant he was out of sight.

'Yes, sure. I suppose. I just feel it doesn't quite square with the idea of him being the killer. It looks more like he was fleeing an assailant. The French windows are closer to the bedroom wing than the front door. Then there's the business of his presence in the house after the murders. Why would he have fled the scene like that, only to come back later?'

'You can't expect a man who's just massacred his family to be in his right mind.' Huldar looked wearier than ever. 'Everything points to Reynir's guilt. That it was a familicide, as you yourself suggested. We'll almost certainly find his body, dead from exposure or suicide. One search party found a tumbledown shed on the boundary of the property, where it's possible he'd been hiding out for a while since there were empty cans of Nocco energy drink and sweet wrappers. The sell-by dates show they can't have been there long. We'll have to see what emerges from the fingerprint analysis.'

'What about the food left out on the kitchen table? Did they find any fingerprints on the packaging?' Týr knew better than to ask about DNA. The samples had only been collected earlier that day and wouldn't be sent abroad for analysis until tomorrow. It would take days, if not weeks, to get the results. Although nowadays they had the competence and the necessary equipment for DNA analysis here in Iceland, there was no accredited lab in the country, and certification was essential if the results were to stand up in court. Fingerprints were another matter. Forensics could analyse them without requiring outside assistance.

'Yes, there were plenty. Several members of the household seem to have handled them before the murders. The food wasn't fresh, although it was still good. But a comparison of the fingerprints will have to wait. They still need to lift prints from the bodies and find Reynir's on something that only he is likely to have touched. The night is young, though. All will become clear in time.' Huldar appeared to suppress a yawn before continuing: 'And we have a possible explanation for the disappearance of the horses, or one of them at least. The phone number of the older daughter, Íris, turned up in the records of the emergency line. Someone had rung from her phone to report a stolen or missing horse. That was on the Wednesday evening before the murders.'

'And? Was it followed up?'

'The call-handler was going to connect the caller to Akranes police station, but Íris, or whoever it was, hung up. When he tried to ring them back, no one answered. He consulted his supervisor but they decided there was no reason to take any further action. I don't know if it's significant but it does seem a little odd.'

'And this was definitely on the Wednesday evening?'

'Yup, definitely.' Huldar rubbed his forehead wearily. 'Oh, and another thing, before I forget. Reynir turned up on LÖKE – it seems he wasn't the model citizen after all.'

LÖKE was the police database.

'What for?' Týr hoped it would turn out to be in connection with domestic violence as, in his view, this would remove all doubt of the man's guilt.

'The illegal cultivation of cannabis plants, would you believe? The case is still going through the system and would probably have been dropped or ended in a fine. He wasn't suspected of dealing, just of growing for his own use. According to him, it was for medicinal purposes. The whole crop was confiscated and destroyed.'

'How was it discovered?'

'A tip-off. From the farmer next door – that Einar Ari the couple were having a spot of bother with. He's in the system too, for some old trouble between him and his brother, and also for making threats against our couple. But things seem to have quietened down in the last few months. Neither party had brought any accusations against the other recently.'

Týr nodded. Clearly, the bad blood between neighbours had found a variety of outlets. 'What about other illegal drugs? Was he on anything else?'

'Not so far as we know. Except all those strong painkillers.' Huldar lapsed into a brief silence, then added: 'That was one of the things I was going to tell you. We spoke to Reynir's doctor about his illness, and what he told us lends further support to the idea that he's our man. Of course, the doctor could only reveal very general information at this stage, but it was informative. Basically, Reynir suffered damage to his prefrontal cortex when his brain tumour was removed. That kind of brain damage often results in a loss of self-control, coupled with aggressive behaviour. As far as he knew, Reynir hadn't displayed any violent tendencies, but he admitted it had been quite a while since he last saw him. Reynir had his operation while they were still living in the US. But the doctor was aware that there had been a loss of inhibition, and he repeated that he couldn't rule out aggressive behaviour. Apparently, it's not unknown for families to conceal this kind of information from doctors in a misguided attempt to protect their loved ones. So, the upshot is that although we shouldn't close our eyes to other possible angles, our priority now is to track Reynir down.' Huldar's image froze again.

Týr nodded, then realised that his picture must have frozen too. 'Oh yes, a hundred per cent,' he said. 'Fingers crossed he turns up soon.' He refrained from mentioning a similar case in France, in which a man had murdered his wife and children in the face of his imminent bankruptcy, then fled the scene, never to be found. They would have to prepare themselves for the possibility that Reynir might never turn up, dead or alive. But this wasn't the right moment to strike a negative note. 'Any news of the post-mortem?' he asked instead.

His boss sighed. 'No. Idunn's a bit of a special case. But I don't suppose I need to tell you that?'

Týr chose not to answer this. Idunn was undoubtedly odd, but he'd rather not discuss her with Huldar. Criticising people behind their backs had always offended his sense of decency. 'She's made a start, though, hasn't she?'

'Yes. But she hasn't finished, and she's not prepared to share any findings at this stage. She was pretty short with me, but I gather they've completed the autopsies on two of the victims. That leaves the other two. Then there'll be a bit of a wait to get the results of the blood tests and biological samples she took.'

If Týr had known his boss better, he would have made a bet with him that they'd find traces of sleeping pills in the victims' bloodstream – at least in the two daughters'. He'd read somewhere that most parents who killed their own children wanted to prevent them from waking up and discovering what was happening, so they resorted to anaesthetising them with drugs. This was especially true of fathers who believed they were acting to protect their family.

'What about the security system?' Týr asked. 'Did they find anything when they examined the computer that had been linked up to the cameras?' He could have answered this himself. If recordings had been found of Reynir or anyone else running amok in the house, Huldar would have opened the conversation with that.

'No. There's still a chance that something will come to light, but no new recordings have been found. The most recent are a couple of months old, so the dismantling of the cameras doesn't seem to have had anything to do with the murders – unless they were planned months in advance.'

As the conversation continued, Huldar started speaking faster and faster, evidently keen to get this over with so he could go home. But, fair play to him, he didn't end the call until he'd brought Týr up to date with all the details.

Little of interest had emerged from the interviews with family and friends. They had all been in shock, after all. It was often necessary to wait several days before grief-stricken relatives could be persuaded to talk honestly about the deceased. Investigating the couple's finances was also proving problematic, as the ownership of companies was a complicated business, very different from the affairs of Mr and Mrs Average who might, in a worst-case scenario, have separate bank accounts, a car and a flat. So far, only part of the funds Ása and Reynir were known to have owned had been traced. Týr listened as Huldar described a tangled web of offshore accounts, shell companies, subsidiaries and other obfuscations of the type Týr was all too familiar with from his job in Stockholm. He was on the verge of offering his services to make sense of the muddle when he came to his senses.

Better to be cooped up in a pine-clad shoebox with a dodgy Wi-Fi connection, sleeping in stiff bedlinen with a Northern Lights motif, on a wrinkled undersheet that didn't reach the sides of the bed, than to be stuck in front of a computer screen, trying to navigate through a jungle of financial transactions, reports and balance sheets.

Týr was more interested in what Huldar had to say next. It seemed, on first inspection, that the family's computers hadn't been touched since the Friday evening, five days before the bodies were discovered. The phones had dropped off the network that afternoon but had remained connected to the wireless router in the house until early evening, so presumably the family wouldn't have been bothered about not being able to ring by conventional means until then. And there were plenty of other clues that the murders had been committed either late on Friday evening or in the early hours of Saturday morning. A further interesting detail was that Reynir's phone hadn't turned up. According to his service provider, it hadn't been used to make calls or go online via 4G since the mast cut out on the Friday. So far, the police had had no success in locating the phone, though there was a possibility it would be found when the repairs to the antenna were completed in the morning. But only if it was in the vicinity of the farm, in working order and charged up. Which was unlikely. The significance of this was unclear. Either way, Reynir could be dead or, if he was alive, could have ditched his phone. The IT department still hadn't got round to examining the victims' phones, but that task was scheduled for tomorrow. But they weren't getting their hopes up that they'd find anything useful on the three phones they'd retrieved from the scene. The two women and Íris, the teenage daughter, were not believed to be linked to the attack in any way except as victims. The younger daughter, Gígja, hadn't owned a phone, as far as they could tell.

Týr promised himself that this would be his last question. He didn't want to give Huldar the impression that he was the type who didn't know when to shut up. 'Just one final thing – have they found any trace of internet searches by Reynir related to sleeping pills or murder or suicide methods?'

The image on the screen began to move again. He saw that Huldar was using the time while he was talking to tidy away the papers on his desk. 'No, not yet. We haven't found any evidence that he bought flight tickets out of the country either.'

Týr stuck by his decision not to drag out the conversation any longer. But that didn't stop him from wondering. As a software engineer and the former owner of a large tech company, surely Reynir would be all too capable of destroying his digital trail. If he'd been planning to get away with the murders, taking steps to cover up any evidence linking him to the crimes would have been the obvious thing to do. If, on the other hand, he'd been intending to take his own life afterwards, there would have been no reason to hide his trail. Týr decided not to bring this up now. It could wait until morning – or be put off indefinitely – since it was unlikely to advance the investigation at all.

As they were winding up, Huldar mentioned that the search of the area around the farm would resume the following day, which Týr already knew. Lastly, his boss asked if the hotel was OK, and if he and Karólína were getting on all right. Týr said the hotel was conveniently close to the crime scene. He didn't complain since it wasn't as if he was on a package holiday. He was on a job, and at least it spared him from having to sleep in the car. He added that he and Karólína were working well together and also that she had been invited to supper with a friend in Borgarnes, which was why she wasn't here now. Týr had been invited too, but he had inferred from her tone of voice that she was only being polite. When he declined, she hadn't been able to hide her relief.

Týr promised to pass on Huldar's greetings in the morning and to bring Karó up to speed with everything they'd discussed. After closing the laptop, he sat there in silence, contemplating the supper he'd bought himself from the petrol station shop. It consisted of a couple of sandwiches with, according to the label, a *hangikjöt* and salad filling. For him, *hangikjöt* – smoked lamb – had nostalgic associations with family Christmases. It was this that had led him to opt for the sandwiches rather than one of the more substantial ready-meals in the petrol station cooler. In his parents' opinion, Christmas wasn't Christmas without smoked lamb, and they always went to a great deal of trouble to procure a joint from Iceland, along with the traditional sweet, crisp flatbreads known as *laufabraud* or leaf-bread, though these had usually been reduced to crumbs by the time they reached Sweden. Týr had never eaten *hangikjöt* outside the festive season, so he was interested to try it as a sandwich filling.

Far from evoking memories of the season of peace and light, however, the sandwich was a disappointment, consisting of two pieces of dry bread around a paper-thin slice of lamb and a large blob of tinned peas in mayonnaise. As he chewed, the mouthfuls formed what felt like lumps of clay on his tongue, which could only be washed down with a drink of water. He gave up after eating half, still feeling hungry. One sandwich wasn't enough, let alone half a sandwich. But foolishly he had bought two of the same kind, convinced that they would be a gourmet treat.

Týr got up and put the remains of his supper in the small fridge, wishing it was a minibar. But although it didn't contain any booze or chocolate, he was pleasantly surprised to discover an apple, a rye pancake with cheese and a small carton of chocolate milk. He spared a kind thought for Gerdur, the woman who had checked them in, then experienced a moment of doubt. Could the food have been left behind by an earlier guest? He unwrapped the plastic from the rye pancake and thought it seemed reasonably fresh. Maybe Gerdur had a future running a hotel after all.

After eating the pancake and apple, he felt a little better. Even his headache seemed to be receding. There was still a lingering tenderness around his temples but perhaps that was just a memory – like the residual marks left by plasters. To blow away the last vestiges, Týr decided to go outside and breathe in the pure country air. A blast of *skafrenningur* wouldn't hurt him.

He was just zipping up his down jacket when his phone rang and he saw that it was his mother. He made it a rule always to answer calls from his parents, unless it was exceptionally bad timing. But even then he could never relax until he'd rung them back. He was their only child. They'd been unusually protective of him when he was growing up, always fearing the worst and taking precautions. More often than not these consisted of watching him closely from the sidelines, ready to intervene if anything went wrong. Perhaps it was because they were both A&E doctors and therefore hyper-aware of all the possible risks. Plus they couldn't have children themselves, so there was no plan B if anything happened to him. The same was true for him, of course; they were his only parents and he had no plan B if he lost them. Come to think of it, though, they were already each other's plan Bs.

His mother sounded as she always did, cheerful but wary, as if perpetually braced to hear bad news. She asked about the weather and how he was doing, then announced that they were thinking of paying him a quick visit. They missed him, and it would be no problem to rearrange their shifts so they could spend a few days in Iceland, maybe at the beginning of next week. When Týr didn't immediately answer, she hastened to add that if he'd rather come over and see them, that would be just as nice.

'I'm afraid it's really bad timing,' he said. 'I'm in the middle of investigating a case in the countryside and I'm not sure I'll be back in town until we've wrapped up. Even if I do get back, I'm bound to be very tied up at work.' Before his mother could take back the suggestion and start saying it had been a bad idea, Týr went on: 'But it would be great to have you over once the investigation's completed. It shouldn't drag on too long.'

The line went quiet for a moment. Then: 'Is it the murder case that's in the news?' So far, the only information that had been released was that the police were investigating the murders of four people in the west of Iceland. Although they were refusing to divulge any more at this stage, the victims were all believed to be members of the same family. But nothing escaped Týr's parents, who were avid consumers of the Icelandic news, taking far more interest in their old country than in what was happening in Sweden.

'Yes, actually.'

'Can't you work on something else? Aren't there enough ordinary crimes that need solving? Surely all the other criminals don't just down tools because there's been a murder?'

'I'm not sure my boss would be very pleased if I asked to be released from my duties just because my parents were coming over for a visit,' Týr said patiently. 'It's not too difficult to postpone a trip that hasn't even been booked, is it? Unless you've already bought the tickets?' It wouldn't be the first time they'd presented him with a fait accompli as if he had a choice in the matter.

'No, we haven't got our tickets. I wasn't talking about our trip, just in general. Do you really have to work on something as awful as murder? Why can't you focus on financial crimes, like you did here in Stockholm?'

Týr tipped back his head, closed his eyes and took a deep breath. 'Because I'm happy doing this. A lot happier than I was in the economic crimes unit. Would you want to work in an area of your field that you found deadly boring?'

'No. But still.'

Neither of them said anything for a while. Týr righted his head, opened his eyes and expelled a breath. He tried in vain to think of a way to direct the conversation on to a more positive track. But his mother got in first, still harping on the same theme. 'It was a family, wasn't it? The people who were killed? A mother and children?'

'I'm not allowed to discuss it with you. Any more than you can discuss your patients with me. But don't worry, I'm not in any danger and I can handle it.'

'But . . .' His mother broke off and seemed to be thinking it over. When she spoke again it was in a different voice, the brisk one she used when she was taking work calls. 'Of course you can handle it, I'm not in any doubt about that.'

Their conversation moved on to other things: his father, Swedish politics, the fact that their long-time neighbours were selling up, the planned repairs to their sailing boat, and cinnamon buns. His mother promised to bring a few bags of them when they came for their weekend visit and asked him to bear it in mind. He was to let them know as soon as he had an idea when the murder inquiry would be over.

They had said their goodbyes and he was about to hang up when she sneaked in one last question: 'Did you see the bodies?'

The question was so unexpected that he was surprised into answering instead of pleading confidentiality: 'Yes. Why?'

'Don't dwell on what you saw. Try to forget it. Promise me. I know what I'm talking about. We see a lot of terrible sights here in A&E and you have to learn to detach yourself.'

'I promise.' Some promises were easier to keep than others, however sincere one's intentions. He suspected that this was one of them. Images from the crime scene kept flashing into his head and there was nothing he could do about it. It was a reflex action, like involuntarily jerking back your hand when you touched something hot.

Týr put his phone in his coat pocket and went outside. He inhaled the fresh, icy air and watched the loose snow swirling to and fro in the wind. He thought about his mother's last question. He hadn't seen many bodies in the line of duty, just a handful while he was working for CID in Sweden and none at all during his time stuck in front of a computer screen. The ones he had seen hadn't included any women or children, only young men who had gone off the rails and had never had much of a future in the first place. Sad, but not exactly unexpected.

But the longer he stared into the spindrift, the more he was puzzled by his mother's insistence that he should promise to try to forget them. Now he came to think about it, her voice had sounded indefinably different from how it usually did when she was worried about him. He couldn't put his finger on it. He took a few more deep breaths, then dismissed the problem from his mind. But, as happens so often, the answer struck him shortly afterwards.

There had been a hint of fear in his mother's voice. Týr finished zipping up his coat and filled his lungs again. The rush of oxygen sharpened his faculties and it suddenly occurred to him what might be going on: one of his parents, either his mother or his father, must have been diagnosed with an incurable condition. As they were both over sixty, this wasn't unlikely. They were workaholics too, concerned with everyone's health but their own. Over the years, Týr had recognised a tendency among doctors to dismiss the very idea that anything could go wrong with them or their families. Certainly, despite their excessive caution in other areas, his parents had never seemed that concerned about his health, even though his biological mother had died of cancer far too young. While he was living at home, he used to have to remind them to book him in for an annual check-up with a friend of theirs who was an oncologist. Not that anything had ever emerged from these examinations other than reconfirmation that he was fighting fit. His worries had proved unnecessary – so far.

The same carelessness meant his mother had never got round to having a gene test to check for the mutation that might have caused her sister's – that is, his biological mother's – death. Perhaps the day of reckoning had come.

Týr stared at the whirling snow that was glowing faintly blue in the moonlight. He tried in vain to come up with some other explanation and in the end had to resign himself to the fact that this was the most likely. It would make their impulsive decision to visit Iceland more understandable; they must want to break the news to him face-to-face.

Týr kicked at the snow to work off a sudden fit of anger. It was directed against death and the unfairness of life. His birth mother, his adoptive mother, the two women and two girls on the farm – they had all deserved to live longer. And while he was impotent in the face of illness, he was filled with an overpowering desire to catch the person who had committed the four murders. He just hoped that Reynir was alive, so that he would get to experience the full weight of the law.

But the chances of that were slim. Týr took a couple more lungfuls of fresh air, then went back inside his stuffy little cabin.

Chapter 12
Before

Sóldís put down her empty coffee mug. She'd lost count of how many cups she'd put away that morning. She doubted her GP would recommend this level of caffeine consumption but the alternative had been to fall asleep on the job. She pictured herself flopping on to the drier in the utility room after putting on the family laundry, making herself a nest out of hay in the byre after feeding the cows, or setting Gígja and Íris to solving problems while she crashed out on the table during their lessons. Without the coffee, she'd almost certainly have declined the offer of lunch and gone back to her quarters for a nap. Sleep took precedence over food when you were this exhausted.

Thanks to the caffeine, none of this had happened. But fear had been an even bigger disincentive to go for that midday nap. Sóldís had realised she couldn't face having a lie-down alone in her quarters, just as earlier that morning she hadn't been able to get back to sleep after finding the remote control in her hand. Especially not after she'd discovered that the two chairs were still wedged under the door handles. This could only mean that somebody had got into the old house without forcing the doors. Her tired mind had eventually settled on two possible explanations. One was that the night visitor had got in through a window. When she checked, however, all the windows were securely closed. The other possibility was that she had walked in her sleep and fetched the remote control herself – two nights in a row, if that was conceivable. On the night before last she could have taken the remote from the TV room and hidden it, then last night returned to the hiding place and retrieved it. But, as far as she knew, she had never in her life walked in her sleep.

A third explanation had just now occurred to her. Could the house be accessed via the cellar? She had never explored behind the old house but it was quite possible that there was a back entrance to the cellar, with steps leading down to it from the garden. It would take her no time to find out if she popped over to her quarters and ran down to the cellar. But no, she couldn't do that – she was too afraid of bumping into the intruder.

If there was a back entrance on the basement level, locking the doors and jamming chairs under the handles was no more than a futile gesture. The intruder – regardless of whether it was Reynir or a stranger – could have slipped in during the night, assuming the back door to the cellar was unlocked. But surely, she reasoned, it couldn't be a complete stranger or the 'horse man', because who in their right mind would sneak into someone's house, only to nick their remote control, then return it again? Surely even Reynir wasn't that weird? But there was no point wondering about it until she had checked whether there was indeed another door.

'Gígja, do you fancy coming outside for a bit? And taking the dogs for a walk?'

Sóldís didn't have to ask twice. The little girl sprang out of the chair where her mother had ordered her to sit and read. Since the book Ása had given her was aimed at older children, Gígja couldn't possibly be expected to read it for fun.

Far from preparing the ground for her daughter to become a genius, Ása was ensuring that she would be put off books for life. Sóldís didn't like to raise this with her employer, though, as she hadn't been hired as a life coach.

If she had been, there were a few other recommendations she'd prioritise over telling Ása and Reynir to stop trying so hard to coach their children to become geniuses. For one thing, she'd encourage them to understand their daughters better. Íris had just gone out riding, as she did every day after her lessons. To Sóldís, it was clear that there was more to these rides than simply exercising the horses. Íris was always in high spirits when she said goodbye, and always wore mascara. It was blindingly obvious that she was going to meet Robbi. He lived on the neighbouring farm, so it would be easy enough for Íris to ride over there, or for him to come to meet her. Sóldís didn't know whether his family frowned on their relationship as much as Íris's did, but she assumed they must.

She guessed that they met in the hut on the edge of the property that she'd heard Ása and Reynir bickering about. As far as she could gather, the hut had no function, except as a bone of contention. Back when the property was divided in two, the agreement had failed to state which farm it belonged to. Reynir was all for letting it go, Ása for asserting their rights. Sóldís had no idea whether the hut was the source of the friction with Robbi's father, or whether it was because of the dispute that Ása wanted to hang on to it. In the end it was immaterial. By the time relations had soured to this extent, the question of how the quarrel began was of secondary importance. Often, not even the warring parties themselves could remember what had originally caused them to fall out.

'Shall we make a snowman?' Gígja pulled on the mittens she'd extracted from the pockets of her coat. One was inside out but it didn't bother her. The dogs stood at her side, wagging their tails as expectantly as if it were Christmas.

'Maybe. Or an igloo?'

This suggestion was eagerly received and before they'd even crossed the threshold Gígja had started to describe to Sóldís what the igloo should look like. It was to be bigger than the byre, with a balcony and a garage.

Sóldís persuaded Gígja to postpone her plans for a minute or two while they did a circuit of the house on the pretext of finding a good place to build the igloo. The little girl had already started forming snow into a mound on the drive.

They headed round the back of the old house together, the dogs following a little way behind. The deep snow proved hard going for little Lubbi, who kept sinking right up to his ears, but with a tremendous effort, he scrabbled his way out every time. Meanwhile, although Bói found the going easier, he made slow progress because he kept stopping to snap at the snow, either to quench his thirst or to express his frustration.

When Sóldís and Gígja rounded the corner, the first thing they saw was a small greenhouse. It was free from snow, which meant it must be heated. Through the glass they could see empty shelves but no sign of any plants or flowerpots. Sóldís didn't waste much time examining it but turned her attention to the wall of the house and saw that there were indeed steps leading down to a cellar door. She couldn't decide whether she was relieved or shaken.

'What about here, Sóldís?' Gígja turned in a circle on the level ground behind the house, which extended away along the valley floor almost as far as the eye could see and had no doubt been used as grazing land when the farm had been a going concern. It would have been no use for cultivation as it was overshadowed by steep slopes on either side. 'Let's build it here!'

Sóldís answered absent-mindedly as she went over to investigate the steps. 'Yes. Great.' She wanted to see if anyone had walked down them recently. And if they had, to check whether there were footprints leading out of the cellar again. She would be able to breathe a little easier – though not much – if there were.

'No one's allowed in the cellar. Daddy says so.' Gígja had abandoned the attempt to find a suitable construction site and come over to join Sóldís. 'There's bacteria down there that can make you sick. And if you get sick, sometimes they have to cut your head open.' Gígja tugged at Sóldís's sleeve. 'Don't get sick. I think you're fun.'

'Thanks, Gígja. But don't worry. I'm not going inside the cellar, I'm just looking at the steps.' There were slight depressions in the snow, blurred by the fresh fall that morning. As far as Sóldís could tell, there were two sets of footprints, one going down and the other coming up. She felt a surge of relief, but the feeling didn't last long. Even if this meant there was no one hiding in the cellar now, it suggested that someone had entered her house in the night. The indistinct prints looked too large to be Gígja's, which left only three other candidates: Íris, Ása and Reynir.

Assuming it wasn't a stranger, it must have been Reynir.

Sóldís tried to banish these thoughts as she helped Gígja build the igloo. But, as she'd expected, Gígja was bored within half an hour, when all they had built was a half-metre-high outer wall for a much more modest structure than her original grandiose vision. It didn't help that the dogs interpreted the whole thing as a game and kept flinging themselves at the low wall. Rather than being annoyed, Gígja bent down each time to explain patiently that this was an igloo, not a toy. Within a few short minutes the dogs would have forgotten again and launched another attack. When Sóldís and Gígja turned to leave and the dogs charged the wall one last time, they didn't even look back to assess the damage. The igloo had been consigned to history.

'Hey, I've got an idea.' Sóldís pointed at the greenhouse. 'Why don't we buy some seeds, and some compost and little flowerpots for you to plant them in? If you're good about remembering to water them, you'll have lots of seedlings by the spring, ready to plant out for the summer. I can teach you the Icelandic names of the flowers and you can add them to your vocabulary list. What do you reckon? An Icelandic lesson with a bit of compost thrown in?'

Gígja looked Sóldís in the eye. She seemed unsure, her face torn between excitement and doubt. 'What if the police come?'

'The police?' Sóldís asked, puzzled. 'You mean when we're driving to the garden centre? Don't worry, I'll drive carefully and I won't go too fast.'

'I don't mean in the car. What if the police come here? It's against the law to grow plants here.'

'Against the law?' Sóldís was struck by an idea. 'Did the police come round about the plants in the greenhouse?'

Gígja nodded. 'They took all the plants. They belonged to Daddy. They were special ones to make him better.'

Sóldís had trouble hiding her surprise. It would never have occurred to her that Reynir or Ása would be involved in anything illegal, let alone in growing cannabis, even if it had been for medicinal purposes. She wished she could rewind and come up with a different scheme for entertaining Gígja. The greenhouse was an unfortunate subject and she was keen for them to drop it before they got back inside. 'OK, forget that. We don't want to make the police cross. How about doing something else instead to collect new words?'

'Like what?'

'Baking? Or we could go for walks and talk about what we see?'

Baking got Gígja's enthusiastic vote. She immediately forgot all about the greenhouse and didn't refer to it once after they'd gone back inside. Instead, she ran straight to her mother and told her that she and Sóldís were going to bake.

Sóldís watched Ása's reaction as she considered this. Just when she was sure that Ása was going to say no, the woman suddenly smiled. 'What a good idea. Perhaps you'd like to bake some muesli bread?'

Gígja made a face. 'Yuck, no. Cookies! Or chocolate cake.'

'We can bake all kinds of things.' Sóldís smiled at Gígja, then turned to Ása. She'd just thought of a plan to get someone to go down to the cellar with her. While they were down there, she could seize the chance to surreptitiously lock the garden door. Because no way was she going down there alone. And since the couple had been quick to cut short any talk about the footprints outside the front door, there was little point dragging them round the back of the house to examine the barely visible marks on the cellar steps. Or of mentioning the missing remote control that had mysteriously reappeared in the middle of the night. She knew Ása and Reynir well enough by now to realise they'd think she was crazy. She cleared her throat. 'I was thinking: I opened the door to the cellar the other day when Gígja and I were playing hide-and-seek, and there was a really bad smell down there. Is there any chance of getting someone in to check it out? Before it spreads to the rest of the house?'

'Oh, not again. Is the smell still there?'

'Yes, I'm afraid so.' Sóldís added hesitantly: 'Is it an old problem?' She hoped it was, hoped the stench had already been there when they bought the house. Anything to stop her lurid imaginings about what Reynir might be hiding down there.

'No. It started a few weeks ago. I opened the door and the smell was so bad I couldn't go in. Actually, that must have been a couple of months ago. God, how time flies. I'd better ring the plumber. Reynir kept meaning to do it but he forgot. Me too. Thanks for reminding me. I'll see if I can get someone to come out today.'

While Ása fetched her phone and rang the plumber, a possible explanation occurred to Sóldís. Could Reynir be keeping his cannabis plants in the cellar? Could he have started cultivating them in there after the police shut down the greenhouse? She'd never seen a cannabis plant; perhaps they gave off a powerful smell if there were a lot of them in a room that wasn't aired properly. But then it dawned on her that she was familiar enough with the smell of the smoke, and she hadn't noticed that once since starting work at the farm.

Perhaps the crop wasn't ready for Reynir to smoke yet. He must have had to start again from scratch.

If so, he wasn't going to be pleased at the prospect of a plumber going down to investigate the cellar.

Chapter 13
Friday

Through the fog of sleep, Týr couldn't at first work out what had woken him or where on earth he was. Not until he opened his eyes and saw the pine ceiling panels did it come back to him: he was in the little holiday cabin, and the ungodly noise that had disturbed him was the cacophonous mooing of cows. He lay there for a long time after he'd surfaced, trying to summon up the courage to venture out from under the duvet. He'd opened the window wide before going to sleep so he wouldn't wake up with a headache, but as a result it was almost as cold inside as it must have been outside in the snow.

In one of the kitchen cupboards, he found a kettle and some instant coffee. The coffee went some way towards taking the edge off his shivers, and a hot shower finally drove the chill from his body. Sadly, he couldn't top this off with a substantial breakfast but had to make do with the sad remains of the *hangikjöt* sandwich in the fridge, though not before he had scraped off the mess of mayonnaise and tinned peas. After that, things looked up a bit; at least he was no longer cold or hungry. But he still had a hollow feeling inside. Coffee and a sandwich were no magic cure against worrying about your nearest and dearest.

Although he'd set an early alarm, the deafening mooing had started far earlier, which meant he was up and dressed long before Karó or any of their colleagues in Akranes and Reykjavík would be stirring. Since he couldn't use the time for work, all he could think of was to ring Sweden, where it would be an hour ahead. At least that way he might be able to reassure himself that his anxiety about his parents was unfounded.

For once, he decided to call his father rather than his mother. Usually, the only thing his dad had to say on the phone was to correct some point about himself that Týr's mother had got wrong. As a result, he was so thrown by Týr's call that his first instinct was to ask if something was wrong. Once his son had explained why he was calling, he calmed down, and didn't seem offended that Týr was only ringing him because he'd woken up so early. They chatted for a while, their conversation progressing in fits and starts. There were long pauses and a lot of umming and ahing, but this came as no surprise to Týr. He knew few people who liked talking on the phone less than his father.

When it became clear that the conversation was running out of steam, Týr asked after his mother. His father began describing her health with a dry enumeration of metrics, but Týr cut him short. 'I wasn't asking about her blood pressure, I just thought she sounded a bit . . . I don't know . . . anxious or apprehensive when we said goodbye yesterday. I was wondering if I should be bracing myself for bad news. For something serious.'

Apparently not. According to his father, everything was fine. Yet he sounded a little odd as he said it. Something was definitely up. The situation put Týr in mind of an icicle that hung from the eaves of a house he passed every day on his way to work. It was big and sharp enough to do serious damage if it broke off and landed on someone's head, yet no one did anything about it. Not the house owner or any of the passers-by, himself included. The same inexplicable apathy stopped him from pressing his father now. By the time he rang off, Týr was none the wiser about what was causing the awkwardness. On the other hand, he was no longer sure that he'd hit on the right explanation last night.

Perhaps there was nothing seriously wrong and the underlying problem, whatever it was, would go away by itself. Realistically, though, it was more likely to strike with a painful blow, like the icicle when it loosened in the thaw.

It was pointless wasting any more time worrying about it now. Nevertheless, this little domestic mystery made it impossible for Týr to hang around, waiting for Karó to wake up. He decided to distract himself by driving over to the crime scene and taking a look around while all was quiet. It would help him get a feel for the place when it wasn't crawling with investigators and search-and-rescue volunteers.

It was still dark but a halfmoon illuminated the treeless landscape of white fields and low hills. Týr took a few deep breaths, scouring his lungs with the crisp air, then walked over to the car, feeling refreshed. The frozen surface of the snow squeaked underfoot, and when he saw lights coming on in the farmhouse, he feared for a moment that he had woken the occupants, then realised that the squeaking was nothing compared to the deafening racket the cows were making. That must be what had got the household out of bed. Or maybe they always got up this early. As a city boy, he was hopelessly ignorant about farming life.

He retrieved the keys from their hiding place on top of the sunshade on the driver's side and started the big vehicle, uncomfortably aware that the booming of his engine was loud enough to drown out the cattle. Spotting a curtain moving in an upstairs window of the farmhouse, he looked away to avoid catching the eye of the woman who'd checked them in, in case she waved at him to wait. It was quite possible that breakfast was included in their accommodation, but he wanted to get going. The last thing he needed right now was a strained conversation over a soft-boiled egg. Especially as he suspected he'd be milked like the cows for information about the case.

It took him no time to drive to the scene of the murders. If nothing else, their basic accommodation had that going for it. He encountered no other traffic on the way and when he pulled into the drive at Hvarf, the yard appeared to be empty of police vehicles. On second glance, though, he spotted an unmarked car parked by the modern house, which looked too scruffy to belong to the police. It occurred to Týr that the Akranes force might have hired a nightwatchman, a local, maybe, as it would be cheaper than using a member of their own understaffed team.

Týr drew up beside the car, noting that there was nobody inside. He got out and peered through the windows in search of clues to the driver's identity. There was nothing on the dashboard, like an access card for a security firm for example, to suggest that the owner of the car worked as a guard. Between the seats he made out a white tin of nicotine pouches and a hairbrush containing enough blonde hair to make someone a decent-sized toupee. On the floor in front of the passenger seat were two empty tins of some energy drink and a rubbish bag overflowing with crumpled paper.

Týr straightened up and listened. The silence was absolute. He couldn't hear anything that sounded like someone moving around out there, and the animals had all been taken away. In contrast, the snow around the buildings bore ample testimony to the presence of humans. It had been so trampled that there wasn't a single patch that wasn't criss-crossed by footprints or tyre tracks, making it impossible to guess which had been made by yesterday's investigators and which belonged to the owner of the car.

The doors of the house were all clearly marked with police tape, the fluorescent yellow forming a stark contrast to nature's monochrome winter palette. The tape still hung in X's between the doorposts, making it unlikely that anyone had entered either of the houses. The visitor could hardly be indoors, then.

Týr raised his eyes to survey the flat valley floor to the east, which was clearly visible in the moonlight. It extended right to the feet of the surrounding mountains and to the hill that hid Hvarf from the road, giving the farm its name. The carpet of snow appeared as pockmarked with footprints in the distance as it was in the farmyard. Search-and-rescue volunteers had been out combing the landscape in search of Reynir without success, but then the man had probably made his escape on the missing snowmobile. It was impossible to guess if any of the tracks were new.

At that moment Týr's ears picked up the same kind of squeaking as he himself had made earlier, on his way from the cabin to his car. Although quiet, it was instantly recognisable. Somebody was walking over the frozen surface of the snow behind the house. Týr set off in the direction of the sound. He strained his ears as he was moving but the noise of his own footsteps drowned it out. He wanted to hear if the mysterious person made a sudden run for it.

He couldn't see anyone behind the modern house. There was a large deck with a hot tub let into it, which didn't provide any cover to hide behind. There was a henhouse too, which, even in this uncertain light, looked unusually smart; clearly it wasn't the standard job, knocked together from offcuts of timber. There was a large run in front of it, fenced off with chicken wire, but, as he soon ascertained, no one lurking behind it. And there was no clucking from inside, as the hens had all gone to a new home – all, that is, apart from the two lying headless in a Reykjavík lab.

Týr made his way as quickly and quietly as he could along the back of the building until he was behind the connecting corridor and the old farmhouse. At first, he couldn't see anything, but then he thought he detected a flicker of movement behind a small greenhouse. It was empty, so there was nothing to hinder his view through the glass apart from the dimness of the moonlight. He guessed that this was where Reynir had cultivated his cannabis plants. Again, he caught a movement but couldn't work out what it was. It might have just been a piece of rubbish stirring in the breeze – if it weren't for the stillness of the air.

The closer he got, the more confident he became that he was right. It was a person. Rounding the corner of the greenhouse, he came upon a young woman with long, blonde hair – unquestionably the owner of the brush in the car. She was crouching down, but her fluorescent jacket gave her away.

Týr took up position by the corner of the greenhouse. 'Hello there.'

The young woman, who had been ducking to hide her face, now looked up, then rose to her feet. She stared at the glimmer of the police logo on Týr's coat. 'Hello.' She shuffled her feet awkwardly, then added: 'I was just leaving.'

Týr nodded. 'I think that's a good idea. You can hardly have failed to notice that you're trespassing on a crime scene.'

The young woman shook her head without breaking eye contact with Týr. From what he could see, she was extremely pretty and her clothes appeared to be from good brands – not exactly your stereotypical burglar. But her beauty wasn't all down to nature; her lips were a little too full for that, her eyebrows too dark and elegantly arched. Not that this mattered. She was a looker, however this had been achieved, and she was obviously conscious of the fact. In an ultra-feminine gesture, she brushed a lock of hair from her face and gazed innocently at Týr from between thickly mascaraed lashes. 'I haven't done anything wrong.'

'Is there somebody with you or are you alone?'

A worry line momentarily puckered her forehead, as if she feared he was going to take advantage of his position. It was an expression he hated seeing, reminding him that, thanks to a handful of stupid bastards, women were automatically afraid that any man constituted a threat. He hastened to reassure her: 'I only ask because if there's somebody else here with you, they'll need to leave as well.'

'I'm alone. And I'm going.'

'Before you do, I'll need to take your name. And see some form of ID.'

'But I haven't done anything.'

'That's irrelevant. You've trespassed on a crime scene. You can't have failed to see the large sign by the drive warning unauthorised individuals not to enter the area. We need your details on file in case your DNA contaminates the samples we're collecting.'

The young woman drew her elegantly pencilled brows together. 'Then you've almost certainly got my DNA already. I used to work here.'

This was enough to make Týr fish his notebook out of his pocket. 'When did you work here and in what capacity? And your name, please.'

'Berglind. Berglind Mímisdóttir.' She watched Týr write it down, then answered his other questions. 'I started just over a year ago and left a few months ago. I was sort of a general assistant. I taught the girls Icelandic, cooked some meals, did the laundry and helped look after the animals. But they must have got rid of them – at least, I didn't hear them in the byre.' She raised a hand to her cheek. 'I listened at the byre door. Would that leave an ear print? Like a fingerprint?'

Týr smiled. 'Possibly. I'll make a note of it.' He scribbled this down as briefly as he could in his little notebook. 'What are you doing here? In the dark?'

'I just wanted to see if it was them – in the news. I was hoping it was just me being silly, but now I can see that it wasn't. I didn't want to come in daytime because then the police would be here and you might think I was involved somehow.' Her eyes widened. 'I had nothing to do with it. Honestly.'

Týr didn't respond, though he thought she was probably telling the truth. She seemed, for example, to be under the impression that the entire family had been wiped out, since the sex of the four victims had not yet been revealed. Anyone involved in the killings would be well aware that there had been no men among the dead. 'You don't seriously expect me to believe that you had to drive all the way out here to find out whether the family were the people in the news? And what were you doing skulking behind the house?'

'I got a shock when I saw the sign and realised what it meant. And even more of a shock when I saw that horrible police tape all over the place. The whole thing feels so unreal.' She paused, licked her lips and took a deep breath. 'I came round the back to look through the big windows. I don't really know why. Perhaps I was just hoping there wouldn't be any sign of blood. Then I could go home and imagine that they'd died without suffering – if that's possible. Is it possible to murder someone without them suffering?'

'Yes. It's possible.' Týr wasn't going to let himself be side-tracked into explaining how. Nor did he have any intention of disclosing any details about how the victims had died. 'Why were you hiding?'

The young woman placed a hand on her breast and let out a breath. 'I got such a shock when I heard a car driving up to the house. For all I knew, you could have been the killer. Returning to the scene of the crime to fetch the murder weapon or . . . I don't know what murderers do. But there was nowhere to hide, so I crept as quietly as I could behind the greenhouse. Stupid, I know, but there was nowhere else.'

Týr nodded, fairly satisfied with this explanation. 'Did you have any contact with the family after you stopped working for them?'

There was a perceptible pause before the young woman answered: 'No.'

The pause was enough for Týr to suspect that this wasn't strictly true. But as modern communications tended to leave a digital trail, there was no point in challenging her now. If she was lying, it would be a straightforward matter for the IT department to prove, unless she'd used a messaging program that couldn't be traced. But that was unlikely. Any communication she'd had would almost certainly have been perfectly legitimate. What she'd said might even be true. 'I'm fairly sure you'll be called in for an interview at some stage of the investigation,' he told her. 'There aren't many people who can give us much information about the family. But just a quick word before you come in for formal questioning. What was the couple's relationship like while you were working for them?'

Berglind's answer took him aback. In circumstances like these, witnesses generally responded very positively at first. Indeed, so far no one had said a bad word about the couple's marriage. But Berglind replied without hesitation: 'Terrible. A complete train wreck. It was only a matter of time before they got a divorce.'

'Did they have a lot of rows?'

'It was mainly her. He was ill, but she was pissed off with her life and the fact he didn't love her. Ása's a total bitch.'

Týr didn't correct her use of the present tense. 'What did they quarrel about?'

Berglind thought for a moment. 'Everything. Actually, I don't really know. I usually got out of the way. I had no interest in listening to their fights.'

This wasn't the time or place for a more in-depth interview, though Týr suspected that Berglind knew more than she was letting on. He was sure that when she was subjected to more intensive questioning, she'd be able to shed some light on the husband's possible motives for committing this horrific act. 'Did you leave your job because of the bad atmosphere in the house?' he asked. 'Or was it never the intention that you should stay longer?'

An expression of rage briefly contorted the pretty features. 'I was sacked,' she said. 'Ása gave me the boot. For no good reason.'

This finally convinced Týr that the young woman had played no part in the killings. The anger in her voice told him that she was still furious about her dismissal, which suggested that she hadn't yet found an outlet for her resentment – or got her revenge.

He escorted her back to her car and asked to see her driving licence. Then, having written down her telephone number, he asked in parting whether she'd met the young man who got the job after her, or the young woman who came after him. Berglind shook her head, giving Týr a look of surprise. 'Did they hire another woman? I only knew about the bloke who came after me. He left too, did he? Or was he sacked?'

Týr sidestepped this question and said goodbye. Berglind fastened her seatbelt, shut the door and drove away after waving at him with an embarrassed smile. He scribbled down her licence number, then returned his notebook to his pocket and watched as she accelerated away, faster than was wise on the snowy drive.

Chapter 14
Before

The cellar turned out not to be the scene of an illicit cannabis farm. Nor was there any sign that Reynir had hastily cleared out the equipment for such a venture before the plumber arrived. There was just the usual kind of stuff that people keep in their cellars anywhere in the world. Boxes of things that were not interesting or useful enough to have on display upstairs. Items that were too valuable, or at least of too much sentimental value, to be chucked out. It was pretty much like any of the storerooms Sóldís knew, except that Ása and Reynir didn't have their belongings lying around in cardboard boxes. They used plastic crates of a uniform size, all marked with the name of an American removals company. They weren't piled up here and there either but carefully arranged on shelving units into which they fitted exactly. Apart from this precise arrangement, there was nothing in the cellar but a complicated system of pipes, valves, meters and thermostats – the intake for the geothermal heating system, as well as an electrical circuit board, a fridge, a freezer and an ancient workbench that had probably come with the house: Sóldís couldn't imagine Reynir or Ása being into carpentry.

The first thing she did when she went down there with the plumber was to locate the back door, open it, then lock it. It had indeed been unlocked, as she had suspected. Anyone could have gained entry to the old house that way. She tried to push away the thought that if the nocturnal visitor was Reynir, he had a key, which meant that locking it was futile. She would just have to pop down with another chair to jam under the door handle once the plumber had left.

The bad smell still hung in the air, though Sóldís was gradually becoming inured to it. The dogs had remained upstairs, vacillating and whining, as they did when they were ill at ease. But whether it was the steep staircase or the stench that made them nervous was impossible to say. Maybe they were just dubious about the plumber. They had barked and growled at him when he arrived, and Ása had excused them by saying that they always behaved like this with men they didn't know; the plumber shouldn't take it personally. Sóldís hadn't helped them down the stairs for fear they might snap at the man, but, in hindsight, this was a pity as they might have been able to identify the source of the smell. The plumber and Sóldís still hadn't managed to locate it. She'd taught biology for a week as a supply teacher, and one of the lessons had focused on the sense of smell. From this she had learnt that dogs had six times as many olfactory receptors in their noses as people did, so their help would have been invaluable.

The plumber turned away from the pipework and replaced his spanner in his toolbox. He'd decided he might as well give the system a quick once-over seeing as he'd come all the way out here. 'Everything looks fine,' he told Sóldís.

'So the smell doesn't come from those pipes?' They'd searched everywhere else for the origin of the stench: the empty, disconnected freezer had turned out not to be full of rotting meat; none of the plastic crates gave off a pong to indicate that a raccoon had accidentally got in there during the move from the US and died on the way; the fridge was likewise empty and clean. All she could think of was that foul water might be leaking from the pipes somewhere.

The plumber smiled. 'No. This isn't the kind of smell you'd get from the heating pipes. From the sewage system, maybe, but not from the hot-water pipes. Mind you, I see the floor's been tampered with at some point. It wouldn't be the first time people have tried to mend the plumbing without having a clue what they're doing. It's not unlikely that the sewer runs right under there. I expect they broke the floor up, replaced a few pipes, then did a bad job of reconnecting them. If so, I dread to think what state the soil is in down there.'

Sóldís stared at the large, discoloured patch on the concrete floor that was much coarser and dirtier than the rest. The plumber's theory seemed plausible, but there was no way that Ása or Reynir would have tried to fix the foul-water pipes themselves. They were a thousand times more likely to have used the workbench, and the odds of that happening were virtually nil. 'Could a bad smell penetrate concrete?'

'Nope.' The plumber pointed to a drain in the floor beside the area that had been disturbed. 'But if there's a sewage leak under the concrete, and the connection between the pipe and the drain is loose, the smell could escape through that.'

They were interrupted by a loud bark from behind them. Bói had climbed halfway down the stairs but there his courage seemed to have deserted him and he was stuck, unable to go up or down. Taking pity on him, Sóldís went over and picked him up. He seemed to have accepted the plumber's presence now and his attention was entirely focused on the floor. The moment she put him down, he darted towards the rough patch of concrete and started sniffing around it and the drain.

The plumber looked from the dog to Sóldís. 'Do you need any more evidence? I expect that's your explanation.' He bent down to pick up his toolbox. 'But I can't fix that now. We're talking about breaking up the floor and replacing it with fresh concrete. I can't do that alone or without the right tools. Shall we decide on a day for it next week?'

Sóldís explained that it wasn't up to her and that he would have to speak to Ása or Reynir.

They went upstairs, the plumber going ahead, as it took Sóldís a moment or two to persuade Bói to stop sniffing at the floor. In the end, she had to haul him away by his collar. He scrabbled frantically against her before finally admitting defeat. But then he baulked at going up the stairs so Sóldís had to carry him again, while he stared longingly over her shoulder at the cellar floor. It was then that it struck her that neither of the dogs had barked in the night when she suspected the intruder of prowling around the house. So either they knew the person in question or it was a woman. According to Ása, they only reacted badly to men. Yet again, this seemed to point to Reynir.

Lubbi ignored the plumber but went mad with joy when Sóldís reappeared carrying his big friend Bói, getting under her feet and almost sending her head over heels backwards down the cellar stairs. She'd been so preoccupied with thinking about Reynir that she'd forgotten to look where she was going. Fortunately, the plumber grabbed her before she fell. After she had given him her rather flustered thanks, to a chorus of growling and loud barks, he finally let go of her shoulder and they walked through to the new house to find Ása and Reynir.

As soon as they emerged from the connecting corridor, they were met by a wall of classical music. The volume grew more and more ear-splitting as they approached the kitchen until it was impossible to hear themselves speak over the wailing strings of a violin. No wonder the girls – and Ása – had made themselves scarce.

Reynir had his back to them and all that could be seen of him around the armchair were his arms waving as if he were conducting the piece. He was facing the glass wall and had drawn up the blinds. Outside, the monochrome landscape looked bleak under a leaden sky.

The plumber raised his eyebrows at Sóldís. Had they known each other better, he might well have pointed to his temple and swivelled his finger as well. Sóldís smiled faintly back, worried about being seen, and resisted the impulse to raise her eyebrows in return. And even add the finger movement that he had omitted.

Instead, she went over to Reynir and had to tap him on the shoulder to get his attention as he had his eyes closed and was wholly absorbed in conducting an invisible orchestra. He jumped and flashed her an irritable look. She was forced to shriek over the violin that the plumber had finished and wanted a word. Only then did Reynir lower the volume with the remote control and get to his feet.

The smile Reynir bestowed on the plumber was perfectly friendly. 'Sorry. But you really have to listen to this sonata with the volume all the way up. They say the devil had a hand in its composition.' Apparently oblivious to the plumber's indifference, Reynir continued: 'The devil appeared to the composer in a dream and played it to him on a violin. He wrote down the score when he woke up. Not bad going.'

The plumber didn't even pretend to be interested. 'About the cellar. The smell's probably coming from the sewage pipe. It looks like someone's done a botched DIY job on it. The concrete floor needs to be broken up so the leak can be fixed.'

Reynir seemed extremely taken aback by this. 'Hang on a minute, I thought it was your job to sort out the pipes during the renovations? You told us they were OK.'

'They were. But since then somebody has tampered with them.'

'Not to my knowledge, they haven't.' Reynir still seemed rather bemused.

'Well, it can't have happened by itself.' The plumber sounded indignant. 'It's obvious that someone has broken up the concrete. Maybe the devil did it in between composing violin concertos.'

Suddenly Reynir seemed to twig. 'Oh, the floor. I get you.' When he saw that the same didn't apply to the man standing in front of him, he went on: 'That was just a repair to the concrete. No one touched any pipes, let alone the sewage one.'

The plumber frowned. 'Are you sure? The person who did it must have been a complete amateur. I've never seen such a mess. The concrete's been left rough and unsealed.'

Reynir looked stung by this, and Sóldís guessed he'd had a hand in the job himself.

'Do you want me to come by next week and repair it? Break up and relay the floor, and take a look at the pipes while I'm down there?'

The question freed Reynir's tongue. 'Break up the floor?' When the plumber nodded, Reynir said in an unnecessarily loud voice: 'No. It's fine as it is.' Then he added quickly that he needed the plumber to take a look at the hot tub as the water pressure was weak. It was the first Sóldís had heard about this, although Ása used the tub every day to meditate in. She got the feeling that Reynir was trying to shift the conversation away from the cellar. If that was his intention, it had worked. The two men went out through the French windows on to the deck to look at the hot tub.

At that moment, Reynir's phone bleeped from the armchair where he'd left it. Sóldís automatically dropped her gaze to the screen and saw the message without meaning to. It was from a sender with the username *Begga Babe* and it was short and sweet, or at least the part she could see was: *Miss you. Any chance of meeting up?*

Begga Babe. Sóldís felt herself blushing with mortification. Could it be the Berglind who'd done her job previously? Gígja had referred to her as both Berglind and Begga. Sóldís hugged herself defensively. Had Berglind and Reynir been having an affair? Surely not. The driver had described her as a young woman, probably around Sóldís's own age. And she herself would never go for a middle-aged bloke, especially not one as weird as Reynir. No, impossible. Then again, what self-respecting woman of his age would refer to herself as 'Babe'?

Sóldís dithered. Should she pretend nothing had happened? Follow the men outside? Go in search of Ása and ask for a job to do? She opted for the latter. The less time she had to spend in Reynir's company, the better. And the sooner she could put that message out of her mind, the better too. What Reynir got up to was none of her business. She knew better than to tell tales to Ása, as the bearer of bad news was rarely thanked.

Sóldís found Ása in the sitting room where she was playing cards with Gígja. Judging by her expression, she was about as keen on Ólsen-ólsen as Sóldís was. Ása glanced up when she became aware of her presence, her eyes expressing a mute appeal for help.

Sóldís made an effort to sound casual: 'Would you like me to take over?'

Ása put down her cards, admitting defeat to Gígja. The little girl reacted with dismay but her mother pretended not to notice. 'Has the plumber gone?'

'No, he's outside with Reynir, taking a look at the hot tub.'

'The hot tub?'

'It was something to do with the hot water pressure. Reynir said there was a problem with it.'

Ása's brows twitched in a frown. 'What would he know about it? He never uses the tub.' Then, quickly changing the subject, she said: 'By the way, Reynir's got a check-up at the hospital tomorrow. We assume he won't be done until late afternoon, and judging from our previous experiences, he'll be completely exhausted afterwards, so we're thinking of staying the night in Reykjavík and driving back the next day. Would you mind looking after the girls while we're away?'

Gígja let out a shout of excitement and it struck Sóldís yet again what a monotonous, isolated life the sisters led. She smiled at the little girl, who was now chanting '*Please, please, please,*' in English, and told Ása it would be no problem. She didn't add that she'd be heartily relieved to see the back of them both, though mainly him. But she had no sooner spoken than she realised that this wasn't true. It would in fact be a problem. Although she found Reynir deeply unsettling and Ása herself a bit eccentric, they were at least adults and therefore good to have around in case something went wrong. The thought of being the only grown-up in this remote spot filled Sóldís with trepidation. What was she supposed to do if the man who'd been skulking around outside made a reappearance? Or they had an intruder? Ring the police? How long would it take them to get here?

Too long, that was for sure.

The locks on the doors wouldn't be much help, not with that large wall of glass in the kitchen that would be so easy to break. If someone wanted to get in, they would get in.

'When are you leaving?' Sóldís tried to stem the tide of worries by focusing on the practical.

'Early. We'll probably do a bit of shopping while we're there.' Ása gave Sóldís an apologetic look. 'I like to grab the chance on the rare occasions I get it. I love living out here but, God, there's so much I miss. Restaurants. Exhibitions. Shops. Cafes. Swimming pools.' Ása paused. 'Maybe I should ask the plumber if our borehole would be up to supporting a swimming pool.'

Ása left Gígja and Sóldís to go in search of the plumber. The little girl had already started dealing. Since the last thing Sóldís felt like was playing Ólsen-ólsen, she had to think fast. 'Do you know what we should do?'

'Play cards?'

'No. What about going for a walk while it's still light?' Sóldís was desperate to get out of the house and into the open air. The afternoon was wearing on and the thought of Reynir's phone message was gnawing away at her. Soon it would be suppertime and after that it wouldn't be long until she had to go back to her own quarters for the night. She couldn't shake off the fear that once she was alone in bed, she would be in danger. Outside, she could make a run for it in any direction if something bad happened; no one would be able to prevent her escape by blocking the doorway, for example, and cornering her in her room.

Gígja thought for a moment, then got to her feet. 'OK. We can play cards this evening. And tomorrow. All day and all evening. I know . . . I know. We can have an Ólsen-ólsen Olympic Games!'

Sóldís was careful not to say yes to any of these proposals. The first piece of advice her mother had given her in preparation for her new job was never to make the girls any promises she couldn't keep. This had been followed by countless other pieces of unsolicited advice, but the first was the only one that had properly sunk in.

'Why don't I pull you on the sledge?' Sóldís suggested. 'We can look for a good tobogganing slope.'

You couldn't fault Gígja's enthusiasm; in fact, a more positive child would be hard to find. In her hurry to go outdoors, she put on her coat inside out, as that was how it had been hanging on the peg in the entrance hall. 'Gígja, what are you like?' Sóldís exclaimed. 'Your coat's on the wrong way round.'

'It's still warm. Just as warm as when it's the right way round.'

Sóldís helped her out of the down jacket and reversed it. When they were both ready, with no fingers or ears exposed, and their snow-boots laced up, they went outside to fetch the sledge which was kept in the byre. Sóldís decided to let Bói come along but to leave Lubbi behind, mindful of how deep the snow was and how, even close to the farm, Lubbi had sunk up to his ears. As she shut the little dog in the house, he protested with a piercing howl. But once they were out by the byre, they could no longer hear his cries and soon forgot all about him.

The cows and horses raised their heads and gazed at them with large brown eyes. There was an expectant moo and one of the horses whinnied. But when it became clear that they hadn't come to feed them, the beasts soon lost interest. The sledge was leaning against the far wall, covered in a layer of the dust that showed it hadn't been used much. It wasn't a kid's sledge but a large red plastic toboggan with handbrakes on either side. Sóldís hoped Gígja wouldn't keep pulling them during the walk. If she did, they wouldn't be out there long.

As Sóldís was reaching for the toboggan, her eye was caught by a huge axe propped up in the corner next to it. Although she'd visited the byre every day, she hadn't noticed the axe before as the sledge had been in the way. She jerked back her hand with a shudder. She couldn't tear her gaze away from the thing or shake off a sudden, strange foreboding that something terrible was going to happen and the axe was the harbinger of doom. Her spine was crawling. Not until Gígja tugged at her coat and asked impatiently if they were going to take the toboggan did Sóldís snap out of it. The axe reverted to an innocent tool that was obviously rarely used. The presence of a large cobweb between the handle and the wall was clear evidence of this, along with the fact that the blade hadn't been blunted by use; it looked as if it had a good cutting edge.

Her overreaction must be down to stress. She would have to get a grip on herself. All the strange incidents in recent days must have some rational explanation and hopefully she would be able to smile about her jitters later. She simply wasn't used to being around types as eccentric as Reynir and Ása. Up to now, most of the people in her life had been very ordinary. Not all equally nice or kind – but pretty conventional. That must explain her mental state.

Sóldís felt her shivers subsiding. But she was still relieved once she'd shut the byre door behind them and no longer had the axe before her eyes.

She brushed most of the dust off the toboggan before letting Gígja get in, and told her not to use the brakes without warning her first. To begin with, it was heavier going than Sóldís had expected, but before long she'd got the hang of it, and the sledge slid along without too much effort on her part. The icy air and physical exertion had a restorative effect and she felt the last vestiges of her fear receding. From time to time, Gígja asked if they could swap places, but after having a go at pulling and quickly giving up twice, she soon stopped insisting. Bói, meanwhile, kept jumping on to the little girl's lap, which usually had the effect of capsizing the toboggan.

Sóldís had set a course up the small valley to the east of the farmhouse. It was on their property, so it should be OK, as long as she didn't accidentally venture too far and cross the boundary on to Minna-Hvarf land. But finding a slope gentle enough for tobogganing proved more difficult than she'd expected, and they ended up going much further than intended.

'Horses!' Gígja pulled the brake and the resulting jerk travelled up the rope and along Sóldís's arm to wrench at her shoulder.

'What did I tell you? Don't brake without warning me first.' Sóldís rubbed her sore arm.

Gígja struggled to her feet and pointed up the valley. 'Horses. Look.'

Sóldís and Bói stared in the direction she was pointing. The little girl was right. Bói started barking. The herd was some way ahead but appeared to be drawing closer, as if driven by curiosity. Perhaps the horses associated human beings with treats. Sadly, they hadn't brought any with them.

The horses seemed to be moving at a sluggish pace. 'They're going terribly slowly, aren't they?' Sóldís looked round at Gígja.

The little girl shrugged. 'Maybe they're freezing.'

Or the deep snow was hampering their progress. Sóldís interpreted the horses' presence as a sign that they shouldn't go any further. The slope they were standing at the foot of now would have to do. It was steep, but that would be all right, so long as Gígja didn't start too high up.

The little girl clambered up the hillside several times and sledged down again, Bói struggling up after her, then bounding down, sometimes beside the toboggan, trying to get on board but never succeeding.

By the time Gígja had had enough, the lead horses were near enough to see quite well, although the light was fading. They halted when they saw Sóldís and Gígja staring at them, and stared back. Then they came on, the rest of the herd straggling after them, moving lethargically as though they were weak from exhaustion or hunger.

'Mummy will be cross.' Gígja made a face at Sóldís. 'She doesn't want those horses here.'

'Do they belong to the bad horse man? To Robbi's father?' Sóldís needn't have bothered asking, because of course they did. Which meant that she and Gígja must have strayed uncomfortably close to the boundary with Minna-Hvarf, though the horses would hardly pay any attention to invisible property lines.

'Yes,' Gígja said, in answer to her question.

Sóldís gave Gígja a sceptical glance. 'How do you know?'

'Because they look so sad. His horses are always sad. And always girls.'

'Mares. Female horses are called mares. Or fillies. You should add the words to your collection.'

'I know. Begga told me. I've already got them in my book but I forgot.'

While Gígja repeated the words over and over again, Sóldís studied the herd of mares. Her thoughts kept straying back to Berglind and her message to Reynir, so she tried to distract herself by focusing her attention on the animals instead. Although she wasn't the horsey type herself, she'd tended to the family's horses every day since she started work here, feeding them, mucking out their stalls and letting them out in the paddock. She couldn't help thinking that Gígja was right; the mares did look dejected, as though they were on their last legs and knew it. They were scruffier than the two animals Sóldís looked after as well, their manes and tails tangled, their coats matted, and with a generally neglected air. Clearly, the harsh conditions were tough on them.

'How do you say that a mare is having a baby?' Gígja had stopped trying to memorise her vocabulary and was now attempting to lift Bói into the toboggan.

'In foal,' Sóldís replied, still without taking her eyes off the herd.

'They're all in foals,' Gígja said, groaning as she heaved Bói up.

'In *foal*. You say that they're all in foal, singular.'

'Yeah, whatever.' Gígja deposited Bói in the toboggan and tried to pull him along, but the moment it moved, the dog leapt out again.

Despite being well bundled up, Sóldís felt suddenly chilled. Even if Gígja was mistaken, but there was something unsettling about that woebegone herd – whether or not they were all mares and all in foal. Because it was glaringly obvious that the animals were not thriving in this place. They had that in common with her.

'Right, back in the sledge, Gígja. It's getting dark.'

On the way home, Sóldís snatched frequent glances behind them. The herd had trailed after them for a while, then halted and watched them go. In the end, Sóldís could no longer make out their shapes; they'd been swallowed up by the darkness.

Her feeling of gloom and anxiety returned.

Chapter 15
Friday

Týr was back in his cabin, waiting for his working day to begin in earnest. It was getting on for half past eight and he was impatient to see some sign of life from Karó. Just as he was starting to worry that her dinner had gone on late and she was oversleeping, she appeared at last, knocking on his door, ready for the new day. She was looking so bright and breezy that the dinner party must have broken up earlier than Týr had imagined. Since moving to Iceland, he'd noticed that people went to bed far later than in Sweden. The few times he'd been invited out to a meal or a party, he'd been amazed by the Icelanders' stamina. Perhaps the twenty-four-hour daylight in summer and the endless winter nights had destroyed his countrymen's biological clocks.

On the dot of eight, he'd phoned CID in Akranes to ask for their assignment, only to be told that he and Karólína would be left to their own devices for much of the day, as it wasn't immediately obvious how they could best be deployed. Hördur seemed in such a hurry to ring off that Týr had to get in quickly with his news about the young woman he had bumped into that morning at Hvarf. Hördur listened, saying 'Yes' and 'I see' in the right places, but Týr got the impression he felt it could wait. He was right, of course: Týr's conversation with Berglind was of no great significance to the investigation, though it had revealed that the couple had been quarrelling and hadn't been as happy as the other witnesses had claimed. But all that did was lend even more support to the theory that Reynir was the killer.

After Hördur had rung off, Týr called Huldar in Reykjavík, half hoping that he and Karó would be ordered to return to town. He'd had enough of staying in a pine shoebox. But his luck was out. All he got was a vague instruction to continue providing back-up to the local team. He and Karó could assist with the collection of evidence from the scene, for example, or make themselves useful in some other way. But Huldar didn't follow this up with any further suggestions.

On the other hand, Týr's account of his unexpected meeting with Berglind was received with far more interest by Huldar than it had been by Hördur. In fact, Huldar was rather disappointed to learn that Berglind lived further up the coast in the small town of Borgarnes, as it was on the patch of the Akranes force. Similarly, when Huldar looked up Alvar Grétarsson, who had taken over the job as assistant after Berglind left, he discovered that the young man lived in the town of Mosfellsbær, twelve kilometres north of Reykjavík, which made it likely that the Akranes police would want to talk to him as well. Nevertheless, he suggested that Týr and Karó take a swing by his place that morning, as long as the Akranes team agreed.

The upshot was that Týr and Karó were to go to Mosfellsbær. During his second phone call to CID in Akranes, Týr was warned that this would only be a preliminary chat to prepare the ground for the formal taking of Alvar's statement. Which he interpreted to mean that Akranes didn't regard the interview as particularly important – or else that they were only too happy to get him and Karó out of their hair for a while.

When people were rushed off their feet, it could be more time-consuming than useful to have back-up officers who didn't know the ropes always asking what they should do next.

Týr didn't care what lay behind the decision. He smiled to himself, relieved to be given a task that would take them away from the scene of the killings. The last thing he wanted was to enter the family home again. The sooner those memories were buried, the better. Whenever he closed his eyes, images of the dead came back to haunt him.

It was common knowledge that some murder cases could have a lasting impact on the mental health of even the most experienced police officers. More often than not, the cases in question were notable for their shocking brutality, testifying to the sick mind of the killer, and only exacerbated by the innocence of the victims. Since police officers were meant to display a professional detachment, they had no outlet for their shock. That left them with three options: find their own way of coping; get professional help; or suffer psychological damage. Týr was beginning to think that this was one of those cases – the first he'd experienced. Soon he would have to decide which approach to take. The only certainty was that he was not going to accept the third option.

It occurred to him that his mother might have detected this in his voice when they were talking on the phone. She'd always been incredibly perceptive. Maybe that was why she'd been so concerned to hear that he was working on this investigation, and his fears about bad news were unfounded. Until he received evidence to the contrary, he was inclined to go with this explanation.

A heavy rapping on his door put an end to his musings. It was Karó. Týr outlined the new assignment to her as he pulled on his coat and gratefully escaped the reek of pine.

On the way to the car, he rang the number Huldar had given him. An automated message immediately announced that Alvar's phone was either switched off or outside the service area. Týr slowed his pace, wondering about this. Of course, there could be a natural explanation: Alvar's battery could have run out or his phone could be broken; he could be on board a plane or in a location where phone calls were frowned on. Perhaps he switched off his phone at night and hadn't got up yet. In most cases there was a perfectly innocent explanation. Nevertheless, he found it disquieting.

'All I'm getting is his voicemail.' Týr made a face and put his phone in his pocket. 'Maybe we should postpone the trip to Mosfellsbær. There's no point driving all the way over there if the guy's asleep or out.'

Karó didn't seem to share his pessimism. 'He could have more than one number.'

Týr tapped Alvar's name into the online telephone directory and found him straight away. 'Nope, he's only got the one number.' Týr tried looking up the address, in case Alvar lived with his parents or was cohabiting. The name Bogi Lúthersson came up. He couldn't be the father, since Alvar's father must be called Grétar, but he could be a stepfather. Týr mentally reviewed all the other possibilities. They couldn't be brothers, as they didn't share a father, and Bogi couldn't be Alvar's son. Besides, Alvar was only twenty-one, so even if he'd had a son the boy wouldn't be old enough to have a registered phone number. Logically, then, this Bogi must be either his stepbrother, his landlord, his flatmate or his boyfriend. 'There's another name here,' he told Karó, 'registered at the same address: Bogi Lúthersson.'

Calling up a map of Mosfellsbær, Týr noticed that Alvar's address was a detached house. He handed his phone to Karó.

'I'm guessing it must be his stepfather. Or else Alvar rents the garage or a flat in the house from this Bogi.'

The best way to find out was to ring the man.

The voice that answered was younger than Týr had been expecting: late teens, early twenties, at a guess.

Týr introduced himself and explained why he was calling. There was a brief silence, then Bogi asked: 'Is Alvar in some kind of trouble?'

'No, we just need to have a word with him. That's all.'

Bogi obviously wasn't buying this. 'Then you'll just have to keep calling his phone. He's not here and I can't help it if he doesn't want to pick up.'

'Can I ask how you two are connected?'

Bogi had no difficulty answering that: 'I rent a room from him. I replied to an ad.'

'I see. Can you tell me where Alvar is? Is he at work or at home?'

There was another silence. Bogi was evidently weighing up whether he would get Alvar into hot water by answering. In the end, he seemed to have concluded that it wouldn't do his landlord any harm: 'He's not here. He's at work.'

'Where does he work?'

'On a farm or something. In Hvalfjördur. For a bunch of millionaires.'

* * *

Týr switched off the engine and Karó undid her seatbelt, but neither made any move to get out of the car. They studied the small detached house they had parked outside. 'There must be some simple explanation.' Karó's gaze travelled over the building as if she was expecting to find the answer to this new riddle among the cracks in the concrete.

'Yes, let's hope so.' Týr had spent the drive trying to work out what could be going on, but hadn't come to any conclusions. According to Bogi, Alvar was still working at Hvarf, but there was nothing to suggest that this had been true. Týr had refrained from bombarding him with questions over the phone, realising at once that they would need to talk to the young man face-to-face. This Bogi was unlikely to have answers to many of the questions they were keen to ask, but with any luck he might be able to help with some of them. He didn't seem to have made the connection between their call and the murders in the news, but then only very vague details were available so far. No names had been released, the location had been described as the west of Iceland, and there had been no mention of Hvalfjördur specifically. Besides, Bogi's generation didn't pay much attention to the news, and Týr doubted the case was being discussed yet on TikTok, YouTube or Instagram.

'What do you reckon a house like that is worth?' Karó glanced at Týr, who shrugged. 'It may not be the swankiest address in town but I'd never have been able to afford anything like that at twenty-one.' She'd looked up the property on the way there and discovered that Alvar was registered as sole owner.

'Bogi may be able to tell us how Alvar came by it. The first thing that springs to mind is that he could have been dealing. But you say he's not on LÖKE or on any of our other databases?'

Karó had phoned the police station in Reykjavík, as they were winding their slow way around Hvalfjördur and the Kjalarnes peninsula, and asked them to look Alvar up for her. 'No. According to Lína, he doesn't have a record, he's never been under investigation or charged with anything, or linked to any case.'

Since there was no reason to hang about, they got out of the car and walked up to the front door, passing an old banger that was parked in front of the garage. Týr knocked, having failed to find a doorbell, and shortly afterwards the door was opened by a short young man with a singularly colourless face. He was wearing tracksuit bottoms and a T-shirt that could have done with a wash two days ago. But he wasn't a total slob as there were various hints that he cared about his appearance: highlights in his hair, chunky rings on his fingers and two chains round his neck.

Týr introduced himself and Karó but didn't waste time explaining why they were there, as he had already informed Bogi at the end of their phone conversation that they were planning to drop by.

'Do you want to come in or what?'

They accepted the invitation and he asked them awkwardly to excuse the mess. He'd been meaning to tidy up but hadn't got round to it yet.

Týr had been expecting the place to be a complete tip, littered with takeaway boxes, cans and dirty clothes, as if a tornado had ripped through it, but when they were shown into the living room, things weren't actually that bad. He was more struck by how old-fashioned the furniture and fittings were – not exactly the kind of thing he'd expect someone in his twenties to choose. But people's taste differed, of course, and maybe Alvar couldn't afford anything apart from stuff you could pick up for peanuts from a charity shop.

There were clumps of dust in the corners of the floor and peeping out from under the furniture. A pair of socks lay inside out on the parquet, and there were two empty crisp packets on the marble table and a duvet on the sofa. Apart from that, there was no sign of any mess. When they got a glimpse of the kitchen, however, it became clear that Bogi had a hell of a job on his hands in there. The sink was overflowing with saucepans and dishes, and the worktops on either side of it were cluttered with empty food packaging and other rubbish.

Bogi removed the duvet from the sofa and hurriedly shut the kitchen door when he caught Týr looking in there. Then he invited them to take a seat on the sofa while he himself perched on a chair.

'What's this all about?' Bogi asked before they could get in a question.

'As I told you on the phone, we're looking for Alvar. We only need to talk to him. He's not suspected of any wrongdoing and has nothing to fear.'

Bogi wasn't satisfied with this answer. 'But why? The police don't want to talk to you unless it's related to a crime, do they? I mean, do you lot do anything apart from investigate crimes?'

Karó smiled at the young man. 'Criminal investigations involve interviewing a lot more people than just the suspects. As it happens, Alvar is a possible witness in a case we're working on.'

'OK. But why do you want to talk to me?'

'Because Alvar isn't answering his phone and we're hoping you can help us track him down. Do you know his parents, for example? Or his girlfriend? Or a friend, a brother or a sister, maybe? It would speed things up if you could point us to someone who's in contact with him.'

'He hasn't got a girlfriend or any brothers or sisters. Not many friends either, and no parents. So I can't help you. Why don't you just go and see him at the farm where he's working?

Believe me, I'd know if he'd come back to town. He lives here. This is his house.'

'Has he had it long?' Týr seized on this as a way of dodging Bogi's question about why they couldn't simply go and see Alvar at the farm.

Bogi shrugged. 'I don't know. He inherited it when his mother died. It was hers. He used to live here with her. She died about two years ago, I think. Something like that.'

'What about his father?'

'He died when Alvar was a kid. In a car crash or something. His mother got cancer.' Bogi reported this unemotionally, as if answering questions for a history test on the life of someone he didn't know. Týr thought of his own response to the possibility that his mother might have been diagnosed with cancer. But of course you were more likely to be moved by the fate of a close relative than a stranger; Bogi wasn't alone in that.

'When did you last hear from him?' Karó asked, when Bogi had finished.

'Oh . . . er. A few days ago, I think. Maybe more than a week.'

'Isn't that unusual? Not hearing from him for so long?' Karó managed to make the question sound casual.

Bogi shook his head. 'No. We don't have that kind of relationship. Since he moved to the countryside, we've only been in touch when something comes up. We used to talk a bit while he was living here, of course, but it's not like we were always chatting or anything. I've only been renting from him for four months.'

Týr chipped in with a question: 'You say you talk when something comes up. Like what, for example?'

'One of the gutters broke recently. A load of ice and snow slid off the roof and took the gutter with it. I let him know and he told me to contact a roofer and get an invoice. So I did. But the man still hasn't been round. I've sent Alvar several messages about it since then but he hasn't answered. Mind you, I don't really know what he's supposed to do about it. He can't force the roofer to turn up.' Bogi paused, looking suddenly shifty. 'And I sent him a message last week, asking if I could have a bit of an extension on the rent. He hasn't answered that either. I'm just hoping silence means consent. Anyway, I know he's seen the messages.' Bogi continued, even more awkwardly: 'I'm having a bit of trouble finding a job, you see. I haven't got a car, so I'd rather find something near by to avoid having to spend all day on the bus.'

Týr bit back the urge to point out to Bogi that it wouldn't take him much longer to get to work by bus than by car. 'Whose is the car outside, then?'

'Alvar's.'

'Why hasn't he got it with him at the farm? Does he own another car as well?'

'No. They sent a car to collect him. I don't think he dared drive up there in his own car. The tyres are bald and he can't afford new ones. Something like that. Alvar's totally skint, although he owns this place. All he inherited was the house, no cash or anything. The house and the car.' Bogi waved a hand. 'And all this stuff. That's why he advertised a room for rent. To cover the payments and so on. The house is mortgaged, apparently. And he's a bit of a clothes freak too.'

Týr and Karó hadn't come here to discuss clothes. 'What did Alvar do before he took a job at the farm?' Týr asked. He assumed the young man couldn't have been unemployed as the couple would surely have been particular about who they hired to work in their home.

'He didn't do anything. He was at uni. Still is, I think, studying alongside his job. Maybe it's not full-time or something. I didn't really ask him about it.'

'What's he studying?' Karó asked.

'Computer science. Programming, that sort of thing.'

Týr raised his eyebrows. 'That's not exactly the kind of study that would prepare you to work on a farm.'

'No, maybe not. But I understood from Alvar that the family's connected to the tech world. He's hoping to get a reference or a possible job in the IT sector through them when his position ends. It's not such a bad plan.'

Possibly it had been a good idea at the time but it was to be hoped that Alvar had a back-up plan, as there was no way Ása or Reynir would be able to help him get a job now.

'Do you mind if we have a quick look around?' Karó asked. 'At Alvar's room and study, if he has one?'

Bogi made a face. 'I can only let you look at my room. I'm not responsible for the rest of the house. You'll have to talk to Alvar about that.' Then, clearly remembering that Týr had got a glimpse of the kitchen, he added: 'I have access to the kitchen and bathroom as well, of course. And I've been using the living room while Alvar's away. You can look at them. But I don't want to let you into his bedroom or study. You'll have to talk to him about that.'

'No problem.' Karó smiled.

They couldn't think of much more to ask, since Bogi didn't seem to know his landlord very well.

Eventually, having run out of questions, they stood up and thanked him. As they were on their way out of the door, Karó's phone rang. With a quick wave to Bogi, she started walking towards the car as she put it to her ear. Týr said a proper goodbye, asking one final question in parting: 'Have I understood right that you and Alvar have been in touch by messaging?'

Bogi nodded.

'Can you see when Alvar last replied?'

Bogi dug in his tracksuit pocket for his phone and fiddled with it. 'A bit over a week ago.' He turned the screen to Týr, who read the text from Alvar asking Bogi to call a roofer and adding that he couldn't get away at the moment as he had too much to do. The message was dated ten days ago. Although Týr didn't say as much, it was impossible that Alvar had still been working on the farm then. According to information gleaned from interviews with Sóldís's parents, there had been no other staff on the farm when she started work there. So Alvar must have left by then. Admittedly, there was a remote chance that Sóldís's parents had made a mistake or that she had been wrong and that Alvar had still been working for the couple. Perhaps he'd got his wish and been taken on by them in a different capacity – as a programmer, for example. Although they had sold their company, it was quite possible that they had needed help with a new project and that he had been working on that, maybe at another location.

Týr noticed that Karó was waving to him from the car, still on the phone. He said a hasty goodbye. Once they were both sitting in the car with the doors shut, she put a hand over the receiver and told him, almost in a whisper: 'They've found Reynir.'

Chapter 16
Before

By the time Sóldís went over to the new house the next morning, Ása and Reynir had already left. There was a handwritten list of the day's tasks from Ása, complete with instructions about what to cook the girls for supper. Below this, Ása had also suggested what they should have for lunch, underlining the information that Sóldís was to make sure the girls finished what was on their plates as Ása didn't want them foraging in the fridge the way they had been recently. The best way to stop them snacking was to make sure they ate properly at mealtimes.

Sóldís permitted herself an eyeroll over Ása's micromanaging. She'd been wanting to do one for days but hadn't dared for fear that Ása or Reynir might notice. Since there was no risk of that now, she indulged herself again, even more theatrically, and felt better for venting her feelings at last. It had been a strain to be on the receiving end of so many superfluous instructions about how to do every tiny thing. They even had opinions about how she should hold the shovel when mucking out the byre. As if it mattered how you shovelled shit.

The note also explained that the couple had decided to set off first thing to be sure of getting the most out of their trip. They wouldn't be back until late the following evening. At the bottom, Ása had written their telephone numbers in case of problems. The numbers were printed in large letters, as if she'd been envisaging a catastrophe in which Sóldís would hardly be able to see due to a cloud of smoke or blood running into her eyes.

Sóldís decided to let the girls have a lie-in. They were subjected to the same level of military discipline in their studies as she was in her job, and it would do them good to relax. Naturally, Ása had made an exhaustive list of what they were to be taught while she was away, but Sóldís reckoned she could polish it off in an afternoon. There was no chance of neglecting the lessons entirely, alas, as she wouldn't put it past Ása to test the girls to make sure their programme had been strictly adhered to.

Sóldís had never had the house to herself before. As a rule, there was always someone within calling distance. The silence was so profound that it felt a little eerie, as though she'd been abandoned, left alone to cope with any bizarre incidents that might occur. It wasn't a pleasant thought, but she reminded herself that the girls were there too, even if they weren't making their presence known at the moment. The thought was comforting, until it dawned on her they would be no help if something went wrong. It would be up to her to save herself and them.

For the first time in several days, she had flaked out shortly after going to bed and slept right through the night. She'd managed to push away the problems in her private life and her gnawing curiosity about what Jónsi was up to now. And the knowledge that all the entrances to the old house were locked and barricaded with chairs – even the cellar door – had taken the edge off her fears about the nocturnal intruder. The windless weather had helped too, as the house had ceased its uncanny creaking and groaning. When she surfaced after nine hours' uninterrupted sleep, her first reaction had been astonishment. She could do it. But as she stood in front of the bathroom mirror, her mouth full of toothpaste and the toothbrush in her hand, the sense of trepidation had reasserted itself. How could she be sure that someone hadn't entered the house while she was asleep? For all she knew, the intruder could have stood over her, watching her in bed.

Sóldís squared her shoulders, hoping that this would give her a boost of courage. She forced herself to look out into the black morning beyond the glass wall and to accept it. The darkness was harmless in itself; the only thing she had to worry about was what it might be concealing.

Sóldís continued to stare out of the tall windows, aware that the effort to think positively had been good for her. She should do more of that. On an impulse, she started searching online for courses in self-empowerment. There turned out to be loads, but none of them fitted her needs, which were that they had to be free and available online. The few courses that appeared to be free either required her to attend in person or else looked a bit woo-woo. Whereas the more promising ones all required taking out a year's subscription, which was out of the question. She couldn't bring herself to fork out the money and, besides, she needed immediate results.

Disappointed, she stuck her phone back in her pocket to avoid the temptation of checking her emails. She could see that she had an unread message, and that could only be from the supervisor of her Master's thesis – on which she'd made zero progress. She was still in exactly the same place as she had been when she first arrived in the countryside; in fact you could say she was in an even worse position because she'd not only stopped thinking about the thesis but also lost the little interest she'd ever had in the subject.

While Sóldís was sipping her coffee, she had a thought. Perhaps Reynir had some self-help books she could look at. He must have had to pause and take stock of his life when he fell ill. Not that this seemed to have done much good in his case, unless he'd been even worse before. Still, it couldn't hurt to take a look at the bookcase in his study. She wouldn't get another chance anytime soon as Reynir was weird about his workspace. She was allowed in to clean, but he would stand in the doorway, monitoring her, as if he suspected her of being up to no good. Unlike Ása, he wasn't constantly telling her what to do, he just stood there, watching her every move. No way could she examine the titles on his bookshelves with him breathing down her neck.

She tiptoed along the hallway to his study, afraid of waking the girls. She didn't want them telling their father, either deliberately or inadvertently. To her surprise, the door wasn't locked as it normally was if Reynir wasn't in there when she wanted to clean, and she was able to open it without making a sound. The room was windowless – perhaps, she thought, to avoid the glare of daylight on the screens. Closing the door warily behind her, she stood in pitch darkness for a moment before groping for the wall switch. The moment the room sprang into view, she breathed more easily, reassured that there was nobody in there, despite what her imagination had been trying to tell her.

Instead of going immediately to the bookcase, Sóldís leant back against the door and surveyed her surroundings. Everything was where it should have been: the desk with the three large monitors, the office chair, printer, filing cabinet and shelves. The creepy little robot was in its place in the corner, but she was growing used to it now. Its lenses no longer seemed like eyes. The walls were hung with framed articles from foreign magazines about the company Ása and Reynir had founded. Some were accompanied by photos of the couple at different times; in the oldest pictures they appeared youthful and smiling, but the closer the articles got to the present, the graver their faces became. Sóldís hadn't had an opportunity to read them but assumed they were favourable, as no one would frame negative reports about themselves and hang them on the wall. Though now that she was alone and had the leisure to read them, she realised she wasn't interested.

But other things of more interest might be kept in the study, like paperwork relating to Alvar's abrupt departure. Reynir and Ása were not the kind of people who would allow him to terminate a contract simply by leaving. They must have wanted to tie up any loose ends and block any chances of him getting additional compensation. Even a document with his full name and address would help. She could use it to track him down and distinguish him from all the other Alvars out there.

She went over to the desk and glanced at the loose papers. Most appeared to be printouts of meaningless lines of code. Nothing to do with Alvar. Reynir had scribbled something on almost all the pages but it was the same story there; she couldn't make head or tail of what he'd written. One page was different, though: it contained a handwritten text in two columns, in which a series of numbers or words were paired. Her curiosity aroused, Sóldís allowed herself to take a closer look since there was no Reynir lurking in the doorway.

It didn't take her long to work out what it was. The series of digits and symbols were obviously passwords to websites, devices and programs. The first column listed the relevant site, including an online chemist, two Icelandic banks, Facebook, Google, Icelandair Saga Club and that sort of thing. The second column contained passwords for each account. They weren't particularly complicated but neither were they ludicrously simple: $$Gig3ja$$, $$Ir3is$$, 28pizzas#%, Boi%8!Lubbi and so on.

Sóldís only meant to skim the list as she didn't want to accidentally memorise the passwords, but she didn't immediately put the sheet down because her eye was caught by what appeared to be a summary or analysis of the passwords at the bottom of the page. She couldn't imagine why Reynir should have gone to the trouble of analysing them, unless he was trying to work out if it would be possible for hackers to crack the other passwords by getting hold of one or two of them.

He was clearly even more eccentric than she'd thought. She put the paper down, only then spotting an acronym in the website column that she recognised: AWC. Every other day she went up to the road to collect the post. The family didn't receive many letters but twice there had been envelopes in the mailbox marked with this acronym. Under a cringeworthy logo it had said: *Association for Women in Computing*. The letters had naturally been addressed to Ása rather than Reynir.

The knowledge brought a sudden bad taste to Sóldís's mouth. The writing on the paper in front of her didn't belong to Ása, Íris or Gígja, which left only Reynir. But the password to a website for the AWC must be Ása's. And the same probably applied to the rest, now that she came to think about it. For reasons best known to himself, Reynir was collecting his wife's passwords, studying them and trying to work out if there was some kind of system behind them.

At that moment a shrill sound pierced the silence, making Sóldís jump. She realised it was her phone bleeping. Her guilt about being in a room she had practically been banned from entering had left her nerves taut. Taking out her phone, she saw a vaguely familiar number and opened the message. It said: *What are you doing? Leave my papers alone.*

Sóldís froze. It must be from Reynir, and the number must look familiar because it had been printed at the bottom of Ása's memo. Her eyes flicked to the webcam at the top of the computer screen in the middle of the big desk and she realised that she was probably looking Reynir straight in the eye, and that she had been caught red-handed. The camera tracked slowly sideways, first to the right, then to the left, as if imitating a disapproving headshake. This was no coincidence: Reynir must be controlling the camera remotely. Sóldís felt the blood rising to her cheeks and hoped the camera would fail to capture her betraying blush. But since Reynir was a computer nerd with money coming out of his ears, it was a vain hope. The camera was bound to be state-of-the-art.

Her humiliation complete, Sóldís stood as if turned to stone, gaping at the convex lens. Luckily, a loud whistling, carrying through the closed door, gave her a jolt. She hurried out of the study, switching off the light before closing the door behind her. It was some consolation to think that Reynir would be left staring into a black void.

The whistling kept getting louder and Sóldís hastened towards the kitchen before it became unbearable. She recognised the piercing screech of the kettle that always stood on the hob. The only person who used it was Ása, for making her herbal tea. Sóldís, still in shock after being caught in Reynir's study, thought at first that the couple must have come home early. Perhaps they'd been forced to turn back because the road was blocked by snow, or the car had developed a fault. Before rounding the corner, she paused to take a deep breath and brace herself for a reprimand, sarky comments or an interrogation by Reynir. He might even fire her. It was funny how this possibility troubled her when deep down she knew that it would actually be for the best. She would no longer have to worry about how to get out of her contract or what she would do, homeless and broke, if she left. The decision would be made for her.

The kitchen was empty. Steam was screaming through the two vents in the spout of the large, handsome kettle, but there was no other sound. The darkness outside was as unrelieved as before and Ása's note was where she had left it.

Sóldís's initial reaction was relief that the couple hadn't come home after all. But this was short-lived. The girls now appeared in their pyjamas, with tousled hair and sleep in their eyes. The dogs had followed them and ran eagerly to their empty food bowls and started licking them optimistically. The deafening shriek of the kettle didn't appear to bother them in the least.

Íris's voice was still husky with sleep as she snapped at Sóldís: 'Turn off that piece of crap. It's impossible to sleep. I woke up thinking the house was on fire.'

Sóldís hurriedly switched off the hob and removed the kettle. The ensuing blissful silence was broken by Gígja asking sleepily: 'Where's Mummy?'

'They've gone. They set off before we woke up.' Sóldís paused, frowning. 'You mustn't switch on the hob under the kettle, Gígja. If all the water evaporates or it's empty to begin with, it could catch fire.'

Gígja yawned before answering: 'I didn't switch it on. I don't drink tea. I think it's disgusting.'

Sóldís turned to Íris who shook her head with a sulky expression. 'Don't look at me. It woke me up. I don't drink tea either.'

The girls were now staring at Sóldís. 'Well, I didn't turn it on,' she said, though she could hear that her voice lacked conviction. Could she have done it without realising? It was an induction hob with touch controls, so it was always possible that she had brushed against it when walking past. Only she couldn't remember going anywhere near the island with the built-in hob. She'd gone straight to the posh coffee machine and made herself a cup. Then opened the fridge to get out the milk. Then turned and stared at the darkness outside. That was it. She couldn't recall doing anything else.

Gígja's eyes widened. 'But . . . if you didn't do it, and I didn't do it and neither did Íris . . . who did?' She glanced at the dogs who were still licking their empty bowls. 'Bói? Or Lubbi?'

Íris gave a derisive snort. 'Of course not, Gígja.' Then her gaze turned to Sóldís, her eyes reflecting Sóldís's own fear.

'Perhaps your mother left the hob on.' This explanation might have worked if the hob had been on low but it hadn't. When Sóldís switched it off just now, it had been on the highest setting. After watching Ása heat water for endless cups of tea, Sóldís knew that the kettle took no time to boil, but she suggested this anyway to deflect Íris's fear. It wouldn't help to have her worried as well. On the contrary, it would only amplify Sóldís's unease.

'I'll ring her and ask.' Íris automatically reached for her phone in her trouser pocket, only to discover that she was still in her pyjamas.

'No. Please don't.' The words tumbled out in a rush as Sóldís didn't want to risk Reynir answering. She knew that, because of his illness, Ása would be driving and so the phone call would probably be relayed over the speakers, involving them both. Ása mustn't learn about Sóldís trespassing in his study – though he may already have told her. She was afraid she'd lose Ása's respect and trust, even if she didn't lose her job. 'I must have brushed against the controls,' she said. 'That would explain it.'

Íris rolled her eyes. 'Jesus. Be careful next time. What if it had caught fire?'

Sóldís pretended she hadn't heard this and asked them instead what they wanted for breakfast. Though she herself was still preoccupied with the problem of the kettle, she didn't want to worry the girls. Especially not as it had just occurred to her that Reynir might be able to control the hob remotely. It might not even require particularly sophisticated technology. Maybe it was just a question of setting a timer.

Gígja wanted cereal with sugar, though this was usually forbidden. Íris wanted to skip breakfast altogether, which was also against the rules. Bói and Lubbi just wanted something to eat.

While Gígja was sitting at the table with the sugar bowl beside her, the dogs were wolfing down some mince and Íris was playing with her phone in her father's armchair, Sóldís drank another coffee, immediately followed by a third. It wasn't that she particularly wanted more caffeine, more that she needed to occupy herself with something other than staring into space and brooding. But after three cups, her heart was racing and she had broken out in a sweat.

'Are you coming with me to feed the animals, Gígja?'

The little girl nodded, her mouth too full to speak.

'What about you, Íris?'

The snort that emanated from the armchair would translate as 'absolutely no chance' in just about every language in the world. Sóldís didn't let it get to her, since she had only asked out of politeness. Instead, she laid a hand on Gígja's shoulder, telling her to finish her cereal, while she herself popped over to the old house to fetch her boots. Then she'd help Gígja sort out what she was going to wear that day.

Still with her mouth full of cereal and sugar, the little girl nodded again.

Sóldís set off but didn't get beyond the kitchen. From where she was standing, she could see down the hall to the door of the connecting corridor. It was open. Yet she had closed it behind her that morning. She always did.

Chapter 17
Friday

A couple of police cars and a large search-and-rescue vehicle were already parked at the side of the access road to Minna-Hvarf when Týr and Karó arrived. This was the home of Einar Ari Arason, the neighbour the couple had fallen out with, who had shopped Reynir for growing cannabis. Ironically, the discovery of Reynir's body had just made it less likely that the animosity between them could have a bearing on the case. If the farmer had slaughtered the family and the young woman who worked for them, he would hardly have dumped Reynir's body on his own doorstep – or as good as. According to the information Karó had been given, the body was lying in a bathtub in a snowy hayfield close to the farmhouse. There was no explanation of what the bathtub was doing in the field.

It didn't take them long to spot it. Three police officers who had got there before them were standing at the edge of the field, watching two men in protective gear trying to raise a tent over the tub.

The sky hung low and grey overhead, the clouds swollen with snow. The forecast was for more bad weather, and travellers were warned against driving around the Kjalarnes peninsula that evening due to the threat of high winds. Although the ground by the bathtub was buried in snowdrifts, the police needed to preserve the scene the way they'd found it. In fact, they could be thankful that there was no immediate prospect of a thaw. Freezing temperatures and a thick layer of snow were infinitely preferable to slush and mud in the present circumstances. Or indeed in any circumstances.

Týr got out of the car and turned to examine the farmhouse. The contrast between this place and the set-up at Hvarf was striking. This was the real McCoy, not a hobby farm. There was an old jeep in the yard. The house could have done with some maintenance and a fresh lick of paint. The byre and other outbuildings were showing their age too, as was the tractor that was parked beside a huge pile of hay bales wrapped in white plastic. The pens and paddocks close to the buildings were empty of livestock. Only beyond where the tent was being erected could a knot of horses be glimpsed in the distance, huddled together, indifferent to the human activity. The opposite applied to the black and white dog standing on the farmhouse steps. Its unblinking gaze was fixed on Týr and Karó, but as it was chained up, it couldn't go anywhere. Presumably this was to prevent it from contaminating the crime scene, as the poor creature surely couldn't be chained up like that all the time.

Two figures were standing at the window, watching what was going on. They looked to Týr like an adult and an adolescent or teenager. The adult was holding something – a cushion or pillow, Týr guessed – but as he was too far away to make out any details, it could just as well have been a half-filled shopping bag. Regardless of what the person was holding, he was inclined to think it was a woman. If he was right, this suggested that the husband, who'd been at loggerheads with Ása and Reynir, had chosen not to watch.

Týr quickened his pace to catch up with Karó, who had marched off without pausing to survey the surroundings. 'Isn't it a bit strange that they didn't notice there was a corpse in their bathtub?' Týr asked when he reached her side. 'I mean, it's not that far from the house.'

She glanced round at the farmyard, then back to where the tent was coming up. 'It's not that close. Anyway, isn't it supposed to have happened at night? I expect Reynir's body was hidden by the snow. It wouldn't have taken long to cover him. I imagine the bathtub's there because they're planning to throw it out once the weather improves, so I don't suppose they check on it much, let alone use it.'

Týr grimaced. 'Then why lug it all the way out to the field? They could have dumped it just outside the yard.'

Karó didn't reply. On the way there, she'd filled him in on what she'd learnt from the phone call. The farmer's son had gone to fetch two mares from the field because the vet had come to have a look at them. As he passed, he'd noticed an odd shape in the tub, so he'd scraped away some of the snow, only to recoil in horror when he saw what it was.

Týr recognised the three people watching the tent being erected – Akranes CID in person: Hördur, the leader of the investigation, and his detectives, Sævar and Elma. Karó joined the group without a word, as if they'd only been parted for a few minutes. Týr, less casual by nature, greeted them all formally. They nodded to him, then returned their attention to the field – apart from Hördur, who said: 'They're on their way up from Reykjavík. Your people – forensics and the pathologist.'

This went without saying, Týr thought. They could count themselves lucky that the body had been discovered this early in the day. The forensics team and Idunn would at least be able to perform part of their duties by daylight, feeble as it was at this time of year. But they would no doubt bring along the portable floodlights anyway, as it would take time to examine and photograph the scene and collect samples. They would be at it until long after the sun had set.

A few tiny snowflakes started floating to the ground. Týr knew this was only a taste of what was to come; these harmless white specks were like scouts, sent ahead of the main army to spy out the lie of the land. Raising his eyes, he saw that the sky had darkened and the snow would soon be starting in earnest. If the gales that had been forecast were added to the mix, some or all of the Reykjavík party might well be forced to spend the night up here too. He found himself hoping they would, since then he wouldn't have to mope around on his own for a second evening in a row. If, as he suspected, Karó went to see her friend in Borgarnes again, at least this time he'd be able to have supper with the others and maybe enjoy a bit of company after the meal too.

Týr brought the Akranes team up to speed with what he and Karó had learnt from their visit to Bogi. He voiced his concerns about Alvar, who had worked as an assistant to Ása and Reynir and now appeared to have vanished off the face of the earth. They listened thoughtfully but didn't volunteer any theories. On the drive up from Mosfellsbær, Týr and Karó had traded possible explanations, but none had seemed plausible, so it was hardly to be expected that people hearing the news for the first time would have any brilliant suggestions to offer. After listening, Hördur said he would have the young man's phone traced or, if the battery had died, at least establish its last recorded location. Gesturing to the bathtub, he pointed out, as was fair enough, that the investigation was about to become more focused on Reynir, but suggested that Týr and Karó should be responsible for following up the Alvar angle. There was no mistaking his relief at being handed this opportunity to keep them both usefully occupied.

Hördur now glanced at his watch. 'Forensics won't be here for a good half an hour yet. While we're waiting, could you two maybe go and take a short statement from the boy?' He addressed this to Týr but nodded at Karó, who was standing with her back to them, watching what was happening in the field. 'He was in shock when we arrived, so it was hard to get anything out of him. I doubt he'll be able to tell us much in any case, but we should at least speak to him while it's still fresh in his mind.'

Týr accepted the task gratefully. It was better than standing around freezing while they stared at a white tent in a white field. 'What about the parents? Is it OK for one of them to be present?'

'If they want. I don't see any reason to stop them. He's only fifteen. But don't ask them any questions. We'll take care of that later.'

Týr didn't object, though personally he'd have thought it was more sensible to keep the father out of it. He might not be a suspect, and it seemed unlikely now that he would become one, but a lot could change. As yet, they had only a very vague picture of the events, though they believed they were on the right track. But Týr supposed there wasn't much the boy could say about the discovery of the body that would jeopardise the investigation, even if it transpired that his father had been involved. It would be different if they were to ask him, say, about his father's relationship with the couple.

As Týr and Karó approached the house, the figures vanished from the window and the lace curtain fell back into place. Unlike his owners, the dog wasn't ashamed to have been caught watching them, and couldn't contain his excitement when he realised they were heading his way. His tail started wagging wildly, and when they ascended the steps, his joy knew no bounds. Visitors were obviously rare in these parts and welcomed indiscriminately.

Týr scratched the grateful dog behind the ears while Karó knocked on the door. The moment it opened, the animal darted aside and started barking loudly at the newcomers, as if to show that he had been doing his duty as a guard dog. The woman in the doorway merely ordered him sternly to shut up, then asked Týr and Karó what they wanted. A plump infant was fast asleep in her arms. The woman looked badly shaken, as was only natural in the circumstances.

Karó introduced them both, then asked if they could speak to her son, Róbert. At first, the woman said no, on the grounds that her son, who she referred to as Robbi, was in shock. Karó promised that they'd be gentle with him and added that the boy had no need to be nervous. It might actually be better to get it over with now than to have to rake the events up again tomorrow. To be completely straight with the woman, she pointed out that he might still be required to give a formal witness statement later, but that a quick chat should hopefully be enough for now.

The woman agreed, on condition that she was allowed to be present, and they accepted this without comment. Then she belatedly introduced herself as Dísa and invited them to step inside. They followed her through to a tidy but old-fashioned kitchen, took seats at the table and declined the offer of coffee. Dísa went out to fetch her son, with the infant still sleeping peacefully in her arms. When she reappeared, she was no longer carrying the baby, so she had presumably put it down in its cot.

Instead, she was accompanied by her teenage son Róbert who was clearly suffering from shock, as his mother had said. If anything, this was an understatement. The boy looked devastated. His eyes were swollen from weeping and seemed unable to focus on anything. His forehead was clammy and his breathing irregular. The boy's distress was so palpable that it was painful to behold. He wasn't old enough to bury his feelings, yet the severity of his reaction seemed a little odd. Týr could understand that the discovery of the body had been traumatic, but the longer he studied him, the more he got the impression that the emotion in the boy's face was grief. What reason could he have to grieve for the man from the next-door farm? There couldn't have been much contact between the families, given the animosity between them. Róbert's mother laid a hand on his shoulder and steered him to a chair facing Týr and Karó. There was another seat free at the table, but Dísa went to stand by the kitchen sink instead, from where she could observe without participating. She wrapped her arms around herself, her forehead furrowed with anxiety.

Róbert stared down at the white tabletop, his legs jigging convulsively. To their surprise, he started speaking without any prompting: 'I didn't know it was them – in the news. I thought they were abroad or something. Nobody told me.'

Before Týr or Karó could respond, his mother interjected: 'We didn't know for sure, Robbi love. We'd only heard rumours. We wanted to protect you in case it turned out to be nonsense.'

Róbert didn't look up or show any sign of being placated by this.

Týr hastily stepped in before his mother could continue: 'So you didn't know until now that the murders in the news had happened on the farm next door?' Of course, this would explain the boy's reaction. Most people would be shaken and saddened by the news that their neighbours' whole family had been killed. In the same way that accidents in one's own country tend to evoke more of a response than those that happen abroad. The closer terrible events are to home, the more deeply they touch people.

Róbert shook his head. 'No. Not until I scraped the snow off the body and saw who was lying in the tub.' He raised his eyes. 'Actually, when I saw it was Íris's dad, I thought at first he'd had an accident or died of exposure or something. I ran straight home to tell my parents. Then Dad rang the police and I heard him saying that the man I'd found came from the farm where the murders had happened. That's when I understood.'

'It must have been a terrible shock.' Karó's voice was warm and compassionate. 'Was Íris a friend of yours?'

Róbert hung his head again and nodded. 'Yes. But don't tell my dad.'

Týr and Karó's eyes met for a moment, then she asked: 'Why not? Didn't he want you to be friends?'

'No. He didn't want me going out with her. Or seeing her at all. Íris's mum was just as bad. She banned Íris from talking to me. They're both as fucked up as each other.'

'Robbi!' his mother exclaimed, then immediately fell silent again.

This wasn't the time or place to start grilling the boy about his father's quarrel with the dead couple. If it emerged that the dispute had been linked to the murders, he would be questioned later, hopefully without his mother hanging over them. What interested Týr more was how the boy could have failed to notice all the comings and goings by the police and search-and-rescue volunteers to and from the crime scene. The two farms were a couple of kilometres apart, and Hvarf wasn't visible from here, but the stream of traffic heading up the road must have been out of the ordinary. 'Tell me, Róbert, hadn't you noticed the police presence in the area? Although you can't see the farm from here, you can hardly have missed all the police cars going past?'

'I was in Borgarnes, with Gran. We had an exam week at school, so I went to stay with her. I only came home this morning.' The boy looked up at his mother, his expression eloquent with a sense of betrayal, as if he had just realised that his parents must have known what was going on.

But the mother and son would have to settle their differences later. Týr continued: 'I see. How did you and Íris manage your friendship, Róbert? Did you meet up or were you only in contact via the internet or phone?'

Róbert looked up at his mother again. He gnawed his lower lip, apparently unable to decide how to answer. Luckily, his mother intervened: 'Just tell them the truth, Robbi. Secrets don't matter after what's happened.'

The boy shot a sidelong glance at Týr, then immediately dropped his eyes, though his head was no longer hanging, which was an improvement. At least his face was now visible as he replied: 'Both. We met up when we could and talked online the rest of the time.'

'Where did you meet? At Íris's house?'

'At first, yes. But then she was banned from seeing me any more, so we started meeting up at this hut on the boundary between our properties. We used to arrange to meet, then ride over there on our horses. We weren't breaking the law – just talking and having a laugh. I used to bring her chocolate and energy drinks because she wasn't allowed them at home.' Róbert's eyes were bright with unshed tears.

'When was the last time you saw her?' Karó chipped in.

Róbert sniffed, then straightened his slumped shoulders. 'Er – before I went to Gran's. On Wednesday last week. I went round to hers because her mum and dad were in Reykjavík. Then we were going to meet up on Friday evening at the hut, but the weather was terrible and she didn't show up. I tried calling her but her phone was switched off. And she didn't answer when I messaged her that evening. Didn't even read my message. I thought maybe her mum had found out that we were chatting and confiscated her phone, or heard that Íris had invited me round to the house against her orders. Or that they'd gone abroad on holiday. It never occurred to me that something bad could have happened.'

Týr, afraid the boy was about to break down, quickly asked a question to distract him: 'You and Íris must have talked about a lot of stuff when you met up. Did she mention that things at home were difficult? Or say anything that might suggest the family were in danger? Now that you think back?'

Róbert shook his head, very slowly, as if limbering his neck joints. 'No. Not really. She said her mum and dad were unbearable. They were horribly strict with her, and they kept having rows. She was more pissed off with her mum than her dad. I got the feeling she was sorry for him.'

'Because of his illness?'

'Yes. And because her mum forced him to sell their company. He wanted to keep it. There was some hassle about money too. Like he didn't get any of it, or something.'

Týr wasn't sure what the boy was referring to. He hadn't heard anything to suggest that Reynir had been stripped of his power of attorney due to mental incapacity. Nor could he see how the proceeds of the sale of their company could have ended up solely with Ása. The couple would surely have had joint ownership, though he supposed they could have made an agreement with a provision to say that the company was her private property. 'What do you mean when you say that Reynir didn't get any money?'

Robbi shrugged his thin shoulders. 'Maybe it wasn't quite like that. I expect he got something, but Íris said her mum controlled their finances. Her dad wanted to buy a small tech company and start working again but her mum wouldn't let him.'

It was possible that other members of the investigation team had already got wind of this, but it was news to Týr and Karó. 'What about the young people who were working for them at the farm? Did you meet any of them?'

'Yes and no. I never saw the girl who was with them first. She'd left by the time I got to know Íris. But I met the bloke – that Alvar. And the new girl once too. I can't remember her name.'

'She was called Sóldís.' Although Karó used the past tense, Robbi didn't seem to grasp the significance. 'What did you think of them? Did anything strike you about them?'

Like most young people, Róbert wasn't used to adults, especially strangers, asking his opinion. And about people he hadn't taken much of an interest in. He was obviously making an effort to answer conscientiously, though an adult wouldn't have used his choice of words. 'She seemed all right. Kind of ordinary. But nice, you know. I didn't like Alvar, though. He was kind of creepy.'

'Creepy? In what way?' Karó asked.

'I got the feeling he couldn't stand me. Like he didn't want me going anywhere near Íris. But then we were banned from seeing each other, so I could be wrong. But I don't think so. He was a bit fake, like he was always pretending. Smiling when he didn't mean it – that kind of guy. I asked her not to tell him we were meeting up because I didn't trust him to keep his mouth shut. He was the type to tell tales, I think. Íris didn't like him either.'

'Do you know where he went after he left? Or why he left?'

'He was sacked, I think. I don't know why and Íris didn't know either. She said he'd had a fight with her dad and been sent away. Or gone of his own accord. She wasn't sure. She didn't know what they'd been fighting about. I don't think she cared either. The new girl arrived almost straight away to replace him, so it didn't matter. That was only a week or so later.'

After this, they turned the conversation back to the boy's discovery of Reynir's body, but nothing new emerged. He had gone to bring in the horses and noticed an odd shape under the snow in the bathtub as he walked past. His story gave every sign of being true and accurate.

As soon as he'd finished, Týr asked: 'One question. What's the bathtub doing out in the field?'

The boy looked up, visibly relieved by the change of subject. 'We use it as a water trough for the mares in summer. In winter too sometimes, when it's not freezing.'

Týr nodded, trying not to betray a certain smugness about having been proved right: the tub wasn't in the field because it was being thrown away or moved somewhere.

They heard the crying of a young child from somewhere in the house, and, as they were running out of questions, they decided to bring the conversation to a close. They didn't want to leave themselves open to the accusation that they'd exploited the opportunity to interrogate a teenager while his mother was out of the room. You never knew what accusations people might bring later.

Týr and Karó left the shattered boy sitting at the kitchen table, alone with his grief. Týr felt for him. Although getting your heart broken was a normal part of growing up, it didn't usually happen with such shocking suddenness and brutality. Týr's first love, for example, had given him the boot via her friend, a nice girl who had sat with him for a while afterwards, letting him cry on her shoulder. She'd given him a toffee she'd found in her pocket. Ever since then, he hadn't been able to see that brand of toffees without feeling a brief pang. He'd been the same age as Róbert. That first jilting was actually a more painful memory than his recent break-up with the woman he'd been living with. In Týr's opinion, it would be absurd to suggest that the boy would get over it.

As they were putting on their shoes in the entrance hall, the front door opened, and Týr and Karó looked up to find themselves face-to-face with a big man wearing a set of shabby winter overalls. He was holding his work gloves and a hat that he threw down with a scowl. 'What the hell are you doing here?'

Týr straightened up, thinking it would be best if he answered. He didn't like the way the man was eyeing Karó. 'We were having a chat with your son. I take it you're Einar Ari?'

The man neither confirmed nor denied it. 'Robbi has fuck-all to do with this business. You're crazy if you think he has.'

Týr made an effort to be civil and not to let the man rile him. 'He discovered a dead body in your field. It's standard practice to talk to people under the circumstances. He's a witness, not a suspect.'

The man finally shifted his gaze from Karó to Týr, making no move to step out of their way or remove his dirty boots. 'Robbi wasn't home when it happened. He didn't go anywhere near the place.'

'So we understand.' Týr was mindful of Hördur's direct orders not to question Róbert's parents, but the temptation was too strong. He could handle a reprimand if necessary. 'But you and your wife were here,' he pointed out. 'Have you noticed anything out of the ordinary? Either last weekend or since then?'

'Like what? Screaming? Hvarf's more than two kilometres away. Of course we didn't hear anything.'

'It's not that far to the bathtub. I was thinking more about that. I was wondering whether you've been aware of anything that could help us pinpoint when the deceased ended up there, or even how he got there.'

'I heard a snowmobile.' It was Dísa who had spoken.

Týr snatched a brief glance over his shoulder at Róbert's mother in the hall, then looked back at her husband. He wanted to keep an eye on him, given that they were standing in a cramped space and the man had a reputation for violence. It was extremely unlikely that he would attack two police officers unprovoked, but better safe than sorry. Einar Ari's expression following his wife's interruption showed that he was annoyed, to put it mildly.

'When was this?' Karó asked Dísa.

'In the early hours of the morning – on either Friday or Saturday night, I can't remember which. I woke up because the baby was crying, and I thought I heard an engine outside. It sounded like a snowmobile. That's not uncommon round here so I didn't give it much thought. I only remember because it was well after midnight, which was a bit odd. It was getting on for three in the morning, I think.'

'You didn't see any reason to inform the police?'

Einar Ari was directing a murderous glare at his wife, and Týr turned to see the woman's expression as she answered Karó's question. Not taking her eyes off her husband, she replied: 'No, I didn't make the connection. Not until now.'

Týr was fairly sure this was untrue. He thought it more likely that Einar Ari had forbidden her to get involved. That in itself wasn't necessarily suspicious. It would be understandable if he wanted to keep a low profile for himself and his family after the people he'd fallen out with had been murdered.

'Hang on, are we being questioned here?' Einar Ari growled.

'No,' Týr said, catching Karó's eye. 'We're just leaving. Thanks for your help. Someone will be in touch soon to take a formal statement from you.' To his relief, Einar Ari moved aside at last, opened the door and let them out. Then slammed it pointedly behind them.

More people had arrived to swell the numbers outside. Forensics had turned up and Idunn was just climbing out of an SUV. She waved at Týr, then headed purposefully towards the cluster of people who were standing at the edge of the field, peering through the thickening haze of snowflakes at the tent which had now been secured in place.

Idunn got into her protective suit, then continued in the direction of the tent, her figure blending into the all-encompassing whiteness.

Chapter 18
Before

Sóldís toyed listlessly with the food on her plate. She didn't want the girls to notice that she had no appetite, though she needn't have worried since they were too engrossed in eating the grilled sandwiches she'd made them. She'd resorted to frying them in a pan as the kitchen wasn't equipped with a sandwich toaster. Every other kind of gadget imaginable seemed to be hidden away in the large drawers, from an electric Himalayan rock salt grater to a juicer, a raclette grill, a fondue set, an egg boiler and even a pizza oven – although pizzas were never on the menu – but no sandwich toaster.

She herself was making do with the veggie burger Ása had proposed for the girls' lunch. After all, it had to disappear from the fridge somehow. She'd take the leftovers out to the byre later. With any luck, they might appeal to one of the cows or horses. As a last resort, Lubbi and Bói could have them. They would eat anything – even Ása's health food.

'You need to come out to the byre with me.' Sóldís hoped the girls wouldn't start protesting or asking why. She didn't want to have to explain that she had no intention of letting them out of her sight, let alone of leaving them unattended in the house. There was something extremely odd going on here and she was still afraid that someone would get in through the locked doors or a secret entrance she knew nothing about. Either that or she was losing her mind in this place, beginning to forget what she had or hadn't done. Could she really have put the kettle on and left the door open? She'd been so sure that she hadn't, but by lunchtime her certainty had gradually been eroded. The more she tried to recall her exact movements, the more elusive the memories became, until she could no longer be confident of anything. It was like trying to grasp hold of mist.

As she had no way of telling which explanation was right, she had decided to assume the worst: someone was able to waltz in and out of the house whenever they liked. And if that was the case, she was responsible for the girls' safety.

'We need to let the cows and horses out for a bit. And feed the hens.'

'I'll come!' Gígja smiled at her, smears of tomato ketchup around the corners of her mouth.

'I can't be arsed.' Íris pushed her empty plate away, reached for her phone and prepared to leave the table.

Sóldís raised her voice for the first time since she'd arrived at Hvarf: 'Regardless of whether you can be arsed or not, you're coming with us.' She hadn't managed to borrow a self-empowerment book from Reynir's study, but it didn't seem to matter. Apparently, she was capable of standing her ground when she needed to. All it took was a healthy dose of fear. Amazingly, her stern tone was effective. Instead of stalking away from the table, Íris sat there looking sulky.

'I'm going out for a ride this evening,' the girl said, her tone truculent, 'so I'll see to the horses. Or one of them, anyway. I don't see why I should have to do everything.'

Sóldís said flatly: 'There's absolutely no way you're going riding this evening.'

Íris gaped at her. 'But I promised. I'm going to meet my friends. You can't ban me.'

'Sure I can. If you want to see your friends, they can come here. But you're not going out. The storm could arrive earlier than forecast and I'm responsible for your safety until your parents get back tomorrow.' Sóldís suspected that it wasn't her *friends* Íris was planning to meet but her *friend*, Robbi. No one had said anything to her about the boy being *persona non grata*, so she wouldn't be doing anything Ása or Reynir could scold her for. And what did it matter when she might be going to lose her job anyway after being caught snooping in Reynir's study?

Gígja put down her glass of milk. 'We can play *Star Wars*. The three of us and your friends, Íris. I've got loads of characters and spaceships, enough for everyone.'

Íris sighed and gave her a withering look. 'We're not playing any kids' games with you, Gígja.' She turned back to Sóldís. 'So, are you saying I can have someone round?'

'Yes,' Sóldís said, her tone softening a little. 'But let's just keep that between us. Like the toasted sandwiches. Your parents have got enough other stuff on their minds without having to worry about little things like that.' She winked at Íris, who immediately cheered up. Now she could look forward to having her friend round to visit instead of brooding on the injustices of the world and the outrageous idea that she should have to do *everything*.

To the girls' surprise, Sóldís locked the front door behind them when they went out to feed the animals. She explained this away by saying that she was worried the storm might blow it open. This seemed to satisfy them, though at that moment there wasn't a breath of wind, the door weighed a ton and, unlike most external doors, it opened outwards.

As they crossed the yard to the byre, it struck Sóldís that they would be sitting ducks if anyone wanted to harm them:

Gígja in her childish Moon Boots and yellow anorak; slender Íris in her fashionable down jacket; and she herself in her drab outdoor gear. The combined weight of all three of them in their boots would hardly be a match for one strong man, and they couldn't expect any help from Lubbi and Bói, who had come along for the outing. But the snow covering the yard bore no sign of recent footprints, and Sóldís forced herself to relax a little. The pure, crisp air was invigorating and the cloudless sky raised her spirits. The sun was shining, warming her face, carrying with it a promise of spring. They could see for miles in every direction and, reassuringly, nothing was moving in the landscape.

But as soon as they entered the byre and closed the big doors behind them, the sense of misgiving returned. There was something unsettling about being shut in like this, the only windows high up under the ceiling, so they couldn't see what was going on outside. Sóldís found her eyes drawn repeatedly to the corner where the huge axe was still propped up against the wall.

As far as the cows and horses were concerned, however, life was going on as usual. The beasts observed the humans impassively. The two cows were loose in the byre, so strictly speaking they didn't need to go outside in the depths of winter. But Ása was keen to emulate the practice of some farmers abroad she had read about, who believed in taking their cows out for a short walk every day at this time of year. She thought it was more humane than leaving them cooped up all the time. Sóldís wasn't convinced. The cows never seemed particularly eager to go out in the cold and snow. Ása's word was law, though, so while Íris let the horses out in the paddock behind the byre, Sóldís and Gígja drove the cows out of the main doors.

They herded them along at a leisurely pace for such a short distance that it hardly counted as a proper walk. The dogs kept running around the cows, leaping up and trying in vain to get them to play. Sóldís had concluded that Bói and Lubbi were under the impression that the cows were overgrown dogs and it was their duty to liven them up a little. Their lack of success never seemed to dent their enthusiasm. Meanwhile, Gígja chattered away non-stop about *Star Wars*, constantly asking which character Sóldís would be if she had the choice. Sóldís, who knew next to nothing about the *Star Wars* franchise, could only think of Darth Vader, but Gígja informed her that Darth Vader was *her* role. They still hadn't solved the problem by the time they returned the cows to the byre and gave them their hay. Then they helped Íris get the horses in, and Sóldís let Gígja offer them the rest of the veggie burgers. They sniffed at them indifferently, then put their ears back and turned away.

Íris was in an unusually good mood and kept looking at her phone as if reading messages. Sóldís guessed they were from Robbi and that she was excited about his visit. It must be a nice change for her to be allowed to meet her friend – or boyfriend – in a warm house rather than on horseback, outside in the cold. She was even happier when Sóldís suggested to Gígja that the two of them play cards or a game when the visitor came round, to give him and Íris a bit of space. Íris positively beamed and Sóldís realised she'd never seen the girl so happy before. Yet again she shook her head over Ása and Reynir's decision to home-school the girls and starve them of the chance to socialise with other kids their age.

Having dealt with the horses and cows, they went round the back of the house to see to the chickens.

Gígja's mouth turned down as they passed the sheep shed. 'I wish we still had the goats,' she said. 'They were so sweet.'

Íris gave an exaggerated groan. 'No, they weren't. They were a nightmare. Always butting you or getting up to mischief.'

'They didn't mean to.' Gígja turned to Sóldís. 'Íris is talking rubbish. They were very well behaved, really. I hope they'll come back in the spring.'

'They're not coming back, Gígja. Mum just said that so you wouldn't be upset. She's planning to convert their stable into an office or something.'

Sóldís intervened to forestall an argument that could end in tears. 'Goats are adorable, aren't they? But perhaps the new place they went to was so nice that they wouldn't want to come back. They might have made some new goat friends. It's hard to leave friends behind. Even if you're a goat.'

Íris pulled a scornful face but it didn't matter since Gígja didn't notice and seemed to accept Sóldís's explanation. She must, like Íris, have had to leave her friends behind in the States when they moved home to Iceland, so they would both know all about that kind of loss.

The chickens welcomed them enthusiastically, making up for the indifference of the bigger beasts. They were Icelandic hens, a colourful breed originally brought to the country by the Viking settlers. Sóldís didn't immediately open the gate of their run but waited until the flock had calmed down, for fear they might faint or have a heart attack and drop dead in their frantic eagerness to be fed.

Once Sóldís judged it safe, they entered the run, and her eye was caught by something colourful lying on the ground. It must have been covered in snow until the hens kicked it off in all the commotion. Handing Gígja the bucket of chicken feed, she bent down to get a closer look.

It turned out to be a small box with a sky-blue velvet lining. Sóldís took off her mittens, picked it up and realised that it was a jewellery case. Jónsi had once given her a ring in a very similar box for Christmas. The ring had been a bit too big and she'd wanted to exchange it but couldn't because he'd bought it online. When she wore it anyway, although it was loose on her finger, she got a rash that, according to the doctor, was caused by a nickel allergy. He'd added that she should avoid wearing cheap costume jewellery in future. It was pretty obvious, then, that this wasn't something Ása or Reynir would buy. They would go for the most exclusive items on offer, not fake gold off the internet.

Sóldís was about to open the box when Íris appeared beside her and snatched it out of her hands.

'What are you doing with that?' she snapped.

'It was lying there. In the snow.' Sóldís watched Íris lift the lid. The box was empty.

'Where's the necklace?' Íris looked up at Sóldís as if she should know the answer.

'I've no idea. Is it yours?'

Íris nodded. All the happiness had vanished from her face as she dropped her eyes to the ground and started peering around for the necklace in the trampled snow. 'It must be here,' she said.

Sóldís helped her search. When she asked Íris what it looked like, she said it was a little heart pendant on a gold chain. It must have been very precious to her, judging by how upset she seemed.

'What's it doing out here?' Sóldís pushed the snow back and forth with the toe of her boot.

'I don't know. I didn't bring it outside. It was on my dressing table.' The girl's voice trembled on the verge of tears.

'Could it have been in your pocket and fallen out the last time you came in here?'

'No. It was on my dressing table this morning and I haven't been out here today.'

'Are you sure?' All Sóldís could think of was that Íris might be suffering from the same brain system failure as she was, and that the dates of her saved memories had got muddled up. 'Isn't it possible that you've misremembered? None of us have been outside today and the box was already here when we arrived.'

'No. I saw it this morning.' Íris was looking again in places where she'd already kicked the snow aside. 'At least, I think I did.'

Gígja came over to see the empty box. 'I know who's taken it.'

Sóldís and Íris both looked up and asked in unison: 'Who?'

'The *búálfur*. Mummy says he's playing tricks on us. She's lost her wallet and can't find it anywhere.' A *búálfur* was a house elf in Icelandic folklore. Clearly pleased to have their attention, Gígja continued: 'He pinches things and they disappear, then he puts them back in a different place. Mummy told me. He lives in the old house. I expect he came with the house and was cross when we moved in. That's why he's playing tricks on us.'

They all turned inadvertently to the old farmhouse. Even the dogs, who were standing outside the chicken wire, looked round, following their gaze. The building no longer struck Sóldís as quaint or homely. Nor was it any consolation to hear that her peculiar experience with the remote control was not unique. Other members of the household had lost things too. There was no way on earth that she was going to sleep in the old house tonight and leave the girls alone in the new one. She'd rather make up a bed for herself on the sofa in their TV room.

Íris went back to scanning the snow at her feet. 'Don't stop looking. It has to be here somewhere.'

And so they carried on searching. But the necklace was nowhere to be found.

Chapter 19
Friday

Týr hadn't given a thought to the pungent reek of pine since Idunn and Karó had knocked on the door of his cabin. Like him, they had just emerged from the shower. Karó's wet, curly hair was caught up in a large bun, while Idunn wore her long, still-damp mane loose. It seemed he wasn't alone in feeling an urgent need to wash after seeing a dead body. Evidently the cabins were all provided with the same soap and shampoo, as the three of them smelt identical.

Idunn had been carrying a laptop under her arm, Karó a bag of pick-and-mix. She explained that she'd bought it when she was sent to the petrol station shop to buy provisions for the crime-scene team and a set of bedclothes for Idunn. As the day wore on, the pathologist had asked if accommodation could be arranged for her so she wouldn't have to drive back to town. By then it had started blowing hard, and her decision came as no surprise to Týr, given how nervous she'd been in the passenger seat in far less severe conditions. The rest of the Reykjavík contingent had hurried home ahead of the storm.

'We decided to come over to yours,' Idunn had announced, then added, when Týr hadn't immediately budged out of the doorway: 'Aren't you going to let us in?'

He'd stepped aside then, delighted to have visitors. He had fetched a bowl for the pick-and-mix, and the three of them had taken a seat at the little kitchen table. The chairs weren't designed to be sat on for long but he couldn't care less about the pain in his buttocks. The company would more than make up for the discomfort.

Idunn's laptop was open on the table and their eyes were fixed on the screen, Karó's and Týr's in particular, looking through the photos Idunn had taken of the bathtub and its immediate surroundings. There was Reynir's body in the tub before it had been disturbed. He was wearing underpants and a bloodstained T-shirt, and had a woollen blanket over his shoulders that he seemed to have made a feeble attempt to wrap around himself. His feet were bare but his hands were hidden by the frozen blanket, so it was impossible to tell if he was wearing gloves. Týr thought it was unlikely, given his state of undress. There were also photos of the body after it had been lifted out and placed on a stretcher. It was in exactly the same foetal position as it had been in the tub, the frozen blanket lying in the same folds, as if the body had been photoshopped into a different location. These were followed by some pictures of the vacated tub, and it was one of these that was holding their attention now. 'As you can see, this removes practically all doubt.' Idunn jerked her chin at the screen. At the bottom of the tub, an axe was lying in a thin layer of snow which still bore the imprint of Reynir's body. 'If that's not the murder weapon, I'll eat my hat.'

Týr and Karó didn't dispute this. The odds of a body randomly ending up in a bathtub with an axe that had nothing to do with it were vanishingly small. Especially as the blade was covered in dark stains that appeared to be dried blood.

'What the hell was the man thinking?' Karó was frowning. 'He kills his family, then walks out into the freezing cold in nothing but his underwear, wrapped in a blanket and carrying the axe. He makes it all that way, only to crawl into a bathtub on the land of his enemy?'

'I don't suppose the bathtub was his intended destination.' Idunn scrolled back to a photo of Reynir lying curled up on the stretcher, ready to be taken to the morgue in Reykjavík. According to Idunn, the fact his body had remained in the foetal position after being moved was due not to rigor mortis but to being frozen stiff. 'If I had to guess, I'd say you were right, Týr. Reynir left the house after murdering his family, intending to end his life by freezing to death. He covered an amazing amount of ground, considering the state he was in, but by the time he spotted the bathtub he must have been succumbing to confusion. Although we'll never know for sure, he may well have connected it in his mind with heat. A hot bath, in other words. But we also know that people who are dying of hypothermia tend to seek out narrow spaces, as if they're trying to hide. Nobody knows why, but that could have been the reason for Reynir's decision to crawl into the tub.' Idunn indicated the semi-naked body. 'It's possible he was more warmly dressed when he first left the house. Many hypothermia victims are found to have undressed in part or in full before they died. This is thought to be because they're overwhelmed by a sensation of burning shortly before their organs shut down. Maybe Reynir's clothes will turn up in the next thaw. It shouldn't be necessary to search far from the tub, though, since the undressing usually occurs in the final stages of hypothermia.'

Týr reached into the bowl and selected a piece of liquorice. 'What about the time of death? Were you able to make a rough estimate?'

Idunn shook her head. 'No, not at the scene. The fact that the body was frozen complicates matters. I need to know if it froze the night the murders were committed or more recently. It's going to be tricky to judge. But I'll work it out.'

'How?' Karó voiced the question Týr had decided not to ask just yet. He wanted to swallow the liquorice before being forced to listen to any grisly details.

'Like I said, it'll be tricky to establish, but there are methods, some of them complicated, others more straightforward. The contents of the stomach and small intestine, for example. If they turn out to be similar to those of the other victims – same food, at a similar stage of digestion – he'll almost certainly have died not long after them. But he may not have eaten the same meal. I'll be looking at other clues too, though. If we're lucky, his internal organs won't have frozen. But I don't think there's much hope of that since he was semi-naked and the temperatures have been below zero all week.' Idunn paused and glanced around the cabin. 'Don't you have a minibar in here either?'

'No. Just a small fridge. No wine or beer.' To Týr, this was evidence that even the most intelligent people could overlook obvious facts if they were hoping for a different outcome. Three identical cabins, all equipped with the same soap and shampoo – what were the chances that only one of them would have a minibar?

'Bugger. God, I'd give anything for a glass of wine.' Idunn craned her neck and half rose to get a glimpse of the farmhouse through the window. 'Do you think they'd sell us a bottle?'

It was the worst idea Týr had heard in a long time. Technically they were still at work and would need to get up good and early in the morning. He tactfully ignored Idunn's question. 'What's emerged so far from the post-mortems on the other bodies? Is there anything you can share with us?' The autopsy reports still hadn't arrived that lunchtime and, in light of today's developments, it was unlikely Idunn would have had time to send them.

Idunn lowered herself into her seat again. 'The draft reports will be sent out tomorrow but the results are no secret. It was all pretty much as I predicted.' She listed the main findings: 'The time of death was in all likelihood Friday night, as we thought. Probably between twelve midnight and three in the morning, give or take, but that estimate is based on more than simply the state of decomposition. If I'd based my conclusions purely on that, the time frame would have been wide open. But I worked on the assumption that they'd eaten supper at around seven, and looked to see how advanced the stage of digestion was at the point of death. Taking into consideration the fact that they were all in their night clothes and were killed in their bedrooms, we can be fairly confident it wasn't their lunch. In addition, they had accessed the internet in the period just before it dropped out in the early evening, which is a pretty clear indication that they were still alive then. But calculating the time of death from the stomach contents is not a very reliable method, so this is just for reference. The broader time frame, based on more solid evidence, is the one I'd be prepared to fall back on in court.'

'Did you find traces of sleeping pills in the girls' blood?' Týr was ready to bet that this would be the case.

'No, none at all. There was no trace of any foreign substances in their blood.' Idunn expelled a breath. 'Sadly, as it would have shown a degree of mercy, at least. Especially as their bloody father had a load of sleeping pills in his possession. All he had to do was grind up a few pills and put them in the kids' food, or in their chocolate milk or their Coke or whatever.'

Karó fished a piece of chocolate out of the bowl and put it in her mouth, then asked: 'When can we expect the results of Reynir's post-mortem?'

'That'll take a while. I need to find out how you're supposed to defrost a body in that state. It'll probably have to be thawed out slowly. I just hope it won't have to be done under refrigeration. Because if it does, that'll cause quite a delay. But the temperature outside isn't that far below zero, so it shouldn't take for ever. I'm assuming I'll be working over the weekend, though.'

At Idunn's mention of refrigeration, Týr felt a sudden urge to hurl his little fridge out of the window. He didn't want to be reminded, every time he looked in it, of Reynir's corpse, lying huddled on a shelf in a big refrigeration unit. 'What about the snowmobile?' he asked, to dispel these thoughts. 'Who was driving that?'

'Possibly someone totally unrelated to the case. You said the woman wasn't even sure which night she heard the engine noise – or if she heard right.' Idunn hadn't displayed any interest when they had reported the news of the snowmobile to the investigation team. It seemed she hadn't changed her mind on the subject, but then she was the type who would only consider evidence that was watertight. Hördur, on the other hand, had pricked up his ears and said he would call in the couple from Minna-Hvarf for formal interviews at the first opportunity. However, that had been before the axe was discovered next to Reynir in the tub. After that, Týr suspected that Hördur had lost interest in the snowmobile, since all the indications were that the murderer was right there in front of them.

But Týr couldn't shake off the conviction that the detail about the engine noise in the night was significant. 'Don't you find it at all odd that she heard a snowmobile, given that one is missing from the farm? What do you think's happened to it?'

Neither of the women was able to come up with an answer to this immediately, any more than he could. Karó was the first to propose an explanation: 'Maybe they'd sold it but hadn't yet got round to registering the change of ownership. Or they'd lent it to someone. At any rate, there was no sign of it on the route between the two farms, according to the search-and-rescue team.' Karó's mouth widened in a smile. 'All the loose ends will be tied up eventually. It shouldn't take long, now that we know who the killer was.'

Týr couldn't understand why he felt so dissatisfied. Karó was quite right: the investigation was drawing to a close. Yet various details continued to niggle at him: the snowmobile, Alvar's whereabouts, and the question of who had been present in the house after the murders. With any luck, that last mystery would be solved by Reynir's autopsy. Perhaps the contents of his stomach would turn out to be bread and cheese, consistent with the food that had been left out on the kitchen table.

'Oh, I forgot something.' Idunn looked up from the screen. 'Not that it really matters – it's just rather strange.' She closed the picture of the axe, then the folder containing the day's photos. Then she opened another, called the depressing name of 'Ása – post-mortem'. Týr screwed up his eyes and peered at the screen through his lashes, reluctant to see the dead woman's insides in sharp focus. Idunn sat back to give them a better view. 'Here it is.'

Realising that the photo didn't show anything gruesome, Týr opened his eyes properly and studied the steel tray which was empty apart from a small piece of jewellery. 'Is that a ring?'

'A wedding ring,' Idunn said. 'Nothing special about that.' She scrolled to the next photo, which was a close-up, giving a much clearer image of the ring. 'But what's engraved on it seems unusual. Mind you, what do I know? I've never been married. Anyway, the ring was Ása's.'

'What's so unusual about the inscription?' Like Idunn, Týr knew little about wedding rings and what would be considered conventional or not in relation to them. Karó shrugged, apparently in the same boat.

Idunn zoomed in on the image until they got a clear view of the inside of the ring and the inscription: $%8Reynir&$$7. 'You can't tell from this picture but the numbers and symbols were added to the name at a later date. As far as I can tell, anyway. The letters of the name show more signs of wear, as if they had been there longer. But with the additions, it resembles a password.' Idunn returned the photo to its original size. 'It's not so much the inscription that's remarkable, though, as where it was found.'

'Oh?' Karó's eyebrows lifted enquiringly. 'Where?'

'In her oesophagus. Just above the lower oesophageal sphincter – the opening to the stomach. In other words, Ása had swallowed it.'

Týr's interest in the ring abruptly intensified. 'What? Why? And when?'

'I don't know why, but she must have done it during or just before the attack. She couldn't have been walking around with it in her oesophagus – it would have slipped all the way down to her stomach. It wasn't stuck in the opening or anything like that.'

'So, you're saying that in the middle of the attack – or immediately before it – she takes off her ring and swallows it?' Týr grimaced involuntarily. He simply couldn't picture it. 'Wouldn't she have had more urgent things on her mind?'

Idunn shrugged again. 'I'm guessing Reynir might have forced her to swallow it. Perhaps the gesture was in some way symbolic for him. Their marriage could have been on its way down the toilet, and one of them could have found a new partner. Though there are no marks on her finger to suggest that the ring was forcibly removed.'

Karó chipped in at this point: 'Perhaps she took it off before she went to bed. I sometimes wear a ring and take it off at night. I keep it on my bedside table.'

Idunn nodded. 'Right. That could be what happened. There are also examples of people surviving an attack of that kind. It's clear from the post-mortem that Ása didn't die instantly. She received a massive injury to the brain but what actually killed her was loss of blood. So, theoretically speaking, she could have swallowed the ring in her death throes, whether consciously or not.'

Images from the crime scene flashed before Týr's eyes again. 'You've got to be kidding.'

'I swear to you. There are countless examples of this sort of thing. One of the most bizarre took place in America around the turn of the millennium. A man survived an axe attack by his son, despite receiving appalling injuries. I have a feeling it was something like fifteen blows, though that's not necessarily relevant. The man's neocortex was damaged and he lost the ability to think rationally. But his palaeocortex remained intact, which meant he could still perform habitual actions. Anyway, he got out of bed, horrifically mutilated as he was, and started getting ready for work. He got dressed. He emptied the dishwasher. He even brushed his teeth and must have seen himself in the mirror but was totally incapable of comprehending the state he was in. In the end, he dropped dead – from blood loss, like Ása – before he could get in the car and drive himself to work.'

It was hard to tell whether Karó's expression reflected horror or incredulity. 'So basically you're saying the bloke was dead but didn't realise it? He was a walking corpse?'

'You could put it like that, I suppose.' Idunn glanced at Týr. He couldn't hide how implausible he found the story. 'Do you think I'm making it up?'

Týr tried to put his doubts into words. 'No. Not at all. I just wonder if the blood pattern evidence could have been misinterpreted. There can't have been any witnesses and sometimes people simply draw the wrong conclusions.'

'It's possible. But I know of a similar story where there was a witness. An Icelandic story.'

Karó's eyes were out on stalks now. 'What happened?'

'It was practically a family murder. A man attacked his girlfriend and child with an axe. The woman received similar head injuries to the man in America. After her boyfriend had made off, she got up and took out the rubbish. Her neighbour found her struggling to open the bin with her left hand, which was dangling by a thread. Then she dropped dead. Just like the guy in America.'

'Christ.' The story was obviously a bit too macabre for Karó. 'That's horrible.'

Eager though Týr was to cut this conversation short, he couldn't stop himself from asking: 'How come Lína missed this? She only mentioned one family murder in Iceland. It seems odd that she should have overlooked it. Especially seeing as it involved an axe.'

'I'd never heard about it either,' Idunn said. 'I just came across it in the pathology department archives, under *axe*, when I was preparing for the post-mortem. It's probably not that well known because the husband was never charged. He killed himself in custody while the case was still under investigation. But anyone who read the papers at the time will remember it. Or at least they should.' Idunn looked from Týr to Karó before continuing: 'You're both too young. Of course, that must be it. Hang on a sec.' She fiddled with her laptop again and opened a folder labelled 'Hvarf – miscellaneous'. Then she opened a scanned document that appeared to be an autopsy report. She scrolled down the text until she got to an appendix with *CONFIDENTIAL* stamped in large, semi-opaque letters across the page. Through this, Týr thought he could read: 'Photos from the scene'.

'Are we allowed to see this?' He hoped the answer would be no and that Idunn would think better of it.

'Sure. You're both in the police, aren't you?'

Since Týr couldn't deny it, he had no choice but to look. The only alternative was to get to his feet, and risk breaking up the party.

The first photo showed a woman lying face down on a paved area in front of a black dustbin. Like Ása, she was half naked, wearing only her knickers and a top that didn't reach down to the small of her back. Beside her was a plastic supermarket bag, knotted at the top. Her arms lay at her sides, as if she had fallen on her face without using her hands to break her fall. As Idunn had said, her left hand had been practically severed at the wrist and was sticking out at an almost ninety-degree angle to her arm. Týr moved his gaze up until he could no longer see the screen.

'You see. I wasn't inventing it. She was on her way out with the rubbish.' Idunn went on scrolling. 'There's a picture here somewhere of the body after it was turned over. With the horrific head wound clearly visible – just in case you were in any doubt.'

Against his wishes, Týr lowered his gaze again until he could see the screen. The wound was the first thing that caught his eye. Idunn hadn't lied. The top of the woman's head was split open and he thought he could see brain tissue in the wedge-shaped gash. He didn't want to know if he was right, so he focused instead on the face with its staring eyes. That, at least, was fairly intact.

'Ugh.' Karó recoiled slightly. 'What happened to the child?'

'It survived. Though what its quality of life can have been like after the attack, I don't know. Its prospects can't have been that great. But all I get to see are the documents that relate to the bodies that pass through our doors. And they're all dead.'

Týr was staring fixedly at the screen. Unlike Karó, he moved closer, not further away. 'What was the woman's name, Idunn?'

Idunn regarded him in surprise. She scrolled up. 'She was called Ingigerdur. Ingigerdur Jónsdóttir.'

An involuntary cry broke from Týr's lips and he shoved himself away from the table, leaping to his feet with such violence that he knocked over his chair.

Idunn spun round, startled. 'Is something wrong?' She turned quickly back to the laptop and snapped it shut. 'Sorry. Photos like that aren't for everyone.'

She and Karó were both staring at Týr, evidently unsure what to do or say. He couldn't help them with that. It was all he could do to hold himself together. He ran his shaking hands through his hair while he was searching for the right words. He would have to explain what the matter was. Or lie to them.

He decided to tell them the truth. He was too worked up to lie convincingly.

'My mother. That's my mother.'

Chapter 20
Before

It had been a thoroughly depressing day. They'd carried on the search for the necklace inside the house. When it wasn't under Íris's bed or anywhere else in her room, they'd gone on looking in the other rooms, but it was the same story there – the necklace was nowhere to be found. Like the remote control, it seemed to have vanished into thin air. By the end, Íris had been fighting back tears. When Sóldís tried to comfort her, she'd had her suspicions confirmed: the necklace had been a gift from Robbi. Although it was getting on for suppertime by now, she noticed that Íris was still pausing to pick up the cushions on the sofa as she went past, checking underneath any loose objects and peering under the furniture. Sóldís felt a sharp pang every time it happened. Spoilt and difficult though Íris could be, she was all right really – probably a sweet kid at heart.

Sóldís had had a sinking feeling in the pit of her stomach ever since that morning when she'd noticed that the door to the connecting corridor was open, and the missing necklace had only made matters worse. On top of that, she was still mortified about the incident in Reynir's office. Although she didn't share her fears with the girls, she was becoming increasingly convinced that the intruder, who seemed to have unhindered access to the house, had taken the necklace. But she did her best to quell these thoughts for now. She had made up her mind to tell Ása the whole story when she got back. About the remote control too. It would be such a relief to share her anxiety with somebody, especially when the person in question had the power to take action – to call the police, install security cameras, hire a nightwatchman. It occurred to her that even getting fired by Reynir would be a godsend.

Until then, she would just have to take a deep breath and push the problem away. In an attempt to raise everyone's spirits, she'd got out the pizza oven and made pizzas from scratch for the girls' supper. As a first attempt, it was pretty successful, if you overlooked the fact that the bases were a bit misshapen and there was no pepperoni. Gígja had assisted with the cooking, though this had been more of a hindrance than a help. The little girl had also laid the table. When Sóldís served up the pizzas, she noticed that some of the knives and forks were the wrong way round and crooked too. Ása would have exclaimed in annoyance but Sóldís didn't care.

The prospect of her imminent conversation with Ása got Sóldís thinking. Were there maybe security cameras installed in the house already? If so, they'd be able to watch the recordings and find out what, if anything, was going on. She hadn't noticed any cameras when she was cleaning, but they might be carefully concealed. She'd heard of cameras being hidden in teddy bears to spy on nannies, for example. So presumably there was nothing to say they weren't concealed in some of the paintings that she was required to clean with a feather duster.

'Can I ask you something, Íris?' Sóldís put a slice of pizza on the plate the girl was holding out. 'Have you got a burglar alarm? With security cameras?' Now that she'd said it aloud, the answer seemed blindingly obvious. In a house like this where everything was so carefully designed and electronically controlled, it would be extraordinary if they didn't have a security system. Especially given that Reynir was clearly concerned enough to monitor his office. Why wouldn't the same apply to the rest of the house?

Íris put her plate down on the table. 'We used to. With cameras everywhere. But Dad took them down.' She pointed to a corner of the ceiling high above them. 'There was one just there. Those ugly plastic caps were put in instead.'

Sóldís twisted round and saw the yellowish plastic cap, like the kind used to cover an electrical socket, contrasting with the pristine white of the paintwork. Sóldís had seen plastic covers like that dotted around the house without paying them any attention. But now she came to think about it, they were out of keeping with the flawless finish everywhere else. The design had been so minutely planned that the presence of unused electrical sockets, sited in such impractical locations as the ceiling, simply didn't fit. Sóldís turned back to the table. 'Do you think it would be possible to reinstall the system?'

'No. Dad threw out the cameras.'

Sóldís handed a slice of pizza to Gígja. 'Do you have any idea why?'

Íris had taken a mouthful and was too well brought up to speak until she had swallowed. 'No, I haven't a clue. Unless they were no good and Dad wanted to replace them. But they never got round to it.' She darted a glance at Gígja, her eyes narrowed. 'Lucky for you. Otherwise I'd have a recording of you pinching my necklace.'

'Uh-uh. I didn't take it.' Gígja didn't let a mouthful of food prevent her from defending herself. 'I'm not interested in necklaces. I'm only collecting *Star Wars* models.'

'Let's say no more about the necklace. It'll turn up sooner or later. If not, I'll help you find another one exactly the same online. The person who gave it to you need never know.' Sóldís didn't want to mention Robbi by name in front of Gígja. The boy was on his way round and it would ruin things for Íris if Gígja started teasing her about her boyfriend in his presence.

Sóldís dropped the subject of the security system as well, since plainly there was nothing more to be said about that.

* * *

Sóldís's attempts to prevent Gígja from teasing her sister were in vain. After they'd finished eating, there was a knock at the door and when Íris ran to answer it, Gígja called after her in a sing-song voice, asking why she was so dressed up and was she making herself pretty for her boyfriend.

It didn't require any particular powers of observation to notice this, since Íris had changed into some of the smart designer gear that she seemed to collect with the same zeal as Gígja did her *Star Wars* merchandise.

The boy who appeared with Íris shortly afterwards was dressed far more conventionally, in jodhpurs and a jumper, emitting a definite whiff of horse. Sóldís knew he'd ridden over, as Íris had announced that he would need to put his horse in their stable. Robbi hovered awkwardly after Sóldís had introduced herself and shaken hands. His sigh of relief was almost audible when Íris suggested they go through into the other room. As far as he was concerned, Sóldís was a grown-up and a stranger, which made her an uncomfortable presence. She bit back an impulse to call after him that she was still young – and a nice person too. Instead, she watched as they disappeared in the direction of the TV room. Then called after them that she could make popcorn, if they liked. But the only answer she got was the scowl Íris sent her over her shoulder. Clearly, Sóldís's presence was not required, not even to pass a bowl of popcorn through the door.

'Well, Gígja. It's just the two of us.'

Ordinarily, Gígja would have made no secret of her pleasure at this, since it would have meant that something fun was about to happen. But the tense atmosphere hadn't escaped her notice, and her face fell when Sóldís pointed out that they were alone.

'Do you know karate, Sóldís?' Gígja looked at her hopefully. 'I don't.'

Sóldís considered telling a lie but decided against it. She was a hopeless liar and Gígja was sure to want her to demonstrate some moves, which would immediately give her away. 'No, I don't either. But luckily it doesn't matter because I don't think either of us have any need for it.'

Gígja looked dubious. 'But what if there's a bad man outside? What if he stole Íris's necklace? What will we do?'

'We don't need to do anything, Gígja. If a bad man took the necklace, he'll be far away by now. Burglars only steal things – they don't hurt people.' This wasn't strictly true, but Sóldís knew it wouldn't make Gígja feel any braver to hear that – rare as it was for burglars to attack people – it did happen. 'Anyway, I'm positive the necklace will turn up. And there's no bad man outside.'

Gígja nodded slowly and seemed a bit happier. 'But what about the *búálfur*? He lives indoors.'

Sóldís smiled, though she found the idea unsettling, given the source of her greatest anxiety. 'There's no house elf here. And if there was, I'm sure he would live in a rock like other elves.'

'Yes. They live in rocks.' Gígja gave a firm nod.

It must be nice to be a child, able to select what to believe in.

'So we won't need to know karate,' Gígja concluded.

Her natural cheerfulness restored, the little girl dragged Sóldís into her room to play the longed-for *Star Wars* game that Sóldís had been promising her. She pulled out her toy box from under her bed and starting taking out all kinds of figurines, weird and wonderful creatures, robots and spaceships. The toys were rather battered and some of the figures were missing an arm or a leg, and one its head. The spaceships had also been knocked about in the course of Gígja's games, and Sóldís soon saw why. Gígja treated them like darts, hurling them around the room as if they would fly instead of crashing to the floor.

The box turned out to contain various other objects Gígja had accumulated as part of her collection, though they didn't belong to the *Star Wars* world. She had drafted them in to the invented universe, finding roles for them that bore testimony to her imagination. A broken computer mouse called Grúm became a device for securing asteroids to prevent major collisions. There was also a corkscrew with a broken arm that she referred to as Skrúf, which was used to discover water on new planets. Among the various other everyday objects mixed in with the *Star Wars* models, there was one item in particular that caught Sóldís's eye.

It was a small black remote control, with only two buttons and a tiny screen, that Sóldís guessed might have belonged to the security system before it was dismantled. It was obviously broken and held together by sticky tape. Gígja swung it over her head, making a noise that was better suited to playing with cars than spaceships.

'Is that a remote control, Gígja?'

'No. It's a Trezor. A rocket that can blow up moons with its laser.' Gígja carried on brandishing the device in front of her.

Taking care not to sound angry or accusatory, Sóldís asked: 'Do you sometimes use remote controls in your games? As spaceships?'

Gígja shrugged. 'No. Why?'

'I was just wondering if my remote control could have been used as a spaceship at some point. It went missing, remember? If it was, I don't mind.'

'No. I didn't take it.'

Sóldís pointed to a cheap ring with big fake red gems that she guessed had once belonged to Íris. Gígja had explained to her that it was a crown – for the queen of the universe. 'I was wondering if you could have borrowed Íris's necklace for your game? Maybe you were meaning to give it back to her tonight?'

'No. There aren't any necklaces in *Star Wars*.' Gígja gave Sóldís a quick, pitying glance. 'The *búálfur* took it. Like Mummy's wallet.' She stopped waving the little remote control around and looked back at Sóldís. 'There aren't any wallets in *Star Wars* either.'

'No. Of course not.' Sóldís decided to drop the subject. She didn't entirely believe that Gígja was telling the truth and was beginning to think the child might be behind all the strange goings-on: the kettle, the missing remote control and necklace, and possibly even the footprints in the hall. Admittedly, she couldn't quite picture how Gígja was supposed to have done that, but there had to be a rational explanation for everything. It was a much, much more palatable idea than that a stranger – or Reynir – was the culprit. Perhaps the little girl didn't even remember doing it.

'Do you sometimes walk in your sleep, Gígja?'

The girl shrugged. 'I don't know. Because then I'm asleep.'

Sóldís decided to abandon her questions and they carried on with the game. From time to time, she rummaged in the heap of toys in case the necklace was lurking there but didn't find anything of interest. Nevertheless, she became increasingly confident that she'd hit on the right explanation for all the mysterious incidents and her heart lifted with relief. Her happiness was complete when Gígja got bored of the game at long last and stopped playing.

What came next was not actually much of an improvement. They played Ólsen-ólsen in the kitchen until Íris and Robbi reappeared. At first, Sóldís was surprised his visit was over so early, as it was only 10 p.m. Then she realised that the boy must be visiting Íris behind his parents' backs, and presumably wouldn't be able to go home much later than this without rousing suspicion.

He said goodbye with a polite 'thank you for having me' and managed to meet Sóldís's eye for a split second before lowering his gaze again. She answered, as custom dictated, 'Thanks for coming', and left it at that. It would not be popular if she got up and accompanied him to the door with Íris. No doubt every second they could grab alone together inside the warm house was precious.

'He's weird. Like Íris.' Gígja was clearly unimpressed with Robbi. 'I'm not going to have a boyfriend when I grow up.' She beamed at Sóldís. 'Like you.'

Sóldís succeeded in returning the smile, though laughter was far from her mind. She heard the front door close, only to open again shortly afterwards. Íris was yelling something that Sóldís couldn't make out, but there was no mistaking the girl's distress. Sóldís ran towards the hall, almost colliding with Íris who was racing round the corner, crying breathlessly: 'Robbi's horse! Robbi's horse!'

Sóldís grabbed her by the shoulders in an attempt to calm her down. 'What? What's happened?'

'The byre. The door was open. His horse has gone. Somebody's opened the door and taken it.'

Sóldís breathed through her nose in an attempt to steady herself. 'Right, come on.' She looked over her shoulder and told Gígja: 'Wait here.' Then she changed her mind; they'd better stick together for safety's sake. 'Actually, no. You come with us, Gígja.'

Robbi was outside, in a frantic state. Sóldís went straight over to him. 'Is there any chance that the door wasn't properly shut?'

'No. I shut it. I'm sure.'

'He wouldn't have made a mistake about closing the byre doors. No way,' Íris said loudly, the words tumbling out in a rush. 'No way. Someone's stolen his horse.'

'What am I supposed to tell Dad?' Poor Robbi was fighting back tears. If he started crying, Íris was bound to do the same, then it would be impossible to get any sense out of them.

'We'll find your horse.' Sóldís walked the short distance across the yard to the byre. The door was open and she reached in to switch on the outside lights. The cows stood in the doorway, watching, bemused. They were loose and could have escaped too but they didn't seem interested – any more than they were in the winter walks that Ása believed did them so much good.

Something compelled Sóldís to stick her head into the byre and check that the axe was still there in the corner. When it was, she felt absurdly relieved. She wished she could quietly dispose of it in the dustbin. Was it meant to be a tool or a weapon? She couldn't think of any circumstances on the farm that would require the use of an axe. There were no trees here or anything else that might need to be chopped down. Feeling a prickle down her spine as she had the first time she laid eyes on the sinister-looking blade, she quickly withdrew her head.

The outside lights provided enough illumination for Sóldís to be able to examine the snow outside the byre. There were all kinds of tracks: footprints made by her and the girls earlier, and by Íris and Robbi and his horse, both in and out of the byre. But there was no way of telling whether any of them belonged to somebody else, since there were too many, over too large an area.

'Let's try following the hoofprints. He may not have gone far.'

'But what are we to do if the person who stole him won't give him back?' Íris said despairingly.

'Have you got a gun? A rifle?' Robbi asked.

'No. Jesus!' Sóldís realised many farms would probably have a gun of some kind. 'There's nothing like that here and we're not going to shoot anyone.' Thank God, Robbi didn't know about the axe, she thought. It would be little better than a firearm in the hands of a teenager. If he tried to use it, he was more likely to injure his horse than the thief.

They followed the hoofprints to the limits of the glow provided by the outside lights. Then, faced by the wall of darkness beyond the circle of light, Sóldís halted. 'This is far enough.' She had no intention of blundering about in the gloom with the kids in tow, let alone of going ahead on her own.

'But we can use our phones.' Íris dug a hand into her coat pocket.

'No.' Sóldís gestured to the hoof marks at her feet. 'Look. There are no footprints beside him. I expect he just got out somehow and is heading straight home. No one's stolen him.'

Robbi scowled. 'The thief could be riding him.' After a moment, he admitted: 'Though he left the saddle and bridle behind.'

Sóldís drew a deep breath. 'If that's the case, there's no point us trying to chase him. The horse will be moving too fast.' She paused to think. 'Maybe we should ring the police. They might be able to track the horse down – and the person who's riding him, if that's what's happened.'

Íris held out her phone. 'You make the call.'

Sóldís dialled 112. She explained what had happened and was told she was being put through to the duty officer in Akranes. A ringing tone followed and Sóldís put her hand over the receiver while she explained to the kids what was happening. Íris immediately snatched her phone back. 'No. I don't want the Akranes police involved. Dad will be furious.'

'Yes.' Gígja nodded, her eyes wide. 'They might take away his greenhouse.'

Before Íris could tell her to shut up, Robbi interrupted, sounding almost frightened. 'Dad'll go mental too. I don't want anyone coming out from Akranes. I really don't.'

Sóldís tried to control her temper. 'Exactly which police did you think were going to come, then?' she asked, exasperated. 'The police from Reykjavík? Or from the other side of the country?'

'Isn't there some kind of force that deals with crimes involving animals?' Íris clearly wasn't very wise in the ways of the world. Or perhaps she was too used to a different world. Maybe there was a police force dedicated to animals where she used to live in America. But before Sóldís could enlighten her about the organisation of the Icelandic police, the phone started ringing in Íris's hands. She looked at the screen, then hastily dismissed the call. 'It's 112. I'm not answering.'

Robbi had begun to shift from foot to foot and show signs of agitation. 'How am I going to get home?'

'You can borrow one of our horses.' Íris wrapped her arms around herself. 'We'll find yours tomorrow.'

Gígja stamped her foot. She had pulled on a pair of Moon Boots in her hurry to go outside, so the stamp could hardly be heard. 'No. You're not taking our horses. Your daddy might kill them.'

Sóldís hastily intervened. There was no time to waste on arguing. 'Can you drive a snowmobile, Robbi?' He nodded. 'Then take one of ours. You can bring it back tomorrow. It'll get you home quicker too.' She didn't actually care if his parents were angry with him because he was home late, she was much more concerned about his safety on the way. The faster he travelled, the less danger he would be in. Or so she reasoned.

Robbi agreed, and a few minutes later they watched him ride away on the snowmobile with his saddle in front of him and the bridle and halter in the luggage compartment. He'd said he was going to take the shortest route, along the valley, and Sóldís and the girls walked beyond the byre and sheep shed so they could watch his progress for as long as possible. When the lights of the snowmobile had finally faded from view behind a rise in the ground, they hurried back inside and Sóldís carefully locked the door. After they had taken off their outdoor clothes, Íris hugged herself again and said: 'The byre doors were definitely shut. Robbi wouldn't have forgotten to close them.'

'Right, we'll sleep in the TV room.' No way was Sóldís going to lie awake, wondering who might be creeping around the house and even entering the girls' rooms. The relief she'd felt when she suspected Gígja of being behind all the strange happenings had proved short-lived. Gígja couldn't possibly have opened the byre doors and let out the horse as she hadn't left Sóldís's side for a minute, except to go to the loo, and then Sóldís had heard the flush and the sound of the tap running. 'We'll fetch our duvets and pillows and make ourselves comfortable in there.'

Neither of the girls raised any objections.

* * *

Sóldís was woken by a scream from Íris. It took her a moment or two to work out where she was after rising up on her elbow. Gígja sat up at the same time, rubbing the sleep from her eyes and yawning, then looked around her in surprise. 'Oh, right. We're in here.'

Íris was screaming something incomprehensible. Sóldís asked in a voice still croaky with sleep: 'What? What's wrong?'

'Look! Look!' Íris held out one arm and showed Sóldís the back of her hand. On it someone had written in thick, black marker pen: 'Whore'.

Sóldís dropped Íris's thin-boned hand, shooting a glance towards the door. It was standing wide open and the light was on in the hall. Yet when they went to bed, the door had been shut and all the lights had been off.

Chapter 21
Friday

'How is it possible that you didn't know?' Idunn was still deeply shocked. She had apologised for the pictures so many times that Týr's head was spinning. Karó had said nothing, perfectly complementing the awkward atmosphere. The confined cabin only made matters worse as it provided no way out of the mortifying situation. Týr had even considered shutting himself in the tiny toilet, just to catch his breath and try to get his thoughts under control. He didn't dare, though, for fear of being overwhelmed by claustrophobia. He already felt as if the walls and ceiling were closing in on him.

It was a nightmare finding out something as devastating as this in the presence of people he barely knew. Though, on reflection, perhaps it was better than being among friends. At least the two women refrained from patting him on the shoulder or gazing deep into his eyes with sorrowful expressions and speaking to him in voices oozing pity.

He rubbed his eyes and tipped back his head to fix his gaze on the pine ceiling panels in an effort to concentrate. Idunn's question hung in the air and he felt compelled to answer it. This grotesque situation wasn't her fault. He would have to get that across to her. It was the least he could do. Anything else would be unfair. 'I was quite simply told a lie,' he said. 'And I had no reason to disbelieve it.'

Idunn cleared her throat. 'Is there any chance that this could be a completely different woman? That the whole thing is just a horrible coincidence? Her son was called Angantýr. She didn't have any other children.'

'No. It's her, all right. My name must have been changed, shortened from Angantýr to Týr. It's definitely her.' Týr was in no doubt at all, though the same thought had flashed through his mind once he had got over his initial shock. It wasn't uncommon for people to look alike. It could have been a coincidence too that the dead woman was called Ingigerdur Jónsdóttir, though his birth mother had always been referred to as Inga in his hearing, and that her patronymic had been Jónsdóttir. But they had the same birthdate and had died on the same day, which pretty much ruled out that possibility. And when it transpired that the murderer, her former live-in boyfriend and the father of her child, shared his own father's name, that clinched it, even if his name – Gunnar Sigurdsson – was relatively common. 'It's definitely her,' he said again.

'But . . .' Idunn broke off and seemed to be trying to choose between the countless questions she must be dying to ask. 'Even if you were lied to, wouldn't somebody have told you – accidentally let it slip, I mean? Someone other than your adoptive parents?'

'Who was there to do that? We moved. Left the country while I was still a kid. I always thought it was because my parents wanted to work abroad, but now I'm sure they had an ulterior motive – as you just said. They wanted to make sure it wasn't flung in my face at some point. It was around the time I started middle school. I suppose they thought teenagers were more likely to hear rumours and be cruel.' Týr expelled a breath, trying to shake off the horror, then lowered his eyes from their contemplation of the ceiling. 'It probably helped too that the case was never that high-profile because nobody was charged. Presumably the identities of the people involved were never made public. But Iceland's a small country and there was a risk that word would get around anyway, so they changed my first name. And I got a new patronymic when they adopted me. Who would ever suspect that I was linked to the case? Today I'm Týr Gautason, not Angantýr Gunnarsson.'

'Wait? Is that allowed?' Idunn was clearly clinging to the hope that the whole thing was a misunderstanding. 'Changing the name of a minor and not giving them a say in the matter?'

'It must be. Because the name on my passport is Týr.'

Karó seemed to have found her tongue again. 'What about . . . you know . . .' She gestured vaguely at Týr's face. 'The scar?'

Týr's hand went instinctively to the rough skin on his forehead. 'I was told I'd fallen off my tricycle, but I suppose it must have been made by an axe.' He fell silent as he registered the implications. Closing his eyes, he tried without success to recall any memories, however fragmentary, associated with the experience. 'Why can't I remember? Aren't childhood traumas supposed to stay with you?'

Idunn coughed, then said carefully: 'Head injuries as serious as that are often associated with amnesia. In both adults and children. That's why it can be difficult to get any sense out of the victims of this kind of attack. And you were only four years old. It's hard enough to remember anything from that age, even without a head injury. I'd have thought it would be futile for you to try to recall it.'

Týr suspected she was right, judging by the total blank he'd drawn when trying to think back. Perhaps he just needed a bit of peace and quiet, and he'd have more success when he was alone.

If, that is, he even tried. Was it desirable to have memories of something that traumatic? Almost certainly not. He straightened his slumped shoulders. It took almost all the strength he had left to say: 'I'd rather you two kept this to yourselves, if you don't mind. I need a bit of time to process it before I tell anyone.' The fact was, he wanted to wait until the investigation of the farm murders was over, because if he suddenly announced that he had survived an axe attack by his own father, he would instantly be transferred to other cases. Especially as he would be forced to admit that, rather than withholding the information when he applied to the police, he had been totally unaware of it himself. He was bound to be taken off any case that was remotely interesting and packed off to see a psychologist. And that mustn't happen, because it was vital for him to see this investigation through. If he didn't, he might never be able to face working on another murder case again. Like a rider who has fallen off a horse, he had to get straight back in the saddle. Not sit at a desk, poring over files. 'Preferably after this investigation is over.'

They both nodded and muttered their agreement. Karó looked him briefly in the eye before lowering her gaze and saying quietly: 'Do you think they don't know? The people who hired you? They must have looked you up on LÖKE. You should be there in connection with the case, even if it didn't go to court.'

Týr had no answer to that. He was struck by a faint, foolish hope that it might all be a big misunderstanding. But common sense immediately reasserted itself. 'I expect my name change is the reason why I'm not in LÖKE. I don't think the database is linked to the national registry.'

Karó looked sceptical. 'Your ID number shouldn't have changed. Isn't it likely that they'd have searched under that rather than your name?'

The storm outside suddenly reminded them of its presence with a screaming buffet of wind strong enough to shake the walls, yet Týr felt an overwhelming compulsion to get out of the cabin. He wanted to stand in the roaring storm, blinded by the snowflakes, the raging elements reflecting the turmoil inside him. 'Huldar was responsible for hiring me,' he said, after a pause. 'It would be just like him to take the lazy option and make do with my name. Týr's not that common, after all. I'm probably the only Týr Gautason in Iceland. And since there's unlikely to be anyone in the database under that name, he must have assumed I had a clean record and was free from undesirable connections. Besides, he wouldn't have been expecting to find anything on me, as I moved abroad when I was twelve, which wouldn't have given me time for much of a criminal record in Iceland. And all my documents and references from Sweden were OK.'

Neither of the women found fault with this line of reasoning. On the other hand, they were aghast when Týr said the first thing he was going to do when he got back to town was to call up all the records of the old case. He would see for himself what it said about him on LÖKE. Karó was even more vehement than Idunn in her desire to dissuade him, warning that it would be tantamount to handing in his resignation. It was strictly prohibited to search the database except in connection with cases under investigation, and police employees' use of the system was carefully logged.

'I'll get hold of the records for you,' Idunn chipped in, as soon as Karó had finished. 'I've got most of the archives on our server and I can call up anything that's missing. I'll put in a request, explaining that I want to look at the historical case because it has similarities to the current one. No one will question my right to do that. You can have a look at the files on my computer.'

Týr didn't know what to say apart from: 'Thanks.'

'No problem. You can owe me one.' Idunn smiled faintly. 'If it's any comfort, you're not the only one with an unusual family background.' She didn't elaborate and Týr was too preoccupied with his own thoughts to ask what she meant.

No one had touched the bowl of sweets since the moment Týr had emitted that dreadful cry at the sight of his mother. He eyed the contents, wondering how he could have had any appetite for them a few minutes ago, yet somehow he couldn't tear his gaze from the bowl. Idunn noticed.

'Týr, I've got a sedative if it would help. I can fetch it from my cabin. It would let you get some sleep tonight.' She checked her phone. 'It's late.' Then, after a pause, she added: 'But we can stay and keep you company, if you'd like.'

'No. Thanks all the same. And I'll pass on the pills. I'm sure I'll get to sleep.' He wasn't fooling anyone. The fact was, he would probably lie awake until morning. He might even give in to the impulse to ring his parents in the middle of the night and ask what the hell they'd thought they were doing. Though that would be unwise. He needed to get a grip on himself before having that conversation.

Karó seemed to read his thoughts. 'It's none of my business, of course, but I think I can understand what motivated your parents. They must have wanted to protect you. That's all. It's not easy being constantly stared at.' She broke off, but she didn't need to say any more. Týr and Idunn were well aware that she was referring to herself.

There they sat, the three of them, in the poky little cabin. The only thing linking them was their job, but this latest development had brought them closer together. Not only did they now share a secret, but both women had hinted that their own childhoods had been far from idyllic. Nothing like as traumatic as what he'd been through, perhaps, but still.

Idunn and Karó got up and started pulling on their coats. They said a rather awkward goodbye, transparently searching for some parting words of encouragement. It didn't help that he was feeling so dazed. He avoided meeting their eyes and said the bare minimum in reply.

Once he was alone, he was seized by a disorientating sense of unreality. He had never experienced anything like it before. He wasn't who he thought he was but someone else entirely. Not Týr but Angantýr. And the name rang no bells, which only added to his feeling of disorientation.

The reek of pine reasserted itself, now that it was no longer overlaid by the scent of the women's shampoo. He closed his eyes and inhaled through his mouth. Then, without thinking, he took his coat from the peg and went outside into the teeth of the blizzard.

He didn't go far. Luckily, he was still conscious of the need to take care. He only took a few steps away from the door, far enough to break his imaginary tie to the cabin. Then he just stood there, letting himself be buffeted by the blast, pellets of snow stinging his face. His hood ballooned out with air and he rocked on his feet, all his attention focused on trying to keep his balance. In a strange way it was cathartic. He didn't know how long he'd been standing there before he started feeling a little better, his breathing returned to normal and his heartbeat slowed. Even his thoughts had untangled themselves enough to develop coherently. He shook off the snow, resolving to deal with them later. His sense of equilibrium was so precarious that it wouldn't take much to destroy it and set him back to square one.

As Týr went inside, he noticed that the lights were off in Idunn and Karó's cabins. It would have done him good to get some sleep as well but he knew he was still too wired. He should have accepted Idunn's offer of a pill, but it was too late now. Having brushed off the worst of the snow, he sat down at the table again, pushing the bowl of pick-and-mix aside, and pulled over his laptop. An internet search on his mother's murder yielded little he didn't already know. The incident had been reported, as had the arrest of his biological father, but there was scant information beyond the statement that a murder had been committed and a child attacked.

The articles contained the standard text used by the police to get reporters to back off: *No further details can be provided at this point.* Although the public generally had to wait until the trial to get the full picture, usually at least the main facts of the case were reported once the investigation had been concluded. But not in this instance. There was no trial, and the main suspect, Týr's father, had killed himself. The fact that this had occurred in police custody would explain the lack of willingness to update the media. The police had waited out their interest, merely issuing a bald statement that a man had confessed to the recent attack on his girlfriend and their child, which had resulted in the woman's death. This was followed by a single sentence noting that the guilty party had taken his own life following his confession, and that since it had been consistent with the evidence, the case had been closed. As these few details had been published before the Icelandic media went online, Týr had to read scans of the articles in the newspaper archives. And there were no comments or links to blog posts or discussions on social media. By the end, Týr was no closer to understanding what had caused his birth father's murderous frenzy than before he had started.

Týr leant back in his chair and groaned. His mind was going a mile a minute and his head felt as if it was about to explode. There was no way he would get to sleep now, but there was nothing more to be gained from browsing. He bent forward to his laptop again. He might as well immerse himself in the current investigation until he couldn't keep his eyes open another minute.

He connected to his computer in the Reykjavík office, which enabled him to access the departmental server. Since he had been sent to Hvalfjördur, a tonne of files had been uploaded to the area created for the investigation, a veritable smorgasbord of information. He didn't know where to start, but, in the circumstances, he thought it best to finally get stuck into the driest, most tedious material – the couple's finances. Sums of money and other figures were unlikely to trigger thoughts of his mother's murder. With luck, he might even nod off. He'd been close to falling asleep on his keyboard often enough during his stint in economic crimes in Stockholm.

There was a brief status report, providing a useful summary of the couple's financial arrangements, and concluding that the investigation team still hadn't managed to track down the bulk of their assets. It had been confirmed, however, that these assets had definitely existed following the sale of their company. It appeared that a good half of the money had disappeared from their joint investment account before they moved home to Iceland. According to the author of the report, the investigators were trying to follow the trail but the fact that the transaction took place abroad was seriously complicating matters. The information had to be approached in a roundabout way and required all kinds of permits. They would get there in the end, but it would take time, and it was still only a little more than forty-eight hours since the bodies had been found.

One thing was clear, however: neither Ása nor Reynir had filed a complaint or reported the money missing or declared that they were victims of fraud.

Týr stared at the screen after he had finished reading. He wasn't particularly surprised. Like those who had compiled the report, he believed that the money must have been squirrelled away in a tax haven following the sale of the company. The way they'd transferred their wealth before moving back to Iceland was textbook behaviour, part of a plan, no doubt, to hoodwink the tax authorities in both countries. It would have been harder to make the money disappear once they were living in Iceland. Indeed, it was difficult to imagine any other explanation for this opacity, unless the couple had bought shares with the missing money as a dodge to avoid paying capital gains tax on their profits. Either that or they were worried by the prospect of a left-wing government imposing a wealth tax. They could have had any number of motives, but ultimately the purpose was to contribute as little as possible to society. People didn't keep their money and other assets in tax havens merely for convenience.

Týr closed the file and skimmed through the titles of the other documents. He spotted a number of witness statements but wasn't familiar enough with the Reykjavík end of the investigation to be entirely sure of their connection to the case. The police had spoken to relatives, friends and acquaintances – both Icelanders and foreigners, he guessed from their names. Those with foreign names had been interviewed more recently; most of the files dated from earlier that day. So it was possible they might contain something relevant that had yet to be shared with the rest of the team. Any older information of significance had already been communicated to everyone, including him.

The third file Týr opened finally produced something of interest. The first two had been conversations with an American woman friend of Ása's and a departmental manager from their company. Both had nothing but good to say about the couple and had expressed their shock and horror over the family's fate. They hadn't been told that Reynir was a suspect and, since it didn't seem to occur to them that he could have been guilty of such appalling crimes, they were unlikely to spread any rumours to that effect.

The third interview was with the former HR manager at their company. She had left her job after the change of ownership and seemed to have a rather different take on things from the manager who was still employed there. Or perhaps she was so busy with her new job at an even bigger software company that she didn't have time for pretence.

The woman's statement was blunt, to say the least. According to her, everything had been going well until Reynir fell ill, but then he had started behaving erratically, though no one could work out why at first. When he got his diagnosis and the tumour was removed, the staff had all fervently hoped that he would return to work fully recovered and back to his old self. But no such luck. Although the tumour had been successfully operated on, his personality had been affected and his behaviour had become unpredictable. He started taking rash decisions, though Ása usually intervened in time to stop them or at least limit the damage. Instead of being his old professional, meticulous self, he had become reckless, taking crazy risks. And his decisions didn't work out, though Ása did her best to sweep his mistakes under the carpet. In the HR manager's opinion, Ása had been hoping, not unnaturally, that her husband would make a full recovery in time. But it was clear to most of their employees that this was totally unrealistic.

In the end, Ása had decided to sell up. Reynir had taken it badly but been forced to agree. The HR manager said it was no secret that their marriage had been on the rocks. Reynir had wanted a divorce, only to change his mind later. She had no idea what had caused this change of heart, because before that they had looked as if they were heading for a break-up. Reynir had embarked on an affair with one of the programmers, a young woman who Ása had wanted to fire when she found out. She had reconsidered, though, when it was pointed out to her that the young woman could sue them for unfair dismissal and sexual harassment in the workplace, since there was such a major imbalance of power between Reynir, one of the main owners and partners in the company, and the girl who had only recently been appointed.

The HR manager didn't know where the young woman was now, as she had handed in her notice. Nor could she say whether her resignation had been related to a non-disclosure agreement, requiring her to leave the company and refrain from commenting on the relationship or bringing a lawsuit against Reynir. Whatever had happened, the couple had patched up their differences not long afterwards, Reynir had fallen back into Ása's arms and nothing had come of the divorce. They had sold the company and moved back to Iceland, and this was the first news the HR manager had heard of them since they had left. Unlike the other two interviewees in the US, she had asked straight out whether Reynir was a suspect. Naturally, she had got no response.

Týr frowned at the document. Could the missing money have been used to buy the young programmer's silence? If so, it was one of the most generous settlements he'd ever heard of. Reading the paragraph again, he realised that this couldn't be the case. Reynir's girlfriend had left before the company was sold. And it went without saying that the money couldn't have disappeared before the couple had taken receipt of it. Unless, that is, Reynir had been forced to agree to the sale in order to buy her silence.

Hopefully things would become clearer in due course, though Týr wasn't optimistic.

One thing was sure, though. The HR manager's statement about Reynir's condition and the cracks in the marriage fitted in well with the theory the police were working on: that Reynir was the killer.

Yet, strangely, Týr was aware of a niggling doubt. There were details that didn't fit, but then there always were, he reminded himself. As a rule, he managed to keep his eye on the ball and didn't let a few loose ends trouble him. Because most things were usually clarified in the end, and everyone was happy with the result, except the guilty party, of course. Could his reluctance to accept the self-evident this time have something to do with his own circumstances? Was he nursing a hope, deep down, that his biological father had been wrongly accused of his mother's murder? If so, he ought to go on leave immediately – tell Huldar about his discovery and withdraw from the investigation.

Uh-uh. No way.

He carried on reading through the files.

Chapter 22
Before

The back of Íris's hand was an angry red and Sóldís guessed that she was still scrubbing at it, though the ugly message had long ago been erased. Sóldís had been forced to step in earlier that morning when Íris had rubbed her skin until it bled. Sóldís had pursued her into the kitchen after the commotion, to find her at the sink, scrubbing frantically at the letters with the washing-up brush. The water running down the plughole was no longer black but pink with blood. It was too late for Sóldís to take a photo of the word. She'd been intending to send it to Ása to hammer home the message that she had to do something to guarantee her family's safety.

Instead, Sóldís had called her. It had taken her several attempts as Ása didn't pick up until nearly midday. By then, the weak winter daylight had banished the shadows and they were all feeling a little calmer. Sóldís had got over the worst of the shock, but as a result she felt she hadn't done a good enough job of conveying the seriousness of the situation to Ása. Certainly, she'd been hoping for a very different reaction from the girls' mother, like a shriek of horror and an announcement that they were coming straight home. Instead, Ása had said they'd just emerged from the Sky Lagoon and hadn't quite finished all their errands in town, but they would be home in time for supper. As an afterthought, she'd recommended that Sóldís lock all the doors.

Her muted response couldn't be due to not listening to what Sóldís had said. A charitable interpretation was that she was just dopey after wallowing too long in the hot waters of the geothermal spa.

Sóldís wondered what the response would have been if she'd been the one with 'whore' written on her hand rather than Íris. None at all, presumably. Yet she could just as easily have been the victim of this prank. The insult didn't apply to her or the girls – or to anyone, for that matter, so the choice of Íris's hand must have been a random one. But there was one snag with that theory: Íris had been sleeping at the back of the TV room, furthest from the door. If someone had entered the house simply with the intention of frightening them, surely the intruder would have chosen Sóldís's hand, as she had been nearest the door.

Once her initial shock had passed, Sóldís's thoughts had gone to Gígja. The little girl had used the word 'whore', obviously thinking it sounded cool and grown-up. Although Gígja hadn't a clue what it meant, she'd realised it was negative. Could she have scribbled it on Íris's hand to tease her or to get back at her? Íris was often spiteful towards her younger sister, after all.

But Gígja had flatly denied it when Sóldís questioned her. She said she didn't own a black marker pen, and anyway she didn't like black – it was an angry colour. She only liked happy colours. And she'd been asleep all night. Sóldís saw no reason to doubt this, but it occurred to her again that the child could be a sleepwalker. She hoped to goodness that was it, because then there would be no real menace, just an unsettling little episode. Ása would know. It must be OK to raise the possibility with her.

But what were the chances that Gígja would have spelt 'whore' correctly – and in her sleep? Practically zero, given the problems she had with much simpler words.

Still, one thing Sóldís knew now was that Reynir had no part in any of this. It was impossible that he could have sneaked away from Reykjavík, driven home to Hvalfjördur, stolen into the house, scribbled on his daughter's hand, then raced back to town. The idea was preposterous, if only because he was barely capable of driving nowadays. According to Ása, most of his journeys ended up off the road, so she had made him promise not to get behind the wheel. And although Reynir could easily have disobeyed Ása's orders, it was highly unlikely that he would have chosen to drive around the unlit fjord in such slippery conditions. He must be aware that the feat was beyond him nowadays.

Sóldís had done a patrol of both houses, forcing the girls to come with her. They found no open windows or unlocked doors or signs of a break-in. The chairs Sóldís had wedged under the door handles in the hall of the old house and in the cellar were still in place. When Íris saw them, she gave Sóldís a quizzical glance but didn't comment. Gígja didn't seem to notice anything odd about it.

After a thorough investigation, Sóldís concluded that no one had broken in that night. The French windows in the glass wall of the kitchen could be discounted, as when they were locked they could only be opened by means of a handle inside. If an intruder had entered, it would have had to have been via the locked front door of the new house, as this was the only one Sóldís hadn't wedged a chair against; which she didn't bother doing because the door opened outwards.

Next, Sóldís made both girls check their house keys, but these turned out to be where they belonged – as did her own keys. And the spare key was in its usual place, among the collection in the bowl on the sideboard in the hall. Íris said she had no idea if anyone else – their neighbours, for example – held keys in case the family locked themselves out. Gígja just shrugged.

In the end, they gave up trying to work out what had happened, as Sóldís simply couldn't come up with any other plausible explanation.

Following her unsatisfactory phone conversation with Ása, she had prepared an uninspiring lunch. There turned out to be no bread for toast, though neither Íris nor Gígja could remember finishing it. Sóldís didn't pursue the subject as she couldn't cope with any more mysteries. If the girls were secretly raiding the fridge, as Ása believed, she wasn't going to make an issue out of it. At their age, she'd had free access to the fridge at home and it had never done her any harm. Ása and Reynir's control freakery wasn't her problem right now. She didn't even bother to insist that the girls get dressed. She had only got dressed herself because she'd slept in her underwear and felt vulnerable enough, alone in the house with the girls, without walking around half naked. If she did, she was bound to start being paranoid that someone was spying on them during the daylight hours as well.

Sóldís couldn't tell whether the girls had no appetite because they'd stuffed themselves with bread beforehand or because the meal was so boring. They prodded indifferently at their plates, and hardly any of the food found its way into their mouths. She felt the same; the fried liver sausage might as well have been made of cardboard. The dogs disagreed, however, and wolfed down the leftovers with such gusto that little

Lubbi almost choked. Their excess energy wasn't due solely to the treats but because they hadn't been walked that day. Sóldís had let them out on to the deck to relieve themselves, but felt it was too risky to do any more. They would just have to do without their exercise until Ása and Reynir got home. The same applied to the hens and the animals in the byre; they would just have to go hungry until then.

Once she had cleared up after lunch, Sóldís got out the girls' schoolbooks. She sat with them at the kitchen table and tried to concentrate on teaching. It wasn't easy but she succeeded in the end. She discovered that if she spoke almost non-stop about a subject, there was no room left for anxiety or fear. It didn't take much to interrupt her train of thought, though; the cackling and squawking of the hens outside was enough.

'They're arguing.' Gígja turned to look through the glass wall, though their view of the henhouse was blocked by the fireplace. 'If we understood chicken language, we'd hear all kinds of bad words now. People use bad words when they argue.'

Íris gave her a scornful look. 'They're not arguing, they're fighting. Hens don't argue because they can't talk. Don't be so dumb.'

Sóldís intervened: 'For goodness' sake, don't you two start fighting. It's bad enough having to listen to the hens.' The cackling and squawking showed no signs of abating and Gígja started to get up from the table. 'Sit down, Gígja. There's probably a bird of prey or a fox out there. The chickens are perfectly safe in their house. And in their run too. They don't need us to go outside and save them. Trust me. Concentrate on your exercises.'

In the end, the hens quietened down. Since Gígja had brought up the subject, Sóldís decided to seize the chance to ask her about the bad words she'd overheard. What did it matter if the conversation found its way back to Ása or Reynir? Reynir already had proof that she was snooping in his study. 'Where did you hear bad words, Gígja? Who was quarrelling?'

'Um. Mummy and Begga. Mummy and Alvar. Mummy and Daddy. Grown-ups are always quarrelling.'

Íris looked up, ready to intervene and teach her little sister manners. 'That's not true. Grown-ups aren't *always* quarrelling. They only do it sometimes. And Mum and Dad don't swear or use bad words. Not even when they're fighting.'

'Yes, they do,' Gígja insisted. 'Mummy said Daddy was a shit when they were fighting. She said Begga was a whore. And Daddy said Alvar was a little shit. And Alvar said Daddy was an arsehole.' Gígja giggled. 'An arsehole. That's rude. Nobody wants to be one of those. And they weren't even shouting, just talking to each other, very angrily.'

'What were they angry about?' Sóldís thought she knew why Ása had been angry with Berglind, and she had no wish to know what Ása and Reynir were quarrelling about. But she was curious about the reason for Alvar's departure. She couldn't rid herself of the feeling that there was something off about his leaving and not returning for his belongings. Had something serious happened to him after he left? Had he been incapacitated in some way? Could he be dead? She pushed the train of thought away as she couldn't bear to think it through. Not now. Yet the worry refused to disappear completely and lingered at the back of her mind like a shadow or a ghost. Could something bad have happened to Alvar while he was here?

'I don't know. When Daddy saw me watching, he told me to go away.'

Noticing that Íris was beginning to eye her suspiciously, Sóldís dropped the subject. Gígja probably didn't know anything. She returned to the lesson and it wasn't long before peace had been restored. For the first time in what felt like ages, the atmosphere seemed almost normal, and Sóldís started to relax.

But the peace wasn't to last long.

The shrill sound of the doorbell cut right through what Sóldís was saying. She broke off instantly, the rest of the sentence suddenly unimportant. Íris and Gígja were no less startled. They all turned their heads simultaneously in the direction of the hall.

Although her heart was beating hard, Sóldís tried to sound casual as she said: 'I expect it's just your friend, Íris. Returning the snowmobile.' She sent up a silent prayer that she was right. It was up to her to check. 'You two wait here.'

'I don't want you to open the door.' Gígja put down her pencil and made a face. 'It could be the man with the black pen.' Her eyes widened. 'Or the thief. Maybe he's come to steal something else.'

'No, there's no one like that around here.' Sometimes firmly asserting a thing out loud was enough for Sóldís to convince herself. But this was not one of those times. She was sure the person outside meant them harm, so she was secretly relieved when both sisters disobeyed her orders and followed her into the hall. They wouldn't be much help if her fears were proved right, but in spite of that their presence lent her a little strength.

Once in the entrance hall, Sóldís stopped in front of the door, drew a deep breath and took hold of the handle. But instead of opening it, she snatched away her hand as though she'd burnt it. They didn't get many visitors and the few people who did drop by would ring the bell again if it wasn't answered immediately.

The bell had only rung once.

Sóldís laid her ear to the door but couldn't hear a thing. This wasn't surprising, since it was a thick, solid slab of wood. And it wasn't really that unusual for people to wait quietly to be let in. Yet she found the silence uncanny. 'Íris. Ring Robbi. Ask him if he's outside the house.'

'What? Why? What did you hear?' Íris's voice was rising in panic. 'Who's outside?'

'No one. Try ringing.' Sóldís, in contrast, kept her voice perfectly level and calm. She might have been a customer support representative at a call centre.

Far from reassuring Íris, however, it had the opposite effect. She pulled out her phone and tapped at the screen with trembling fingers before holding it to her ear, anxiously licking her lips. When her friend answered, she turned her back to them. 'Hi, quick question: are you outside my house?' She said this almost in a whisper and was silent while listening to his reply. 'OK. I'll call you back later.' A short silence followed. 'No, nothing. I'll call you later.' She turned back to the others, her face rigid. Then jerked her chin at the door, whispering: 'It's not Robbi. He's at home.'

Sóldís felt a small, clammy hand closing around her fingers and gripping them tight. 'Who is it, then?' Gígja took a step backwards, trying to pull Sóldís away from the door. 'Don't open it.'

Sóldís had no intention of doing so. Not even if the person outside claimed to be from the police. Freeing herself from Gígja's grip, she moved to the peephole in the door, though the thought of looking out filled her with dread. She imagined the person outside pressing their eye to the other side. Finding herself eye to eye with someone was an even more frightening prospect than seeing the whole person. Nevertheless, she summoned her courage, stood on tiptoe and peered out.

She couldn't see anybody. Only the empty drive and a distorted view of the byre wall. There was no one standing on the steps. She turned to the girls. 'Maybe the doorbell's broken. Unless it was the postman with a package that wouldn't fit in the mailbox.'

Íris slowly shook her head. 'No. The postman never comes to the house. And there's nothing wrong with the doorbell. Just try it.' Then, immediately regretting it, she said: 'No. Don't open the door.'

Sóldís squeezed out a smile through facial muscles that were stiff with fear. 'It must have been somebody. Maybe a neighbour. They must have given up and left, thinking we weren't home.'

'Yes, that must be it.' Gígja's gaze swung from Sóldís to Íris and back to Sóldís. Her eyes were like saucers and she looked close to tears. 'Mustn't it?'

'Yes, definitely.' Sóldís took her hand again, shooting Íris a warning glance. It worked and the girl didn't contradict her. 'Shall I make us some cocoa?' She couldn't face any more teaching at the moment but felt the need to occupy herself with some simple, practical activity. Making hot chocolate ticked both boxes.

Gígja nodded and Íris shrugged, but for a teenager that was as good as a 'yes'. The moment they returned to the kitchen, though, any thoughts of hot chocolate were abruptly dispelled.

Someone had scrawled in big, red letters across the glass wall:

CAИ'T RUN CAN'T HIDE

The N in the first word was back to front, indicating that the letters were on the outside of the glass, not the inside. Whoever did it had realised their mistake and written the rest of the letters correctly. It was a faint consolation to know that the letters were on the outside, but this was immediately overturned by the certainty that the person who did it must be the one who had written on Íris's hand in the night. Which meant that they could get inside the house whenever they liked. So the three girls were no safer in here, surrounded by reinforced concrete, than they would be out in the open. The message was intended to taunt them, to remind Sóldís that there was little point locking and barricading the doors.

Even worse, Sóldís could see white fluff sticking to the smeared red letters here and there. She didn't dare approach the glass to get a closer look, but from where she was standing they resembled outsize snowflakes. Or feathers.

* * *

Íris was still clutching her phone although she had hung up on Robbi. She was holding it tightly to her chest, as if convinced that a fully charged phone was enough to ward off any danger. It might have come in useful in town, but out here calling someone wouldn't make any difference. They were too far away for anyone to reach them in time. 'He said his horse came home on its own last night.'

'Great.' Robbi's horse wasn't top of the list of things Sóldís was most concerned about right now.

'And he promised not to come over.' Íris looked at Sóldís. 'I can't understand why you don't want him to come. He's got a gun.'

'That's exactly why.' Sóldís said no more. She didn't want to have to spell out to Íris the danger of summoning a besotted teenager to come to the rescue of his girlfriend, armed to the teeth. No matter how good a shot he was, he must have gained his experience in very different circumstances from these. From crouching in a ditch, probably, waiting for a flock of geese to fly over. It was all too likely that his rescue attempt would end in disaster and one of them would get hit – or Ása or Reynir, since they must be about to drive into the yard any minute.

After another phone call from Sóldís and a photo of the red letters daubed across the glass wall, Ása had finally grasped that the situation was too serious for them to justify continuing their shopping spree or lounging about in cafes. The decisive factor was Sóldís's announcement that she was going to call the police. This did not go down well, and in the end she had promised not to make the call – at least until Ása and Reynir had got home.

That had been almost an hour and a half ago.

'What about the snowmobile?' Íris still hadn't given up all hope of getting Robbi to come over. 'What if Dad notices it's gone?'

'Your dad won't have time to think about the snowmobile today,' Sóldís replied. 'Nor will your mum. Robbi can just bring it back tomorrow.'

'But . . .' Íris didn't finish her thought. She obviously couldn't think of any arguments that would change Sóldís's mind.

'Your parents should be arriving any minute. Let's just stay calm. Don't worry about the snowmobile. Don't worry about the person outside. We're quite safe here. Nobody can get in.'

Sóldís had shepherded the girls into the TV room where they had slept the night before. It had no windows and the door opened inwards. She had locked it, then jammed a kitchen chair under the handle. There they were going to stay until the girls' parents got home.

On the big TV screen, a black hole was sucking matter into itself. Sóldís had put on a documentary about astronomy in the hope of distracting their attention and making up for her failure to teach them properly over the last two days. None of them were concentrating, though, as they all kept glancing at the door to reassure themselves that the chair was still there. Only Gígja succeeded from time to time in becoming absorbed in the programme, presumably in the hope of spotting a rocket or two, but so far it had featured nothing but nebulae, planets and now this black hole.

'I need the toilet.' Gígja got up from the sofa and crossed her legs.

'Can't you wait a bit longer? Your mummy and daddy will be here any minute.'

'No. I can't. I'm bursting.'

Sóldís glanced around in the hope of spotting some receptacle they could use as a potty. A bowl, a tray or some other container. But the TV room was as minimalist as every other space in the new house and she couldn't see anything suitable. The choice was either to let Gígja pee on the floor or to take a chance and dash out into the hallway. There was a guest loo next door to the TV room, so it wasn't far to go. If they all went together, they could lock themselves in there and wait for the girls' parents.

'Come on. We'll all go.'

Íris was reluctant to join in a group trip to the toilet but quickly realised it was better than being left behind on her own.

Sóldís's heart was thudding as she removed the chair and opened the door. She did it fast, like someone tearing off a plaster. There was no one outside. They'd just entered the hallway when they heard the sound of the front door opening. Gígja clutched at Sóldís's arm, only to release it when Ása called out that they were home. At that, Gígja seemed to forget that she was bursting for the loo and raced off to meet her parents with Íris hot on her heels.

Sóldís was less keen to encounter them. Despite her overwhelming relief that they were back, she dreaded a confrontation with Reynir. She was already at the end of her tether and a reprimand from him about snooping in his study would be the final straw. Although his firing her would actually be a blessing, she couldn't cope with that conversation right now. Breaking down in tears was the last thing she wanted to do. If he was going to sack her, she wanted to be able to walk out of here with her head held high. Not with the humiliation of a runny nose and hiccupping sobs.

She heaved a deep breath, and went out to face the family.

Chapter 23
Saturday

The day dawned with innocent blue skies, as if yesterday's screaming blizzard had never happened. It was perfectly still outside and the snow that had fallen in the night sparkled like an eiderdown in a newly washed satin cover. Týr blew out a long breath, then drank in the bracingly cold air. It helped take the edge off the headache he'd woken up with after a fitful night's sleep in the stuffy cabin. He filled his lungs again. If it hadn't been for Karó, he would have continued practising this deep breathing until the ache had receded, but he couldn't stand here like some freak doing transcendental meditation in front of his colleague. They had work to do.

Týr noticed that Idunn's car had gone. She must have left for Reykjavík at the crack of dawn since there was nothing more for her to achieve here and the tasks would be piling up in town. He and Karó were in the same position. He had been woken by a phone call from Huldar, telling him there was no reason for them to stay another night. He'd left it up to them to decide what time they would return to Reykjavík, though. If Akranes CID required their services in Hvalfjördur for the rest of the day, that was fine. Týr hadn't been able to reply at first, still groggy with sleep and disorientated from the previous evening's revelations. Not even the bellowing of the cows at milking time had woken him. Trying not to sound suspiciously husky and betray the fact he'd overslept until nine, he managed to say that he'd confer with Karó about how best to use their day.

He hoped she would have an opinion as his own mind was completely blank.

Karó was vaping outside her cabin. The cloud of steam hung in the still air but she waved it away when she spotted Týr. 'I wasn't sure if I should wake you or let you sleep in.'

Týr smiled faintly and nodded. 'Thanks. I thought I'd never drop off.' He assumed there was no need to explain what had kept him awake.

'Are you doing all right?' Karó looked Týr in the eye. Her expression indicated that she didn't think he was. 'You look like shit. Understandably.'

Týr replied curtly, 'I'm fine. Just tired.' This was a blatant lie and they both knew it, but it had the effect he had hoped for. Any discussion about his past or how he felt was now off limits.

'Idunn left bright and early.' Karó put the vape away in her bag. 'She couldn't wait to get started on Reynir's post-mortem. Or at least to find out when she could start, given that his body's frozen.' She shuddered. 'I don't understand how she could have chosen that as a career.'

'Well, she did say she wasn't much of a people person.' Týr didn't want to think about post-mortems. It would conjure up images of razor-sharp scalpels or the rib cutters used to open the chest cavities of the deceased. And the prone body of his mother. Before he knew it, his mind would start merging the two. Despite having no memory of his mother, he didn't want to visualise her on an autopsy table. He wanted to picture her as she was in the framed photo beside the urn on his parents' mantelpiece. 'Should we let the owner know we're leaving?'

'Already done.' Karó slung her sports bag over her shoulder. 'I told her she could keep the sheets too. I don't fancy the thought of using them at home. I'm afraid they'll give me nightmares.'

Týr picked up his own bag. 'Good. I left mine behind as well.' He'd done it for the same reason. He just hoped the bedclothes hadn't permanently ruined the Northern Lights for him.

They crunched over the snow to the car, where Karó announced that she would drive. Týr didn't object, though concentrating on the road in these treacherous conditions would have helped dispel any intrusive thoughts. Before Karó started the engine, she looked at him, eyebrows raised questioningly. 'What do you want to do now?' Then: 'Would you like to take the day off, maybe? That would be fine by me.'

The last thing Týr wanted was a day off. He desperately needed a distraction. If he went home, he'd only sit there staring at his phone, waiting for his parents to answer the message he'd sent them when he finally crawled out of bed. He hadn't explained what it was about, just said that the three of them needed to talk. Since they usually replied immediately, their silence was deafening this time. Could they somehow have guessed that he had found out about his past? 'No. I'm good. What about checking in with the Akranes guys? They might have something for us.'

'A few crumbs, maybe. I expect the bulk of the stuff that needs doing at this end has already been taken care of. The case is as good as solved.' Karó reached for her seatbelt.

'Yes, probably.'

Karó clicked her belt into place, then met Týr's eye. 'You don't sound sure. Are you thinking that the killer could have been somebody other than Reynir?'

'No, not really. I just feel there's still too much that needs clarifying. All the loose ends are bugging me.' Týr knew he'd find it hard to articulate his doubts. Everything pointed to Reynir's guilt. Everything. But just as all the pieces appeared to be falling into place, he felt that the bits that belonged to a completely different puzzle were becoming naggingly conspicuous. 'Alvar. The snowmobile. The missing money. The fact that Reynir – or somebody else – had been in the house after the murders. The fact that the daughters hadn't been given sleeping pills although there were plenty in the house. The missing keys. All that and more. Nothing glaring. Just details that it wouldn't hurt to follow up.'

Judging by Karó's expression, she agreed with him that it wasn't exactly compelling evidence. But she was polite. 'Perhaps we could get to the bottom of some of the mysteries you mentioned? I'm sure the Akranes guys would be grateful to offload a few of those small jobs.'

Hördur turned out to be busy, so it was Elma who picked up when Týr called. She had a pleasant voice and didn't give the impression of being in a hurry to get him off the line or dispatch them back to Reykjavík. What's more, she didn't dismiss his concerns about all the loose ends. On the contrary, she said they had been discussing this very point at their morning meeting. Týr was sure she wasn't just saying that to make him feel better, since it emerged that they had called up to chase Alvar's bank statements and phone data, as well as putting pressure on the people investigating the couple's finances to come up with some results.

It was decided that Týr and Karó should go and have a word with the hairdresser, Ella, the wife of Karl who had discovered the bodies. Since Ása seemed to have interacted more with her than with anyone else in the district, it was quite possible that she had confided in Ella while she was having her hair cut and her highlights done. Maybe even shared things with her that she hadn't mentioned to her friends or relatives in town, who she rarely met face-to-face. Týr agreed. He found it much easier to communicate in person than over the phone or via email. Words were valuable but they had their limits. It was incredibly easy to misinterpret something when you couldn't see the person's body language or hear their tone of voice.

Týr said goodbye to Elma, then turned to Karó, who switched on the engine. 'We're going to have a chat with Ella.'

* * *

They had taken seats in the room where they had spoken to Karl the day after he had stumbled on the bodies. This time it was Ella sitting with them, and they accepted the coffee they were offered. It was good and strong, served in mugs that sat comfortably in the hand. Týr had already drained a cup and a half while the woman rambled on about how tragic and incomprehensible the whole thing was. Her reaction was hardly surprising. Ella said there hadn't been any incidents involving major loss of life in the district for many, many years, and that no one could have dreamt that anything like this would happen. She and her husband were both so distressed they couldn't sleep. The deep trenches under her eyes backed up her story.

News of the body in the bathtub at Minna-Hvarf had obviously spread, since Ella referred to that too, with a shake of her head and a heavy sigh.

Týr felt it was time to get down to business. He needed a proper distraction from his troubled thoughts and small talk wasn't working. 'We were hoping Ása might have told you something that could shed light on what's happened.'

Ella put down her mug on the table. 'Like what? Who would be capable of wiping out a whole family who'd never hurt a soul? Surely it could only be someone who was very sick?'

Týr quickly closed down this particular avenue. 'Maybe. But we need to examine every aspect carefully or there's a risk that all kinds of doubts will crop up later. We want to close the case properly.'

Ella nodded. 'I understand. But you'll have to tell me what you want to know, because I can't immediately think of anything that might help you. Mind you, I did know their marriage was a bit rocky because of Reynir's illness, but that wasn't anything that would threaten their safety. All couples have their ups and downs.'

Karó agreed, then weighed in with the first question: 'Did Ása talk much about Reynir, then? About their marriage?'

Ella didn't immediately answer. She seemed to be thinking. 'Yes. I just don't know where to begin.'

Karó told her it didn't matter; they'd be grateful for any information. The story Ella then embarked on didn't come as much of a surprise. Apparently Ása had confided in her that she was at the end of her tether at times. Reynir was a different person since his illness and she felt as if life had catapulted them into a premature old age. She was wrestling with the same kinds of problems as people whose partners had dementia. She couldn't trust him any more. Not to drive, or to cook, or to look after their finances – or anything.

'Did she say anything else about their finances?' Remembering what the HR manager had said about the circumstances in which Reynir's girlfriend had parted ways with the company,

Týr decided to be more precise: 'Did something Reynir had done mean that they had to pay a substantial sum of money to a third party? As compensation, for example?'

Ella wrung her hands in her lap, looking agitated. 'She didn't go into any details, just said she'd been forced to block him from accessing their bank accounts. All I could think of was that he'd started gambling on the internet or something. Nothing like what you're implying.' She paused for a moment. 'I find discussing this very uncomfortable. I don't know if it's right. Ása trusted me. I know she's dead and all that, but still.'

Karó said she understood, but that in cases like this withholding information wasn't being respectful to Ása's memory, quite the reverse. Her words seemed to work and Ella relaxed again, loosening her clasped hands and letting out a breath.

Týr thought it was pointless asking any more about the couple's finances. If the woman had suspected Reynir of being an inveterate gambler, plainly she didn't know anything about the missing money. The sum was too large for him to have lost it in online poker games. Though, actually, for all he knew Reynir might have fallen in with gamblers who played for huge stakes.

Nevertheless, he decided to move on to the next question. 'Did Ása ever mention a young man called Alvar who worked for them?'

Ella's eyes widened. 'Do you think he's mixed up in this?'

'No,' Karó said firmly. 'We're just trying to get hold of him. He lived with the family for a while and we need to talk to him as a witness – that's all.' Karó was obviously keen to quash any rumours before they started. Her tone left no room for doubt. 'Did Ása mention him at all? Or say where he went after he stopped working for them?'

Ella thought for a while before answering: 'No. I don't recall her saying anything about where he went. I'd have remembered that, as it was fairly recent. But he didn't go amicably. I do know that much. He was sacked.'

'Sacked?' Týr hadn't been expecting this. Berglind, the young woman he had found skulking behind the greenhouse, had also been sacked. And Sóldís had packed her suitcase before she was murdered. Was it possible that, rather than planning to take a weekend off as most people thought, she had been the third assistant in a row to be dismissed by the couple? 'Do you have any idea why?'

'Yes. Or I think so. Ása used to complain about him. She asked if I knew anyone who needed a job, preferably a young man. I'm very glad now that I didn't know anyone, as I gather the girl they employed in Alvar's place is dead too.' Ella's gaze swung from one of them to the other, seeking confirmation, before she continued: 'They went through an employment agency that contacted the people on their books, but they couldn't find a young man who was prepared to take the job. That's why they hired a girl.'

'What did Ása say about Alvar?' Týr interrupted, as the conversation was getting off track. 'What did she complain about?'

'Oh, goodness. What didn't she complain about? Some of it was just the usual sort of problems you get when a stranger moves into your house. He got on her nerves straight away – so smarmy, I think she said. And he had no idea how to clean; he used to go through cleaning products like there was no tomorrow. But as time went on her complaints became more specific. You know how it is. She started getting a better idea of what it was about him that she really didn't like.'

'Which was?' Týr tried to keep Ella to the point.

Ella didn't seem affronted by his prompting: 'She said he'd had ulterior motives for taking the job in the first place. From what she let slip, I understood that she thought he was after money.'

'Isn't that why most people apply for jobs? For money?' Karó smiled to take the sting out of her comment.

'Yes. Of course. But I think she meant more than that. She said he'd been overly interested in their older girl, Íris. She thought he was flirting with her – not because he fancied her but because he wanted to become part of the family. Naturally, Íris wasn't interested in him. She was only a teenager and in her eyes he must have seemed old. He was over twenty, after all.'

'Was that why he was sacked? Did he cross a line with the girl?' Karó's eyes narrowed a little as she said this.

'Something like that. He kept touching her more than necessary and his behaviour was inappropriate. Ása said she'd given him a talking to and he'd completely lost it. Started hurling insults at her and accusing her of being jealous of her own daughter. Apparently he apologised afterwards but I think it was too late. Ása was determined to get rid of him.'

'But she didn't sack him immediately?' Týr would have found instant dismissal a natural reaction in the circumstances. Swearing at your employer is usually a point of no return.

'No.' Ella wrinkled her brow. 'I was a bit taken aback to learn that he was still with them the next time I heard from Ása. I asked why she hadn't got rid of him and she said that first she needed to make sure he hadn't stolen something from her.'

'Stolen what?'

'I gather she'd lost a wallet. But I must have misunderstood, because you wouldn't expect there to be any more in her wallet than bank cards and maybe some cash. I can't believe she'd have let a pervert stay near her daughters just for the sake of recovering something like that. But I didn't ask any questions. I thought it would be rude – that I'd sound nosy.'

Týr and Karó exchanged rapid glances. He'd hoped she might be able to make sense of this, but unfortunately she looked as confused as him. They continued to question the woman; some things she knew, others she didn't. She thought she knew when Alvar had been let go, which fitted more or less with what had already emerged about Sóldís's appointment. Ella had no idea how Alvar had got home but thought it was out of the question that Reynir would have driven him and extremely unlikely that Ása would have gone to the trouble. They'd probably contacted the driver they hired to run errands for them. Unfortunately, she didn't know the driver's name, only that Ása had been satisfied with him. As far as Ella could remember, he'd been recommended to them by their architect.

As they started to wind up, Týr got the feeling that Ella was withholding something. She seemed unnaturally relieved that they were finally leaving, which was inconsistent with her status as a neutral witness. 'Is there maybe some final thing you want to share with us?' he prompted.

The woman feigned an expression of surprise. 'No. Nothing. I think I've told you everything.'

Karó, it seemed, was thinking the same as Týr: 'Oh, one more thing. Why was the young woman who was hired before Alvar given the sack? We understand she didn't leave of her own accord either. Did Ása suspect her of stealing too?'

Týr wanted to punch the air when it became apparent that Karó had hit the bullseye. Ella looked embarrassed and Týr thought at first that she was going to offer them more coffee as a delaying tactic. She opened her mouth, only to close it. Then opened it again: 'Oh dear, I was hoping I wouldn't have to go into that. I promised Ása to guard the secret with my life.' Ella paused, as if struck by the inappropriateness of this phrase.

'Embarrassing secrets don't matter to her any more in the circumstances,' Týr said, pointing out the obvious. He was sure that Ella would spill the beans in the end; the question was whether it would be now or later. It turned out they were in luck.

'Oh, to hell with it.' Ella licked her lips, then went on: 'Reynir was messing around with the girl. Or young woman, I should say. He kept inventing excuses to go over to the old house. Eventually Ása got suspicious, so she started checking up on them using the security cameras they had around the house and saw Reynir touching the young woman in an inappropriate way when he thought no one could see. So Ása sacked her. Understandably. Apparently it wasn't the first time this had happened. He'd had an affair with an employee too, back when they had their company in America.'

Týr and Karó were silent, unsure whether there was more to come. But when Ella showed no signs of continuing, Karó said: 'It didn't occur to her to divorce him?'

'No. She said it was linked to his illness. Both his affair abroad and what happened here. She said he had no self-control any more. No inhibitions. And it wasn't his fault. It had been her decision to move home to Iceland and live in the countryside. She hoped that way she could isolate Reynir from temptation and save him from any further trouble. In other words, the plan was to shut the family off from the world – as far as possible – then everything would be better.'

Karó showed no sign of understanding Ása's decision. Nor did Ella, it seemed. After a moment, she went on: 'If there's some way of avoiding making this public, I'd be grateful if you didn't put it on file. It's so easy to misunderstand Ása's behaviour and think she was being pathetic, but she was no coward. The way she saw it, she was simply standing by her husband during a difficult illness. I'm sure this has nothing to do with the killings, and it's definitely nobody else's business.'

The brain is a fascinating phenomenon, especially when it goes wrong. Serious brain disorders are unlike the usual kind of illness where a patient lies in bed, pale and weak, receiving nourishment via a drip and otherwise causing little trouble. When the brain malfunctions, it has a major impact on the daily life of the victim's nearest and dearest, as Ása had discovered. Týr's thoughts went to the scar on his own forehead and the lucky escape he'd had. 'This case is unlikely to go to court,' he said reassuringly. 'The files won't be made public. You shouldn't worry too much.' Sadly, he knew this for a fact from his own history.

Ella didn't make the connection, still evidently under the impression that an outsider had attacked the house. 'What about our safety? Should I be worrying about that? You're definitely going to arrest someone, aren't you? Everyone living around the fjord is nervous. Not just me.'

'You can set your mind at rest about that.' The conviction in Týr's voice was unmistakable and Ella was visibly relieved.

They said goodbye and went back outside. As Karó was driving out of the farmyard, Týr sent a message to Alvar's lodger. He reckoned they had good reason to talk to him again. His description of Alvar didn't quite square with what Ella had heard from Ása. A quiet computer science student, an orphan with few friends – from Bogi's description, Alvar wasn't a pervert who hit on underage girls. But, of course, losers like that came in all shapes and sizes. Regrettably – or it would be easier to identify them.

They hadn't even driven out of the gate before the young man answered. He was in and at a loose end.

Chapter 24
Before

Reynir had behaved as if nothing had happened. There was no dramatic face-to-face sacking or any sort of reprimand. Apart from giving Sóldís the occasional strange look, he didn't say a word about the incident in his study. Sóldís could only interpret this as meaning that he didn't want to involve Ása. Perhaps he was afraid Sóldís would reveal that he'd been analysing his wife's passwords.

Íris had only just stopped crying. Between sobs she had told her parents the whole story and Sóldís had filled in the gaps. But since Íris had left out the part about the missing necklace, Sóldís tactfully didn't refer to it. One more secret hardly mattered now.

Ása and Reynir had listened without comment until Íris had finally finished her story. They still had their outdoor clothes on and were doing their best to follow the thread but it wasn't easy. Presumably it helped that Sóldís had already given Ása a potted account over the phone when she was begging them to hurry back. Then, as Ása and Reynir had gone with Íris into the kitchen to see the writing on the glass wall for themselves, Sóldís had grabbed Gígja by the hand to stop her following them. She was sure that the white bits were feathers and the red was blood, and she didn't want Gígja to realise. If she did, it wouldn't take her long to work out what that meant for the hens.

Sóldís heard a gasp from Ása, followed by the sound of the door opening on to the deck. One of the adults had gone out to the henhouse to check on the situation. A minute or so later, the door closed again, Ása muttered something that Sóldís couldn't hear, and Íris broke into a fit of wild sobbing. There was no longer any doubt in Sóldís's mind that one or more of the chickens had met a grim fate.

The thought filled her with horror and a sort of cold dread. Not just because of the poor hens but because a person who could mistreat animals was capable of anything – of crimes far worse than writing on someone's hand or pinching a remote control or a necklace. Her fear rose to a whole new level. It reminded her of the time she had broken her leg while skiing. Before the accident, she had been afraid of heights and a little nervous on the slopes. Afterwards, she had broken out in a cold sweat at the mere thought of putting on a pair of skis. There's nothing worse than discovering that an imagined threat is real.

Sóldís could feel herself growing numb all over and thought she was going to suffocate. She had to concentrate on breathing. In, out. In, out. If she didn't consciously make the effort, she wasn't sure her body would do it. She filled her lungs and emptied them a few times, reminding herself that she was no longer alone with the girls. Ása and Reynir were back. They were in their late thirties – proper adults, not 'adult' in inverted commas like her. They would know what to do and take the appropriate action. The person terrorising them would be exposed, arrested, charged and locked up in prison. Or something like that. It wasn't a question of whether but when this would happen. The adults had taken charge. At last.

But even that thought didn't fully dissipate Sóldís's fear. Maybe another, more balanced pair of adults could have allayed her worries, but was she really safe with the two standing in front of her? Her mind screamed, 'No, absolutely not,' and she bit down hard to stifle the urge to blurt out her resignation. She knew from experience that she should not make big decisions when agitated.

Sóldís felt a tug at her jumper and glanced down to see Gígja staring up into her face, her eyes anxious under knitted brows. 'What's the matter?' the little girl asked.

Sóldís smiled down at her. Her lips were so dry that she felt the lower one split. Running the tip of her tongue over the sore spot, she tasted blood. 'Oh, nothing. Everything will be OK now. Your mummy and daddy are home.'

'Your mouth's bleeding.' Gígja made a face. 'Do you want a plaster?'

Before Sóldís could decline this offer, Ása reappeared. 'Gígja, go with Íris and Daddy. He's going to play cards with you.'

Sóldís took this to mean that Ása wanted a private word – correctly, as it turned out. She also assumed she would be asked for a detailed description of everything that had happened since the couple had left the day before. Once they were sitting facing each other across the kitchen table, her boss did indeed request her version of events. But first Sóldís asked if the chickens were all right. A flicker of horror passed across Ása's face and she shook her head.

Before Sóldís repeated the story of the words daubed on the glass wall, she braced herself to tell Ása everything, leaving nothing out. So she mentioned the remote control, the tracks in the snow on the cellar steps, the kettle, the open door that should have been shut, and the creaking in the old house at night. She also reminded Ása of the wet footprints in the entrance hall that she and Reynir had so airily dismissed. After she had finished pouring out the story, she waited for Ása to suggest their next step.

But the woman just sat there without speaking, staring over Sóldís's shoulder at the glass wall as if mesmerised by the horrible red scrawl. She was still wearing her coat but didn't seem aware of the fact; at least she'd made no move to unzip it, despite the warmth in the house. In the end, Sóldís lost patience: 'Aren't you going to ring the police?'

Ása's head didn't move but her blue eyes shifted sideways to meet Sóldís's gaze. 'Not right now. It's nearly suppertime and they probably won't think it's serious enough to come all the way out here. Maybe tomorrow.'

The word *maybe* echoed in Sóldís's head. Maybe? She was so surprised by this reaction that it took her a moment to recover. She'd expected Ása to pull out her phone immediately and demand police assistance, even if it was outside office hours. She'd also imagined that the couple's status as important taxpayers would ensure that everything was done to oblige them. Or at least she assumed that was how things worked. 'Aren't you going to do anything?' she asked.

'Yes, of course. But I still haven't got my head around all this well enough to work out what exactly we should do.' Ása kept her gaze fixed on Sóldís's. 'Do you have any suggestions?'

The question destroyed any remaining illusions Sóldís might have had about the proper adults knowing what to do. 'Suggestions? Me?'

'Yes.' Ása's face was rigid, her expression impossible to read. 'You've had more time than me to think about it.'

Sóldís had only one suggestion to offer and Ása had already dismissed that. But she voiced it again anyway: 'Ring the police. They can come and take fingerprints, find out who's behind this and arrest him.'

'Him? Are you so sure it's a man?' Ása looked down, wiping the flat of her hand over the tabletop as if brushing off crumbs, though the surface was spotlessly clean as always. 'It could be a woman. In fact, I think that's more likely. Or at least equally likely.'

It was a possibility Sóldís hadn't even considered. 'Why?'

'I have my reasons.' Ása removed her hand from the table. 'It's not only men who are capable of that sort of thing.'

Sóldís didn't know what to say when Ása stopped talking. She clearly had a specific person in mind – she must have. And that person wasn't the horse man Gígja claimed to have encountered in the snowstorm. Sóldís had been convinced that Ása would blame what was happening on him. She longed to ask who the woman was but decided against it. She couldn't be anyone Sóldís knew. It wasn't as if she moved in the same world as this family, even though she was temporarily living with them. The only possible candidate she could think of was Berglind. Perhaps Ása knew about her relationship with Reynir. Come to think of it, Gígja had mentioned a fight between the two women in which Ása had called Berglind a whore. But there was a world of difference between being on bad terms and butchering someone's hens and smearing gory threats on the windows. 'I think,' Sóldís ventured, 'that the man . . . or woman . . . who's doing all this has a key to the house. You need to change the locks.' She sat up straighter. 'If you don't, I'm leaving.'

'Don't be ridiculous. Nobody's leaving.' Sóldís's threat clearly annoyed Ása, but it didn't seem to come as any surprise to her that there might be extra keys floating around out there. 'Good idea, though. I'll call a locksmith first thing in the morning.'

'Does anyone else have a key? Apart from your family and me?'

'Possibly.' Ása grimaced slightly. 'Probably, in fact.' She sighed and shook her head with a defeated look. 'I'll have to ask Reynir. If I know him right, he won't have remembered to ask for the keys back.'

'The keys?' Sóldís almost threw up her hands in despair. 'You mean there are multiple keys in circulation?'

'There could be two. Three, if we include the one we keep in the Reykjavík flat.'

Ása lapsed into silence again, and they sat there for a while without speaking. Sóldís was afraid she was going to call it a day and put off dealing with the matter until the morning. That mustn't happen because Sóldís didn't want to spend yet another night in the old house, frantic with fear about what might happen under cover of the darkness. 'What about the security system?' she asked hopefully. 'Would it be possible to get it working again?'

'Yes. But not this evening. It needs new cameras and possibly some wiring replaced too.'

'Can't you put the old cameras back up?' Sóldís could hear a pathetic whine entering her voice. Too bad. She was just hoping that Íris had been wrong when she claimed that the cameras had been thrown out. So fervent was her hope that she crossed her fingers under the table. 'I mean, just for tonight, until the new system is set up?'

'They were disposed of. Reynir saw to that. He took the cameras down because he was paranoid that I was using them to spy on him. He was quite right, of course.' Ása smiled coldly, then drew her brows together as if to frown. Yet her forehead remained perfectly smooth. Sóldís now noticed a telltale puffiness about her skin, and it dawned on her that

Reynir wasn't the only one who had been to see a doctor while in town.

In spite of her churning emotions, Sóldís derived a moment of pleasure from this discovery. Ása's fresh, youthful appearance wasn't just another gift from her fairy godmother. She felt herself flushing at the ill-timed thought and reminded herself that Ása didn't exactly live a charmed existence. By no stretch of the imagination could Reynir's illness be attributed to good fortune. These thoughts had distracted her, making her lose the thread. 'What should we do now, then?' she asked. 'What if this person is still around?'

'We'll make damned sure they're not. There's nothing else we can do.' Ása turned her head slightly, her gaze shifting over Sóldís's shoulder again. 'And we'll clean that muck off the glass. I can't look at it a minute longer.'

* * *

Outside there were no clues to suggest that anyone was lurking near the house, but this didn't reassure Sóldís as she and Ása couldn't see far in the gathering dusk. They tried to illuminate the snow with their phones to check whether there were any footprints leading away from the deck. They'd brought the dogs with them for moral support, but this turned out to be a big mistake. Bói and Lubbi charged around, overjoyed to be let out after being cooped up all day, destroying any tracks that might have been on the ground. The loose snow had drifted in the wind too, quickly filling in any footprints and smoothing out the surface all around.

Sóldís and Ása did a circuit of both houses and paused to take a look in the byre, but there was nothing out of the ordinary to see, just the horses and cows in their stalls – no one hiding out.

The shed was empty too and, to Sóldís's surprise, Ása didn't even notice that one of the snowmobiles was missing. Íris would have to wait until tomorrow to make arrangements with Robbi for it to be returned. Sóldís couldn't worry about that now. Next, the two women checked the sheep shed, where the goats had briefly been stabled. It was full of boxes and other stuff, like the cellar of the old farmhouse. In different circumstances, Sóldís would have marvelled at how much clobber one family could accumulate, but she had more important things on her mind. The contents included beds and other pieces of furniture, presumably brought over from America but then found to be superfluous to requirements. It was pretty clear what would happen to all this stuff. When Ása and Reynir decided to redecorate, they would replace everything with brand-new items, while this furniture continued to collect dust for the foreseeable future. Sóldís chivvied Ása out again before her boss could get any ideas about adding this space to the list of areas she was already responsible for cleaning. The last thing Sóldís could face was spending any time, alone and defenceless, dusting unwanted furniture in the spooky, unlocked outhouse.

Next, they walked round behind the old farmhouse and established that the greenhouse was empty, but then no one in their right mind would try to hide in there – it was visible to all. After that, they set off back towards the new house, hurrying past the chicken run with eyes averted. Sóldís, hearing clucking from the henhouse, consoled herself with the thought that at least some of the poor creatures had survived.

Ása started speaking as soon as they were past the run: 'I'm going to ask Reynir to remove the dead hens before the girls see them. He can bury them or something. The bodies are in there – decapitated. Their heads are nowhere to be seen.

They must have been used as paintbrushes. Let's hope he finds them in the snow so the girls don't stumble across them later. I'll get him to wash off the writing too. I just can't face doing it myself.'

Sóldís gave a private sigh of relief, as she'd been afraid the task would fall to her. For the same reason, she didn't like to point out that the ground would be frozen hard, making it almost impossible to dig. She didn't want to run the risk of being ordered by Ása to fetch a bin bag and scoop up the bodies, then bring a bucket of water and a cloth to clean the windows. Or to be told to search for the missing heads.

Ása paused when they reached the front of the house again. 'I think we can be confident there's no one here. Whoever it was must have left.' She peered down the drive in the gloom. 'Didn't you hear a car at all?'

'No. But then we locked ourselves in the TV room the moment we saw the writing on the glass. There are no windows in there, so I doubt we'd have heard the engine even if there had been one.'

'Probably not, no. We had the TV room soundproofed so we could turn up the volume without making the whole house shake.' Ása seemed satisfied with this explanation. 'Whoever did it must have driven away, so there's nothing more to be afraid of. Not this evening, at any rate.'

Sóldís didn't agree. If their tormentor had arrived by car, presumably there was nothing to stop them from coming back later this evening or during the night. 'I need you to walk round the old house with me too or I won't be able to get any sleep.'

Reading from Ása's expression that she thought Sóldís was making an unnecessary fuss, she added quickly: 'Or I'm leaving, no matter what you say. I'll organise a lift for myself this evening.' The only person who might be able to pick her up at short notice was the driver who had brought her here in the first place. And he would have to be paid. How much, Sóldís had no idea, but almost certainly more than she had in her account. They were approaching the end of the month and she'd used up all her overdraft.

Ása rolled her eyes. 'There's no need to make any more of a drama out of it. Come on. Let's get it over with.'

Sóldís began by dragging Ása down to the cellar. There was absolutely no question of her going down there alone, so it would be better to get it out of the way first, in case Ása lost patience before they'd explored every corner of the old house. The back exit turned out to be locked and the chair was still jammed under the door handle. When Ása saw this precaution, she gave Sóldís a look as if it was finally dawning on her just how frightened Sóldís had been. 'There's a disgusting smell down here.' Ása turned away from the door, wrinkling her nose. 'I thought the plumber was supposed to fix that?'

'Reynir didn't want him to break up the floor. But it'll have to be done.' Sóldís stepped aside and pointed to the large, rough patch where she had been standing.

'What the bloody hell is the matter with him?' Ása surveyed the plastic boxes filling all the shelves. 'It'll have to be dealt with or the smell could infect everything that's stored in here. It's not like he has any reason to be proud of the mess he made of the floor.'

Sóldís couldn't agree more. The floor was incredibly badly finished, but then what could you expect? Reynir wasn't exactly the practical type. 'Can I ask why Reynir did the concrete here rather than the builders who were restoring the house?'

Ása shook her head in exasperation. 'You may well ask. He became obsessed with the idea of getting involved with the building work himself. I don't know – some kind of macho bullshit, I suppose. I banned him from going anywhere near it as I knew he'd only cock it up, but to keep him quiet I said he could have a go at repairing this floor after we'd moved in – so he wouldn't get in the way of the builders.' Ása looked down with an exasperated expression. 'It was badly cracked, but for Christ's sake, this is a cellar floor, so it wasn't important. I thought he'd forget all about it, but no, he wanted to prove his manhood or some such nonsense. And this was the result.'

Ása moved over to the new patch and sniffed again. 'How is it possible? To cock up a small repair job so badly that the concrete stinks?' She glanced up. 'It wasn't there before. This smell. Not when he first laid the floor. Something must have leaked into the concrete, don't you think? Are you aware of anything that could explain it?'

Sóldís shook her head. 'I don't come down here if I can help it. I was hit by the smell the first time I opened the door. It has nothing to do with me.' Sóldís didn't ask how she was supposed to have created the stench. By peeing on the floor? Or puking on it?

Ása couldn't hide her eagerness to get out of there and practically ran up the stairs. She hurriedly closed the door behind them and even tested the handle to check it was definitely shut. Then the two of them went from room to room, never once being aware of a presence or spotting any signs that someone had been there.

'Nobody here.' Ása looked at Sóldís. 'Are we done then? Or do you want to check the loft too?' This last part was said half mockingly, so she seemed surprised when Sóldís gasped.

'Is there a loft?' They were standing upstairs at the time and Sóldís automatically raised her eyes to the ceiling.

Ása suppressed a sigh and gave in to Sóldís's request to be shown the place in the book room where a trapdoor was neatly concealed in the ceiling. Sóldís had never even noticed it. Ása fetched what looked like a broom handle that had been leaning against a bookcase and passed it to Sóldís. 'Push the trapdoor with this.' She pointed to the right spot. Sóldís pushed at the spot with the pole and found she didn't need to use much force. The trapdoor opened smoothly and a ladder slid down halfway. Ása tugged at a ring and the other half extended to the floor. It all happened almost noiselessly, Sóldís noted. Apart from a faint squeaking – a squeaking she had heard before without being able to identify it.

'Be my guest. Take a look.' Ása gestured to the ladder. 'Let's hurry up and get it over with.'

Sóldís climbed the ladder, slowly and gingerly, as she didn't trust it to hold her weight and was afraid of falling. But it didn't give way and she was soon high enough to poke her head through the opening. She paused to pluck up her nerve, dreading what she might find up there.

There was nothing to see, only insulation lining the gaps between the rafters, and some plywood panels that had been laid across part of the space to create a floor. It was dark up there and Sóldís clung to the ladder with her left hand while groping for her phone with her right. When she shone it over the rafters, she noticed something glimmer in the middle of the floor. She vacillated for a moment, then realised that she wouldn't be able to stop thinking about it if she didn't investigate. Of course it would just be a piece of metal – a screw or something. But if she didn't make sure, her imagination was bound to convert the harmless screw into a knife or a razorblade. She ducked her head back through the opening and told Ása she was going up into the loft.

Ása sighed. 'Why? Surely there's nothing up there?'

'There's something shiny. I'm going to check it out.' Sóldís heaved herself up through the hole, still terrified of falling back down the ladder when she let go. Before crawling across the rafters, she called down to Ása: 'The floor will be able to support my weight, won't it?'

'I assume so. Or you would have fallen through it by now.' Ása sounded impatient and annoyed, as if she couldn't care less if Sóldís suddenly came plunging through the ceiling of the book room. Then, apparently relenting, she called: 'Stick to the plywood panels.'

Sóldís crawled cautiously towards the place where she'd spotted the glint of metal. It wasn't far but it felt precarious, though the rafters proved strong and the panels supported her weight so well that they didn't so much as creak as she moved over them. If they had, she'd probably have lost her nerve. But it wasn't easy. She had to shuffle along on hands and knees while lighting her way with her phone. In the end, she gripped it in her mouth so she could use both hands.

When she got there, the phone fell out of her mouth. On top of the rafter she'd been aiming for she saw a small gold heart with a delicate chain lying pooled beside it.

Sóldís picked up the necklace and put it in her pocket, telling herself it wasn't necessarily Íris's. It could have belonged to one of the builders who had renovated the house. But it was no good trying to deceive herself. Of course it was Íris's heart pendant.

She heard the muffled sound of Ása's voice calling: 'Are you nearly done?'

'I'm coming.' Sóldís prepared to turn back but her phone chose that moment to conk out. She hadn't charged it since yesterday morning as she hadn't dared to go over to the old house after dusk to fetch her charger. Or this morning either.

In front of her was pitch darkness, behind her the faint light from the trapdoor. Then, in the darkness ahead, she noticed something that couldn't be right: a small ray of light rising from the floor.

Sóldís crawled towards it. There was no plywood board over the rafters where the light was shining and the insulation had been pulled back. She eased herself closer, until, by lying on her front, she could make out the wood panelling that covered the ceiling of the floor below. The light was coming from a small hole and beside it was something that looked like a cork. When she picked it up and fumbled it with her fingers, then held it up to the light, she saw that it was a knot of wood.

Without pausing to think, she craned her neck until she could peer with one eye down the hole. Below her she made out a familiar duvet cover.

The hole was directly above her bed.

Chapter 25
Saturday

Týr and Karó had got a rather muted response from their colleagues in Akranes and Reykjavík when they each rang a team to relay what they had learnt from Ella. They were told to write a report, and that a decision about how to proceed would be taken in due course. Like most of the evidence that had emerged during the investigation, Ella's testimony had only corroborated the theory that Reynir was the killer, especially given what she had had to say about Alvar and Berglind. But it was important to bear in mind that this was only a second-hand report, and it would be difficult to confirm the details now that Ása was dead. When Alvar and Berglind were interviewed, their versions of events would no doubt be quite different. The way things were progressing, it would soon be possible to spare some officers to track Alvar down, but in the meantime Týr and Karó were to relax and hold on to the thought that the case was close to being solved.

This was not the reaction they'd been hoping for, though it was understandable enough. They learnt that Berglind, the young woman who had originally worked for the couple, would be questioned by the Akranes team. Her interview would be a formal affair, carefully prepared in advance. If Berglind had been having an affair with Reynir, he might well have confided in her about his marriage, which meant that she could be in a position to provide an insight into his state of mind prior to the murders. Although it was a while since she had stopped working for the couple, it wasn't inconceivable that she and Reynir had stayed in touch behind Ása's back.

Týr felt sorry for Hördur as the phone call drew to a close and he started racking his brains to think of another assignment for them. Eager not to be a burden, Týr proposed a job for himself and Karó. Anything to avoid being given the rest of the day off, which would leave him with too much time to brood on his own problems.

He still felt guilty about having contravened Hördur's direct orders by talking to Einar Ari, though Hördur had taken the news with equanimity. His response had no doubt been influenced by the fact that Týr and Karó had discovered a potentially significant detail about the snowmobile. Hördur had taken a great interest in the engine noise that Einar Ari's wife believed she'd heard in the night. Instead of reprimanding Týr and Karó, he'd said he would get his officers to check the few CCTV cameras located in Hvalfjördur, in case the snowmobile had been captured on film. He wasn't optimistic, though, as snowmobiles were rarely used on roads or near any sites monitored by security cameras.

Before they rang off, Týr proposed that he and Karó should pay a visit to Alvar's lodger, Bogi, and Hördur agreed. They were to have another chat with him in the hope of extracting more information, both about the young man's possible whereabouts and also what it was he'd been accused of. The latter was a remote possibility but you never knew. If Alvar had been wrongly accused, he might well have aired his grievances to his lodger. The fact Bogi hadn't mentioned any incident of the kind could have had a natural explanation. People were often reluctant to betray confidences, as Ella, the hairdresser, had shown.

'What about meeting him at a restaurant?' Týr could hardly hear himself speak over the rumbling of his guts. He hadn't eaten any breakfast, and the strong coffee they'd drunk at the farm was making his stomach churn with acid. It was bad enough trying to deal with his inner turmoil and lack of sleep, without hunger being added to the mix. 'I'm starving and there's a chance we might find it easier to persuade him to open up if we're not talking to him in Alvar's house.'

'Sure, why not? Do you have anywhere in mind?' Karó was concentrating on the road ahead. 'I eat anything.'

Týr searched on his phone for a restaurant near Alvar's house that wasn't too upmarket. He'd received a message from his father but he didn't open it. He wanted to read it in private, when he had some time to himself, not when he was on duty and needed to concentrate on the job in hand. Having found a suitable-seeming place that sold basic stuff like burgers, he rang Bogi and suggested meeting there. Bogi was hesitant at first, but quickly changed his mind when Týr explained that the food would be on them. Týr guessed that the poor sod would be out of the house like a shot, despite knowing they wouldn't reach the restaurant themselves for another twenty minutes. Clearly, the prospect of a free meal was a big draw. After this, Týr firmly pocketed his phone, ignoring his father's message.

'You sure you're OK?' Karó turned her head briefly towards him. 'If you want to talk, feel free. It sometimes helps.'

Sometimes but not always. The only reason Týr was still functioning and not curled up in a ball somewhere was that he had the case to focus on and keep his difficult thoughts at bay. There was no way he was going to risk losing it by stirring up his past again. 'Thanks, but I'm good.'

'Whatever you say.' Karó reached for the radio and turned up the volume. They spent the rest of the drive listening to uninspiring music, interrupted now and then by equally uninspiring comments by the radio host.

When they reached the restaurant, Bogi was already sitting at a table by the window, watching as they entered. The laminated menu he was holding looked a bit dog-eared, as if the cook saw no reason to vary the dishes on offer. There were no other customers, but then it wasn't yet midday and presumably few people felt like tucking into burgers before 11 a.m.

Once they'd exchanged greetings, Týr took their orders. Bogi wanted a burger, chips, a grilled sandwich and a Coke. Karó said a coffee would do, and Týr ordered a burger for himself. He paid, got a number, then took a seat beside Karó, facing their hungry witness.

There was no point wasting time on chit-chat about the weather. 'Have you heard from Alvar at all since we last spoke?'

Bogi shook his head. 'No.' Looking a bit awkward, he added: 'But then I haven't been trying to get hold of him. Because of the rent – you know. I can't pay it and he'll only chase me for it. Why, was I supposed to call him?'

'No, not necessarily.'

Bogi shifted on the hard plastic seat. 'Can I ask you a question? Or is it against the rules?'

Karó smiled. 'No, it's not against the rules.'

'OK.' Bogi didn't immediately ask the thing that was obviously bugging him. He appeared to be trying to work out how best to phrase it. Eventually he said: 'I saw the news.' He waited to see if Karó or Týr would take this bait, but they were silent and left it to him to ask the question that was hanging in the air: 'The farm where those murders happened . . . is that the farm where Alvar's working?'

Týr saw no reason not to tell the young man the truth. He would find out sooner or later. 'Yes. That's why we need to talk to him.'

'So he's not one of the people who was killed?' It was hard to tell whether Bogi was relieved or disappointed. The dead are unlikely to hassle you for rent.

'No. We'd hardly be trying to get hold of him in that case, would we?' The smell of frying meat reached Týr's nose and his guts welcomed the fact with a loud singing. Neither Karó nor Bogi appeared to notice, but then the subject under discussion was serious.

'Then is he . . . you know, is he suspected of being the murderer?'

'No.' Again, Týr felt there was no reason to conceal the truth. 'But he might know something about what happened there.'

Bogi nodded. 'I see.'

'So you appreciate how serious this is?' Karó unzipped her coat, slipped it off and hung it over the back of her chair. 'We urgently need to speak to Alvar, but since he doesn't seem to have his phone switched on or to be answering messages, we're a bit stumped. Of course, we could put out an appeal for information about him, and that's what we'll do if we can't contact him any other way, but that's not a very desirable solution from his point of view. Nobody wants their mugshot in a police "wanted" notice.'

'No. Of course not. He wouldn't like that. It would probably make him keep his head down.' Bogi grimaced and shot a glance at the counter to check if their food was ready. It wasn't. 'But he's got to be somewhere and he's sure to turn up soon. I swear to you, though, I have no idea where he is.

I'm not hiding him or covering up for him. He hasn't been in touch at all.'

Týr saw no reason to doubt what he said. 'Have you ever caught Alvar doing anything dishonest? For example, has he ever stolen anything, to your knowledge?'

The question seemed to take Bogi by surprise. 'No, never. Never. He's not the type.'

'Do you know him well enough to be sure about that?' Karó asked.

Bogi thought. 'No. Maybe not. Still, I've been renting from him for four months. Or a bit longer. So I know him fairly well. Better than most, I expect, because he doesn't have many friends. Only two, really, and they both left in the autumn to study abroad. Then there are the people who were at uni with him. But I think they're more like acquaintances.'

Karó took down the names of the two friends, though Bogi could only remember the first name of one. She also made a note of the fact that they were studying in Denmark, but Bogi couldn't tell them the name of the university or what courses they were taking. He had the feeling they were both doing something related to computing. Or technology.

'Do you think he could have gone abroad to visit them?' Týr heard plates being banged down on the counter behind them.

'Well, I don't know.' Bogi stared hungrily at the food that was awaiting them. 'He could have, I suppose. I don't know where else he could be.'

They fetched their food and sat down again. Týr, unable to wait, tucked in at once, and so did Bogi. Karó sipped her coffee. Not until Bogi had put away half his burger and was starting to eye his sandwich did she resume the questioning. 'What about girlfriends? Any exes or new girls he's mentioned to you?'

Bogi gave a short, contemptuous laugh. 'Blokes like me and Alvar don't have girlfriends. The kind we're interested in wouldn't touch us with a barge pole.'

Týr, noticing Karó's tightened lips, hastily swallowed his mouthful and took over the questioning: 'And what kind of girls are they?'

Bogi shrugged. 'Just . . . you know . . . hot chicks.'

'Any particular age?' Karó managed to make the question sound casual, but Týr knew she was digging, trying to get a sense of whether Alvar was attracted to underage girls.

'No. As long as they're not old, of course.' Bogi stuffed the rest of the burger into his mouth in one piece. His cheeks bulged, hamster-like. 'Our sort of age. Or thereabouts.'

Týr put the rest of his burger back on his plate. He'd had enough. 'Alvar must have had the odd day off and come home?' When Bogi nodded, Týr continued: 'Did he ever mention any disagreements with his employers or seem worried that he might lose his job?'

Bogi emptied the can of Coke down his throat. 'He didn't talk about anything much. Though one time he wasn't too happy – he seemed pissed off with work – but the next time he came home he seemed in a good mood. He's only been back those two times. They don't give him every weekend off, if that's what you think.'

'Did he speak well of the couple he worked for?' Karó asked.

Týr was becoming familiar with her technique and was sure she'd follow up this question with another. They didn't need a second-hand report about Ása and Reynir, since there were plenty of people who'd known them personally and witnessed their marriage first hand.

'He didn't really talk about them – not like that. Though he did mention that they were loaded.' Bogi paused and thought.

'Oh, yeah, and that the bloke was kind of weird. He had this massive scar on his head from a brain tumour and was a bit mental because of that.' Bogi suddenly broke off in embarrassment, transfixed by the scar on Týr's forehead.

It wasn't the first time someone had looked at Týr like that, but he felt uncomfortably conscious of it now that he knew he hadn't got the scar from falling off his tricycle. That had been a cute story. But the idea that his father had hit him with an axe was a far darker tale.

Karó hurriedly slipped in a question before Bogi could start backpedalling in an attempt to mitigate the awkwardness. This was obviously what she'd been building up to ask: 'What did he say about the two daughters?'

Bogi almost sighed aloud in his relief at being offered a way out after his gaffe about the scar. Perhaps that was why his answer was unusually frank: 'He was hoping to pull the older girl. He didn't mention the other one.'

Týr frowned. He knew this made his scar more conspicuous but he couldn't help himself. 'You do realise she was only fifteen?'

Bogi looked uncomfortable again. 'Oh, come on, I didn't mean it like that. Neither did he. He meant when she was older. He just thought she was fit, and she was rich too. But I reckon he only meant it as a joke. Honestly.' But his voice lacked conviction. 'Anyway, she had a boyfriend, I think. Some local kid. So it was only a joke.'

Neither Týr nor Karó smiled.

Bogi reached for the sandwich, but instead of biting into it, he contemplated the white bread with the black tiger stripes left by the grill. Then he raised his eyes with a wounded expression. 'What are you looking so pissed off about? Don't you think Alvar was good enough for the little rich girl?'

'Good enough? Sure. Too old? Definitely.' Karó didn't mince words.

But her answer didn't seem to satisfy Bogi, who still looked sulky, as if suffering from an inferiority complex on behalf of himself and his landlord. At least, that's how Týr interpreted it. He reckoned he could take a pretty objective view of Icelandic society as he was coming to it with the eye of an outsider, and he hadn't noticed people being labelled posh or not. Most Icelanders had picked their nose in the same sandpit, walked the same pavements on their way to school, gone clubbing in the same nightspots and bought their food at the same supermarkets. There was no sense of mystique attached to anyone, even if they belonged to the small group of national celebrities. So the question of his social standing shouldn't cause a young man like Bogi any angst, unless he had a chip on his shoulder. Then again, Týr could have misread the national character.

'Did he say anything else about the daughter or her boyfriend?'

Bogi seemed to have got over his affront because he answered this straightforwardly enough: 'Only that the girl's mother didn't want them to meet up. She was having a fight with the boy's dad. Something to do with horses and pigs.'

'Horses and pigs?' It was the first Týr had heard about pigs in this context. Ása and Reynir hadn't kept any pigs and he hadn't noticed any on the farm where Róbert lived. 'Are you sure he said pigs?'

'Yes, I think so. That's why Alvar thought he might be in with a chance with the girl.' Bogi corrected himself hastily: 'Later, of course – when she was older. Assuming he was still interested. But I think he'd got bored of her. If you ask me, she sounded like a stuck-up bitch. Spoilt, I expect.' Bogi was doing what so many people did when they were rejected – denigrating the girl, in this instance on his friend's behalf.

Neither of them said a word in reply. Bogi fiddled with the chips on his plate. 'So where do *you* think Alvar is?'

'We don't know. Unfortunately,' Karó replied.

Bogi lowered his gaze to the table. 'If he's done something wrong, can I carry on renting from him? Or will the house be taken off him?'

Karó pushed away her cup as if she'd had enough of her coffee – or the company. 'In your shoes, I'd be more worried about what would happen if I didn't pay the rent. That can't end well.'

They returned their plates to the counter, then offered Bogi a lift home. He accepted, got into the back of the car, then started asking how much police officers earned. 'I'm thinking of applying. I'd make a great cop.'

Týr and Karó suppressed their smiles and avoided answering. But the next question demanded a response.

'If I help you track down Alvar, will I get paid for it? Is there a reward?'

'No to both questions. But if you know where he is, it would be better for you if you told us.' Týr twisted round in his seat to scrutinise the young man's expression. But Bogi's face was blank as he stared out of the side window, perhaps trying to think of other ways to pay his rent.

When they reached Bogi's house, he didn't seem particularly eager to get out of the car and go inside, perhaps because there was no one waiting for him. 'There's one thing. Alvar's got an iPhone. And an iPad too. I know he has a tracking app, because he lost his iPhone just after I'd moved in and managed to find it using his iPad. If you want, you can try it for yourselves.'

It wasn't such a bad idea. The police in town might already have done a search for his phone, but it couldn't hurt to give it a shot. Karó switched off the engine and they followed the young man inside.

They stood in the living room while Bogi fetched the iPad. They could see into the kitchen where the same chaos reigned. Týr shook his head. It wasn't as if Bogi was exactly busy. Assuming Alvar wasn't a total slob too, he was bound to be mightily pissed off when he eventually came home.

If he came home.

Once Bogi had handed them the tablet and showed them the map generated by the phone tracker, Týr wasn't so sure. According to the tracker, the phone had last been used in the vicinity of Hvarf. And what was worse, this appeared to have been on the very day the mobile phone signal had dropped out.

Alvar's phone had not been used since.

Chapter 26
Before

The blinds were drawn and all the lights were on – the kitchen brilliantly lit, the darkness kept firmly at bay. But Sóldís couldn't stop shivering, couldn't get rid of the awful thought of the shadowy figure spying on her all this time as she slept. She had to get out of here. Had to quit her job and flee back to town. She could hang around outside her old flat, waiting until Jónsi went out, then go in and fetch the rest of her stuff. It didn't have to be difficult or complicated. If he'd changed the locks, which she very much doubted, she would kick the door down. Her plans didn't extend any further than that. Where she would go afterwards, where she would live, how she would support herself – she'd worry about all that stuff later. If the worst came to the worst, she could go back to her parents and face the inevitable 'we told you so' about her break-up. They had always been sceptical about Jónsi and like most people they loved being proved right. That's why she'd kept the news from them. In the few short phone calls she'd had with them since arriving at the farm, she'd merely told them she needed a change from the city. But even moving back in with them would be preferrable to the current situation. Anything was better than being stuck here a moment longer with these weird people – and the stalker who was terrorising them all.

Sóldís didn't mention a word of this aloud. She was afraid that if she did, her resolve would falter. Besides, she couldn't face the inevitable confrontation with Ása. She'd retrieved the driver's business card from her coat and stuck it in the pocket of her jeans, and every now and then she slipped in her fingers to touch it. It was her lifeline: she was going to ring the driver first thing in the morning and ask him to come and pick her up. Only then would she break the news to Ása that she was leaving. She couldn't care less what clauses her contract might contain about terminating her job early. The couple couldn't keep her a prisoner here just because of some words on a page.

'Perhaps the builders didn't tidy up after themselves and forgot to block it up.' Ása was still clutching at straws to explain the spyhole. 'That's the most obvious explanation. They were under a lot of pressure to finish and the loft wasn't exactly a priority.'

Sóldís took a deep breath and released it slowly. It would be easiest not to answer, but she couldn't let Ása get away with trying to deny the problem with a cheap excuse like this. 'You didn't see it. Someone had deliberately taken up the insulation and pushed it aside, then pulled the knot out of the panelling. It's not a patch the builders didn't get round to finishing.'

Ása was silent. The two of them were sitting at the kitchen table. Reynir and the girls were watching a film in the TV room. Ása had finally taken off her coat and thrown it over Reynir's untenanted armchair. The chair stood in its place by the fire, angled to face the blanked-out windows. Its position appeared odd without the view outside, as if it had been put there for a blind person to sit in.

Ása hadn't given up. 'There's still nothing to show that it was done recently. It could have been one of the builders – spying on the others. Maybe one of them was lazy and the others suspected him of taking a nap when they weren't looking.'

Sóldís didn't even dignify this with an answer. It was plain from Ása's voice that she didn't believe it herself. Instead, Sóldís took a sip of water. Ása had offered her a glass of wine but Sóldís couldn't face so much as a drop of alcohol. Far from taking the edge off her anxiety, she knew it would only make things worse.

'Anyway, at least one thing's clear: Reynir didn't do it. He wouldn't climb up there to spy on you while you were asleep.' Ása took a slug of red wine and gave a short, derisive laugh. 'You're not his type.'

There was an insinuation in what Ása said, but Sóldís couldn't tell whether she was supposed to demand to know what she meant or ignore it. She decided not to ask. She couldn't give a damn about Reynir and the type of girl he went for. In fact, she couldn't care less about anything to do with him or Ása. The girls were a different story, but she couldn't take them with her. All she could do was try to persuade their parents to take action to guarantee their daughters' safety. 'You've got to put in a security system,' she said. 'The sooner, the better.'

'Believe me, I'm going to. No matter what Reynir says.'

Ása's sense of defiance was completely inconsistent with what Sóldís knew about the balance of power in the relationship. To her, Ása appeared to be in sole charge. Reynir didn't have a say in anything, not even in what they had for dinner. Sóldís wasn't sure he even tried to get his opinion heard. If anything, she got the impression he was quite happy – relieved, even – for Ása to make all the decisions. So it was hard to picture him banging on the table and refusing to have the security cameras reinstalled.

On the other hand, she reminded herself, it was Reynir who'd taken them down. The cameras had apparently provoked him into taking action. Into hoisting himself out of his armchair, turning down the deafening music and walking around the house, systemically tearing the cameras down from their mounts and destroying them. According to Ása, it had been because he didn't want her spying on him. But what on earth had he been doing that he didn't want her to see? Sóldís could only think of one thing: he'd been sneaking into the loft in the old house to play peeping Tom. She wasn't the first young woman to have slept there, after all. Berglind had worked there before her, and a young man too. Perhaps Reynir's voyeuristic tendencies weren't limited to girls.

'Were you trying to catch Reynir sneaking over to the old house?' Sóldís could no longer resist the urge to ask. After all that had happened, she no longer cared if Ása thought she was being nosy or crossing a line. If she didn't ask now, she'd never know. Because wherever she ended up, she wasn't going to waste another minute dwelling on anything related to her time on the farm. 'Was that why he ripped the cameras out?' she persisted. 'Was that why they were set up in the first place?'

Ása bared her teeth in a smile that was more like a grimace – a dam to prevent a scream from bursting forth. 'Yes. And no.' Ása held Sóldís's gaze with her own. 'The system wasn't set up for any particular reason. It was just one of the details incorporated into the original design. It had nothing to do with Reynir.' She lowered her eyes to her glass. 'But he tore it down, all right. You see, I discovered that he was up to something, and he thought it was because of the surveillance cameras. Which was right. But the hole in your ceiling has nothing to do with it. Reynir isn't particularly devious. He never was, and the operation didn't change that. He's not the type to spy on anyone.'

The wind had gathered strength outside and was now whining in the unsealed gaps around the French windows. It sounded almost like whistling. Sóldís glanced automatically at the doors, half expecting them to open and the blinds to be sucked out. But nothing of the sort happened. She wondered if she should tell Ása about the message that had popped up on Reynir's phone from *Begga Babe*. It hadn't entered her head to do so until now, but a lot had happened in the interim. 'Was it by any chance connected to Berglind? The girl who was here before me?'

Ása looked up and raised her eyebrows. 'You're sharper than I thought.' She sipped her wine. 'Yes. They were up to some nonsense.'

Sóldís didn't know what to say. *My condolences*? Hardly. *Oh, I'm so sorry to hear that*? No, not that either. Nor could she say: *Well, at least it's over now.* Because, judging by *Begga Babe*'s message, that wasn't true. On reflection, she decided not to tell Ása. She'd have to find out for herself. In the end, all Sóldís could think of was to ask: 'Was that why she left?'

'She didn't leave, I fired her.' A flicker of satisfaction crossed Ása's face as she said this. Clearly, it had been no hardship.

Sóldís found herself staring at the wedding ring on Ása's slender left hand. She was itching to ask the question she'd been holding back. It seemed like a natural response to what Ása had just told her. Besides, Ása obviously had no compunction about hurting other people's feelings. So Sóldís went ahead: 'You fired her. Why didn't you divorce Reynir?'

Ása didn't seem affronted. 'Can I ask you something?' she said instead. When Sóldís nodded, Ása went on: 'If Reynir had had a heart attack while driving and killed a pedestrian, do you think I should have divorced him? Or accepted that his illness was to blame for the accident and stuck by him?'

To Sóldís, the question was rather more complicated than it sounded. It wasn't simply about whether you should be loyal to your partner. Supposing, for example, the driver had been warned about the risk of this happening but insisted on driving regardless? She understood what Ása was trying to say, though. The brain damage Reynir had suffered as a result of his tumour had changed him. Ása was going to stay by his side and remain true to their marriage vows: for better, for worse, in sickness and in health. Instead of responding to Ása's question, she asked: 'Will he get back to normal? In time?'

Ása tightened her lips and shook her head. 'No. He's as normal now as he's ever going to be. He'll be like this for the rest of his life. Not the man I married but another, more troublesome version of him. You could say the coding of Reynir's brain is like the alpha version of the intended final product. Full of flaws and coding errors. Errors that can't be corrected. I just have to learn to live with that and keep reminding myself that he is the man I loved and still love. In spite of everything.' She looked vaguely around her, an almost imperceptible glimpse of sadness in her face. 'That's why we're here. Because there are fewer chances for him to make a serious mess of things. But not no chances, sadly. As I've discovered. Shutting yourself away, cutting yourself off – it doesn't work. Your troubles come looking for you. Because of the way Reynir behaved with Berglind, I decided to employ a young man next time. That went well.' Ása gave a brief, sarcastic laugh. 'Let me give you a piece of advice. Always trust your instincts. When we interviewed him, I had a feeling there was something wrong. He seemed so stressed and kept avoiding eye contact, as if he was shifty or having trouble concentrating. But I put it down to nerves and ignored my doubts. Big mistake. Always trust your instincts.'

Sóldís wasn't interested in hearing advice from Ása. She'd already had it up to here with advice. 'What about me?' she asked. 'Weren't you worried about me? In connection with Reynir?'

Ása looked unflatteringly surprised. 'No.' Her astonishment changed to pity. 'You needn't worry. That's exactly why I chose you. He's attracted to . . . well, I don't quite know how to put it without offending you, so I might as well be blunt. Since his illness, Reynir has been more interested in the packaging than the contents.'

Sóldís could feel the blood rising to her cheeks. She felt acutely conscious of her thin, limp hair, her slightly too-large nose and crooked front teeth. It was more or less what Jónsi had flung at her, only in different words. She was tomato ketchup: Jónsi and Reynir both wanted Béarnaise sauce. She slipped her hand into her pocket and touched the driver's business card again like a talisman of her imminent escape. But as she made to stand up, Ása reached out and laid a hand on hers. 'Don't be offended, please. Being intelligent and kind is so much more important than looking like a model.'

Sóldís derived little comfort from this. She didn't think she was cleverer than anyone else. Was she kind? Yes. Sort of. But that wasn't much consolation. It wasn't as if beautiful people couldn't be kind too – and intelligent. Take Ása, for example: she ticked at least two out of the three boxes. Intelligent and beautiful. But was she kind? Sóldís wasn't so sure. She freed her hand from Ása's and stood up. 'I'll get supper ready,' she said curtly.

This had the desired effect: Ása was disconcerted enough to take her wine glass and go through to join the rest of the family. Sóldís was now alone in the kitchen, and, in spite of everything, she was glad. The room was brightly lit, the blinds were drawn and nothing could happen. Ása and Reynir weren't far away. For good measure, she took out a big kitchen knife and laid it on the counter beside her. Better safe than sorry.

Íris came through to fetch some water. While she was running the tap, waiting for the water to get cold, Sóldís took the necklace out of her back pocket. She hadn't mentioned it to Ása. Tapping Íris on the shoulder, she laid the necklace in the palm of the girl's hand. 'Don't ask me where I found it. That doesn't matter. But Gígja had nothing to do with it.'

Íris closed her hand over the necklace and opened her mouth to ask a question, then, changing her mind, just gave Sóldís a smile of gratitude. Once she'd filled her glass, she went back out.

Sóldís decided to make spaghetti and mince, in what could be interpreted as a rather feeble protest, since Ása had never served this dish. Sóldís deliberately left out the vegetables but put in plenty of salt, a generous pinch of seasoning and a traditional helping of sugar. Childish though it was, she got a small kick out of making sure that the last meal she cooked for the family would be anything but health food.

But her half-hearted attempt at revenge backfired. The girls were happy, but then she'd been expecting that. What she hadn't bargained for was that Reynir and Ása would shovel the meal down with such gusto.

They put away plenty of wine too. Another bottle was brought out, although they had no reason to celebrate.

After supper, Reynir was the first to rise from the table, announcing that he was going out to the byre. The wine seemed to have diminished his fear about what might be lying in wait outside. It had obviously allayed Ása's concerns too, as she gave him an inconspicuous sign to go behind the house as well and get rid of *you know what*.

It was on the tip of Sóldís's tongue to ask if this was really such a good idea, but she stopped herself. It was none of her business if Reynir wanted to take unnecessary risks. Anyway, the cows and horses needed to be fed, as they'd been neglected far too long already. The headless chickens would have to be removed from the run too, and buried or at least disposed of somewhere else. The writing would have to be cleaned off the glass, and the hen's heads would have to be found or there was a danger that they'd be forgotten about in all the fuss and the girls would stumble over them in the morning when they went to feed the chickens. If they saw the feathers stuck to the letters daubed on the windows, they were bound to work out where the red colour had come from.

For once, Íris offered to help clear away, and Sóldís accepted, realising that this was her way of thanking her for recovering the necklace. When she came in to supper, she'd been wearing the fine chain round her neck, the little heart tucked out of sight inside her collar.

Ása disappeared with her glass and the half-finished second bottle. Gígja, meanwhile, clambered on to a bar stool by the big kitchen island and leant forward, resting her head in her hands. 'Mummy and Daddy had a fight. While you were cooking.'

'Don't tell tales, Gígja.' Íris turned from the sink to shoot her sister a poisonous glare.

'I'm not telling tales. I'm just saying.'

'What were they fighting about?' Sóldís guessed it was to do with the security system. Maybe Ása had said they'd better reinstall it and Reynir had lost his temper.

'About Mummy's wallet. The one that was stolen.' Gígja shrugged. 'Mummy says Daddy took it. But he says she stole it from him first, so he can steal it back if he likes. But that he hasn't got it. Not directly.'

'What are you on about, Gígja?' Íris put a saucepan lid in the dishwasher. 'Dad wouldn't be interested in Mum's wallet. You must have heard wrong.'

'No, I didn't. I know what they said. You weren't there, I was.' Gígja looked back at Sóldís. 'Then Daddy said that Alvar must have taken the wallet, but Mummy said she didn't believe that any more. If Alvar had the wallet, he'd have called. Or something.'

Sóldís couldn't make any sense of this. 'Why would he call if he'd stolen the wallet? Could Íris be right that you misunderstood what they were saying?'

Gígja shook her head. 'No. Mummy said so. She said Daddy knew perfectly well that Alvar couldn't use it, so he'd have to get in touch – if he had it. She thinks Daddy's stolen it. But I believe Daddy. He hasn't got the wallet.'

'Use what, Gígja? What wouldn't Alvar be able to use?'

'I don't know. The wallet, maybe. Maybe it's locked and he can't open it.'

Sóldís put down the cloth she had been holding. She couldn't imagine a wallet that couldn't be opened just because it was locked. All it would require was a pair of pliers or something.

Íris put her hands on her hips. 'You're talking crap, Gígja.'

Just then, Sóldís heard the front door open and decided not to ask any more questions. Reynir was obviously back from the byre. It was just as well they'd stopped talking because he appeared without warning in the doorway, leaning against the frame with his hands behind his back. 'One of the snowmobiles was parked outside,' he said. 'With the keys in the ignition.'

Sóldís saw Íris stiffen beside her. It was easy to guess that her friend Robbi had returned the snowmobile but hadn't dared knock when he saw that Ása and Reynir were back. 'Oh, sorry, I went for a short spin on it.' Sóldís tried to sound normal. 'While the spaghetti sauce was cooking. I just needed a breath of fresh air, but I didn't have time to put it away in the shed. I was worried the mince might burn.' She kept her eyes fixed on Reynir, hoping to see a sign that he believed her absurd story.

To her surprise, he swallowed it whole. 'I see. Don't worry about it. I'll put it away.' Then he beamed at the three of them. 'Guess what?'

'What?' Only Gígja seemed eager to hear what he had to say. Luckily, she hadn't corrected Sóldís, as Sóldís had feared, so she must have taken her story at face value and failed to make the connection with Robbi borrowing one of the snowmobiles the previous evening.

'Well, ladies. You can sleep peacefully tonight. I've brought something in from the byre.' Reynir drew out what he'd been hiding behind his back.

He was holding the big axe.

Sóldís had been intending to spend her last night in the TV room, close to the family, rather than on her own in the old house. But now she rapidly revised her plans. She would feel safer alone over there than anywhere near an axe-wielding Reynir. That was absolutely certain.

Chapter 27
Saturday

Out of the corner of his eye, Týr saw Idunn entering the office. She stood there looking around but no one appeared to be paying her any attention; they were all too engrossed in their work. Although it was the weekend, the office was as busy as it would be on a Monday afternoon. Every desk was occupied and the rattling of the keyboards resembled a monotonous composition by an AI app that hadn't been taught about rests.

By the time Týr and Karó had returned to the office bearing Alvar's iPad, quite a few jobs relating to the young man had been added to the list of assignments, since he seemed to have vanished off the face of the earth. Few if any of the team members believed that his disappearance was directly related to the murders, but a serious effort was being directed at finding him, nonetheless.

Týr had heard some people airing the theory that Alvar had dropped his phone in the dung channel of the byre, and decided to throw it away when it turned out it was damaged. This presupposed that he had changed his number when he got a new phone, and no one seemed to find this odd, though Týr would have thought that most people would choose to keep their old number. The iPhone itself had not been found on the farm or in the vicinity, but it could still be there somewhere under the blanket of snow, out of sight until the next thaw.

So far, however, no new number had been registered in Alvar's name. Which meant he'd either got himself a foreign number or a burner phone, or that he'd turned his back on mobile phones altogether. Although such a thing wasn't unheard of, it was rare, especially among Alvar's age group. Týr hadn't had time to wonder whether Alvar had gone missing or what could have happened to him. He just concentrated on the job in hand. Whenever he let his mind wander, it strayed back to the secrets of his youth that were there for the finding on the LÖKE database, and the temptation became almost unbearable. It was better to focus his mind on specific aspects of the current investigation. He still hadn't opened the message from his father for fear of being distracted.

He got up and headed in Idunn's direction. Her face lit up when she saw him and she made a beeline towards him. He noticed with surprise that her hair was wet as if she had just stepped out of the shower, her face was bare of make-up and she smelt of soap.

'Hi. I thought I'd drop by as I couldn't get hold of Huldar on the phone.' She darted a sideways glance at the departmental manager's office. 'Is he not in?'

'He's in a meeting.' Then Týr added, so that Idunn wouldn't get the mistaken idea that he'd be back any minute: 'It's bound to run on a bit.'

'Damn.' Idunn pulled a face. 'I really need to talk to him or to somebody else in charge of the investigation. Given the nature of the issue, I'd rather talk to them face-to-face than send an email. But there's no way I'm driving all the way up to Akranes.'

'Then it's him or nobody. Huldar's in sole charge at the Reykjavík end.' Týr gestured towards a small meeting room.

'If you like, we can take a seat in there and you can give me a message for him. I'll be here when he gets out of his meeting.'

Idunn thought for a moment, then accepted his offer. After she had declined coffee, they went and sat down in the room. 'First I have to ask you: have you talked to your parents yet?' Her expression revealed sympathy rather than a desire to pry.

'No. I'll call them this evening.'

Idunn nodded. 'You do that. I think you'll feel better when you've heard their side of the story. It can't have been easy for them. Sometimes people's attempts to make the best of a bad situation turn out to have been misguided. In hindsight. When you've talked to them and you're ready, you can come by my office and have a look at the files. But it would probably be better to wait a bit. Your work should take priority. And that conversation with your parents.'

Týr mumbled that she was probably right. He'd been thinking along the same lines himself but he was dreading the phone call, afraid of saying something he'd regret in the heat of the moment.

Idunn seemed to sense his reluctance to discuss his private affairs. She looked relieved and he remembered what she had said about not being much of a people person. Emotional dramas wouldn't be her thing at all, so this must be difficult for her. But he didn't get a chance to thank her, because she cut to the chase: 'I've just finished the post-mortem on Reynir. They thawed him out last night, so there was no reason to hang about.'

Týr tried not to show how gruesome he found the idea of defrosting a human being like a packet of mince. That explained Idunn's wet hair; he assumed the pathologist must jump in the shower after performing an autopsy. He was relieved to think she had washed off all the horrible stuff that might have been splashed on her during the procedure, and also any lingering smell of death. 'What did you learn?'

'That's the thing.' Idunn sat back in her chair. 'Some of it didn't come as much of a surprise, like the fact that almost everything points to death from hypothermia. We'll get a more definite answer on that once they've analysed various tissue samples.' Idunn must have seen from Týr's face that he'd been expecting a more conclusive answer. 'Proving death by hypothermia is a tricky business. Sometimes all you can do is eliminate other possibilities. And take account of circumstantial evidence. Don't worry – I'm not the type to assert something that I can't prove beyond all doubt. In this instance, I'm fairly confident. He showed signs of erythema – minor haemorrhages in the synovial membranes – as well as what looks like blood in the synovial fluid in the knee joints. It all points to hypothermia. But, like I say, we should hopefully get confirmation of that when the results of the tests come back.'

'So he didn't kill himself, then? Didn't slit his wrists or anything like that?'

'No. Though of course I can't give any opinion on whether he deliberately went out in the cold semi-naked for that purpose. The post-mortem can't tell us that. I do believe he got into the bath by his own efforts, though. In other words, that he climbed in while he was still alive. That's what the position of his body suggests. He was lying huddled up in the foetal position, which is natural enough given that he was dying of cold. It's hard to picture someone dumping him in there, then forcing his body into that position.'

Týr tried to picture the sequence of events. The bathtub was close enough to the farmhouse at Minna-Hvarf for Reynir to have been able to see it when he crawled into the bath.

Týr took this as a sign that the man hadn't wanted to save himself. Or that he'd been seized by an instinct to hide, as Idunn had suggested when they originally discussed it. He decided to ask a question, though he was almost sure of the answer: 'Can you tell how far gone he was by that stage?'

'No. But I think it's likely he was on the brink. Based on his lack of clothes, the cold and the distance he'd covered. But I can't tell from his physical remains whether it was his intention to freeze to death there.'

'I can't see what other purpose he'd have had. If he'd meant to get away, he'd have worn more clothes. We received the news earlier that no clothes have been found in the vicinity, so he must have been almost naked apart from the blanket when he set out. If he'd wanted to get away, surely he'd have taken one of the cars? It must have been him who took all the keys, assuming he was the killer. At least, I can't picture anyone but the perpetrator doing that. The farm's snowmobile still hasn't turned up, but we've established that it's nowhere near the bathtub. A search has been made of the whole area. So Reynir can't have left the house on that.' Týr wasn't going to complicate matters further by reminding her about the engine noise the farmer's wife from Minna-Hvarf claimed to have heard. The Akranes police had found nothing useful on the CCTV recordings from Hvalfjördur, so they would probably never know for sure if it had been a snowmobile. Týr had found this incredibly frustrating, as had Elma when she rang to break the news. 'Doesn't it all point to the fact that he wanted to die of exposure?'

'He could have been running away. From the killer.' Idunn looked Týr in the eye. 'I'm coming round to that idea. That's why I'm here. Because I assume it'll have quite an impact on the direction of the investigation.'

Týr was momentarily lost for words, despite having had his own doubts about Reynir's guilt. 'What evidence do you have?'

'He had defensive injuries. For example, his left thumb had been practically severed, the tendons were cut through, and the wound was consistent with his having held up his hand in front of himself. This only came to light when the blanket was removed. It all suggests he tried to grab the axe to ward off a blow. And there are other, less obvious signs that he tried to defend himself, and – however he managed it – he seems to have succeeded. Apart from his thumb, he doesn't have any other axe wounds. The rest are bruises and grazes.'

Týr paused to digest this. He stared over Idunn's shoulder at the white wall while he was thinking. 'Could he have incurred the injuries in a struggle with his wife?'

'Yes. It's possible. She could have wrestled the axe off him. We can't rule that out. But there's more.'

'Like what?'

'The contents of his stomach. They match those of the other bodies. Which suggests they all ate the same meal that evening and therefore it can't have been Reynir in the house several days after they died. Although his time of death is fairly imprecise because his body was frozen, the chronology just doesn't fit. All the evidence is that he died the same night as the others. Of course, that doesn't prove conclusively that he wasn't the killer. A complete stranger could have been in the house after the murders. Or Reynir could have had an accomplice. Or he could have eaten the same meal as the others several days later.' Idunn paused before continuing: 'Another thing that struck me as odd was that his bladder was fairly full.'

Týr couldn't see the connection. 'How's that significant?'

'I can't picture a man attacking his family with an axe without having taken a moment to empty his bladder first.

I find it far more likely that he woke up in the middle of the night and didn't have time to go to the toilet.'

'So you're saying you don't think Reynir did it?'

Idunn shrugged slightly. 'I wouldn't put it that strongly. The axe that was in the bathtub with Reynir seems to point to his guilt. His fingerprints were found on it, from what I understand.' Idunn noticed Týr's doubtful look. 'Isn't that right?'

'Yes. Apparently. But forensics say the axe shows signs of having been wiped clean. The fingerprints are consistent with someone gripping the handle, but there's only one set of them, which is strange. You'd expect him to have shifted his grip at some point. There's no blood on the handle either, which is extremely odd. Forensics reckon Reynir cleaned the axe before heading out into the snow with it. But his reason for doing so is completely obscure. They also found traces of blood in the trap below one of the basins and in the drain below the shower. Was Reynir clean?'

'No. He was covered in bloodstains. His T-shirt, abdomen, hair, you name it. He definitely hadn't taken a shower.'

Týr sat there for a while, deep in thought, before speaking again: 'I suppose he could have washed the axe in the shower after trying and failing to do so in the basin. It was a hell of a size.'

Idunn didn't comment on this explanation. 'Anyway, the evidence is all over the place, so I suggest you start taking a serious look at other suspects. Assuming there are any.'

Idunn was silent as Týr slowly nodded, like one of those bobblehead dogs on a dashboard. The movement, foolish as it looked, helped him to think. Not that it was exactly complicated. 'I have a candidate.'

* * *

Karó put down the board marker and stepped back to get a better view of what she'd written. She and Týr were alone in the meeting room; the others were busy with the tasks Huldar had assigned to them.

After hearing what Idunn had to say, Týr had decided that it couldn't wait: Huldar would have to be informed immediately. Huldar had broken up his meeting and retired to his office with Idunn, who had presumably repeated the information she had given Týr. They were in there for more than half an hour, and by the end Týr was starting to fret that she might also have regaled Huldar with the sordid story of his own background. But when they finally reappeared there was nothing in Huldar's manner to suggest that Idunn had betrayed Týr's trust. He realised he was being paranoid. Just because he was the centre of his own life, that didn't make him particularly interesting to anyone else. Idunn and Huldar had more pressing things on their minds right now. As did he.

Huldar had then held an emergency team briefing, explaining that there was a possibility that the status of the investigation had changed. He'd been quick to take the implications on board. Although most of Týr's colleagues were counting down the days until the woman Huldar was standing in for returned from maternity leave, to Huldar's credit he had responded decisively to this new development. In Týr's view, the tasks Huldar had allotted to the team were sensible; he wanted them to home in on three possible suspects. One was the ex-boyfriend of Sóldís, the family's assistant. When her phone was examined, they had discovered that he'd sent her a death threat. Since people often said things like that in the heat of the moment without really meaning it, Huldar warned the team to take it seriously but also with a pinch of salt. He also stressed that they should bear in mind that Reynir's guilt hadn't been disproved yet. Although the theory no longer seemed as compelling, it remained a possibility.

'So, we've got Alvar. Then Sóldís's ex-boyfriend, Jón – referred to as Jónsi in their text messages. Then Einar Ari, the farmer from Minna-Hvarf.' Karó read out the three names at the top of the table she'd created. Below each name she had noted what was known about the man and his movements during the days around the murders. The information was far from complete, as the police had paid the men little attention until now. Karó had also written down possible motives: an acrimonious break-up in Jón's case, and a bitter dispute between neighbours in the case of Einar Ari.

Both men had turned up on LÖKE. According to the notes, Einar Ari had threatened Ása and Reynir, and also allegedly attacked his brother while he was still the owner of Hvarf, but his brother had later dropped that accusation. Meanwhile, the complaint against Sóldís's ex, Jón, had also been dropped. The girl who'd been in a relationship with him before Sóldís had accused him of threatening her, but, when it came to the crunch, she hadn't been able to face going through with a trial. She had preferred to forget about it and get on with her life, and anyway the threats had ceased as soon as the police got involved. Neither case gave them any reason to believe that the men in question were likely to pick up an axe and use it on women and children. But then if murders were that easy to predict, there probably wouldn't be any.

As yet, no one had hit on a plausible motive for Alvar. He had worked for the couple for just shy of two months and had no history of violent behaviour or psychological problems. His name didn't turn up once on LÖKE, as a witness, perpetrator or suspect. Yet it wasn't unknown for people who had never created so much as a ripple to suddenly go berserk and commit an atrocity. He was known to have money troubles, but how slaughtering his employers was supposed to solve those was anybody's guess. Then again, the enormous sum that had vanished from the couple's bank account before they moved back to Iceland was still unaccounted for. One member of CID had advanced the theory that it might have been kept in cash at the family home and that Alvar had stolen it. It was no worse an idea than any other, and it might explain why Alvar appeared to have done a runner. The chances of getting out of the country undetected were much greater for those with deep pockets. A good idea, then – but not one supported by any evidence. The banknotes left in the unlocked safe at the house didn't fit this scenario. On the other hand, they hadn't been large denomination notes, so perhaps that's why they had been left behind. A few hundred thousand krónur was peanuts in comparison to the sum that was missing from the couple's bank account – assuming that part or all of it had been hidden in their house in the form of cash.

None of the three men stood out as having a stronger motive to commit the appalling crimes than either of the others. But, by the same chalk, none could be eliminated from the inquiry at this stage.

The section of the table Karó had designated for fingerprints and biological samples was blank, as these still hadn't been taken. As a result, it had not yet been possible to check whether there were any matches with the wealth of samples and prints that had been lifted at the scene. Plans were now under way to remedy this. Meanwhile, the results of the DNA analysis had not yet come through, so it remained unclear whether any DNA from individuals apart from the family members and the assistant had been present. If something did turn up, the investigators could expect another delay while the profiles of the three men were compared to the unidentified sample. However, the preliminary results of the fingerprint analysis confirmed that there had been other people in the house apart from the family and Sóldís. The question was whether the prints could be explained by an innocent visit from before the murders took place. It was perhaps significant that no unidentified fingerprints had been lifted from the bedrooms where the victims were killed.

The most interesting information included in the table so far related to the three men's phone use. Reports had been hastily prepared from the data that had already been gathered, as the men had all been in the picture from the outset, if only for form's sake. Their phone movements had been tracked for the evening and night when the murders were believed to have taken place. According to this, Sóldís's ex, Jón, hadn't been anywhere near Hvarf, so he could be eliminated. His phone had been at his address the entire time and had, moreover, been used. It wasn't impossible that he'd persuaded someone to sit with it and use it regularly while he himself made a quick trip to Hvalfjördur, but this was regarded as highly unlikely.

The farmer from Minna-Hvarf had also stayed at home for the most part, only moving around on his property, and making one trip to the town of Borgarnes, some forty minutes up the coast. The phone had never gone anywhere near the dead zone around Ása and Reynir's farm, but had remained, unused, at Minna-Hvarf from ten in the evening. The most likely reason was that the man had gone to bed at that time. But that wouldn't have prevented him from paying a visit to Hvarf during the night, minus his phone. His imminent interview by Akranes CID would hopefully reveal evidence confirming either his guilt or his innocence.

Alvar's phone data gave the same picture as his tracking app. His mobile phone had dropped off the radar when the mast that served Hvarf stopped working, and hadn't reappeared on any other network. As only a single mast covered the area around Ása and Reynir's farm, Alvar's phone couldn't be located precisely using data from his provider, but the app on his iPad, on the other hand, relied on GPS, which provided quite accurate coordinates. According to them, the phone had been outside the house at Hvarf. Its movements couldn't be tracked, however, only its location at the point when it was last switched on. But the data did show the phone being picked up by another mast on the evening of the day Alvar was believed to have been sacked from his job. His phone had approached Minna-Hvarf and remained there overnight and for the next few days. The police assumed that the farmer, Einar Ari, would be able to shed some light on this. Or, failing that, his wife or son. The fact that Alvar had turned up at the neighbouring farm was consistent with the testimony given by Ása and Reynir's regular driver when the Akranes police had got hold of him a short time ago. He told them he hadn't driven Alvar home when he left his job at Hvarf, so the young man couldn't have got back to Mosfellsbær that way.

According to the driver, the last he'd heard from the family at Hvarf was when Sóldís had rung him early on the Friday morning and asked if he could pick her up. He'd gleaned that she was quitting her job. But he'd been busy that morning and extreme weather had been forecast for the afternoon, so he'd told her he couldn't collect her until the following day, which was the Saturday. When he didn't hear anything more from her, and her phone seemed to be either dead or switched off, he'd assumed she must have had a change of heart. Hördur, who'd interviewed the man, was unimpressed that he hadn't dared drive out to the farm just because of a storm. A professional driver shouldn't have had a problem with that, he'd said, with all the scorn of an Icelander from the countryside. But then he'd revised his opinion a bit, admitting that the man wasn't like the commercial drivers who were used to plying the rural roads outside Reykjavík and having to put chains on their tyres: he ran more of a city limousine service.

The strange thing was that after several days at Minna-Hvarf, Alvar's phone had reconnected to the mast that covered Ása and Reynir's property. Again, it was impossible to tell whether he had approached the house or been staying there, but his phone had remained connected to the network there right up until the mast had dropped out. The most likely explanation was that Alvar had been living with the family during this time, though no one was aware that he had been reinstated or allowed to stay on. Of course, there were few people left to report what had happened at the farm in the days leading up to the murders, but those the police did interview not only hadn't heard about this development but regarded the very idea as absurd. According to the Akranes team, who were handling that side of the inquiry, both Ása's friend, Ella the hairdresser, and Karl, her husband, insisted that the couple would never have contemplated taking him back.

Apart from this, Alvar's phone data showed little movement. During the two months he had lived at the farm he had gone home to Mosfellsbær twice for the weekend. Once there, he had mostly stayed at home, which was consistent with the testimony of his lodger, Bogi. He had also travelled around Hvalfjördur a bit, and once gone to Borgarnes, presumably having borrowed a car from his employers or been given a lift by them. Other than that, Alvar's phone had remained within the area covered by the Hvarf phone mast for the entire time he worked there.

Týr looked back over the list of Alvar's movements. 'Have the coordinates of his trips been plotted on a map? His movements around Hvalfjördur, for example?'

'Yes. I think Lína took care of that. He seems to have kept his phone switched on during his trips, which is lucky for us. Though I have to say that this suggests his movements were perfectly innocent. If he'd wanted to hide them from us, he'd have switched off his apps and communication software which are constantly connecting to the system. He's studying IT so he must know all about that sort of thing. Why do you ask?' Karó put down her board marker. 'Do you think he could have been up to no good?'

'No. Not directly. I was wondering if he'd been on the lookout for summer cabins or farms where he could lie low after the murders – if he'd been planning his getaway. It might sound far-fetched, but the guy seems to have disappeared without trace.' The police had contacted Alvar's friends who were studying in Denmark, and they had sworn that he wasn't with them. In fact, they said they hadn't a clue where he could have got to. The same applied to his closest relatives – his aunt and his grandfather. 'He has to be somewhere,' Týr said.

'Why don't we get hold of Lína's map and have a look at where he went?' Karó put her hands on her hips and tipped her head from side to side to ease her stiff neck. 'I'm up for getting some fresh air. Perhaps we can drop by the police station in Akranes too. See if they'll let us watch the interview of the couple's arch-enemy, Einar Ari.'

That sounded good. Just what Týr needed, in fact.

Chapter 28
Before

Sóldís awoke to darkness. Even with her eyes shut, she could tell. She lay there for a while, afraid of what she might see when she finally opened them. At least, she consoled herself, she hadn't woken up to feel anything in her hand, and all was quiet in the house. There were no mysterious creaks or squeaks. She turned on her side so that the first thing she saw wouldn't be the spyhole in the ceiling directly above her. She'd had to screw her eyes shut when she got into bed to stop herself staring at it and waiting for the gleam of an eye on the other side.

All she had to do was stick it out for a few more hours. Until this evening, at the latest. Her courage rose at the thought and she opened her eyes to check what time it was. Her first action would be to ring the driver and ask him to collect her. The sooner, the better.

As her eyes grew accustomed to the darkness, she peered over at the door to make sure that nobody had opened it while she was sleeping. Seeing that the page she had torn out of the boring literary novel was still in its place between the door and the jamb, she breathed a sigh of relief. Out of sheer spite she had chosen the last page in the book, hoping that Ása and Reynir hadn't yet read it.

The next moment, Sóldís felt the adrenaline start pumping through her veins as her gaze fell to the floor and she made out a patch in the gloom that resembled a dead rat. Anyone capable of slaughtering chickens would hardly stop at killing a rat or two to inspire terror. But then she reminded herself that no one had opened the door, and relaxed. On closer inspection, she realised it was just one of the socks she had taken off last night.

Sóldís reached for her phone to check the time. She groaned when she saw that it was still far too early to call the driver. Since she would probably have to persuade him to let her pay for the lift in instalments, she needed to keep him sweet, not irritate him by disturbing him at an ungodly hour. The family were presumably still asleep too, so she might as well use this time to pack. It wouldn't take long as she'd brought so little luggage with her – a good thing, as it turned out.

She got dressed, then braced herself to open the wardrobe. She hadn't looked inside it before going to bed, so for all she knew it might contain a nasty surprise. And if not something nasty, then perhaps Ása's missing wallet. Sóldís was in no doubt at all that it had been taken by the same person who had swiped the necklace and the remote control. Whatever the couple thought, her predecessor, Alvar, was almost certainly innocent of stealing the wallet if that was the case. He was long gone from the farm, and she couldn't imagine anyone making their way from Reykjavík to this remote location just to steal a worthless remote and necklace out of spite.

When the wardrobe turned out to contain nothing but her clothes, her heartbeat returned to normal. She pulled the few garments from the hangers and chucked them on the bed, then emptied the only drawer she'd used, took her jumper from the shelf and her suitcase out of the bottom of the cupboard.

With every piece of clothing she packed, she felt her spirits rise, and by the time she closed the case she was actually feeling optimistic. This miserable chapter of her life was drawing to a close. Whatever came next, it couldn't be worse than her time on the farm.

While trying to get to sleep last night, she'd contemplated her next steps. If she didn't yet have a fully fledged plan, she did at least have the outlines of one. She would rent a room, get an ordinary day job in a shop or a nursery, and work on her dissertation in the evenings. And she would go to bed at the end of every day under a solid white ceiling panel, unmarred by knotholes, and give thanks that she was no longer at Hvarf. For the first time in ages, Sóldís felt almost happy.

But that feeling didn't last long. On the stroke of eight, she rang the driver, only to learn that he couldn't collect her until the following day. He was busy until lunchtime, and there was a severe storm forecast for that afternoon. She almost broke down in tears at that point, but got a grip on herself before she was reduced to begging him. It wouldn't have made any difference.

Sóldís sniffed and swallowed her tears. He would fetch her tomorrow. That meant one more night. She ought to be able to survive that. On her way over to the new house, she paused in the little book room to put the novel back in its place and carefully avoided looking at the trapdoor in the ceiling, before making a quick exit.

* * *

'Where are the other hens?' Gígja bent down to peer inside the henhouse.

Sóldís took a gentle hold of her shoulder to prevent her from poking her head inside the door. 'They're asleep. Let's not disturb them. We'll just make sure there's plenty of food so they can come and get theirs later.' It wouldn't be possible to conceal the fact for long that two chickens were missing, but Gígja could find out after Sóldís had left. Sóldís didn't want her last hours with the girls to be spoilt by tears.

She would miss Gígja. Íris too, actually. And Bói and Lubbi, of course. The dogs seemed to read her mind as they rooted around in the snow beside the henhouse. Stopping what they were doing, they cocked their heads to one side and gazed at her in puzzlement through the chicken wire. Behind them, a spade was propped up against the wall of the house, and it suddenly dawned on Sóldís why the dogs were so eager to dig up the snow. Hastily giving the last of the food to the hens, she shepherded Gígja out of the chicken run. It would be hard to convince the little girl that everything was fine if one of the dogs appeared with a headless chicken in its jaws.

She called to the dogs to follow them and they obeyed reluctantly. They must be longing for a walk but there was no chance of that. None of the household was prepared to abandon what little security the house offered. It was bad enough having to feed the animals, though the byre was only a few steps away. Ása seemed to realise how frightened Sóldís was, since she didn't ask her to see to the beasts until the winter sun was at its midday peak. Its weak light certainly helped, but it wasn't enough to drive out the fear that had taken hold of Sóldís.

She had been afraid Reynir would offer her the axe when she and Gígja went outside, but luckily he didn't. The implement was nowhere to be seen, so she guessed it was lying on the floor by the couple's bed – on his side. How Ása could sleep with that weapon within reach of her half-crazy husband was beyond Sóldís's comprehension. But the faint shadows under Ása's eyes today no doubt betrayed how she felt.

'Come on,' Sóldís said with fake breeziness. 'Let's feed the cows and horses and let them out for a while. Then I'll make cocoa. Maybe we could get in a game of *Star Wars* after that.' No one else was likely to indulge Gígja like this once Sóldís had gone. And bored as she was at the thought of having to play with the bizarre figurines and spaceships, she wanted this to be her parting gift to the little girl. There would be no card to explain that this was what it was, but that couldn't be helped.

Ása had finished the day's lessons rather earlier than usual. She was visibly on edge, like the rest of the household, with the exception of Gígja. But this had nothing to do with Sóldís, since she hadn't yet told the couple about her decision. She wanted to wait until she had spoken to the driver tomorrow morning and agreed when he was coming. Half an hour before he was due, she would break it to them. That way they wouldn't have much time to reproach her or threaten her with legal consequences for breaking her contract. She wasn't worried about them persuading her to change her mind as wild horses wouldn't make her stay here a minute longer than she had to. There was something uncanny going on at Hvarf – something terrible was about to happen. She could feel it.

'You can be Darth Vader.' Gígja looked up at Sóldís with a smile as she slipped her mitten-clad hand into hers. Sóldís got a lump in her throat at the touch and at the sight of the child's sweet, confiding little face, but managed to swallow it and return her smile. She sent up a silent prayer that she was wrong about the imminent danger.

She would have to call the police herself when she got back to town. Ása and Reynir were against the idea, but just because they were being pig-headed, that didn't mean she couldn't take action. Having more or less resolved to do this, she felt a bit happier. If, God forbid, something terrible did happen, she would find it easier to live with her conscience if she had done everything in her power to prevent it. Ása had told her that they weren't going to contact the police because their lawyer had advised them to keep a low profile and avoid getting into trouble with the authorities again. If they did that, there was a chance that the business of Reynir's cannabis farm would be left to gather dust in a drawer. A faint chance. But Sóldís hadn't done anything illegal, so she had no reason to avoid the police. Besides, she thought, having Reynir charged with growing a bit of cannabis was surely preferable to living under a state of siege like this.

Sóldís opened the byre door with the same caution as she had her wardrobe that morning. She held her breath, mentally counted to three, then flung it open with a squeal of hinges. She peered inside, ready for anything. Shafts of grey light fell from the high windows, providing a little illumination. Motes of dust floated in the air. The two cows turned their big heads to the door and fixed their eyes on her and Gígja. In spite of the dim light, she could make out the gleam of their wet muzzles. One of the beasts had a tuft on top of her head that was standing straight up in the air, as Gígja hadn't had a chance in the last few days to climb on to a stool and comb it down as she usually did.

'Where are the horses?' Gígja stepped inside. 'Are they asleep like the hens?'

Sóldís followed her in. She knew enough about horses to know that they sometimes slept lying down. Their stalls were floored with rubber mats covered in straw, as Ása had read that this was the best bedding for the animals. And certainly the horses always looked in fine fettle. But you could usually hear the rustle of straw as they moved. Now, though, there was no sound from their stalls, although normally they would have been heaving themselves to their feet at the noise of the byre door opening, aware that humans meant food, a ride or a spell outside in the paddock. 'Gígja,' Sóldís said. 'Wait here. Don't follow me in.'

'Why?'

'Just in case the horses are ill. I don't want you to catch anything.' Sóldís knew it was impossible that the horses could have been struck down by illness. And even if they had been, Gígja wouldn't be at risk of catching it. In reality, she was afraid of finding something far, far worse. Despite her desperation to get this over with, her legs refused to obey and she found herself moving with dreamlike slowness. She prepared herself for a sight so horrible that she would let out an involuntary scream. That mustn't happen. If the horses were lying decapitated on the blood-soaked straw, she had to be able to behave as if nothing was wrong. For Gígja's sake.

Both stalls were empty. It took all the strength Sóldís had summoned up to prevent herself from bursting into laughter or tears. She was so relieved that she could have done either. Once she was sure that she had got herself under control, she turned. 'They're not here, Gígja. So it's all right.'

'Where are they then?'

'Íris and your father must have gone out for a quick ride while we were feeding the hens. They'll have wanted to hurry before the storm. They won't be long because it's going to arrive very soon.'

But Íris and Reynir hadn't come back by the time Sóldís and Gígja had finished mucking out and feeding the cows.

They hadn't come back, because, as it turned out, they had never left the house.

* * *

'They must have escaped.' Ása was determined to keep deluding herself. She was sipping espresso from a tiny cup, having foregone her tea for once.

'And closed the doors behind them?' Sóldís said drily. She'd had enough of Ása's rationalisations: the person who was persecuting them had deliberately set the animals free. But she was reluctant to betray Íris by mentioning that Robbi had been round and his horse had also been let out of the stable. 'The horses were deliberately let out,' she insisted. 'And probably driven away as well. They don't usually run off even when they're loose.' She could talk like this because neither of the girls was in the kitchen. Gígja was in her room, setting up their *Star Wars* game, while Íris was probably in her own room, exchanging messages with Robbi. 'The byre doors were shut.'

Ása blinked at her in disbelief. 'Why would anyone let out the horses?'

Sóldís really didn't want to have to bring up the business of the hens. She would rather suggest something unrelated to all the mysterious incidents. 'Perhaps they've been stolen. Are they valuable?'

'Well, they weren't just any old nags. We paid a fair amount for them. But I find it hard to believe that anyone could have known they were here – apart from the man who sold them to us, and he's well known in the business. He's got a very good reputation, and he didn't get it for selling horses, then stealing them back again.' Ása picked up her coffee cup from the kitchen island and, turning her back on Sóldís and Reynir, went over to the shiny chrome coffee maker and put it under the tap. While the machine was making more espresso, she added: 'I'm sure they must have just got out themselves. Somehow.'

To Sóldís's astonishment, Reynir now entered the argument on her side. He still hadn't said a word about catching her snooping in his study, and as a result she had been feeling a little more charitably disposed towards him. 'I agree with Sóldís, Ása. The horses can't have got out by themselves. They'd have had to open their stall doors, then the doors to the byre. That's way too far-fetched.'

'Someone could have forgotten to close the doors,' Ása said obstinately. She removed the cup from under the tap prematurely and took a sip that could hardly have been more than a drop.

'Oh, come on. The doors of both stalls and of the byre? I don't buy it. I fed them yesterday and I closed the doors myself. Of their stalls *and* the byre.'

Sóldís felt her certainty waver. Reynir was all too capable of walking out, leaving everything wide open behind him. She changed gear: 'Don't we need to find the horses?'

Ása couldn't hide her relief that they'd moved on to solutions instead of arguing about the cause of the problem. 'Yes, absolutely. There's a blizzard due to hit any minute and they can't be left out in that when they're used to being kept indoors.'

Silence fell in the kitchen. None of them knew how to go about looking for runaway horses. Ása was the first to come up with a suggestion, a question she directed at Reynir: 'Should we ring Karl and ask him to help us?'

'No, damn it.' It was the first time Sóldís had heard Reynir directly contradict a suggestion of his wife's. 'We'll go out in the car and look for them ourselves. They can't have gone far.'

He couldn't know anything of the sort – the horses might have been out there for hours – but it was the only sensible plan. Sóldís said: 'I can come with you, Ása. But we should go now if we don't want to be caught in the storm. And we'd better take Íris with us along with their tack. Someone will have to ride and lead them home.' Sóldís couldn't picture them trying to herd the horses with the car; being flighty animals, they were completely unpredictable, quite capable of dashing off in completely the wrong direction.

'Fine,' Ása said. 'Let's go. Reynir, you wait here with Gígja. There's no need for us all to pile into the car.'

Sóldís said she'd fetch Íris, and met a beaming Gígja in the bedroom hallway. The little girl raised her arms triumphantly and announced: 'All ready!'

While Sóldís was breaking it to her that there would be a short delay, she heard the sound of raised voices coming from the kitchen. Trying to ignore them, she ushered Gígja into her room, so the child wouldn't have to witness her parents fighting. She'd already overheard more than her fair share of rows, judging from what she'd said. Having told Gígja to wait for her there, Sóldís thought that rather than fetching Íris and exposing her to Ása and Reynir's quarrel, she would go back and face it herself. Perhaps they would cut it out when she appeared. Few couples like to fight in front of people they don't know well, and Ása and Reynir barely knew her at all. Apart from Reynir's creepy questions when she first moved in, neither of them had shown any interest in her personal circumstances. Ása clearly felt that their online job interview had been sufficient. She'd asked about what she felt was relevant and didn't care about anything else.

'I haven't a clue what's happened to them. I didn't take them.' Reynir sounded a bit bemused, more like his usual self, except that his presence didn't feel as unsettling as Sóldís had found it before.

The couple were standing by the sideboard in the hall. Ása was holding the bowl that usually contained the household keys. It was empty: there were no house keys, car keys or keys to the snowmobiles. They both turned to look at Sóldís and she hastily said that she hadn't taken them either.

'Then who did?' Ása sounded simultaneously accusing and bewildered.

Before Sóldís could answer, Íris appeared. 'I can't make a call. Is there something wrong with the signal or is it my phone?'

Sóldís didn't have her phone on her and neither did Reynir. Ása put down the bowl and reached into her pocket for hers. 'There's no signal. Perhaps it's the weather. Use the Wi-Fi instead.'

She had no sooner spoken than the storm struck with house with a violent gust. The high glass walls reverberated in the kitchen and the nearby window was sucked slightly inwards. Car keys or no car keys, it was clear that nobody was going out to search for the horses in this.

Sóldís, seized by a terrible sense of doom, slipped her hand into her pocket to touch the driver's card for reassurance. But they weren't going anywhere. Not in a vehicle, not on horseback. They were trapped on the farm.

Can't run, can't hide . . .

Chapter 29
Saturday

Einar Ari had refused to come into Akranes to be interviewed. He claimed he couldn't get away because he had a sick mare, so in the end it was decided that Hördur and Elma should go to Minna-Hvarf and question him there. Hördur judged that there was no time to lose as the man would only make up more excuses, and he'd rather not have to bring him in for interview in handcuffs. It would only antagonise him. Týr thought this was sensible: handcuffs rarely helped to loosen anyone's tongue.

It was agreed that Týr and Karó should meet Hördur and Elma at Minna-Hvarf. All the same, Hördur didn't want them to sit in on the conversation with Einar Ari – it would be complete overkill, like attacking a bowl of skyr with a JCB, as he put it. Two police officers were enough. Instead, Týr and Karó were to have an informal chat with Einar Ari's wife, Dísa, while Hördur and Elma were giving him the third degree. As Dísa hadn't been involved in her husband's dispute with the couple from Hvarf, chances were that she'd be more willing to talk and might even let slip something that Einar Ari would prefer not to reveal.

Karó got behind the wheel and for once Týr was glad to be a passenger. It was a beautiful day, still and sunny, and he was able to enjoy the view without having to worry about keeping his attention fixed on the road ahead. It was good to get out of the office and have mountains before his eyes instead of a computer. They drove in silence for the most part. Týr suspected that Karó was itching to ask him about his birth mother but was afraid it would be inappropriate. He had swiftly and consistently rejected her previous offers of a shoulder to cry on, so she must have got the message by now that he didn't want to talk about his mother's gruesome death. And as little had changed since he discovered her true fate, he was careful not to create any openings for conversation. He hadn't replied to his father – and there was complete silence from his parents as well. He guessed that they were waiting in an agony of suspense for him to make a move and allow them to explain their side of the story. As he would, eventually.

However, Týr decided that now was no worse a time than any other to ask Karó about a matter that had been bugging him. He hoped they would continue to be partners, and if he left it too long, the question would seem foolish – like asking someone to repeat their name in the middle of a conversation.

'I wanted to ask you something, Karó. When people mistake you for a foreigner – do you want me to intervene? I find it pretty uncomfortable, and I'm guessing it's far worse for you, but I don't want to interfere if you feel it would only make matters worse.'

Karó threw him a look. She didn't seem annoyed, only surprised. 'I've been asked a lot of strange questions in my life, but never that.'

'I really didn't mean to offend you.' Týr wished he'd kept his mouth shut.

'Offend me? I'm not offended. Just surprised. I don't have a manual to tell you how to behave. You'll just have to work it out for yourself. But, for goodness' sake, don't feel you have to come to my rescue in situations like that. Just do what feels right to you. Within reason, of course.'

Týr nodded, trying to hide his embarrassment. A manual would actually have come in handy. He stared out of the passenger window at the slopes of Mount Esja, where he spotted two small figures in colourful outdoor clothing descending the mountain's white flank. He envied them the fresh air in their lungs and the muscle burn in their weary legs. He turned back to face the front, wanting to say something but unable to find the words. What he really wanted was to apologise for the way other people treated her, though of course that was ridiculous. 'Most people behave like that because they're stuck in the past,' he said eventually. 'In the days when the Icelanders were all the same. It'll change in time.'

Karó only said: 'Hmm.' But after a moment she replied: 'I know. But it still hurts. I'm getting pretty fed up of waiting. I've done that more or less since I was born.' After another pause, she continued: 'Perhaps that's why I joined the police. No one can mistake me for an asylum seeker or a tourist if I'm wearing a uniform.' She glanced at Týr and smiled. 'I'm neither, by the way.'

'It was a mistake to apply to CID, then. The traffic cops have the really fancy uniforms.'

Karó smiled at him again, showing that he needn't worry about being misunderstood. After that, they continued to talk intermittently, and strictly about the case, as they drove around the Kjalarnes peninsula, then along Hvalfjördur. It was the first time Týr had had a proper chance to appreciate the beauty of the fjord since the investigation began. On all the previous occasions, the weather had been bleak or a storm had been raging, either outside the car or inside him. The latter was still true, but although Karó said little, her comfortable presence temporarily helped to soothe the turmoil in his head.

When they finally reached Minna-Hvarf, they found a police car from Akranes parked in the yard but no sign of Hördur or Elma. Evidently, they hadn't waited for their Reykjavík colleagues, but then they had no reason to. The cowshed doors were open and outside them stood an impressively large pram. It was easy to guess where they'd find Dísa.

The bathtub had disappeared from the hayfield. Týr knew that there had been plans to take it to town; the forensics department must be getting quite cluttered by now. He hoped this visit wouldn't lead to even more stuff being crammed into their storerooms.

He and Karó got out of the car and walked over to the cowshed. As they passed the pram, both gave in to the temptation to peer through the net and glimpsed a pair of plump red cheeks. The farm baby was sleeping peacefully, undisturbed by the loud mooing issuing from the shed. But its mother was obviously more sensitive to noise, as she became aware of their presence almost immediately, despite having her back to them. She was wearing large rubber gloves, a woollen jumper, and jeans crammed into high wellington boots. Her hair was pulled back in a loose bun and when she turned round, she brushed a lock from her eyes with her forearm. A look of alarm crossed her face when she recognised them. 'What's going on?'

'We're with Hördur and Elma, who got here earlier.' It was Karó who answered.

'Why are there so many of you? Were you called out?'

Týr realised what was worrying the woman. She thought something had emerged during her husband's interview that had led to back-up being summoned. 'We're just a bit late,' he reassured her. 'We didn't want to disturb them, so we decided to have a quick word with you instead.'

'I'm busy.' The woman was clinging to the handle of her large broom as if it were a lifeline.

'This isn't formal. You're welcome to carry on sweeping and we'll try not to get in your way.' Týr moved a little closer and Karó followed. 'It would be interesting to hear what you've got to say about various details that have recently emerged.'

'Like what?'

'Like the fact that a young man who used to work for the couple seems to have stayed with you for a while.'

'So what if he did? That was long before the murders. What were we supposed to do? Leave him outside to freeze to death? He knocked on our door late one evening, saying he'd been given the boot by that lot at Hvarf. He'd stormed out, determined to walk back to town. Not very clever, but then being an idiot shouldn't be a death sentence, should it?'

A loud mooing from one of the cows meant that Týr was forced to pause for a moment before he could continue: 'When we spoke to your son, he didn't say a word about this. Although we asked him about Alvar.'

'He wasn't here. It's as simple as that. He was with his grandmother in Borgarnes that week because he had to be present for a practical at school. If you'd asked me, I'd have told you. We've got nothing to hide. Alvar slept in Róbert's room and the plan was to give him a lift home the next time we went into town. But after a few days he took off. Just disappeared, taking most of the contents of our fridge with him.'

'It didn't occur to you to look for him?' Karó took a step backwards when the cow in the stall next to her raised its tail – which turned out to have been a wise precaution.

'Of course it did.' The woman began sweeping again. 'Not straight away, though, because we thought at first he'd gone back to Hvarf and made it up with Ása and Reynir. But when we heard that a new girl had started work there, we were a bit concerned. Enough for Einar Ari to go over to the farm to ask if they'd seen the boy. But the family freaked out when they saw him through the window, so he turned round and came home. The couple had it in for him. Had it in for all of us. Her, especially. If he'd knocked on the door, the same old quarrel would have broken out and he just couldn't face it. I can understand how he felt.'

Karó turned away from the cow that was now lighter by what must have been several kilos of dung. 'Why did he go over there then?'

'He was hoping to talk to Reynir. He was much less hysterical than Ása. But Einar Ari was out of luck. The younger girl was playing outside and told him Reynir was asleep. She invited him to build a snowman with her and come in for cocoa. Einar Ari refused, of course, and left again. But it was too late, because the woman had spotted him and all hell broke loose. Einar Ari said Ása screamed and dragged the little girl inside as if she was in danger. Silly woman.'

'When was this?'

'On Sunday . . . what . . . nearly two weeks ago.'

Neither Týr nor Karó pressed her for a more precise answer. They knew from Alvar's phone data the exact dates of when he had come to Minna-Hvarf and when he had left. 'Did Alvar say anything to you or your husband about where he was planning to go after he left yours? Anything more than just that he was going back to town?'

'No. Only that he was planning to go home. To Mosfellsbær. He said he'd got a house there. I took that with a pinch of salt.

He'd hardly have taken a dead-end job here in the countryside if he'd been able to afford a house.'

'Nothing about going abroad, then?' Týr didn't believe this but it wouldn't hurt to ask.

'No. Nothing. We put him to work helping out on the farm while he was here and he was done in by the evening. Just went straight to bed. That shows the difference between the sort of business we run here and that toy farm at Hvarf. He'd worked there for two months, I gather, and said he'd never been as tired there as he was at ours.' The woman leant her broom against the wall and surveyed the results of her efforts. She seemed satisfied, put her hands on her hips and continued: 'But quite apart from being a bit soft, he wasn't someone I'd ever have hired to work for us.'

'Oh?'

'There was something wrong with him. I'd never have trusted him with the animals.'

'Did he do something to harm them?'

'No. But the way he treated them made me think there might be a cruel streak there.' The woman plainly misinterpreted Týr and Karó's reactions to this because she went on angrily: 'I expect you think us farmers who work to put meat on your plates and milk in your coffee have no feelings for our stock. Well, you're wrong. I'm attached to every single one of our animals. I try to make sure they have a good life right up to the end.'

Týr noted that she only mentioned herself when she spoke about care and concern for the livestock. But when she spoke about farmers in general, she'd said 'us'. He gave her a friendly smile and replied: 'We don't doubt it.'

* * *

Týr stood in the drive beside Karó while she had a leisurely vape and contemplated the dejected-looking herd in the field where the bathtub had been. The horses didn't seem to have cheered up at all with the improvement in the weather. Dísa had cut short their conversation when the baby started crying in the pram. She'd picked it up and carried it into the house. Týr hoped Hördur and Elma would show their faces soon. Although the sky was cloudless, the sun was beginning its descent towards the horizon, and it would soon be bitterly cold.

He was relieved when the door opened and the two detectives from Akranes emerged, accompanied by the farmer. Karó, who was still watching the horses, didn't notice them. 'Those are a bit perkier,' she observed.

'What?' Týr turned and, following her pointing finger, noticed that two horses had left the herd and were trotting towards them.

'Right.' Hördur had come over. 'Seen something?' He sounded genuinely curious, but then many of the objects from Hvarf that had yet to be found could still turn out to be buried under the drifts in the field, like all the household keys, Reynir's phone and even the clothes he might have shed in his confused state.

Karó hastily shoved her vape in her pocket before turning to Hördur. 'No. I was just watching the horses.'

Hördur and Elma surveyed the herd. Then Hördur turned to Einar Ari. 'Are all those horses yours?'

'Yes. I wasn't aware there was a limit on how many I was allowed to own.' The farmer couldn't hide his indignation over their visit and Týr guessed he had accompanied them out to the yard in order to see them off his property.

Behind him, Týr heard Elma's agreeable voice: 'Those two as well?'

Looking round, he saw that she was pointing to the horses that had caught Karó's eye.

'Yes, them too.'

Elma went on: 'I thought you only kept mares.'

'I do. What of it? You're not going to start banging on about cruelty to animals too, are you?' His voice was tight with anger. 'What I'm doing is perfectly legal. It's the only way I can keep my head above water. If you're so bothered about animal welfare you should pay more for your products.'

Elma didn't let this get to her. 'Strange mare. Don't you think?'

They all looked at the horse she was pointing to, which was one of the two that had approached them. The animal had paused to urinate and it was quite clear now to everyone that he was no mare.

* * *

'Do you think he's here?' Týr regarded the uncompromising gate and traffic barrier blocking the access road in front of them. Beyond it they could see the buildings of the old whaling station. They were parked almost on the shore of the fjord, at the foot of a low rocky hill that appeared to be an outlier of the mountain that rose up on the other side of the main road. The area was closed off and notices on the high wire fences made it clear that all unauthorised traffic was prohibited and that the area was monitored by CCTV. Týr's gaze travelled over the tanks and buildings, unable to guess their purpose. 'I'd think twice about hiding out in an area that's crawling with security cameras.'

They were at Midsandur, on the northern side of Hvalfjördur, where they had driven immediately after leaving Hördur and Elma at Minna-Hvarf. The Akranes detectives had required no assistance to complete their interview with Einar Ari, once it had become clear that the two horses missing from Reynir and Ása's farm were among his herd. When Einar Ari was finally persuaded to admit it, he claimed that the animals had appeared in his field the day after the storm on Friday, just over a week ago. He'd felt the onus should be on their owner to come looking for them, not for him to find out where they had come from. If nobody got in touch about them, the old law of finders keepers would apply.

After this, Týr and Karó had set off to follow the trail of Alvar's phone movements. According to the data, he had twice visited the old whaling station during his time working for the couple at Hvarf. On the first occasion, he seemed to have entered the area, perhaps by climbing over the fence to have a look around. The second time he hadn't gone any further than where they were now – unless he'd just parked there and left his phone in the car.

'Well, there's no shortage of buildings here.' Karó switched off the engine.

She didn't remove the key from the ignition, but kept hold of it, as if she couldn't make up her mind whether to get out of the car.

Týr examined the rough plot of coordinates he'd got from Lína and compared it to their location according to the GPS on his phone. He nodded. Lína hadn't had time to superimpose the dots and lines on to a map of the area. 'We're in the right place according to the coordinates.' He raised his eyes to scan the factory area as Karó had done. 'He came here twice. That has to be significant. I could understand it if he'd been curious to explore the area once, but twice? I can't see what would have drawn him back here. Unless he was fascinated by the buildings. Maybe he thought he could hide out here. Logically, that would mean that if he was involved in the murders, they were premeditated.'

Karó let go of the key, asked if she could borrow the phone coordinates and pored over them for a moment or two. 'Maybe he just went fishing. To pass the time.' She handed back the map, pointing at a line that diverged more or less at a right angle from the road they had been following. 'Look. That must be the main road, so, going by this line here, he must have gone out along the pier. At least I think so. It's a bit hard to work out the distances from this. But it looks to me as if that must be the pier.' She stared out of the windscreen at the stone-built mole projecting into the still waters of the fjord, with a wooden pier at the end. Týr followed her gaze.

'If the area's guarded by CCTV, he would hardly be allowed to fish from the jetty,' he objected.

'I suppose it's always possible he was interested in Second World War relics. According to the internet, the US army built the facilities here in the 1940s as an oil depot.' Karó shrugged at Týr's sceptical expression. 'There are plenty of nerdy types out there with weird interests, Týr.'

He conceded that this was true, then suggested they drive on. It wasn't far to the next place where Alvar had stopped, so there was no need to hang around here any longer. If Hördur thought it worthwhile, he could apply to the whaling company for the recordings from the security cameras – if they still existed.

They continued on their way, past a series of restored Nissen huts and sheds. Alvar hadn't stopped here, according to Lína's map, but the cluster of buildings was interesting nonetheless. If Alvar had driven around the fjord in search of possible hiding places, the old barracks must have caught his attention. They pulled into a gravel parking area in front of a building that looked like a cafeteria. The whole place was covered in notices prohibiting unauthorised traffic and warning that the area was protected by CCTV. All the windows of the cafeteria were clearly marked as being solely for the employees of Hvalur Ltd.

'The lights are on outside some of the Nissen huts.' Karó indicated a row of the distinctive old army barracks, with their curved corrugated-iron roofs. 'They're obviously still in use. Presumably as accommodation for workers.'

Týr nodded, and they agreed that the area wasn't as good a hideout as they had originally thought. Nor was the next place Alvar had stopped any more promising. It was a track leading to another pier near by, called Midsandsbryggja. It was blocked off to the public by a locked gate with the inevitable warnings about unauthorised access and CCTV.

'Perhaps you're right. Perhaps he just went fishing.' Týr studied the aluminium roof of a building that could be glimpsed over the high, concrete wall they had parked beside. 'He can hardly have been planning to break in here to find somewhere to stay.'

'How long do people usually spend fishing?' Karó switched off the engine.

'A couple of hours, I'd imagine. I really don't know.' Týr looked round at her. 'Why do you ask?'

'Didn't it say that he'd stopped here for twenty minutes or so?'

Týr looked down at Lína's map and saw that this was correct. He double-checked the coordinates to make sure they were in the right place. 'Yes. Twenty-three minutes. And it was definitely here.' He looked out of the windscreen again, then through the side windows and behind the car in search of anything that could explain why Alvar might have lingered there. 'Strange. There's nothing here. And I doubt he'd have been fishing for such a short time. He can't have got out for a smoke either, because in that case he'd have left even sooner.'

'Let's take a look around.' Karó removed the key from the ignition. 'Who knows, we might spot something.'

They got out of the car. Apart from a gull that amused itself by hovering over their heads, there was nothing moving in the landscape. They gazed out along the impressive wooden pier, then back towards the old whaling station in the distance. They could see more from here than from the road and now spotted two black ships drawn up on the beach. They rested side by side, and couldn't possibly have arrived there by natural forces or as the result of a shipwreck. Each vessel had a tall, white mast with a crow's nest at the top like on a pirate ship. Karó pointed to them: 'What about those boats? He could have hidden in one of them.'

Týr didn't buy this for a minute. It was impossible to see how Alvar could have climbed on board, for one thing. And, even if he had, conditions below decks were bound to be cold, dank and miserable. Týr looked out across the smooth, blue waters to the low mountains on the other side and the flat-topped, white form of Mount Akrafjall far away at the mouth of the fjord. 'Beautiful – but then it's beautiful everywhere around Hvalfjördur. There would be no reason to stop here in particular. Those walls block the view, so if he'd just wanted to enjoy the scenery, he'd have been better off stopping almost anywhere else.'

'Yes. Right.' Karó turned to examine a small cove next to the flat, gravelled area where they were standing. She stepped over the crash barrier and walked across a strip of grass that was mostly buried in snow. 'Look. There's a stone wall. And steps leading down.'

Týr went over to join her. It was low tide and the steep, stone-built side of the mole descended several metres to the sea below them. Gentle waves licked idly at the grey rocks, as if secure in the knowledge that they would wear them down in the end.

But Karó didn't seem interested in coastal erosion. Gripping the metal rail of the worn steps, she peered down them. 'What's a ladder like this used for, anyway?'

Týr moved closer and saw that there were around twenty steps made of weathered wood and fastened to a rusty steel frame. On both sides of the steps were handrails that had once been painted white but were now mostly reddish-brown with rust. 'No idea. Not a clue. It must have been something to do with boats. Unless . . .'

'Unless what?'

'Could it be for sea swimming?' Týr asked, though he suspected this was a foolish suggestion. Then again. That could conceivably have been why Alvar had come here, even if the steps hadn't originally been intended for swimmers. The shortness of his stay would fit with that idea since the sea was too cold for anyone to take more than a brief dip.

Karó ignored his suggestion, saying instead: 'Týr, look.' The movement of the sea and the refraction of the sunlight from the gentle waves made it hard to work out the depth of anything under the surface. Nevertheless, Týr thought he could discern a large, dark object lying about one metre down, just beyond where the steps disappeared into the shallow water.

'What is that?' Karó leant forward to get a better look. 'Is it a box? Or a suitcase?' She straightened up again. 'I could swear it's a suitcase. That must have been one unlucky tourist. Maybe they were going for a swim.'

'Not with their luggage, surely?' It looked to Týr, as he stared down into the water, as if Karó might be right.

It was a suitcase that had sunk to the seabed. 'I'm going to get it,' Týr said. There was no question of leaving without checking what was inside.

This proved easier said than done, as Karó had warned him. The steps held, and, despite her fears, Týr didn't slip off the worn rungs, but the sea was bitterly cold. Numbingly cold. Nevertheless, he managed in the end to heave the case up from the seabed. The most difficult, precarious part was hauling it back up the narrow steps. The saturated suitcase was unbelievably heavy, and Týr had started shivering uncontrollably.

The case lay on the snowy strip of grass, seawater trickling out of the sides. It gave off an odour of sea, salt, seaweed and fish. Karó pointed out a small label with a barcode stuck on one side of the case. 'It should be no problem to discover the owner. The barcode will contain the details of the passenger who checked it in.'

Týr nodded, then pulled a pair of latex gloves from his coat pocket and bent down to unzip the case. The zip was stiff and emitted loud protests as he tugged at it, but in the end he succeeded in opening it by brute force. Before raising the lid, Týr glanced up at Karó and said: 'Shall we try and guess?'

Karó responded promptly: 'Clothes belonging to a tourist. A brand-new *lopapeysa* on top, knitted in China, still in its bag.'

'I say money. Shrink-wrapped bundles of euros and dollars.'

In the event, neither of them proved right.

The suitcase contained a human body.

Chapter 30
Before

The mobile phone connection was still down. There was no landline in the house and the car keys were missing. Their last chance of making contact with the outside world had gone when their internet connection dropped out as well. All because of Ása and Reynir's obstinate refusal to face facts.

To begin with, they hadn't been alarmed by the loss of the internet, they just said they'd have to switch the router off and on again. But when restarting it again and again failed to solve the problem, Reynir had resigned himself to putting on his coat and going outside to reboot the junction box. This was located in the control room, which couldn't be entered from the house, according to Ása because of the potential fire risk from the fuse box.

Reynir returned almost at once, with a light dusting of snow on his hood and shoulders. The others were all standing in the doorway, waiting for him, Íris holding her phone aloft in her impatience to get back online. But Reynir couldn't have had time to do more than open the door and take a quick look inside. His expression when he pushed back his hood and met Ása's eye betrayed his lack of success. Probably a fault in the cable connection, he told them, and his older daughter sighed loudly. But Íris and Gígja were the only ones who believed him. It was clear to Ása and Sóldís that something else was going on. Only later, once the girls had disappeared to their rooms, did Reynir tell them the truth: the junction box had been sabotaged – smashed beyond repair.

Sóldís was surprised by her own reaction to the news. She neither froze nor panicked but accepted it with weary fatalism. She'd reached the stage where one more piece of bad news had ceased to matter. Her nerves were already stretched to snapping point. The situation was bad and getting steadily worse, but there was nothing she could do to remedy it. The whole thing was out of her hands now – if it had ever been in her power to fix.

An exhaustive search for the keys had yielded no results. They had divided up the rooms in both houses between them. Only Gígja was considered too young to take part. Sóldís had been allotted the little girl's room and she'd searched it more thoroughly than anywhere else. But her hope that the keys might be there proved unfounded. She had turned the whole room upside down, even peering inside the spaceships that had been carefully lined up for the next game of *Star Wars*, though most of them were barely large enough to hide the key to a bicycle lock. The missing keys were not there. Not in the sock drawer, or under the bed or duvet, or in the purple pencil case or anywhere else in Gígja's room.

By the time they had finished searching, the storm had released its full fury, and it was too dangerous for anyone to try to fetch help on foot. They were trapped and there was nothing for it but to wait until morning when the blizzard had blown over.

One more evening and night to get through.

'We should check the property for the person who sabotaged the internet. They must still be here. There was no car or any other vehicle outside.' To give Reynir his due, he wasn't ready to give up yet. Unlike Sóldís, he still believed he could control the situation.

'And then what, Reynir? What are we supposed to do with this man or woman, or whoever it is, when we find them?' Ása was on the verge of hysteria now. 'What if it's Einar Ari? Would you be able to take him on? Well, would you?'

Reynir was visibly stung. Sóldís felt a little sorry for him and her sympathy only grew when Ása continued: 'All we can do is wait for the storm to blow itself out, then head over to Karl and Ella's place on foot. Use their phone to hire a security guard. A big, strong, *healthy* man.'

This last comment was below the belt, and Reynir's face twisted with anger. Sóldís realised a marital row was brewing but felt too apathetic to remove herself from the firing line. Besides, there weren't many places where she could take refuge. The old house was out of the question because she didn't want to be alone. Íris was unlikely to welcome her, and although Gígja would, it would inevitably lead to another *Star Wars* game. Sóldís had only just endured one of those before the internet dropped out. Despite Gígja's promise that Sóldís could be Darth Vader, she had ended up with a figurine missing its head, a broken spaceship, the bottle opener and the Trezor. She couldn't face going through that again, so she would just have to brave Ása and Reynir's quarrel.

'And whose fault is it if it does turn out to be Einar Ari? Not mine.' Reynir watched as Ása took out a bottle of wine and struggled to open it. The cork wouldn't budge and her clumsy attempts, so different from her usual refined movements, betrayed how stressed she was.

'Since you brought up the subject, let me ask whose fault it is that we can't call the police about him? Well? I wasn't the one growing illegal substances.'

Sóldís couldn't listen to any more of this. Rows between couples were not intended for other ears. They sounded so ridiculous to bystanders. She and Jónsi had rarely quarrelled. When he lost his temper, she never used to answer back. During their short cohabitation she had taken the blame for all kinds of crap in order to keep the peace. The moment she had shaken the dust of Hvarf off her feet and was back in town, she was going to phone him and tell him in no uncertain terms that none of it had been her fault. Many months – and in some cases two to three years too late – but she couldn't give a shit. She owed it to herself to have a showdown with him. If she was to have a new life and a new beginning, she would have to shake off the old people-pleasing version of herself and chuck it on the rubbish heap.

Then Sóldís remembered that not all transformations are like a caterpillar turning into a butterfly. Tadpoles, for example, turned into frogs.

There was a soft thud from the glass wall. The blinds were still drawn so they couldn't see out, but all three of them automatically jerked their heads round. Ása, who had been about to take a sip of her yellowish white wine, froze with the glass to her lips. 'What was that?'

Neither Sóldís nor Reynir could answer. Something had hit the glass, but it hadn't sounded like a loose object blown by the wind. The thud had been more muted, like a large inflatable beach ball bouncing off the window.

Reynir was the first to react. He went to the switch on the wall and the blinds began their slow ascent. Reluctant as she was to see what was out there, Sóldís remained transfixed, unable to turn away. Seeing would be less scary than hearing and wondering what it was. Besides, Ása and Reynir would cry out if they saw something horrible, and she would be forced to face it sooner or later.

There was a vague shape outside. Ice had formed on the glass and the snow had drifted a metre deep against the windows. But despite the raging white-out, something dark could be glimpsed pressing against the glass, its shape becoming more distinct the higher the blinds rose. Ása was the first to work out what it was. 'A horse! It's a horse!' She couldn't hide her relief. Sóldís shared the feeling. Until she remembered the hens. She wasn't going to give way to relief until she had seen the rest of the animal.

The horse turned out to be in one piece, its head still firmly attached to its muscular neck. Like the window, it was coated in ice, merging into the blizzard.

Reynir went over to the window where the horse was standing. 'It's not one of ours. This one's a grey.' He cupped his hands to the glass and peered out. 'There are more horses on the deck and just beyond it. A whole herd. The poor creatures must be looking for shelter.'

Ása put down her glass and strode over to the switch, and the blinds began to descend again. 'I can't look at them. I can't bear it.'

Sóldís was astonished. Ása might be a bit strange – but she wasn't cruel to animals. Regardless of whether the blinds were up or down, the horses' distress would be the same. It reminded her of that stupid question about the tree in the forest. If no one is there when it falls, does it make any sound? Of course it makes a sound.

'Shouldn't we do something?' Sóldís felt compelled to ask. If they were confronted by a field of motionless mounds under the snow tomorrow morning, she'd never forgive herself. She didn't want to spend the rest of her life regretting that she hadn't intervened. Not the rest of her new life. The time for keeping quiet was over.

'What? What can we do?' Ása asked, her voice unusually shrill.

Sóldís could only think of one thing. 'Let them into the byre. Into the stables.'

'There are far too many of them. Dozens, I should think. And we only have four stalls.' Reynir's voice sounded robotic, as though he was reading out the results in an election and wasn't allowed to reveal any bias.

'But . . . isn't . . . can't we . . .' Sóldís was so exhausted, so close to admitting defeat, that she couldn't think of any other suggestions.

'Sóldís.' Ása's face had adopted the same expression as it did when she was teaching the girls. But the wine glass that had found its way back into her hand rather undermined her credibility. 'This storm is far from the worst thing those mares have to suffer. They're blood mares. I've tried to save them but it's not possible.'

'Blood mares?' All Sóldís could think of was that this meant they were thoroughbreds of some kind. But what did that have to do with anything?

'Yes. Blood mares. They're reared for their blood. It's sold to Denmark and used in pig breeding. Cattle breeding too. As if that wasn't bad enough, they have to be in foal when the blood is extracted from them so they're producing the required hormone.'

Sóldís frowned, puzzled. 'What does the hormone do? Does it work like a steroid?'

'No. It's used to manufacture fertility drugs for pigs and cattle – to induce ovulation before insemination.' Ása stared at the blinds as if she could see through them. 'But the blood-taking is hard on the mares and affects the foals they're carrying. I mean, there's a reason why pregnant women aren't allowed to give blood. They need it for themselves and their unborn child. The same applies to other mammals, mares included.'

Reynir let out a weary sigh. 'Do we really have to go into all this again?'

'She asked a question, Reynir. I'm answering it.' Ása looked back at Sóldís. 'When the mares give birth, their foals are often terribly weak because of all the blood-taking. But presumably the owner doesn't care because they aren't destined to live long anyway.'

'What happens to them?' Sóldís asked, though she really didn't want to know.

'They're generally slaughtered in the autumn. Shot and sometimes sent to the abattoir. Einar Ari shoots his. Then buries them somewhere on his property. Or just leaves them lying there. Are you surprised that I asked him to stop this barbaric practice?'

Reynir rubbed his eyes. 'You know perfectly well he can't do that. The blood mares are the only thing keeping them solvent. And the practice is perfectly legal, remember? Not pretty – but legal. At least, according to the Food and Veterinary Authority.'

Ása's expression made it plain what she thought of the FVA. 'And that bloody Einar Ari completely lost it when I tried to talk to him. That's how the trouble began. And since he behaved like such a shit, we decided to—'

'You. *You* decided.' Reynir interjected, then broke off.

'Oh, come off it. You agreed with me at first,' Ása answered angrily, then addressed Sóldís again. 'So we decided not to let the herd graze on our land any more. Neither of us wanted to have to look out of the window and see the guy turn up with his rifle to shoot a foal. No, thank you.'

'And that's why he's started persecuting us. Breaking in, sabotaging and destroying things and threatening us. Where's it going to end, Ása?' Reynir went back to the window blinds and peered out between them.

Sóldís felt she had to say something here: 'Nobody broke in. The person doing this has a key.'

Ása looked mockingly at her husband. 'And who could that possibly be, Reynir? Let's see . . . Oh, yes . . . Berglind, maybe . . . Or Alvar. Is that it?'

Reynir didn't answer. He sat down in his chair and stared at the blinds without moving. Ása lifted the bottle and waved it in Sóldís's face. 'Want some?'

Sóldís declined. She needed to have all her wits about her in case anything else happened. Besides, she wasn't in the mood. When Gígja came in, saying plaintively that she was hungry, Sóldís welcomed the distraction. At least Ása would stop going on about the poor mares. Sóldís couldn't take any more horror. She was at breaking point.

She prepared supper with Gígja's help, trying to make the cooking as fun as possible for the little girl. It was their last supper together, that much was certain. The driver better not bloody cancel tomorrow. She wasn't going to tell him that she would pay in instalments until they had reached town, just in case he refused, however bad she felt about deceiving him. Because trying to walk the sixty or so kilometres back to Reykjavík was a crazy idea. She wasn't prepared to risk dying of exposure just because she'd made a mistake in her choice of job.

Gígja smiled at Sóldís and said confidingly that she was her best friend. Sóldís smiled back, wrestling with the impulse to tell the little girl what she was planning. But of course she didn't do it. Gígja added that maybe tomorrow they could make some new spaceships and play *Star Wars* again – because it was the weekend. Sóldís felt a painful lump forming in her throat. She resolved to find the best *Star Wars* spaceship money could buy, just as soon as she could afford it, and send it to Gígja with a short note apologising for not saying goodbye. The thought made her feel a little less wretched.

Ása and Reynir had disappeared into their room soon after Sóldís and Gígja started cooking, and, when they reappeared, harmony seemed to have been restored. Ása had left her wine glass behind in the kitchen but showed no interest in it when they sat down at the table. The five of them all ate together, in silence mostly – apart from Gígja. The adults were careful never to let their eyes stray towards the glass wall, and Sóldís found herself crossing her fingers that no more thuds would interrupt the meal. It worked. Either the horses had gone or they were standing in an unmoving huddle.

Towards the end of the meal, Sóldís noticed Ása reach out to Reynir and stroke the back of his hand. Their eyes met and they smiled. She felt a twinge of regret for having spent so much time feeling resentful and angry with them. In spite of their wealth, they didn't have it easy.

She felt herself softening still further when both girls helped her with the washing up. She even managed to ignore Íris's sulks and grumbling. She wondered how her relationship with Robbi would develop, and realised with a jolt that she would never know. Once she had left Hvarf, their paths were unlikely to cross again, even if the family abandoned this isolated life and moved to town. They simply didn't move in the same circles.

When they had finished clearing up and Gígja was beginning to yawn, Sóldís decided to retire to her quarters. She was at no more risk there than in the new house; she might even be safer, she reasoned, since the anger of the person laying siege to the farm could hardly be directed at her. She said goodnight to Gígja, dropped a kiss on the top of her head and told her she was great. She said goodnight to Íris too and must have sounded unusually mawkish because Íris seemed slightly disconcerted. Then she rearranged her features into the familiar long-suffering-teenager face as she said goodnight back.

Sóldís scooted through the connecting corridor, not daring to look out through the glass, then locked and barricaded the door before hurrying straight upstairs. She brushed her teeth, then packed her toothbrush and toothpaste in her suitcase. It occurred to her that it would be a good idea to have something to read but she couldn't face venturing into the book room. If the trapdoor opened while she was standing there, reading the spines of the books, it would completely finish her off. Better to have nothing to do but try to get to sleep.

Sóldís stuck the page torn from the novel into the gap between the door and the jamb. Then she got into bed, pulling her duvet up to her chin. Something was bothering her but she couldn't work out what it was. Probably it was nothing more than a reaction to the ordeal of the last few days.

She reminded herself that she just needed to get through tonight and maybe a few more hours tomorrow morning, then she'd be out of here. And what could happen in such a short time? So what if she woke up with something in her hand? Or an insult scribbled on her body? Perhaps a message would be scrawled on the glass wall. In big red letters, with tufts of horsehair here and there. She would survive that, just as she had everything else. So what if she felt bad? In time, she would gradually stop thinking about it, the memories would fade and she would find it hard to remember exactly what had happened and what had been written on the windows. Though for now, of course, it was still fresh in her mind: *Can't run can't hide*. But the house was all locked up. No one could get into her room.

Sóldís dropped off surprisingly quickly and had pleasant dreams.

* * *

In the middle of the night, she woke with a gasp. She hadn't a clue what time it was as she'd forgotten to charge her phone before going to bed. Since there was no signal or Wi-Fi, she hadn't thought to check it after getting back to her room, or had the sense to plug it in. From the pitch darkness outside, though, she guessed dawn was still a long way off.

Sleep must have freed up her thoughts because it came to her in a flash what it was that had been bothering her before she drifted off. When she went past the living room on her way to the stairs, she had caught a glimpse of the dining table. There had been four chairs round it. Not the full set of six but – and this was the bad part – not just three either. One should have been securing the front door, another the door to the connecting corridor, and the third the garden door in the cellar. Six minus three was not four. One of the chairs had been returned to its usual place – either the one that should have been in the cellar or the one in the entrance hall. The chair in the cellar had still been in place when she went down there earlier that day with Ása, but it was a while since she had checked on the chair in the entrance hall. Her tired mind couldn't now recall when she had last seen it there, but it must have been some time ago.

Sóldís sat up on the edge of the bed, her heart hammering. Then she heard a faint scream that could only have come from the new house. It wasn't the kind of scream someone might emit in the middle of a nightmare. It was louder and more piercing, or it would never have carried all this way.

The scream tore through the night again. By some miraculous power Sóldís was on her feet. The room was cold and her bare feet and arms immediately broke out in goose bumps. At least the page was still in place, which meant the door to her room had not been opened, but that was little comfort. She peered out, seeing nothing, then crept to the stairs and tiptoed down them, so carefully that not a single step creaked. Removing the chair from under the handle of the door to the connecting corridor, she darted along it, her heart in her mouth, aware that she would be clearly visible through the glass to anyone standing outside. But the screams were becoming ever more frantic, bringing it home to her that the threat wasn't coming from outside – it was inside the house.

When she reached the door to the new house, she paused and pressed her ear against it. There were two people screaming. One in terrible agony, she thought, while the other seemed to be yelling something.

She strained to make out the words. It sounded like Reynir. She thought he was yelling: *No, Alvar! No!*

Chapter 31
Saturday

Týr and Karó were standing at the front door of Alvar's house in Mosfellsbær for the third time. But this time they weren't alone. There was a member of forensics with them to collect samples. It was evening and the street lights made haloes in the thickly falling snow. The windows of the neighbouring houses were illuminated by flickering TV screens, most so large that even at a distance it was possible to see the presenters reading the evening news. The programming was running late as Iceland had been competing in an international handball tournament. Týr didn't know how it had gone but hoped for the best.

The story about the body in the suitcase wouldn't have broken yet. It was only a few short hours since he and Karó had dragged it up from the bottom of the sea. To Týr it already felt like a lifetime ago, but he put this down to weariness after a long day – a day when he wouldn't normally have been working. He didn't know if the suitcase had arrived in Reykjavík yet but assumed it must have. It was presumably waiting in the refrigeration unit at the National Hospital pathology department for Idunn to hoist it on to her steel table and get down to work.

Týr and Karó had waited by the jetty in Hvalfjördur for Hördur and his team to drive over from Akranes. After that, there had been another wait for forensics and Idunn to come up from Reykjavík. Once they'd appeared and got down to work, there had been little for Týr and Karó to do but get in the way. Although Týr was freezing thanks to his wet trouser legs, they had hung around for long enough to hear Idunn announce that she didn't trust herself to draw any firm conclusions about the gender or age of the victim after a preliminary glance at the remains; the body was in too bad a state for that. But judging from the checked shirt and the hair, which she could tell had been short, although the scalp had loosened from the skull, she guessed it was a man. These two details alone didn't automatically rule out the possibility that it was a woman, though.

According to Idunn, the degree of decomposition indicated that the victim had been dead for a considerable time. Months, in all probability. Which meant the person couldn't possibly have died the night of the murders on the farm. Hördur had frowned at that and asked sharply if this meant he was now dealing with two unrelated cases. Idunn had merely shrugged, the movement barely visible under her white protective overalls. Týr kept his opinion to himself. In his view, the cases were unquestionably linked. It would be a hell of a coincidence if someone else had dumped the body there and Alvar had merely been fishing. But all would become clear in due course, so he felt it best to hold his tongue for now.

When he and Karó returned to the office, Týr was given the job of accompanying a forensic technician to search Alvar's home for biological traces and fingerprints. The longest delay had been waiting around for the search warrant to come through. It was too urgent, and there was too much at stake, for them to risk having Alvar's lodger, Bogi, block their attempts to examine the house. The search for Alvar was now top priority and the police had rushed out a 'wanted' notice for him. As yet, nobody had phoned in with news of his whereabouts, but with any luck that would change. It was only an hour since the notice had been circulated, and not many people would be poring over the online news outlets at this time on a Saturday evening.

The door opened and Bogi appeared, looking startled to see them again so soon. His astonishment increased when he clocked the third person behind them. Týr greeted him and handed over the search warrant, explaining what was going to happen. Bogi quickly skimmed the text, then let them in. As was to be expected, he was dying of curiosity and Týr was forced in the end to take him aside so he wouldn't get in the way of the technician. But first he had shown them Alvar's room, which he said he never entered, and pointed out his toothbrush in the small, shared bathroom.

Týr sat down on the familiar sofa in the living room and Bogi took a seat opposite him in a matching chair. Týr grabbed the chance to ask him if there was any news and whether Alvar had been in touch since that morning. No, Bogi told him, nothing had changed since the last time they spoke, but, on the other hand, there was a lot he himself wanted to know.

Bogi was in the middle of a question about the legal status of a lodger who rents a room from a man charged with a crime, when Týr's eye was caught by the slightly crooked shelf on the wall behind him. It always got on his nerves when things were out of alignment; he was forever straightening pictures and paintings in his flat. The recent spate of earth tremors, caused by seismic activity on the Reykjanes peninsula to the south of Reykjavík, had almost driven him demented. Every time he got home from work or woke up in the morning, he would walk around his flat, restoring everything to its correct position. At this moment, though, he found himself drawn to contemplating this misalignment, rather than simply finding it irksome as usual. He put this down to fatigue. Bogi's tedious questions were sending him to sleep. Then his gaze landed on a glass bowl on the shelf, and he felt his tiredness falling away. He stared until he was quite sure he wasn't mistaken. 'How many cars did you say Alvar owned?' he interrupted.

'Just the one parked outside.'

Týr nodded. 'Is he a hoarder?'

'A hoarder?' Bogi obviously didn't follow.

'Yes. A hoarder. The type who can't throw anything away.' Týr's gaze shifted from the bowl to Bogi's face. 'Keys, for example.'

The glass bowl contained keys. It was full of them. That in itself wasn't unusual. In most homes you would find more keys than were in use. But what had particularly attracted Týr's attention were the two black remote-control key fobs – expensive items that couldn't by any stretch of the imagination belong to the old banger parked outside. Even if they belonged to a previous vehicle Alvar had owned, he'd have been unlikely to sell it without handing over the remotes. Any buyer would have wanted them included when they signed the contract.

Týr got to his feet, went over to the crooked shelf and picked up the bowl. The two fobs matched the makes of the cars that had belonged to the dead couple at Hvarf. He put the bowl down again.

'Are you quite sure Alvar hasn't been here in the last few days? Quite sure he's not here now?'

Bogi stared at him in apparent bemusement. 'Well, I don't know. I suppose he could have come by without me noticing. It's not like I'm home the whole time. I mean, I was out this morning meeting you.'

The phone rang in Týr's pocket. He took it out, ready to dismiss the call if it was his parents, but he didn't recognise the number, so he answered. It turned out to be Ella the hair-dresser on the other end. When Týr heard what she had to say, he left the room to speak to her in private.

After she had rung off, he shoved his phone in his pocket and went back into the living room. Bogi's chair was empty. Through the kitchen doorway Týr glimpsed a back door. It was wide open and the cold was pouring in. The lodger had done a runner.

* * *

Like so many people who had been in his position before him, Bogi proved incapable of taking responsibility for his actions. None of the appalling crimes were his fault. He was the victim of fate, as he was at great pains to make the police understand. But this was a picnic compared to the first part of the interview, in which he had flatly denied everything, despite being in a hopeless position. Týr was beginning to think he must be a bit thick, when it finally got through to Bogi that he was in a corner. That was when Bogi learnt that the people who had met Alvar at Minna-Hvarf had been in touch to warn the police that the wrong photo had been used in the 'wanted' notice: it was of a completely different young man. Bogi wasn't told who had reported this, but in addition to Ella, the police had received calls from the driver who had worked for the couple, as well as Íris's friend, Róbert, and his mother Dísa. All Bogi was told was that witnesses would be brought in next day for an identity line-up. No one was in any doubt about what would emerge from this. Alvar's photo had been downloaded from the system, where it was on file because it had been used for his passport, so it was clear that the mistake did not lie there.

There was other evidence. After Týr had caught up with Bogi and marched him back to the house, more technicians had been called out from forensics and the house had been subjected to a thorough examination. Týr had barely broken into a sweat during the chase, as Bogi had been in his socks and was hopelessly unfit. The snow had helped too: Týr had wasted no time wondering which way his quarry had gone as it had been easy to track him into the neighbour's garden. Then he had spotted Bogi running along the pavement in the next street and after that the rest had been easy.

The search of the house had yielded rich pickings. The snowmobile turned up in the garage. The glass bowl had been found to contain more keys from the farm at Hvarf. Bogi's phone had been handed over to the guys in the IT department, who had immediately established that it had been connected to the mast at Hvarf more or less continuously during the time Alvar had been employed there. As well as an oral swab, Bogi's fingerprints had been taken, and forensics had already found a match with some of the unidentified prints at the farm.

There wasn't much point in Bogi denying his guilt and trying to pin the crimes on Alvar. In fact, the investigators were confident that they would soon be able to call off the search for Alvar, because the body in the suitcase had to be his. Once that had been established beyond doubt, Bogi's defence would collapse. Dead people didn't go around murdering people with an axe, as they pointed out to him. Shortly afterwards, when he had been told about the imminent identity line-up, he caved. More or less. Though he would probably go to the grave convinced that his actions had been entirely the fault of other people.

Bogi claimed that Alvar's death had been an accident. Alvar had attacked him in a fit of rage and Bogi had shoved him away so violently that Alvar had fallen over backwards and hit his head on the marble table in the living room. He had died instantly and Bogi had realised there was no point calling an ambulance. It was apparent to all those listening that this was nonsense: a blow to the head rarely leads to instant death. But no one contradicted him in case he clammed up. Instead, they made an effort to appear understanding, though it left a bad taste in their mouths. The only person in the interview room who was not dissembling at all was the lawyer Bogi had picked at random from a list he had been shown. The lawyer was there to protect the young man's rights during the interview and possibly to defend him in court at a later date. He spoke up from time to time but was mercifully brief, since the other people present were far more interested in hearing what Bogi had to say.

If Bogi was to be believed, Alvar had been stressed out and uptight on the day of the fight. He'd been angry with Bogi because he was behind on the rent, and nervous about an online interview with some prospective employers. Bogi just happened to wander into the living room where Alvar had set up his computer, and everything had kicked off. Their quarrel had ended in blows. But Alvar's death was an accident, Bogi insisted. He'd been standing there over the body, wondering what the hell to do, when he heard voices coming from the computer. Acting on the spur of the moment, he'd sat down in front of the laptop and conducted the interview as Alvar, to buy himself time. He knew this would be the first time the prospective employers had seen Alvar during the recruitment process, so he'd thought there would be no risk in posing as him. To his astonishment, the interview had gone quite well

– well enough for him to get the job on the spot. As a result of this unexpected development, he decided to buy himself even more time by accepting the offer, to ensure that Alvar wouldn't be missed. *I was in a tight spot* was how he put it. He'd taken Alvar's phone with him and replied to the few messages Alvar received, in addition to exchanging messages with himself as an insurance policy in case things went wrong later.

He'd taken Alvar's body with him to the countryside in a large suitcase. He complained that it had been a nightmare trying to squeeze the body inside and that he'd had to break several bones before it would fit. Týr was struck by the way Bogi told them this without the slightest hint of remorse. It was what finally convinced him that the young man was seriously deranged. But he was careful to keep a blank face as he listened to the rest of the tale.

Once at Hvarf, Bogi had hidden the suitcase in the cellar. When Ása showed him round the old house, she'd mentioned in passing that the cellar was never used, so he'd reckoned it would be safe as a temporary hiding place. He had chosen a bedroom on the ground floor, to be close to the cellar, and slept with his own door open so he could keep an eye on it. His plan had been to find a suitable place near by to dispose of the body, somewhere it would never be found. Alvar would be just one more name in the missing-persons statistics, and when the police came to Bogi for information, he would say that Alvar had shown symptoms of depression. The case would eventually be dropped and they would write it off as suicide. Or so Bogi told himself.

But it had taken longer than anticipated to get rid of the body. Bogi had been working for the couple for more than a month before he was finally trusted with their car. A vehicle was essential because he couldn't drag the heavy suitcase any distance. He'd had enough of a struggle getting it into the boot of the car that took him to Hvarf and getting it out again at the other end. He'd been forced to do it himself because he didn't want the driver to become curious about the weight. But the family had agreed to lend him a car at last and he'd gone on an initial recce without taking the suitcase along. After driving around Hvalfjördur, he'd decided the pier by the old whaling station was the most likely spot. The gate to the area had been open, which meant he would be able to drive out along the pier and dump the suitcase in the sea. It was the only real option at that time of year as it would have taken for ever to dig a grave in the frozen ground.

But after a month and a half in the warm cellar something terrible had happened to the contents of the suitcase and the stench was so bad he could hardly go down there. A disgusting substance had oozed out of the case on to the unsealed concrete floor. There was no way he could make a run for it, though, leaving the case behind. The smell had begun to spread to the ground floor and it was only a matter of time before Ása or Reynir noticed it. He'd tried opening the cellar window and door from time to time in an attempt to air it, and liberally sprayed around window cleaner and other strong-smelling cleaning products to disguise the smell, but nothing worked and the stink became more and more noticeable. He had to get rid of the suitcase. So in the end he'd just had to grit his teeth and deal with it.

Two weeks later he'd managed to wheedle the loan of the car again by pretending he was going to hike up to the Glymur waterfall at the head of the fjord. Luckily, by then the case had stopped leaking, so it didn't leave a trail when he hauled it out of the back exit to the cellar and dragged it round the house to the car, where he managed, with difficulty, to manhandle it into the boot. At this point, Bogi paused to look at his interviewers, as if expecting praise or a pat on the back for his efforts, but no one said a word.

Bogi went on with his tale, describing how his plan had been derailed by the discovery that the gate to the area by the whaling station was locked. It was pure coincidence that it had been open when he'd done his original reconnaissance. This left him with a dilemma. Returning to Hvarf with the suitcase was out of the question. But then he'd noticed another pier, a little further along the coast, and he'd driven over there. It had turned out to be closed to the public too, but he'd found a stone wall with steps leading down it into the sea. Using the handrail as a slide, he'd sent the suitcase hurtling down it into the water, where it had vanished into the depths – or so he'd thought.

But Bogi clearly hadn't taken the tides into account, or else the sea had been unusually cloudy at the time, because the suitcase had been clearly visible from the shore at low tide. In Týr's opinion, this wasn't bad luck. The young man just wasn't that bright or well organised; but he was the type who always managed to save his arse somehow. Though even people like him usually crashed and burned in the end.

Bogi described in disturbing detail just how bad the car boot had smelt after he had taken out the suitcase. He'd left it open for hours to air it, but then he hadn't been in any hurry. His alibi of a hike up to Glymur meant that the family wouldn't be expecting him back until quite late.

Afterwards, he'd become paranoid that the family might notice that he didn't have much stuff with him, given the huge suitcase he'd brought along originally. That's when he'd got the idea of going back to Alvar's house on his next weekend off and helping himself to the rest of his former landlord's clothes, which were much smarter than his own. To his regret, he'd been forced to abandon them at the farm when he left in a hurry after Karl's visit.

At this point they'd paused the interview and knocked back some coffee to steel themselves for what was to come. Only Týr, Hördur and Elma were sitting in the room with Bogi and his lawyer; the rest of the team were following on screen. Týr would have preferred to be in the other room with Karó, and thought that Huldar should have taken the hot seat himself. But apparently Huldar was afraid of how he would react when he heard Bogi describing his murder of the two little girls, so thought it best that Týr take his place. It was essential to extract a full confession, as that would facilitate the follow-up. The request for custody that was currently being prepared would be accepted without delay and the trial would only hinge on the question of whether Bogi should receive a longer sentence than the standard sixteen years for murder.

'Good luck.' Karó gave Týr's forearm a barely perceptible brush with her fingers, as if she were a character in a computer game, who could lend him strength with her touch alone. Oddly enough, it worked.

'Thanks.' Týr smiled at her, finished his coffee, and shuddered. Although he was revolted by Bogi and dreading the next part, he was keen to get it over with. He wasn't the only one. The cardboard cups were chucked in the bin, and they took their places again, either in the interview room or in the room next door to watch on screen.

Bogi and his lawyer had been conferring while they were out of the room. They fell silent and straightened up again when the door opened and Týr, Elma and Hördur filed in. Týr noticed that Bogi's eyes lingered longest on Elma. He appeared to be assessing her, as if she were a model auditioning for a job and he a fashion designer. Týr resisted an urge to lean over the table, jab the back of his hand and tell him that he was dreaming, that it would never happen, not in a million years. But there was no need as Elma managed to convey as much with her expression of pure contempt.

The interview resumed. Bogi gave them a potted account of his time on the farm, some of which sounded plausible, other parts not. One of the things Týr found absurd was Bogi's claim that the teenage girl, Íris, had fancied him and come on to him, but that he hadn't been interested. No doubt the reverse was true.

Then they came to the part they had all been waiting for. Though no one wanted to hear Bogi's description of the murders, they needed him to keep talking. But it turned out that there was a prologue to the story.

Bogi began by saying that he'd have been perfectly willing to stay on at the farm. If Reynir and Ása hadn't accused him of stealing, everything would have turned out differently and they would still be alive. Týr wondered if the young man was really crazy enough to believe that the couple were somehow to blame for their own murders. It seemed he was.

Bogi claimed he hadn't stolen anything. He wasn't a thief. Hördur, who had been taking a sip of water, almost choked at this assertion. But the young man didn't seem to notice and went on with his account in the same flat, unemotional voice.

Ása had accused him of stealing her wallet. But then Reynir had intervened and claimed that the wallet was his. Bogi hadn't understood this at all, but in the subsequent commotion he had tackled Reynir in private and demanded to know what was going on, after which it had been explained to him. Bogi didn't mention anything about having threatened or intimidated Reynir but they took it as read that he must have scared the living daylights out of the poor man.

If Bogi's account was to be believed, the explanation had been long and complicated. Reynir had told him that he'd taken a chunk of the couple's money and stashed it away in a safe place. He'd wanted a reserve in case they got a divorce, because since his operation, he'd become interested in other women and he wanted to continue to enjoy the same living standards if he and Ása went their separate ways. Bogi added in an aside that this was understandable as Ása had been a total bitch. She'd gone completely over the top in trying to protect her husband following his illness, and Reynir was being suffocated, being kept a virtual prisoner in the depths of the countryside. When Ása found out that her husband had stolen the money she'd gone apeshit. It had taken her a while but in the end she had found out where he'd invested it, then prised the password out of Reynir and changed it.

'What kind of investment was it, then?' Hördur asked. He was leading the interview, Elma and Týr only slipping in the odd question.

'Bitcoin. Accessed via a Bitcoin wallet that Ása kept locked in the safe, which only she could open. Reynir may have been a bit out of it but he wasn't totally useless. He used the webcam on his computer to see the code Ása had entered, then opened the safe and stole back the wallet.' Bogi broke off for a drink of water. 'But according to him, Ása had changed the password, and before he had a chance to work out the new one, he lost the wallet. He was too dopey to look after the thing and it disappeared. And they thought *I'd* stolen it. Which was total bullshit. If you ask me, he just hid it so well that he couldn't remember where he'd put it. That's why I stayed on at Hvarf after . . . you know. To look for it.'

Next, Bogi told them he'd completely lost it when they sacked him. He'd repeatedly assured them that he hadn't stolen anything but they'd refused to listen. They'd said it wasn't just about the theft any more but about the way he'd reacted to the accusations. They said they didn't feel they could sleep at night with him under the same roof and that they were going to ask their driver to come and pick him up next day. But he wouldn't be allowed to take his stuff away with him yet because they wanted to search it first – and search him too. Bogi had been so furious that he had stormed out that evening and walked all the way to Minna-Hvarf. He knew about the feud between the farms and assumed he'd be given a warm welcome there. My enemy's enemy is my friend, and all that. And it had worked; the farmer and his wife had taken him in. During his brief stay there, he'd brooded on the situation and seen that the only way out was to get hold of the Bitcoin fund for himself. If he could find the wallet and the password, he would own the money. That's how cryptocurrencies worked.

None of them pointed out that this wasn't actually correct; it was against the law to acquire another person's possessions by theft, regardless of whether they existed in digital or physical form.

Bogi then began to describe how he had lived at the farm for several days without anyone realising. He'd taken a house key with him when he left, so it was easy for him to get back in. He'd slept in the restored sheep shed where they kept a load of furniture, including beds, at first eating food he'd brought with him from Minna-Hvarf, but later he'd been forced to raid the fridges on the farm, in the old and new parts of the house. He'd mostly moved about the place at night, which is how he'd avoided detection. But he'd quickly got bored of that and decided to amuse himself by playing pranks on the family in revenge for how they'd treated him. He'd been enraged to discover that a new assistant had been hired in his place, only a week after he'd been sacked.

A malicious smile had spread across his face as he described Sóldís's attempts to barricade herself in, wedging chairs under the door handles. It had made him so angry that he'd decided things couldn't go on like that. He was beginning to feel like a ghost. He was still alive but he no longer lived among people, just lurked in the shadows like a spider. He would have to act. He'd been ransacking the house for the Bitcoin wallet at night but there was a limit to where he could go and there was always a risk that someone would wake up and catch him red-handed. So he formed a plan to attack the couple and coerce them into showing him where the wallet was hidden and handing over the password. If Reynir had genuinely forgotten where he'd hidden it, Bogi would give him such a bad fright that it was bound to come back to him. He added that fear was a good way of refreshing someone's memory. Which was nonsense, of course.

Týr could see the expressions of the others hardening. Bogi was finally getting round to the most unspeakable part of the story. Týr thought he was probably finding this more difficult than anyone else. He held his breath, determined not to let his thoughts stray to his birth father. He mustn't assume that the same kind of sick mind had been behind the attacks on him and his mother, or that his father and Bogi had been thinking the same thoughts when they raised the axe. Bogi was speaking only for himself. This mantra helped Týr to feel a degree of detachment from what was to come.

'After I'd decided what to do, I took all the keys from the bowl they were kept in. Then I let out the horses in the night and drove them away. When I woke up next day, I went for a walk and took down the phone mast. Reynir had told me about it – typical, he just had to boast. Well, he'd have done better to leave it out.' When he got no response to his gloating smile, Bogi took up the story again: 'Anyway, I went back and trashed the junction box in the control room, cutting off the farm completely. No one could get away or call for help. They were my prisoners.'

Týr felt a chill spread through his body. He assumed the others round the table felt the same, the lawyer included.

Unfortunately, it wasn't to be the last time he was filled with horror as he listened to Bogi talk, because his tale was about to get a lot darker.

Chapter 32
Before

Sóldís was breathing rapidly through her mouth. She could taste salt where the tears were sliding down her cheeks. She was weeping not from sorrow but from desperation. She had no idea what to do. The screams carrying through the locked door were so blood-curdling that something terrible must be happening. This wasn't a fuss about letters scrawled on a hand or window, a missing necklace or any of the other things that now seemed so trivial.

The steel of the door handle no longer felt cold to the touch. She'd been holding it too long for that. She had unthinkingly grabbed hold of it, obeying her first instinct to rush in and help the person who was screaming. Then common sense or fear, she didn't know which, had taken over and told her to wait. What could she do? Wouldn't she become just another victim of the attack that seemed to be taking place?

Sóldís removed her ear from the door. Why didn't Ása and Reynir just give the man what he wanted? What could be so valuable that it was worth going through this ordeal for? Sóldís owned far less than them – almost nothing, in fact – but she would gladly have handed the whole lot over to avoid what was happening to them now. Why didn't they just give the man the wallet and password he was demanding?

And where were Íris and Gígja? Why couldn't she hear any sound from them? Or the dogs? Shouldn't they have been barking like crazy if someone was attacking their owners? The door handle felt as though it was burning her hand. She had to go in there and fetch the girls. Ása and Reynir would just have to fend for themselves. If she could sneak back to her side of the house with the girls and hide . . . No, that would never work. They would have to get away, make a run for it. Outside the glass walls of the connecting corridor she could see the driving snow. The storm had lost some of its violence but it was still too severe for them to get far, especially Gígja with her short legs.

Come to think of it, though, it wasn't that far to the neighbouring farm. Maybe half an hour's walk in good weather. Or more like an hour with Gígja in tow and a powerful headwind. If they were lucky, the wind would be behind them. Sóldís was in too much of a panic to work out the direction the snowflakes were blowing in, but this was the only plan she could think of. To tiptoe into the bedroom wing, fetch the girls, race back to the old house, barricade the door to the connecting corridor with a chair, dress them in some of her own things as there would be no time to pause in their entrance hall to grab their outdoor clothes – it wouldn't matter if hers were too big – and get out via the cellar door . . .

Boots! She only had two pairs. But that wouldn't make any difference, because Gígja couldn't possibly walk all that way in boots that were far too big for her. Not in deep snow.

All right – alternative plan: they would just have to leave via the front door of the main house, where the family's outdoor clothes were kept. The girls could pull them on over their pyjamas. She herself only had on pyjama bottoms made of a thin fleece-type material that was wearing through at the knees, but she could at least borrow one of Ása's expensive jackets. This was their only chance.

Sóldís tightened her hold on the door handle, only to hesitate when the thought struck her that it might be more sensible to make a run for it alone. She would be able to move faster and fetch help sooner. Whatever his feelings about Ása and Reynir, the farmer at Minna-Hvarf would hardly refuse them help if it was a matter of life or death. But the next moment, Sóldís remembered that on the other side of this door was the little girl who regarded her as her best friend. If she left now, there was no telling what might happen before help arrived.

Sóldís opened the door. She stepped barefoot on to the heated floor and set off noiselessly in the direction of the bedroom wing. The screaming and yelling were still going on and nothing seemed to have changed. Ása and Reynir kept shouting that they didn't have the wallet, he had to believe them. But Alvar obviously didn't because he kept yelling at Reynir to remember where he'd put it. If he didn't, Ása would suffer.

The worst part was entering the bedroom hallway. Sóldís felt sick, one moment feverish, the next moment shivering, as she inched her way closer to the girls' rooms. All the time she kept her eyes fixed on the open door of their parents' bedroom. Like everything else in the house it was huge, and the bed wasn't visible from where Sóldís was standing. Although she couldn't see anyone, she was in no doubt that Ása, Reynir and Alvar were in there because that's where the shouting was coming from. If anyone appeared, she would turn and bolt. She heard a pathetic whining from the TV room and felt a moment's relief that the dogs were alive. But there was no way of taking them along. She mustn't get distracted: the only thing that mattered now was rescuing the girls.

Íris's door was closer than Gígja's. That was lucky as the older girl would be able to help Sóldís get her younger sister out. She assumed Gígja would be beside herself with terror but that Íris would be able to put a hand over her mouth if she tried to cry out at any point. Íris could grab some clothes from her wardrobe too while Sóldís was leading Gígja out of the room, in case the little girl's pyjamas weren't warm enough.

Íris's door was open. Sóldís halted, irresolute. Íris always kept her door shut and she was unlikely to have made an exception now, but Sóldís couldn't afford to waste any time, so she tiptoed inside. All the lights were off. Sóldís's eyes had adjusted to the light coming from Ása and Reynir's bedroom, so it took her a few moments to work out what she was seeing in the gloom. The sight was so surreal that she couldn't take it in at first. But once it had hit her, she clamped her hands over her mouth. Íris wasn't going to be coming with her. Sóldís squeezed her eyes shut and tightened her hands over her mouth. She felt the tears spurting from her eyes and her nose becoming blocked. Her heart was thundering in her chest and her breathing was ragged.

Afraid she was going to collapse, she turned and retreated on trembling legs back into the hallway. Seeing that Gígja's door was shut, she sent up a silent prayer that the little girl was safe in her room. She opened the door warily, just enough to slip inside, then closed it behind her and stood in the darkness for a moment, still with her hand on the doorknob. Then she fumbled for the switch, turned on the light and took a frantic look around.

Gígja was nowhere to be seen. Her bed was empty, the duvet pushed aside as if she had got up. But at least there was no blood splashed up the wall, so clearly Gígja hadn't suffered the same fate as Íris. Sóldís felt a flicker of relief. The image of Íris had burnt itself into her retinas, though, and she was finding it hard to focus. She wanted to throw herself on the bed, pull the duvet over her head and howl out her grief while waiting for the inevitable. But she had to pull herself together for Gígja's sake. She peered under the bed. There was nothing to see apart from the odd bit of fluff that had evaded the mop. Gígja wasn't hiding under the desk either.

Sóldís was caught up in a nightmarish version of hide-and-seek, which she had played so often with Gígja over the last week. No need now to pretend to look where Gígja obviously wasn't hiding. She made a beeline for the wardrobe and opened the first compartment. Gígja wasn't there. She opened the second door. The child was huddled up at the back. She'd pulled up her legs and wrapped her arms around them, her head between her knees.

'Gígja.' Sóldís whispered her name, her voice so hoarse it sounded more like a frog than a human. She crouched down until their faces were on the same level. 'Come on. Don't make a sound.'

Gígja raised eyes swollen from weeping. 'I want to stay here,' she said in a small voice. She hiccupped, then repeated: 'I want to stay here.'

With a superhuman effort, Sóldís controlled the desperation in her voice. 'We need to go, Gígja. Now.' She reached into the cupboard and stroked the girl's head, hoping the child wouldn't notice how badly her fingers were trembling. Then she moved her hand round behind one of the girl's shoulders and pulled her gently towards her. The smooth base of the wardrobe provided no resistance and Gígja slid closer, still in the same position. Sóldís took her head in her hands and gently forced her to look up. She whispered: 'You have to stand up. Close your eyes and put your hands over your ears. I'll guide you. But you have to stand up.'

Gígja looked at Sóldís's face and whispered: 'Are you crying too?' Sóldís nodded. The tears started pouring down Gígja's cheeks again but in silence. 'Íris. Íris needs a plaster.'

Gígja had obviously run into her sister's room for safety when she first heard the screams.

'I know,' Sóldís said. 'We need to get a doctor. We must hurry.' The tears were flowing unchecked down her own cheeks too.

Gígja nodded. Sóldís took her little hands and placed them over her ears, making her hold them there. Then she told Gígja to close her eyes, and, taking her by one shoulder, she led her to the door. Heaving a deep breath, Sóldís opened it a crack and peered out into the hallway, only to dart back in and push the door to as Reynir emitted a series of piercing screams. They were followed by a strangely sharp yet muffled thud, which Sóldís couldn't immediately identify. But it didn't take her long to guess what had happened because there were no further sounds from Ása.

She peered out again, only to jerk back her head when Reynir suddenly shot out into the hallway. He was covered in streaks of blood and clutching one hand, which appeared to be bleeding. Sóldís pushed the door silently to when she heard Alvar utter a yell, and assumed he would set off in pursuit of Reynir. The heavy, unhurried footsteps going past in the direction Reynir had taken suggested that she was right.

She and Gígja had to get out of this room and into the entrance hall as quickly as possible. Sóldís opened the bedroom door the moment she thought the coast was clear. The screams had been cut off, and it was strange standing there in near silence after what had gone before. Then she realised that the silence wasn't complete. She could hear a rattling, sucking noise from the couple's bedroom. Lifting Gígja's hand away from one of her ears, she whispered to her to stay where she was and keep her eyes shut and her hands over her ears. Then she replaced the child's hand and dashed to door of the couple's bedroom. Perhaps Ása was all right and would be able to escape with them. Sóldís didn't want to go alone. In a situation as hideous as this one, it would be better to have company, and Gígja barely counted.

But Ása wasn't going anywhere. She was lying on her back on the bed. It took Sóldís a moment or two to take in what she was seeing. Incredibly, Ása was still alive. Her eyes were staring at the ceiling and she didn't notice Sóldís, all her attention apparently taken up with trying to breathe. A red bubble formed between her lips and burst.

Ása's left hand shook convulsively as she moved it to the bedside table, picked up a ring, raised it with difficulty and put it in her mouth. Then she seemed to go slack and the rattling breathing stopped.

Sóldís realised she had been frozen there too long when a blood-curdling scream split the silence right behind her. Spinning round, she saw to her horror that Gígja had been too frightened to stay where she was and had followed her to her parents' door. Sóldís grabbed her arm and drew her away. Her first thought was to protect the child from the terrible sight. But she would have done better to clap a hand over Gígja's mouth and gag the tearing cries she was emitting. A movement made her look up.

At the end of the hallway stood a young man wearing rubber gloves, with an axe in one hand. Like Reynir, he was covered in blood. He shook his head as if displeased at the sight of them, then started moving towards them. Sóldís glanced around frantically for an escape route, feeling like a mouse cornered by a cat. She knew she was going to suffer the same fate as the mouse but she clung to the hope that Gígja would be spared. '*Please, please.*' It was all she could say when the man reached them. '*Please, Alvar. Please.*'

The man smiled maliciously. 'My name's not Alvar.' Then he snatched at Gígja, who had finally been shocked into silence, and yanked her to him. Sóldís had been holding her shoulders but didn't manage to tighten her grip fast enough. She cried out in horror and tried to drag the little girl away from him but the man flung her aside. Meanwhile Gígja just stood there, gaping blankly, as if in a daze. Her expression didn't even change when the man dragged her into her room and closed the door behind them. Sóldís tried to follow but he had locked it. She banged on the door, screaming and sobbing, then she heard the same strange, muffled thuds as she'd heard from the parents' room earlier. There was no further sound from Gígja.

When the thuds stopped, Sóldís backed away from the door. She saw the handle turning and instinctively whirled round and fled, but found herself moving nightmarishly slowly. She didn't seem able to control her legs. Trying to ignore the quick footsteps behind her, she stumbled into the connecting corridor and thought of locking the door to the old house and jamming the chair under the handle. That way she would hopefully be able to buy herself a few minutes, enough to pull on her coat and boots and flee into the night. There was little hope of sitting out the attack in there, in spite of locks and chairs. The man had an axe. He would smash his way in, sooner or later.

But she never got a chance to try out her plan. The man who was not Alvar caught up with her as she went through the door and knocked her to the floor, then followed her at a leisurely pace as she kept crawling, although she knew it was hopeless. She headed stubbornly, desperately, for the nearest bedroom in the faint hope of shutting him out in the hall and escaping through the window. But it was no good: he was right behind her.

She struggled first to her knees, then to her feet and backed away. Then she collided with the bed and could go no further. The man raised the axe.

Chapter 33
Tuesday

Idunn seemed to have noticed that Týr's eyes kept straying to the dark suitcase in the corner of the office. 'Don't worry. It's empty. It's waiting to be taken up to forensics.'

Týr merely nodded. He was relieved to hear this, though he had known Alvar's remains couldn't still be inside it. 'They're completely snowed under,' he said. Although the police had Bogi's confession, they still had to analyse all the evidence. There was always a chance that the young man might retract his confession later. He would have plenty of time to think about it in custody – time that he might use to concoct some absurd excuse that he was deluded enough to believe would exonerate him. It was safer if the police could lay a bundle of evidence on the table in support of their case. 'So don't hold your breath,' Týr finished.

This didn't seem to bother Idunn, who went on from where she had left off before the suitcase was mentioned. 'And he says he didn't attack the family with the intention of killing anyone?'

'That's what he's claiming. He says Reynir suddenly picked up an axe. That it must have been lying beside the bed.' Týr smiled. 'As if anyone would believe that.'

'No. That would be crazy.'

'He says he wrestled it off him straight away but that Reynir's action had changed everything. What was supposed to be intimidation turned into a nightmare of violence.'

'How did he justify murdering the daughters? Did they come at him too with weapons that they'd been hiding under their beds?'

'He said they kept screaming. If they'd been quiet he'd have left them alone. But that contradicts what he'd said before. Earlier he claimed that the couple kept shouting his name, so he'd been forced to get rid of the girls. He thought they were bound to be shown photos of the real Alvar later on and then it would come out that someone completely different had been living in their house. Since they'd be able to identify him, there was a danger he'd be exposed and they'd testify against him.'

Idunn grimaced. 'He certainly valued his freedom, didn't he?'

'Yes. He's not right in the head. It was clear to everyone during the interview.' Týr wasn't going to be distracted into speculating about Bogi's mental health. For all he knew, the young man could be a sociopath, a psychopath or quite simply evil. It all came down to the same thing. There was no excuse for what he'd done. Týr would rather erase him from his memory, not least because he made him wonder what had been wrong with his birth father. 'Huldar thought we ought to get your take on the chain of events, in case you spot any discrepancies. We need to act fast – before Bogi stops cooperating.' Týr could have spoken to Idunn over the phone but he had offered to go round and see her at work. Not out of conscientiousness but because he saw this as an opportunity to look at the files on his mother's murder. He would bring it up at the end of their conversation.

Týr repeated Bogi's description of events, speaking fast because he didn't want to dwell on the account. He told her about Bogi's unsuccessful attempts to frighten the couple into telling him where they had hidden the Bitcoin wallet. And how everything had changed when Reynir allegedly pulled out the axe and Íris, who had been woken by the noise, appeared at the door. She had been beside herself with terror when she saw the axe in Bogi's hand and kept screaming and crying until he said he'd no choice but to drag her into her room and shut her up. Out of consideration for her parents, he had closed their door while he was doing this.

'Consideration? Is that really the word he used?'

Týr saw no reason to make excuses for Bogi. 'Yes,' he said flatly. Then he described how Bogi had gone back into the couple's room where they were waiting for him in a state of terror. Bogi had told them that if they stayed where they were, nothing would happen to Íris. But if they stirred from the room, he would finish her off. They had kept their side of the bargain; he hadn't. But he had forgotten to wipe the axe clean, and the gory blade and the blood splattered all over him had given him away. That's when the screaming had really begun. Bogi had continued to interrogate them about the Bitcoin wallet and password but couldn't get any sense out of them. When Ása started blathering on incoherently in English, he assumed she'd totally lost it and decided to shut her up. Reynir had thrown himself across the bed to his wife and tried to block the axe in the air but had only succeeded in injuring his hand.

'It sounds plausible. So far. At least there's nothing glaringly inconsistent with the evidence of the post-mortems.'

Týr had been expecting this. A bloodstain-pattern analyst had already compared the account with independent findings and hadn't found anything that didn't fit.

As Týr drew near to the end of the story, he knew he was rattling along faster and faster, like a machine gun. With a slight Swedish accent too, as he couldn't take care over his pronunciation when he was speaking at this speed. He just wanted to get it over with. 'When Bogi attacked Ása, and Reynir saw that he couldn't protect her, he ran out of the room. Bogi went in pursuit, and he was just about to step out of the French windows when he heard more screams from the bedroom corridor. So he turned back, sure that Reynir wouldn't have time to get far. He found Sóldís and Gígja outside the couple's bedroom.'

Týr lowered his eyes as he described the murders of the little girl and the young woman. He didn't want to see the horror reflected in Idunn's face. Or, worse, to see her watching him impassively, as if he'd merely been reporting a trip to the supermarket. There was no way of telling which it would be with Idunn. Up to now, her main reaction had been distaste at Bogi's choice of words. He knew perfectly well that she regarded Bogi's crimes as repellent, yet she gave every appearance of listening to the account with complete composure. Like a scientist examining the Ebola virus through an electron microscope.

After Týr had relayed how Gígja and Sóldís met their ends, he paused and drew a deep breath. 'Then he went after Reynir. He took one of the snowmobiles and followed Reynir's trail. He had a few problems because the snow was covering his tracks but he had worked out where Reynir was heading. By then the storm was dying down. He says he got to Minna-Hvarf just as Reynir was crawling into the bathtub. So he wiped the axe clean, put the handle in Reynir's freezing hand and closed his fingers around it. Then he left it there, after satisfying himself that the man was dying.

'After that he went back to Hvarf and began the search, saying he'd found a piece of paper with all kinds of passwords on Reynir's desk, but not the Bitcoin wallet, though he was convinced he'd have found it eventually, given the chance. But it was hard to concentrate because the animals were driving him mad, making a hell of a racket with their mooing and barking and whining to be fed. The dogs kept scratching at the door of the bedroom wing too, trying to get in. He had two choices, either kill them and the cows and hens, or shut the dogs in the byre and give them some food to keep them quiet. As he didn't have a gun, he decided it would be less hassle just to feed them. I swear he believed we'd be impressed by his big-heartedness.' Týr shuddered. 'Anyway, he was careful to wear gloves while he was in the house, though he assumed he'd have time to clean before he left. But it didn't work out like that. When the neighbour, Karl, started nosing around the house and discovered the bodies, Bogi was forced to make himself scarce. Karl had come round two days earlier as well, though that time he'd only rung the bell, before going away. But once he had entered the house, Bogi couldn't hang around any longer. The moment Karl had gone, Bogi took the snowmobile, and grabbed the plate, the glass and some of the other stuff he'd used at the house and burnt them back in Mosfellsbær. He was in such a hurry that he forgot to take the money he'd found in the safe, which he bitterly regretted afterwards. He even boasted about managing to avoid all the cameras on the way. According to him, it required skill, and it was no joke trying to navigate around Hvalfjördur avoiding the roads, but he succeeded somehow.'

Idunn took an elastic band from her desk and tied back her thick, curly hair in a ponytail. 'This is all consistent with the evidence of the post-mortems, as far as I can see.' She thought for a moment. 'Apart from the ring. Did he mention having seen Ása swallow it? Or did he maybe shove it in her mouth himself?'

'No, he's said nothing about it.' But then no one had asked.

'Maybe it happened after he ran out of the room chasing Reynir.' Idunn laid her hands flat on the desk as if about to stand up. 'Apart from that, I can't see anything to suggest he's lying. I can go over the results of the post-mortems again, just to be sure, but I don't expect to find any issues.'

Týr nodded, suddenly awkward. He didn't know how to raise the subject of his mother. Maybe Idunn had had a change of heart, after realising she could get into trouble. But when he sat there without saying anything, she seemed to guess what was up. Instead of rising to her feet, she said: 'Have you spoken to your parents?'

Týr couldn't hide his relief. Idunn had broached the subject. 'Yes. And I was right: it is my mother. *Was* my mother.'

'How did it go? The phone call?'

'Not well. Not well at all. I'll have to talk to them again. Not right away, though. It's going to take me a while to accept their decision not to tell me the truth. I find it so weird. I mean, I can understand why they didn't do it when I was a kid – but they've had years since then.' Týr hadn't meant to discuss the phone call with Idunn but it was a relief in a way. He had no one else to talk to—apart from Karó perhaps—and Idunn was totally free from sentimentality – and nosiness.

'When do you think would have been the right time?'

Týr wasn't ready for the question and hadn't given it any thought. When had he been sufficiently mature and well balanced? 'When I was twenty. Or twenty-five, maybe.'

'Or thirty? You can see that it wouldn't have been an easy decision,' Idunn said. 'You'll understand better when you've seen the files.' She opened a drawer in her desk and took out a memory stick. 'It's not pretty.'

Týr stuck it in his coat pocket. He didn't immediately withdraw his hand but clutched the memory stick in his fist. He felt it was the most precious thing he'd ever held in his life. This must have been how Darwin felt when he got to hold the first edition of *On the Origin of Species*. Because the stick contained his origins. Of no value for anyone else, unlike Darwin's book, but of inestimable value to himself. 'Thanks, Idunn.'

But the question that had been driving Týr spare couldn't wait until he plugged the memory stick into his computer. 'Can you tell me one thing? Do any of the files explain why he attacked her?' He didn't need to specify who he meant.

'Yes.' Idunn hesitated. 'The answer won't bring you any relief, though. It's something you must have come across before. The age-old reasoning of some jilted men: *If I can't have her, nobody can.*'

'So, she was leaving him?'

'That's what he claimed. For another man, though he didn't give a name. Apparently, this was only based on a suspicion that she was involved with someone else. He had no proof and, considering that he must have been out of his mind, I wouldn't put too much weight on his testimony.' Idunn was silent for a moment or two before adding,'I'd ask you to destroy the files afterwards if I thought there was any likelihood you'd do it. But as there isn't, I won't bother.'

Týr smiled and stood up. Before he could say goodbye, Idunn got in one last question: 'Do you think Bogi found the wallet? That he'll come into possession of a huge fortune once he's served his sentence?'

Týr sincerely hoped not. The previous evening, records had arrived from the couple's bank, which made it clear that the missing funds had been used to buy Bitcoin. The police had immediately got hold of the broker at the bank who had handled the transaction, and he'd assured them that he had done his best to dissuade Reynir from making such a risky investment. It was totally out of step with the rest of their portfolio of assets. During the brief phone call, the man had denied three times that he'd had any idea about Reynir's brain tumour. But he'd also pointed out that the value of Bitcoin had skyrocketed afterwards and the reckless investment had quintupled in value, whatever might happen in future. He recommended that the Bitcoin should be sold so that the daughters could benefit from the proceeds. The staff at the bank had only been informed about Ása and Reynir's deaths. Sadly, Íris and Gígja would never benefit from anything, let alone a Bitcoin fortune. So it was unthinkable that Bogi should do so.

But not impossible. According to the IT department, if Bogi had got his hands on what they called the Bitcoin wallet's seed recovery phrase – a unique sequence of words – then he would be able to access the cryptocurrency even without the wallet. Software from a wallet manufacturer had been found on Ása and Reynir's computers. The manufacturer initialised a phrase from a succession of between twelve and twenty-four English words, and the users could then add a word of their own choice, which could be anything they liked, as a private key. It was believed that the couple had done this. It was also assumed that they must have written the private key down on paper, since in the cryptocurrency world people were warned against keeping such information in electronic form. No note containing this type of information had been found, but it wasn't impossible that one would come to light later.

None of the investigators could imagine why the couple wouldn't have just handed over the key to Bogi to save their lives, so they thought Ása might have been trying to do just that when she started reciting a string of seemingly meaningless words in English. Their tormentor hadn't understood. That was preferable to the idea that Bogi might not be telling the truth and had in fact written down the words before killing the couple anyway.

'It mustn't happen. If no one else has the wit to do it, I'll keep an eye on him myself when he gets out of prison. If he starts living like a king, we'll know he's got his hands on the loot.' Týr wasn't talking idly. Although the statute of limitations applied to the crime of theft, the heirs nevertheless had a claim to the stolen goods.

'Let me know if you need any help,' Idunn said drily. 'I'm sure I'll still be here.'

* * *

Forensics looked as if one of the officers been made homeless and was intending to move in to the office. Usually, the practice was to remove as little as possible from a crime scene, taking copious samples instead, but this investigation was unlike most others. The sheer number of victims, the size of the property, the fact that the scene was more than an hour's drive from Reykjavík – in optimal weather and traffic conditions – and the cost of employing a full-time security guard for the remote farm, all meant it wasn't feasible for forensics to work there in shifts for days at a time, so all portable items that required examination had been brought to town. That way, the forensic technicians' time was also better employed.

Týr had gone to Hvarf that morning with an officer from the IT department. The young man had no interest in anything but computers, had been engrossed in his phone all the way up there, and got straight to work when they reached the farm. His job was to search for any security cameras that could be concealed in the furnishings, or any other computer or technological hardware that the other investigators might have missed. He was to keep a particularly close eye out for any devices with an internal memory that could conceivably contain the couple's Bitcoin holdings.

The young officer had a reputation for being sharp, though you wouldn't have known it from looking at him. While he was searching the premises, Týr wandered around aimlessly. With only the two of them there, the silence was oppressive. The cuckoo clock had stopped, there was dust in the air, and the absence of any life in the house was eerie. Týr was extremely relieved when the young man reappeared, saying he'd finished. The small robot Týr had noticed in Reynir's study was peeping out of the cardboard box in his arms. He explained that the device had the capacity to monitor its surroundings, so he was taking it back to Reykjavík on the off-chance that it might have recorded images of the fateful events.

When Týr got back in the car, he surveyed the property for what would, he assumed, be the last time. For him, the disproportionately large, modern building, the old farmhouse and the smartly restored outbuildings had a bleak, forlorn air, forever tainted by what had occurred. He wondered what its fate would be, whether someone would move in with a young family and animals, or a rich foreigner would buy it as a rural retreat. Still wondering, he started the engine and drove away.

One thing was clear to him later, as he stood in the forensics department, surveying the family's belongings. None of these objects would ever be returned to the farmhouse.

Týr went over to a colleague who was taking samples from the dried bloodstains on a painting that Týr recalled had hung in the marital bedroom. At the next desk, another technician was examining the designer pieces that Íris had used to decorate her wall. He put down a blood-splashed bag and picked up a small, blue jewellery case. On the neighbouring desk, Týr could see Gígja's toys, in a similar state. And on another Týr spotted objects from Ása and Reynir's bedside tables: a book, a lamp and a wireless phone charger. There was scarcely a patch on them that hadn't been sprayed with blood.

'Anything new?' Týr asked.

The man looked up from the painting with a weary expression. 'No.'

An awkward silence ensued, and Týr was relieved when the young IT guy he'd driven to Hvarf reappeared, apparently looking for him. He came over, saying he just wanted to let him know that they hadn't learnt anything useful from the little robot. Judging by the records, it hadn't been switched on for months. Then the IT guy glanced around, taking in the items on the desks. His gaze passed over the bags, paintings and ornaments without interest, but paused and lingered on Gígja's toys. As if in a trance, he moved closer, and Týr followed, hoping he might have spotted something of significance. But no such luck.

'*Star Wars.*' The young man was obviously itching to get his hands on the models. 'Did you find any collectibles?'

The woman who was busy taking samples from the toys raised her eyes to him, looking as tired and uncommunicative as the man Týr had tried to strike up a conversation with before. 'I don't know,' she said indifferently. 'There's more in there.' She waved to a box on the floor beside her. Then, taking pity on the IT guy, she handed him a pair of gloves. 'You can take a look if you like, but it's all more or less broken, so I doubt there's anything of value.'

Týr watched as the young man's enthusiasm gave way to disappointment. Then he extracted something from the bottom of the box, his face cheerful again. 'What the hell's this doing here?'

He was holding what looked to Týr like a small remote control with two buttons and a tiny screen, marked 'Trezor'. A piece of sticky tape had been wound round it, and when the man turned it over in his hand, they saw that there was a white label stuck to the back.

'What is that?'

The young IT guy looked up, his eyes blazing with triumph. 'The Bitcoin wallet.' He peeled up a corner of the label and his smile grew even broader. 'And if this isn't the seed recovery phrase. The idiots. You're not supposed to keep it with the wallet. Jesus.'

Týr bent down and saw the three first words on the label: *Plant Duck Economy*. If the number of words in the seed phrase was divided by the total amount of Bitcoin holdings, each of the words would be worth more than his combined lifetime earnings, regardless of whether there were twelve or twenty-four of them. Unbelievable. He straightened up. 'Perhaps they were afraid something might happen to them and wanted to guarantee that the girls could recover the money.' Týr's urge to defend the couple might have had something to do with the fact that he kept most of his own passwords on a label on the back of his computer screen.

'Let's just hope the private key is there too.' The IT guy peeled the entire label off the wallet. 'Damn. It doesn't look as though it is. Unless they'd just decided to use another English word.'

'I think I know where it is,' Týr said suddenly. Ása had swallowed her ring for a reason. She couldn't have been thinking straight in her death throes but must have acted on instinct to deny the private key to her killer.

The forensic technicians came to life. The young woman sitting nearest was the first to shove back her chair and get to her feet, eager to see the unremarkable little plastic object with the paper label that was worth billions of krónur. The rest followed suit, until they had formed a knot around the IT guy. Týr wondered if any of them momentarily entertained a wild idea of snatching the wallet and label and forcing Týr to tell them the private key. Then running out of the building, fleeing the country and never having to touch a swab again.

He felt no such temptation himself. Another small piece of hardware was occupying most of his thoughts. Idunn's memory stick was burning a hole in his pocket – yet he dreaded looking at its contents. He guessed it would take him more than an hour to go through all the files, but he had made up his mind to ring his parents that evening, even if he hadn't finished reading everything. He had been too angry and distressed during their last phone call, and his parents deserved better. In reality, his anger was directed not at them but at his birth father, the man who had killed his mother and tried to murder him. His adoptive parents had only done their best to salvage a difficult situation. They were experts in sewing up wounds and massaging life back into patients with heart failure, but nothing had prepared them for the experience of caring for a young child who had crawled out of the ruins of his former life.

They weren't to blame for his mother's tragic fate or his father's sickening crime. Týr would phone them and forgive them everything. He would go through the files, face up to what had happened, then let it go and get on with his life.

Now that he knew his origins, he should be capable of dealing with almost anything. There would be better times ahead.

* * *

Idunn slid her office chair back a little from the screen. Sometimes she found the additional distance helped her get a better perspective on the images she was studying. She frowned at the photo she had blown up, but viewing it from further away didn't help. Thoughtfully, she placed her palms together as if in prayer and raised her fingers to her lips.

She had made use of a brief lull in her work to reread the post-mortem report on Týr's mother. He would almost certainly want her to confirm that all the details were correct and that no aspect of his mother's case was in doubt. Idunn hadn't spotted anything untoward the first time she read the files, but then she hadn't been looking. They had simply been case notes on an axe murder that might provide a useful comparison for her post-mortems on the bodies from Hvarf.

It was like one of those hidden picture puzzles: once you'd spotted the concealed object, you couldn't unsee it.

Idunn turned her chair to look out of the window. A woman was hurrying to her car in the teeth of the wind. Her coat flapped around her body and her scarf streamed out behind her, looking for all the world like the little prince in the story. Idunn watched as she got into the small electric car, then wrestled with the wind as it tried to tear the door out of her hands. The woman eventually won the battle, closed the door and drove away. Once she had vanished from view, there was nothing in the deserted car park to distract Idunn, and she had to bring her mind back to her dilemma.

What if she was wrong? It did happen – however rarely. She inhaled sharply, reached for the switch on her monitor and turned it off. The image vanished, making it easier to think. She tolerated most people but actively liked only a few. Týr belonged to the more exclusive club. He was all right. Straight up and down. Should she tell him about this? She wasn't sure. It might be significant, but, on the other hand, there could be some other explanation, though it could never be verified. The suspect was dead and in no position to amend his statement. Perhaps he had been in such a state that he had made a mistake. Or remembered the events wrongly. Something along those lines. If so, her observations would only be confusing for Týr. Perhaps it would be better if she kept them to herself.

Because there was no getting round it: Týr's father's confession did not fit the facts.

Idunn continued to stare out of the window. She hated it when there was no closure. Why was nothing ever simple? Or fair, for that matter? She realised that her thoughts had shifted, from Týr's mother to the recent case. She was by no means faint of heart or oversensitive – she'd seen too much – but she wasn't a robot, and performing back-to-back autopsies on the two sisters and the young au pair had got to her.

Everyone dies, as Idunn knew better than most. It wasn't death in itself that was dispiriting but the loss of life. The younger the victim, the greater the loss. She couldn't remember ever being involved in a case where so much life had been lost in one fell swoop. The only upside was that the investigation had been concluded and most, if not all, the questions had been answered. Yet she didn't feel the usual urge to clap her hands together and start on new tasks.

Another issue relating to the Hvalfjördur murders kept bothering her. Those blood mares. In an attempt to put it to rest,

Idunn had done an internet search and found that there had been a flurry of discussion about the practice a few years ago. It surprised her to read that peddling mares' blood was a substantial industry and not limited to only a handful of farmers. This did little to make her feel better. The conclusion of all the articles was that it was a despicable business, albeit legal. No one appeared to have come forward to defend the process or attempt to explain the vileness away, but the blood-mare farmers' silence had paid off in the end. The uproar had fizzled out, the number of comments under the articles had tailed off, and readers had moved on to the next controversial issue. Stamina had never been the public's strong point when it came to the news.

Idunn tried to shake off her sadness. There was nothing more she could do for the young sisters and au pair. Or for the poor blood mares. In the latter case, she could only hope that nature or the universe would step in and put a stop to the practice. Sometimes, life had a way of administering justice. Not often, but sometimes.

Idunn turned away from the window when she heard a soft knock on the door. In a loud voice she told the person to come in, and the familiar face of one of her assistants appeared. The young woman announced the delivery of a body for post-mortem.

'What are the circumstances?' Idunn expected it to be a hospital autopsy or a sudden death at home. No murder had been reported in the news, and anyway, if it had, she would have been called to the scene.

'An accident victim. A farmer.'

'Tractor?' Idunn assumed it would be either that or a mishap involving some kind of farming equipment.

'No. A horse.' Before Idunn could ask if the farmer had fallen off and landed badly, the assistant continued: 'A freak event. Apparently, his wife witnessed it from the window. He'd been throwing a stillborn foal into a pit where they dispose of dead livestock. But the mare, its mother, had followed him, and kicked him in the head just as he was dropping the foal's body into the pit. He tumbled in after it and died, either from the head wound or by drowning in the soup of remains.'

'Where was this?'

'Hvalfjördur.'

'And the name of the farmer?'

The assistant looked down at the paperwork she was carrying. 'Einar Ari. Arason.'

Idunn suppressed a grim smile and said that she was coming. Sometimes life had a way of administering justice. And this was one of those times.

Idunn grabbed her lab coat and left the office.

If you enjoyed *Can't Run, Can't Hide*,
get your hands on *The Prey* . . .

What may be searching for its prey out on the ice?